PRAISE FOR ISLA DEWAR

'A realist, observant and needle-sharp,
Isla Dewar can be very funny'
The Times

'The best, the funniest, cleverest, the most enjoyable writer in Scotland today. I can guarantee that you too would enrich your life beyond all measure by discovering Isla Dewar'
Robin Pilcher

'Dewar has a very sharp sense of humour and writes with a great deal of wit'
Newcastle Evening Chronicle

'No one can tell a story quite like Isla Dewar'
Lancashire Evening Post

'A warm-hearted and gifted storyteller'
Catherine Ryan Hyde

IT TAKES ONE TO KNOW ONE

Isla Dewar's first book, *Keeping Up with Magda*, was published in 1995. Dewar found success with her second novel, *Women Talking Dirty*, the film of which starred Helena Bonham Carter. She contributed to the collection *Scottish Girls about Town* and has also written for children. Her most recent novel, *A Winter Bride*, was set in Edinburgh in the 1950s. Born in Edinburgh, Isla lives in the Fife countryside with her husband, cartoonist Bob Dewar, and a bunch of pheasants outside her kitchen window.

It Takes One to Know One

Isla Dewar

First published in Great Britain in 2018 by Polygon,
an imprint of Birlinn Ltd.

Birlinn Ltd
West Newington House
10 Newington Road
Edinburgh
EH9 1QS

www.polygonbooks.co.uk

ISBN 978 1 84697 454 0
eBook ISBN 978 1 78885 077 3

British Library Cataloguing-in-Publication Data
A catalogue record for this book is available on request
from the British Library.

Typeset by 3btype.com
Printed and bound in Great Britain by Clays Ltd, Elcograf S.p.A.

For Sonny who wasn't in the world
when this book was started.

1

It Never Just Drizzles in Hollywood

The man was not what Martha expected. She'd thought he might be middle-aged, complex and wise or perhaps a little alcohol-raddled and cynical. But Charlie Gavin was fidgety. He drummed his fingers – not an impatient tapping on his desktop, more a well-rehearsed thumb and finger drum solo. He arranged his pens into a perfect parallel row. He wiped a minuscule few specks of dust from the phone.

'You're married?'

'Um . . .'

He stopped arranging his pens and looked at her, eyebrows raised. 'Um?'

'Separated,' she told him. This wasn't actually true. But it was as near to the truth as she was prepared to go.

He said, 'Oh, man, that's tough. Children?'

'A daughter, Evie. She's seven.' Oh, man? Had he really said that? She thought people only spoke like that in the movies.

'A difficult age, seven. It's a time when you're becoming aware of the world and innocence is drifting away.'

'I suppose,' said Martha. 'But then I think every age is a difficult age. That's life. We move from difficult age to difficult age. Just when we relax because one difficult time is over – wham – we get embroiled in the next one.'

In fact she thought seven an excellent age. Her daughter was still a child and, right now, lived a life uncluttered by the hassle of getting on in life. She didn't have a mortgage, didn't have bills to pay and could go out to play when school was over. Meals she didn't have to plan or cook were regularly provided. She got kissed and cuddled and tucked up in bed every night. She was loved, and she knew it. Life was a breeze when you were seven. Reviewing the innocence and comfort of her daughter's existence, Martha felt proud and a tad envious. She wished she'd been smart enough to enjoy being seven when she'd been there. Still, she didn't want to openly disagree with Charlie. It wasn't the thing to do in a job interview.

Charlie agreed on the matter of difficult ages. 'I'm thirty-seven. Forty's looming. It's hard.'

He tapped his desk, gazed into the distance and looked to Martha to be considering his life so far and the difficulties that lay ahead. She took in the room. It was large, airy, painted a fading blue with a desk at either end. One wall was filled with framed prints – Monet, Degas, Cezanne and Matisse. Charlie had the desk by the window. Martha presumed she'd be behind the one near the kitchen door, if she got the job. A fire burbled in the grate. A black cocker spaniel stretched on an ancient Chesterfield sofa and yawned from time to time. He snored and farted as only dogs can without shame or apology for his lack of social graces.

Martha was disappointed Charlie Gavin looked nothing like Sherlock Holmes or Sam Spade. He dressed carefully – grey trousers, grey shirt open at the neck and a black velvet jacket. His hair was too long and curled over the collar of his shirt. He frequently ran his fingers through it. He didn't look thirty-seven. His face was unlined, almost as if it was waiting for life to happen, make its mark. Or maybe, Martha thought, his scars went deeper than the odd wrinkle. Perhaps he nursed a wounded heart.

He was lucky. Well, his face was lucky. Running worried fingers over her own face this morning while looking in the mirror, Martha decided that every dire moment, doubt and downright tragedy was written there. At best she could say she looked like a woman of the world. But she wasn't prone to self-flattery. She was sure she looked baggy-eyed, emotionally battered.

'I mean,' Charlie said, 'I'm this old, almost middle-aged, and I still don't know what I want to do when I grow up.'

Martha knew what he meant. She ran her fingers through her hair and wondered if his habit was infectious. 'I wanted to be a cowboy when I was little.'

He perked up. 'Did you? So did I. It seemed like the life to me. Wandering the range, sleeping under the stars – just moseying, me and my faithful horse. Moonlight, I was going to call him.'

'Excellent name,' said Martha. 'Mine was to be Durango.'

'Oh,' he lit up. A glint of envy in his eyes. 'That's a good name.'

Martha nodded 'I thought so.'

They sighed in unison.

'Of course,' he said, 'there would be insects out there on the range what with the heat and all.' He examined his sleeve and brushed off an imaginary horsefly. 'And the diet wouldn't agree with me. All the beans. Then there's the weather.'

'I know,' said Martha. 'It really rains out on the range. Sheeting downpours. That's the movies for you. It never just drizzles in Hollywood.'

'Exactly,' he agreed. 'After wanting to be a cowboy, I wanted to be a famous jazz trumpeter.'

'Oh, do you like jazz?'

He nodded. 'Some of it. Miles Davis, Thelonious Monk. Mostly I like the hats. Jazz men wear cool hats.'

'I suppose they do,' said Martha. 'I never did get along with hats. I don't have the head for them. And I think you have to be tall.'

'Exactly,' said Charlie. 'I feel self-conscious with a hat on. I love the names, though. Sonny Boy Williamson, Satchmo.'

'Yes,' Martha agreed. 'Blues players too. Blind Lemon Jefferson, Muddy Waters, Howlin' Wolf. I'd love to have been a blues singer.

Big Voice Bessie Green, or something. I'd have worn a low-cut slinky dress, belted out my woes, then I'd have taken a seat at the bar, drunk bourbon and shot the breeze with the band.'

'Yeah,' said Charlie. 'That's the life.'

'Still, you play the trumpet?'

'No.'

'That could have been a bit of a drawback.'

'Yes. It was just a dream. I was fourteen. A trumpet was not on the agenda. It was way out of reach.'

Martha briefly felt inclined to tell him about her struggle to buy a guitar when she was fourteen. But something about him – a flicker of regret and, perhaps, anger that spoke of a damaged childhood – made her stop.

She said, 'Still, this seems fine to me. I'd be happy with this.' She waved her hands to indicate the room, and then folded them on her lap. 'What exactly is it you do, Mr Gavin? As a private investigator, that is.'

'Call me Charlie, everybody does. I look for people. I'm a specialist. I don't do any other kind of investigating.'

'But how do you do that?'

'We all leave trails behind us. I try to find them. Then follow them.'

'And what does that entail?'

'Oh, I talk to the people left behind. I follow the daily paths of those who have gone missing and gather information along the way. I look at old newspaper reports and electoral registers. I find out what was happening in the lives of the missing when they disappeared.'

She leaned forward. 'Do you have a lot of success?'

He shrugged. 'A bit. I've found that some missing people want to stay missing.'

'I see,' said Martha.

'Then again some missing people are desperate to come back. They just don't know how.'

Martha noted Charlie seemed a lot happier now she was asking the questions. She thought this was not a good thing in someone in his line of business. 'I expect you'll be out of the office a lot. Looking for people.'

'Yes, a little,' he said. 'Though I prefer to be here. I like it here with the fire on and the dog sleeping. I sometimes get people to go places for me.'

'You have more staff?'

'Not exactly. The occasional helper.'

His fingers moved up to his hair again. He drummed the top of his head. 'Mrs Florey who had the job worked from ten till four every day. She liked to get away before the rush-hour traffic got too heavy. She cycled.'

'I wouldn't have to do that,' said Martha. 'I live five minutes' walk away. Portobello is not that big, anyway. Why did Mrs Florey leave?'

'She wanted to see the world – the foothills of Mount Everest, the Australian outback and such like. She thought if she didn't do it now, she might die and never do it. She's seventy-two.'

'Oh. I don't think you'd have that problem with me. I'm a home-loving sort.'

'Me, too.' He looked embarrassed. 'I like to be at home beside the fire with Murphy and a good book.'

'Murphy? Is that your wife?'

'The dog.' He pointed to the snorer and farter on the sofa. 'He hasn't got very good manners but he's excellent company. I'm not married. Nobody would have me. I'm not a good catch.'

He looked at the clock and checked its time by glancing at his watch. 'Half-past ten. I get a bacon sandwich from the café across the road every morning at quarter to eleven. It would be part of your duties to pick it up.'

Martha told him that would be fine. 'I'm partial to a bacon sandwich myself.'

He nodded, rearranged the pens on his desk and ran his hand

over the phone. 'You'd have to type up my reports and answer the phone. That sort of thing.'

Martha smiled and said she could do that.

'Well,' Charlie said, 'that's wonderful.' Slapping his palms on his desk, he stood up. 'When can you start?'

'A week on Monday? I have to hand in my notice at my present job.'

'Jolly good. I'll look forward to seeing you then.'

He swept her from the office, along the corridor to the door that led onto the street, repeating, 'Jolly good, jolly good,' as they went. 'Ah, I almost forgot. No pink.'

'No pink?'

'Don't wear anything pink to work. It's the rule. This office is a pink-free zone.'

Martha shrugged. 'OK.' An odd request, she thought. But what was it to her? She didn't have much pink in her wardrobe.

It was raining. The air smelled of wet beach and ozone. The sea was a step away, round the corner. Charlie greeted the wetness from above with amazement, holding out his palm to gather some drops. He leaned over, tapped the brass nameplate on the wall – Charlie Gavin Be Kindly Missing Persons Bureau – bade Martha goodbye and went back inside. Seconds later he was back in the street again, tapping the nameplate again and shouting after Martha. 'Mrs Walters.'

She turned. 'Yes?'

'You can type, can't you?'

'Of course.'

'And shorthand? Do you do that?'

'Yes.'

'Ah, excellent.'

They were standing yards apart talking with raised voices. Passers-by looked on with interest. And it was still raining, a fine drenching drizzle.

'And previous experience,' he shouted. 'What about that?'

'I work in an insurance office. Been there for two years and before that I briefly worked for a small publishing company. Both posts were secretarial.'

'Excellent,' he said. 'Just the thing. Um, why do you want to leave your present job?'

'I feel I'm not getting the chance to develop my full potential.'

He gave her the thumbs up. 'Good answer. See you Monday next.' He went back inside, tapping the nameplate as he passed.

Martha stood staring at the doorway. Had that just happened? Had that man just conducted a job interview in the street, yelling questions through the rain? What kind of boss would he be? She dreaded to think. And what kind of private investigator suddenly thought of the questions he ought to ask when the interview was over? A seriously bad one, Martha decided. Charlie Gavin was a disappointment. She'd hoped he might be the one. But clearly he wasn't.

He reappeared. Tapped the nameplate for the umpteenth time and ran to the café across the road. Now he was wearing a raincoat that was slightly too big for him. Martha thought it a very Humphrey Bogart garment. Well, that was something – a Humphrey Bogart raincoat. He went up a notch in her estimation.

Seconds later he emerged from the café carrying a brown paper bag. The bacon sandwich, Martha decided. They must have had it ready for him. He saw her and appeared delighted she was still there. Pointing up at the sky, he shouted, 'Drizzle. Obviously this ain't Hollywood.'

He went back to his office, came out again, tapped the nameplate and disappeared inside.

2

A Life in a Shoebox

Charlie's heart had skipped a beat when Martha walked into his office. He'd first noticed her years ago. Back then she'd been Martha Campbell. Her married name was new to him. But once, though she didn't know it, she'd been his hero.

Six o'clock on a Friday evening, he'd been buying a newspaper and had spotted her standing at the bus stop across the road. She'd been wearing jeans turned up at the bottom to reveal pale thin ankles, a white T-shirt and a black leather jacket several sizes too big. She was carrying a guitar in a battered case and was scowling the sort of scowl only an adolescent could manage. *This is me, you got a problem with that*? the scowl said. It had made him smile. There had been a time when he'd been master of that scowl.

'Who's that?' he'd asked Sheena, the woman behind the counter.

'Our Martha,' Sheena told him. 'Lives in John Street. Her father died a while back. She's been a worry to her mother ever since. A bit wild.'

'She plays the guitar?'

'Not very well, I hear. She's in a band. Her mother's praying she'll grow out of it.'

'A rock'n'roll band?'

'That's what I hear.'

'I didn't think girls did that sort of thing.'

'Neither did I. It's not right. But Martha's heart is set on it. It's a phase, her mother says. It'll pass. That's what you do when you have kids, spend your days waiting for phases to pass.' Sheena had peered out the window at Martha. 'That lass did no end of paper rounds to get the money for the guitar. I was right glad when she'd saved enough. She was the worst paper-girl I've ever had.'

Charlie's heart went out to Martha and her guitar. Who wouldn't like someone who was a diabolical paper-girl?

At the time Charlie had been trying to sort out his life. He was considering his future, and had been for some time. He was confused. Lonely. He didn't know who he was.

He wasn't working. The only jobs he'd held had been casual labour on building sites. He'd been surprised he hadn't been called up to do National Service like everyone he knew and had asked his Auntie Ella, who'd brought him up, why this was.

'Oh,' she'd said, 'they probably knew all about you. They have records and they'd have seen that you have flat feet and had a touch of diphtheria when you were little. You wouldn't be suitable.'

He'd stared at his feet. They seemed perfectly normal to him and the diphtheria was news. 'Was I ill?'

'For a while. I was right worried, I can tell you. But you were a tough wee thing. You made it through. You're fine now. Only maybe not for army life.'

It occurred to him that if he was fit enough to work on a building site, he was fit enough for the army. But he didn't complain. He was muscular, tanned, there were passing girls to whistle at and it brought in enough money to buy weekend booze, natty shirts and get him into jazz clubs which were more about sitting with a beer listening to music than drinking and dancing.

Oh, he accepted he'd never learn to play the trumpet and bring audiences to their knees weeping at the beauty, pain and honesty of his music. But he felt there must be something he'd be good at, a hidden talent he might stumble upon. It would be satisfying. It might even make him rich. If only he could stumble on that talent soon.

Recently things had changed. His Auntie Ella had left him twelve thousand pounds. It had been a surprise. It had opened possibilities.

Lying on her deathbed in hospital, Ella had gripped his arm. 'There's something I have to tell you.' He'd leaned close. She smelled old. Her voice was a rattle, a whisper. She lifted her head from the pillow. This message was urgent. 'Look in the biscuit tin. It's to make up for what I did. I did a terrible thing.'

'What terrible thing? You've never done anything terrible.'

Four o'clock in the afternoon and visiting time was over. People were heaving on winter coats, kissing the cheek of the one they'd come to see, and trudging along the gleaming polished floor to the door. Matron, a fierce rock of a woman, small and solid as a wrestler, who tolerated nothing less than instant obedience, was standing, arms folded, at the end of Ella's bed. 'You have to go. It'll be tea time soon and doctor's coming on his rounds.' She glared the glare of a woman who had never known defiance. Charlie had pleaded for a few more minutes.

'She's telling me something important.'

'You can see her tonight. Seven till eight.' Matron glared harder. Pointed at the door. Charlie left.

He didn't go back. He got drunk. He was easing the dread. Auntie Ella was dying and he didn't know what to do about it. He'd known for some time this would happen. But now it was actually happening, it frightened him. He'd be alone in a tiny flat that smelled of Ella and Ella's cooking.

Once he'd thought about going to Canada. There were opportunities there. But he didn't want to leave Ella. She was old and forgetful and he was all she had. She'd taken him in when his mother died. He owed her a lot. He owed her everything he was, everything he had – his sanity, for example. If she hadn't taken him in, he'd probably have ended up in a children's home. 'You don't want to think about them,' Ella had said, shaking her head, drawing in her breath. 'Fearful places. Beatings. Hungry bairns. Cruelty to make you weep.' He reckoned she'd given up a lot to raise him. How could he abandon her after such a sacrifice?

After leaving the hospital he'd walked, hands in pockets, not really noticing where he was going. He moved along pavements considering terrible things – murder, theft, fraud – wondering what Ella had done. She was a gentle, timid soul. Born to sit on life's sidelines smiling slightly. She was no criminal mastermind. In the end Charlie decided that Ella might once have taken a bus ride and forgotten to pay. Her conscience would have been burdened with guilt for a long time over such an oversight. He smiled at the thought. And stopped, looked round. He'd walked so far from the hospital, he was yards from the Bull and Barnacle, a rough and rowdy drinking hole. It was his favourite pub for watching people who lived their lives openly, wildly, shouting and fighting and swearing. It fascinated him.

He took a stool at the bar and ordered a pint. The conversations around him were unpleasant but bawdy. He found that after another two pints this no longer bothered him. Life became pleasantly blurry and he became more sociable than he actually was.

Halfway through his third pint, the pleasant blurriness seeping through him, he'd been thinking the world was lovely, absolutely bloody lovely, and his fellow men were all his friends. Except the bloke on his right who'd been saying abusive things to the woman standing next to him. She had her back to Charlie. All he saw was white high heels, a tight red skirt, a flimsy but absurdly bright yellow-and-turquoise top and long blonde hair. Attractive, but not his type. The man had been calling her a cow, a bitch, a pervert. He'd said he hated the bloody likes of bloody her and told her to bloody go and bloody stand somewhere bloody else. He didn't bloody want her anywhere near him. 'Someone might think I'm with you.' He'd shoved her. Raised his fist.

Charlie had stepped forward. 'That's no way to treat a lady. You don't hit women.' He was feeling gallant. Alcoholically gallant.

The man turned and the blow that had been intended for the woman crunched into Charlie's cheek. It wasn't painful. The pain would come later. The shock had taken his breath away. As he reeled back, clutching the bar, knocking over chairs, spilling beer, the woman had turned, smiled and said, 'Thank you, darlin'.'

Even in his dazed state Charlie could see he'd made a mistake. This was no woman. Women didn't look like that. They didn't sound like that. This person had a voice that might suit a sailor, deep, salty, rough. She also had the beard to go with it and was missing a front tooth. The shock had made him reckless.

'God, you're ugly.' Charlie's cheerful blurriness and sociability had abandoned him. Now he was being drunkenly honest. Not good. The woman turned on him, too. Her blow landed on his stomach. He keeled forward and spat out a mouthful of regurgitated beer. The next punch hit him on the side of his face and the next sent him spinning to the floor. Now his assailants found it more convenient to kick him. It saved them bending down.

Curled up and praying for the beating to stop, Charlie had breathed in stale beer and tobacco and the foul smell of the filthy sticky wooden floor. Somewhere above him a woman, a real woman, was shouting, 'Outside. Outside the lot of yez.'

He'd been dragged face down across the room and thrown onto the pavement. When he'd come round he was in the gutter. His jacket was ripped, his pockets were empty and he was bleeding from his nose and mouth. He could barely move. In time, he'd crawled to the pub door, pulled himself to his feet and hobbled back in.

By now the pub had filled up. A thick blue layer of cigarette smoke curled and shifted along the ceiling, the air reeked of alcohol and curses. The man and woman who'd set about him had bonded and were standing at the bar each with an arm round the other's shoulder. Charlie had said, 'Bloody hell.'

The room had silenced, the swearing and drinking momentarily stopped. Everyone had turned to look at him. 'You,' the barmaid yelled. 'You at the door.' She'd pointed, arm rigid. 'Get out and stay out. You're barred. Don't show your ugly mug in here again. You're trouble.'

Charlie said, 'But . . .'

The barmaid had screamed, 'OUT.'

Charlie left. He thought this was the safest thing to do.

He'd walked home. Nothing else for it, he'd no money and, besides, he doubted he'd be allowed on public transport in his present state – ripped clothes, reeking of beer, bruised and bloodied face. It was after midnight when he reached the flat. His key had been spared and was still in the back pocket of his trousers. A mercy, he'd thought. He'd hung his jacket on the hook by the front door, splashed cold water on his face, wincing a lot, lay fully clothed on his bed and slept.

The banging on the door woke him. He'd opened his eyes, winced again – daylight hurt. He considered himself to be a master of light – he could tell the time by the colour of the day. Two in the afternoon. The banging continued. He should answer it, but moving was a problem. He'd heaved himself upright and shuffled from the bedroom to the front door. Not a long trip, but a painful one.

Perhaps it was their bulk, or their dark uniforms, but policemen always made him feel guilty. Seeing two of them standing in his doorway, surveying him, taking in the torn shirt and bruised, pulpy face, Charlie had felt bound to confess. Fair cop, he'd thought to say, 'I'll come quietly.' He knew for a fact he'd done nothing. He'd been set upon while defending a lady's honour. Except that the lady in question had turned out to be a man who'd taken exception to being called ugly. He'd started to prepare his version of events.

'Mr Gavin?'

'Yes.'

'Perhaps we could come in. The hospital couldn't get hold of you last night. I'm afraid we've got bad news.'

And Charlie knew this visit had nothing to do with the happenings in the pub. His Auntie Ella was dead. He'd never know what the terrible thing was.

The funeral had been quiet. Only Charlie, a couple of neighbours Ella had been friendly with and a woman who was the barmaid at the pub where she cleaned. Gazing at his feet and not looking at any of the three people who'd come along, Charlie gave a short speech.

'Thank you all for being here today. It would make Auntie Ella happy to know you came to say goodbye. I'll always be grateful to my aunt. She took me in when I had nobody. I think she saved my life. All that, and she made a mean scone.' He'd shoved his hands into his pockets, stared into the mid-distance rummaging through his mind for something more to say. He'd known he ought to invite the mourners out to a hotel for a cup of tea. That was the expected thing on such occasions. But the thought had filled him with dread. He didn't know these people, had nothing to say to them. He could have invited them back to the flat. He'd had tea and perhaps there were biscuits in the tin. 'Biscuits,' he said. Auntie Ella had said to look in the biscuit tin. There was something there to make up for the terrible thing she'd done. What? Custard creams? Bourbons? He was fond of them. 'The biscuit tin,' he'd said. He was near to tears and desperate. He'd be alone now. And that aloneness would go on for a long time. Maybe for the rest of his life. He'd wanted to get on with it. 'Biscuits,' he said again. The small gathering murmured understanding. In moments of grief and mourning there was nothing like the comfort of biscuits.

He'd discovered the money when he got home. He'd gone straight to the tin, an old and dented thing with a picture of the Forth Railway Bridge on top. Twelve thousand pounds in cash was stuffed under the lid in single and five-pound notes, all crumpled. Charlie had counted it, and then counted it again. He'd arranged it into hundred-pound bundles spread on the table in front of him. And counted it again. He'd never seen so much money in his life. It should have delighted him. But no, it filled him with guilt. How much had Auntie Ella denied herself to save this amount? The piles in front of him were the result of years of scrimping. It hurt to think of what she could have bought – a new coat, a decent sofa, a fridge. This flat where they had lived was bare, uncomfortable. Life had been frugal.

The furniture here was old, worn and dented or chipped from years of use. The kitchen had three pots. The bedrooms each had a narrow bed and forlorn wardrobe. Built in the early twenties, there was an inside toilet, but no bath. Washing was a delicate operation done in the kitchen, always hurriedly and always while singing or shouting, 'Keep out,' so each would know the other was in no state to be seen. Nakedness had been fleeting.

'Be safe and be kindly,' Auntie Ella always said. 'If you're safe you're never sorry. And if you're kindly, kindliness will come back to you.'

Charlie didn't know about being kindly, but safe was a good idea. He'd put the money back into the tin and had taken it to the bank where he'd placed it on the counter. One of the tellers had fetched the manager.

'Best place for it, lad,' Mr McGregor had told him. He'd pointed at the tin. 'Seen it before.'

Charlie had wondered if Mr McGregor had visited Auntie Ella and been offered a biscuit.

'People putting money in tins they keep under the bed rather than in the bank. It isn't safe. And there's no interest on money stashed under the mattress.'

They'd been in his office. Mr McGregor behind his giant polished desk, Charlie on a chair that had placed him rather lower down than the manager. He'd felt like a schoolboy, seeking approval from his headmaster.

Mr McGregor had leaned back. Looked serious. A man in

his fifties, balding with steel-rimmed glasses, his suit dark grey, shiny at the elbows, his shirt perfect white, he'd looked like a bank manager from central casting. 'Buy a house, son. You could get a lovely bungalow. Three bedrooms, nice little garden. You'd be set for life.'

Nobody had ever called Charlie son before. The word almost stopped him breathing. He didn't have a father. He didn't have a mother. Auntie Ella called him darling from time to time. She loved him, fussed over him but rarely gave him advice other than, 'Be kindly and be safe.' So fatherly advice – the first he'd ever been offered – was welcome, but a bit embarrassing. Charlie was tempted to take it. He wanted to please this man. But he was going to Canada. There was nothing now to keep him here.

He needed a passport. To get one he needed his birth certificate. He was here. He'd been born. He must have one. Back home, he'd searched the flat. He'd started with the drawer in the living-room sideboard where Ella kept all her papers. Here he'd found several recipes for interesting things to do with mince, along with old electric and gas bills and a few Christmas cards. He binned the lot.

He'd searched the other drawers and found nothing. He moved to the kitchen, but there the drawers and cupboards only contained ancient utensils – a potato peeler, a couple of knives, old pots with shaky handles.

Next came the search he dreaded – Auntie Ella's bedroom. He knew that he'd have to empty Ella's drawers and wardrobe before he went to Canada. But without that birth certificate he couldn't get a passport and there was only one place it could be – that room.

It smelled musty with a faint undertow of Ella's Lily of the Valley perfume; a tiny, frighteningly tidy, sparsely furnished room. The flat had always been immaculate, nothing ever lying around. Sometimes Charlie thought his aunt behaved as if she expected tidiness inspectors to break down the front door and rush in checking for mess. But then, Ella had a fear of unexpected visitors. She'd jump at any knock on the door.

He'd felt like an intruder. This had been Ella's sanctum and after he was seven years old he'd rarely come in here. He'd moved softly on tiptoe across to the small dressing table beside Ella's bed and opened the top drawer. He'd found a bible. In other drawers he'd found a hardly used lipstick and an old powder compact with a faded picture of a rose on the lid, a hairbrush, a set of curlers and Ella's scant collection of underwear. Nothing more. There were two skirts in the wardrobe along with three blouses, a cardigan, a coat and two pairs of shoes neatly lined up at the bottom. He'd raked in Ella's coat pockets knowing she'd be unlikely to keep a birth certificate there, but he was desperate.

On his hands and knees he'd looked under the wardrobe and under the bed. Only dust. He'd sat on the floor feeling hopeless. It wasn't the missing birth certificate that depressed him; it was the heart-stopping austerity of his aunt's life. The woman had nothing.

Ella had earned money as a seamstress. The only people who'd called at the flat were customers who wanted curtains made or clothes altered – hems taken up, waistbands loosened, jackets taken in or let out. The only time Ella left the flat was on Tuesday, Thursday and Saturday nights after ten when she cleaned the pub in the High Street.

How he'd hated these nights. Even now, years later, a low growl of worry spread through him at the thought of a Tuesday, Thursday or Saturday spent alone. He'd sit by the door wearing his striped pyjamas and thick red dressing gown waiting for Ella to come home. He'd start at every creak or night-time groan in the flat and hold his breath at footsteps passing in the street. He'd read, or study the pictures in his book. It was the story of two children lost in a deep dark forest. Dangers lurked. Witches, dragons, wolves, evil goblins watched the innocent pair from behind bushes and trees as they wandered through the density of trees and further and further from home. He'd put his fingers over the lost ones, keeping them safe from grasping claws and reaching arms and wild glinting eyes.

Ella always came home at half-past midnight. Charlie would hear her key in the lock, exhale a gasp of relief and run back to bed. By the time Ella had come in, put her bag in its place in her room, taken off her coat and stuck her head round the door of his room, he'd be under the blankets, eyes shut, pretending to sleep.

From when he was seven Charlie had done the shopping. Auntie Ella would give him a small list and some money and send him to the butcher's and the grocer's. She didn't like any of his friends dropping by and hated when he'd gone to play at someone's house. 'Be back by five,' she'd say. He'd sigh. But who was he to complain? Auntie Ella had saved him from life in a children's home. Her descriptions of the cruelties that went on in such places made him weep for the ones who had no Auntie Ella to open her arms to them. He'd prayed for them. It had been a nightly ritual, kneeling by his bed, fingers laced, eyes squeezed shut, begging God to keep the orphans safe.

Remembering all this, he'd sighed and heaved himself to his feet. As he'd pushed himself upright, his eyes had swept the top of the wardrobe and he caught a glimpse of something. A box. Ah, all the important papers will be in that. How like Auntie Ella to hide it away. Keeping it safe.

He'd taken it to the living room, set it on the table and opened it. Inside he'd found his life – a baby tooth wrapped in tissue paper, a lock of pale blond baby hair, a tiny pair of shoes, all his school reports, the valentine card he'd made for Ella when he was six, Christmas cards he'd given her, a photo of him on the beach standing at the water's edge, painfully thin in woollen swimming trunks holding a bucket and spade, a few buttons he recognised from childhood shirts, a pressed flower, his certificate for perfect attendance at Sunday school. All that and no birth certificate. He'd lurched from memory to memory, but had been shocked that his entire life so far could be stuffed into a small shoebox. It was time to move on, time to reach out for bigger moments. He'd go to Canada.

A week later he received a letter from the General Register Office for Scotland replying to the one he'd sent asking for a copy of his birth certificate. There was no record of anyone called Charles Gavin born in Glasgow on the fourth of March 1932.

The following afternoon he'd gone to Register House to look for himself. He'd searched through 1932, moved on to 1933, 1934 and 1935 but couldn't find anything. He'd looked for Ella Balfour – 10 November 1898 – and couldn't find her either. 'But she existed,' he'd shouted. 'She was my aunt. She brought me up. Saved me from the children's home.' He'd beat his chest. 'Look. It's me. I exist. I'm here.' He'd been escorted from the building.

He hadn't known what to do. He was a man without a past. Without a future, he'd thought. Every so often he'd grip his own arm, punch his thigh. 'I'm here. Flesh and blood.' He'd wondered if his mother, whoever she was, hadn't registered him. Auntie Ella had been vague about his parents. 'Your mother was a beauty. Long fair hair, perfect skin. Mairi, she was.'

'What about my father?' Charlie would ask.

'He was rich. I didn't know him really.'

She'd been equally vague when asked about herself. 'Oh, I had a little flat in Glasgow before you came along. But I moved here to be by the sea. My sweetheart died in the war, you know. Oh, he was a lovely man. Tall, handsome just like you're going to be.'

Charlie had decided he was a fool. He should have asked more questions. He should have found out more about his mother and father. He shouldn't have been so accepting.

He'd bought a house in Bath Street – three storeys of disrepair, bad plumbing, scary wiring and rotting floorboards. But he liked the space, large rooms and a wild garden at the back. He'd moved in with just a suitcase, sat on the floor and thought he really ought to get some furniture. 'Cups,' he'd decided. 'Spoons, towels, a kettle.' He'd bought a mattress, a record player, a kettle, some cutlery, two towels and a cup. All a man needs, he'd told himself.

He'd spent his days lying on his mattress looking up at his dust-streaked windows listening to Louis Armstrong and Charlie Parker. He'd eaten at cheap restaurants, drank a lot, felt sorry for himself but had rather enjoyed that. He'd indulged himself in his sorrow. He was a man who didn't exist.

Every day he'd go to the newsagent's to flirt shyly with Sheena as he bought an evening paper to read in the pub nearby. On the day of spotting Martha, he'd told Sheena she was looking good today, which she wasn't. She'd laughed as he headed out the door and said, 'Get a job. You need to do something. Your flirting technique's terrible.'

Charlie stopped, stared across the road. 'Who's that?'

It had been Martha. Looking fierce. A girl who knew everything about herself – who she was, where she was going, and didn't care what anyone thought. Her jaw was set and she stared up the road, willing the bus to come. How dare it not come? Didn't it know she was waiting?

If Charlie fell in love with her, it was only for five minutes. She'd been too young for him. And at the time his preference had been for women of experience, older than him with plump pillowy breasts and smoky voices. They'd be wiser and perfectly capable of drinking him under the table. But the girl across the road had stopped him breathing. He was lost in wonder. He'd stared. He'd envied her confidence, her ambition. He should be like that. He should look for himself, find out who he was and then move on from that.

He'd seen her often. Sometimes she'd had a boy with her. He'd been puppy-like, following her. Then, a few years on, she'd been pregnant. After that she'd disappeared, didn't turn up at the bus stop for a while. Later, about three years on, his heart had leapt when he saw her with a young child, a girl. She'd been leaning down talking to her, laughing at something she'd said.

It'd been a good laugh. Hearty, warm.

Ten years after that first sighting across from the newsagent's, when Martha walked into his life once more, it had happened again. Charlie stopped breathing. He fiddled with his pens. He flicked non-existent dust from his phone. He couldn't think of a decent job interview question to ask her. And when he'd come to himself, she was gone.

Oh, the joy when he'd come out of the café with his bacon sandwich. There she'd been, standing in the rain. He'd smiled and said something inane about the weather and Hollywood. Back at his desk, feeling like a responsible employer, he'd opened his paper bag and as he sniffed deeply the aroma of hot bacon and melting butter, it came to him that actually, after being too tongue-tied when she was sitting in front of him, he'd interviewed the poor woman as she stood on the pavement being soaked by relentless drizzle.

'Fool,' he'd said. 'Fool. Fool. Fool.' And banged his stupid head on his desk. He cursed himself for not getting the interview right. He thought he never got anything right. He stood. Pulled on his raincoat. Whistled on Murphy to stop snoozing on the sofa and come with him. He felt it coming on – the sadness. It always came on when he'd messed up.

Before it got too bad and the blackness gripped him, he'd go home and see how the people there were doing.

3

The Second-Stupidest Thing You've Ever Done

'So,' said Sophie, 'did you get the job?'

Martha said, 'Yes, as a matter of fact I did.'

'Oh dear, I was hoping you wouldn't.'

Sophie was sitting at the kitchen table. She wore her work outfit – a pair of men's dungarees, a voluminous checked shirt that had belonged to her husband and a blue apron.

Martha took off her coat, hung it on the post at the top of the stairs and kicked off her shoes. 'Well, I got the job. So nyaah.' She stuck out her tongue at her mother and looked round. 'Tea?'

'I never say no to a cup of tea,' said Sophie.

'How's work going?' asked Martha.

'Got two in the oven. Another one to go. Then I have to put it all together.'

She baked cakes for birthdays, anniversaries, indeed for any occasion that her customers thought would be enhanced by a specially decorated piece of baking. Her cakes came in any shape, size or colour. Today's cake was to be in the shape of a bicycle for a district nurse who was retiring. 'The wheels are tricky, but I'm worrying about the handlebars.'

'Why take all those difficult cakes on?'

'Money,' said Sophie. 'We need money. Especially now you've given up a well-paid job with a good company for a small-time one-man detective agency. You had prospects. Now you've a silly job. You've no sense.'

Martha put tea into the teapot and sighed. 'Mother, I've told you already. It takes over an hour to get to work at the moment. I have to leave before eight every morning and I don't get home till after six. I hardly see Evie these days. She's seven. She needs a mother. Anyway, it isn't a detective agency, it's a missing persons bureau. The Be Kindly Missing Persons Bureau.'

'Evie's got me. I can sort out her problems. That's what a grandmother is for.'

'I'm missing seeing my own daughter growing up.'

Sophie shrugged. 'That's the way of things in the modern world. Also, you have to consider you might be a bad influence now you're working at a detective agency. You'll be mixing with criminals.'

'No, I won't. Charlie traces people who have gone missing.'

'I know why you did this. You think this Gavin chap could be the one. The one who'll find Jamie.'

Martha shook her head. 'Oh, he's not the one. Definitely not. I don't think he could find anyone. I have a feeling he's a terrible detective.'

'Then why take a job with him?'

'I've already told you. No commuting. I can leave here a few minutes before nine and be home just after five.'

'You'll never meet anyone working there. The only people you'll meet will be lonely people who have lost the ones they love. It will be depressing and tragic.'

Martha said she wasn't looking for anybody. 'I'm happy as I am.'

'I don't believe you. Nobody's happy as they are. Everybody wants a little bit more of what they've got. New gadgets or curtains or a bigger house. Or they want something completely different, a new way of life. If people were happy as they are the world would come to a stop.'

'So you're not happy as you are?'

'Of course not,' said Sophie. 'I'd like to be thinner and richer. And I don't think you can be happy living with your mother in the house where you were brought up.'

'It was your idea. When the Jamie thing happened, you said Evie and I should move in here with you. You said it would save me paying the rent and you'd look after Evie while I was at work.'

'And I do. I love doing it.'

Martha said, 'So why are we arguing?'

Sophie sighed. 'We are arguing because I can't believe you are leaving a very good job in insurance to go and work in a sad little agency. It's the stupidest thing you've ever done.' She sniffed, 'I take that back. It's the second-stupidest thing you've ever done.' She looked round the kitchen. 'This place could do with a good clean up. And I need to sort out the cupboards. Everything's all jumbled up.'

'It's not too bad.'

'It's a mess. I think I should put the things in the food cupboard in alphabetical order. Then I'd know where they are. A for . . .' She couldn't think of anything beginning with A. 'B for biscuits and beetroot, for example.'

Martha said, 'It's a longstanding jumble. I know it well.'

Sophie got up. 'In that case, I'm going for a walk. The doctor says walking's good for me. You can take the cakes out of the oven.' She disappeared down the hall and minutes later reappeared heaving on her coat. 'I don't believe that this has nothing to do with finding Jamie. You think that detective man can help you.'

'No, I don't think he could,' said Martha. 'But Jamie is my husband. I'd like to know where he is and what possessed him to disappear like that.'

'He was selfish and irresponsible.' Sophie was incensed. She stomped down the hall heading for the door. 'He couldn't face a life of marriage, bills, endless routines and bringing up a child.'

‘Something’s weird about it all,’ Martha said.

Sophie stomped back up the hall. ‘You’re looking for a mystery where none exists. Jamie was bored. He’s a quitter, that’s all.’

Martha said, ‘Perhaps.’

She heard Sophie march to the front door and go out, and looked at her watch. ‘Twenty minutes.’

Sighing, Martha sipped her tea and stared at the cooker waiting for the cakes to be ready. It left her mind free to roam through what she now called the awful time. The black time.

4

The Chip Thief

It had started when Martha had told Jamie she was expecting their second child. She'd thought he'd be delighted. 'We'll be a proper family – husband, wife and the regulation two children.' She grinned at him.

He nodded. 'So we will.'

They were eating lunch in a diner in Stockbridge. Martha's treat – she'd started saving for this, sneaking small secret amounts of her weekly housekeeping allowance into her knicker drawer every week since missing her first period. This time she was going to do everything properly. This pregnancy was going to be beautiful. She'd be relaxed, glowing. Baby would arrive in the world smiling. She planned to move through her expectant months wearing soft, wafting clothes listening to Mozart and eating healthy things. She imagined herself an earth mother. Barefoot and pregnant. Clear-skinned and calm.

The wonderful, uplifting, remaining seven months would start with her telling Jamie her good news here in this place where rock'n'roll roared out and the walls were festooned with American heroes – Steve McQueen, Buddy Holly, Elvis, Paul Newman. Jamie loved it here. He loved everything American. He loved that his burger was served with fries and not chips. Never chips.

Unfortunately, Martha's financial reckonings were wrong. Things cost more than she'd budgeted for, so she claimed not to be hungry and ordered a cup of coffee for herself. She smiled watching Jamie and Evie eat, almost enjoying the feeling of martyrdom. It was good to feel saintly about forsaking a meal so loved ones could enjoy a burger. Then again her stomach was making strange and embarrassing gurgling noises.

Jamie had bought a new Stones LP and seemed more interested in reading the sleeve notes than he was in Martha's announcement.

'You don't seem very pleased.'

'Of course I'm pleased. Who wouldn't be? It's great news.' He smiled, a slight upward flicker of his lips. 'I'm going to be a daddy again. Cool.' He returned to the sleeve notes.

Not wanting an argument, she'd left it at that. Jamie lit a cigarette and watched a group of people at a table nearby. Martha followed his gaze. The people were probably the same age as she and Jamie, but looked younger. They had youthful confidence, were dressed to shock – jeans, cowboy boots, beads, T-shirts. One of the girls had a pink feather in her hair. She was rolling a cigarette and telling everybody she wouldn't have a burger, she'd turned vegetarian this morning. This seemed to impress the group. Jamie nodded agreeing and pushed away his plate, disowning it. He had, however, finished the burger that had sat on it.

Wafts of patchouli drifted across to Martha. She absently picked up one of Evie's fries and ate it.

The child wailed, pointing at her. 'You ate my chip. It was my favourite. My best chip. And you ate it. I was savin' it.'

Martha blushed. 'Sorry.' She pointed at the plate. 'There are other chips. Look, there's a good one. I think that's the chief chip.'

Evie shook her head. 'I don't want the chief chip. I want that chip you ate.' Red-faced and tear-stained, she pointed at Martha's mouth. The place where the chip was last seen.

The patchouli group turned and stared at Martha. Harsh, accusing looks. She was a cruel mother. A chip thief. They were young enough to think they knew everything and young enough, also, to disapprove of anyone boring enough to have married and produced a child. They sneered. She cringed.

Bored by this drama, Jamie drew his cigarette along the base of his ashtray, looked at his watch. 'Must go. Have to be back at work in fifteen minutes. Don't want to be late.' He pointed at Evie's plate. 'You shouldn't have done that. I hate it when someone pinches my chips, too.'

Martha went to the counter to pay. And on her way back to the table glanced at the patchouli people. She heard one of them say that when she had children she'd let them do as they liked. 'They'll be free spirits. They'll grow up with no hang-ups.'

Jamie had disowned her. He was outside, leaning on the wall, smoking another cigarette, acting aloof.

They walked up the road slowly, tiny steps at a young child's pace, heading for Princes Street. Martha spoke about the new baby, the changes that were about to come into their life. It would be good for Evie to have a brother or sister. A boy would be wonderful, but in a way it would be handy to have another girl. 'We wouldn't have to buy new clothes. I think it's cool to have a family while we are young. We can grow up with our children.' She prattled on, not really looking at Jamie, just letting her thoughts flow. 'We'll have to get a bigger house in time. The kids can share a room at first but they'll want their own space soon enough.' She stopped, frowned. 'What d'you think of Luke if it's a boy? And Emma for a girl. Evie and Emma. Sounds good.'

Jamie stopped walking. Looked a bit panic stricken. 'Shit. I've forgotten my LP. Left it back at the diner.' He whirled round and started to run back. She watched him go, thinking that really he didn't need to run so fast. His head was back, arms working like pistons. He was travelling. Something about the urgency in his voice and his sudden speedy departure upset Evie. She reached out, calling, 'Daddy. Daddy!'

'He's only gone to get his record,' said Martha. 'He'll be back.' She leaned on the railings, looking into Queen Street Gardens. 'I'd love a big garden,' she said.

Ten minutes passed, twenty, half an hour. Where the hell was he? She decided to walk back to meet him, thinking he'd probably met somebody he knew and couldn't get away. She would rescue him.

She turned the corner expecting to see Jamie coming towards her. The street was empty. As was the diner. Sonny and Cher were booming out on the radio, 'I Got You Babe'. Martha stood in the doorway looking round. She couldn't believe Jamie wasn't here. 'Did my husband come here to pick up an LP he'd forgotten?' she asked.

The waitress said, 'Yes.' She pointed to the table where Martha and Jamie had been sitting. It had been cleared and wiped. 'He left with his friends.'

'What friends?'

The waitress pointed to the table the patchouli people had occupied. 'The people there.'

Martha said, 'Ah. Right.' How odd, Jamie hadn't mentioned that he'd known these people. He hadn't said hello to them. Surely he would have introduced her. She went back into the street, looked to the left and right. Nobody there. She went back into the diner. 'Are you sure he left with these people?'

'Yeah, positive.' The waitress looked offended at being doubted.

Martha looked round once more. But the place was definitely empty. She dipped and glanced under the table. Bobbed back up, caught the waitress's eye and blushed. 'He might have been playing a joke.'

The waitress shook her head. 'No. No joke. He's not here.'

Martha shrugged. She must have missed him. How odd. He'd probably gone back to work. He'd taken a different route. One he'd decided was quicker than the one they had been walking.

She caught the bus home. Spent the rest of the afternoon playing with Evie, dreaming about being a proper family – husband, wife and two kids like the people in her school reading book – and ignoring the raw churning in her stomach. Something odd and fearful had happened.

At six o'clock she started getting Evie ready for bed and put two lamb chops under the grill to cook slowly. Jamie usually arrived home at half-past. He'd sit Evie on his knee and read her a story. After that he'd slip out to his shed to check his record collection. There wasn't space in their tiny living room for his hundreds of albums. Tonight, however, Jamie didn't return at his regular time. Tonight he didn't come home at all.

A miserable ache of a February night that Martha would never forget – the awful, awful night. The night of silence, her imagination in overdrive and a burning anxiety raging through her. She moved between the kitchen and the living-room window, staring out. Waiting for Jamie to appear. 'Where the hell has he got to?'

She put Evie to bed, read her a story, and when she asked where her daddy was, told her he'd be home soon. Jamie would come, banging the front door shut, shouting apologies, the chill night air clinging to his coat. He'd laugh and tell her he was sorry, he'd had to work late and hadn't time to phone her.

Eleven o'clock and still no sign. Martha sat in the living room, hands folded on her lap, nerves singing in her stomach and doom scenarios in her head – Jamie dead after being hit by a bus, Jamie suffering amnesia in hospital, Jamie attacked by thugs and lying bruised and bleeding and undiscovered in some park somewhere. She phoned every hospital in Edinburgh and, no, a Jamie Walters had not been admitted to any of them.

She phoned her mother, who told her not to worry. 'He'll have gone out to the pub with some workmates. He'll come home blind drunk smelling like sin and begging your forgiveness. It happens. And, no, don't phone the police. Not yet. You'll both end up being embarrassed. Just remember men snore and men make stupid remarks and forget your anniversary and are annoying. And sometimes they go off on their own to do manly things like get drunk and pretend to be younger than they are. Just relax. He'll be home soon enough.'

Martha had gone to bed unconvinced by her mother's notions of Jamie's whereabouts. She lay tense and listening for footsteps on the path outside. Nothing. And the night rolled on. At three in the morning she got up and made tea. She sat at the kitchen table listening to the night sounds of the house, waiting for daylight and for the world to start up again. The image in her head was of Jamie. 'Shit,' he'd said, 'I've forgotten my LP. Left it at the diner.' And he'd taken off running back to get it. The more she thought about it, the faster Jamie had run. Eventually, he wasn't running he was fleeing. He was waving his arms and shouting, 'Aaaah! No!' It dawned on her that he wasn't running back to the diner. He was racing away from her. Away from what she'd been talking about – the life they were going to live, the new child, the bigger house and more mouths to feed.

In the morning, after taking Evie to nursery, Martha looked in Jamie's wardrobe. His clothes were gone. All that was left was a selection of white shirts. They looked lonely. They had nothing to do with the Jamie she knew. The rock'n'roll boy who'd driven their van, shared their music dreams. They were Jamie's compromise shirts. The things he'd put on to go out to work at a job he'd hated. Something he'd done to pay the rent and put food on the table. She went out to the garden shed. The sweet herby smell lingered. Jamie's dope. Martha knew all about his habit and didn't blame him. She figured he needed the escape and smoking a little grass was something he had in common with the people whose music he loved. This morning that scent was all that remained of Jamie. His record collection was gone. Hundreds and hundreds of LPs. He must have been taking them away bit by bit for weeks. And Martha knew Jamie had left her.

The letter arrived the next day. Seven words. *I've gone. Don't look for me. Sorry.*

'For God's sake, I know you've gone,' Martha said. There was nobody around to hear. But speaking out loud helped. He hadn't even written love Jamie. That hurt.

Later that day, Martha phoned Jamie's work. He was under-manager at a Princes Street department store. She was told he'd handed his notice in last week. 'Didn't say where he was going,' the girl on the end of the line said. 'Sorry.'

Days later Martha miscarried. Sophie took her to hospital, and brought her back to her own house when it was over. 'You're best here where I can look after you.' So Martha sat by the fire, pale and drained, hardly speaking. She was numb. Sophie looked after Evie, took her to nursery, and in the afternoon brought her home again. She brought Martha bowls of chicken soup and told her to rest. 'You're suffering from shock. It'll pass. What you need is hot, sweet tea, soup and a bit of comfort.'

It was inevitable. Sophie suggested Martha and Evie move in permanently. 'Well, you need to get on with your life. You'll have to get a job and meantime you won't be able to pay your rent.' She sighed. 'It'll be company. We both need company.'

Martha got a job with a small publisher. She'd thought it would be a lively place to work. She'd meet interesting people, authors for example. But George McPherson only published dead authors whose work was long out of copyright. The books were usually about bird watching, rock climbing, geology and walking. Nothing that interested Martha; so, she was bored and lonely. George often worked from home, and she was the sole employee. A couple of months after she started at the company George joined his authors. His wife found him dead at his desk and a few days later told Martha she was no longer needed.

After that Martha found a job with a huge insurance company, working in the typing pool. Machines clattered round her, girls gossiped, bosses came and went flapping bits of paper. And Martha kept herself to herself. She arrived at nine, went home at five and rarely spoke to anyone. She didn't make any friends. She refused to make friends. She didn't trust people any more. And she didn't want anyone to know her story. It was too shameful. Her husband had walked out. People would think it was her fault. She'd been a nag. Or frigid. Or both.

'So, here I am,' she said to the kitchen in Sophie's house. 'Back in the flat where I grew up. It looks the same. Smells the same. It is the same. I've changed. I've lost my sense of wonder.' She sniffed deeply. 'Talking of smells, the cakes are ready.'

5

You Should Be Dancing

On cue, twenty minutes after Sophie had left the flat, the phone rang. 'Please bring the car. I can't be bothered walking back home.'

Martha shoved her feet back into her shoes, heaved on her coat and took the car key from the hook marked B, in the hall. B for Beetle rather than C for car. Sophie thought her car deserved a small amount of recognition as she considered it to be more characterful than just a car.

The house looked out onto the sea, but the entrance was at the side. Sophie and now Martha and Evie lived on the upper two floors. The flat was large, draughty and badly in need of decorating. But that was beyond the family budget. Sophie covered the walls instead with paintings found in junk shops and collections of objects that she put together and framed – postcards, feathers found on the beach, withering flowers from her garden and selections of things she found interesting – a clipping from a newspaper alongside some Christmas wrapping and a few pebbles from the shore. She gave these groupings names that had no connection with what they contained – Yesterday's Doubts, A Little Bit of Yearning, Waiting for Judas – and always refused to explain what was meant. Mostly because she didn't know. The names were an assortment of words that had popped into her head.

The rain had stopped and a fresh wind was whipping off the sea. Martha pulled her coat round her as she walked up the path to the car. This rescuing of mother happened quite often. Sophie would set off striding towards Joppa. It was part of her good-health regime that she'd started when she hadn't actually wanted to be healthy. She'd wanted to die, to join her husband, Martin. And to punish herself for being alive when he wasn't. But she had responsibilities – a daughter who needed a mother.

So Sophie walked for Martha, though she hated it. It was purposeful but lonely. Before his death she and Martin had walked every evening. They'd discussed everything from politics to missing socks. They'd talked so much they'd always cover more ground than they intended and had sighed as they'd turned to tackle the long journey home. So walking brought painful memories. When they got too much to bear Sophie would phone home.

Martha drove up the High Street to where she knew Sophie would be waiting, at the end of the prom. She parked and joined her mother leaning on the railings, staring out at the sea.

'Walking's boring,' said Sophie. 'It's a matter of putting one leg in front of the other and that's all there is to it.'

'Well, that's easy,' Martha said.

'But you are just moving through the day. Air on your face is nice. But because you are only using your legs, your mind is free to think. It's the thinking gets to me. I hate random thinking. It's awful. No wonder philosophers are a bunch of fruitcakes.'

Martha said she didn't think philosophers thought randomly and they weren't all fruitcakes. 'What do you think about?'

'All the things you shouldn't think about. Life. Loneliness. Grief. Sorrow. Regret. Stupid decisions.'

'Goodness,' said Martha. 'No wonder you hate walking.'

'And you. I think about you.'

'You lump me in with all those awful things?'

'I worry about you. You should be enjoying yourself. You should be going out at night mixing with people, not sitting at home with your mother. You should be dancing.'

'I don't want to dance.'

'You're living with regret. You're hanging on to your past, hoping to find Jamie. Hoping he'll come back. But he's gone.'

'I just want to know why,' said Martha.

'The why of it all is obvious. Jamie had an is-this-it moment. He looked round at the clutter of plastic toys and at you all tired and bedraggled after a day with Evie and at the little house you lived in and he thought, this isn't what I planned.'

'But we were in love. We were settled.'

'Oh, settled.' Sophie flapped her hand, shooing settled away. 'Don't be daft. Nobody's settled. Well, Evie is. But she's seven. That's when you're settled. You're loved, but you take it for granted. You know what's going to happen from day to day. And on good days you might get a warm plate of custard and bananas with melty brown sugar on top. It's all you want. But once you are grown-up that's it for being settled. You go crashing into love. Unsettled. You marry. Unsettled. Then you find yourself in a house somewhere having to clean up, wash socks and underpants and worry about paying bills. Unsettled. You have a child and it's all guilt and more worry. Unsettled. Your child grows and grows and becomes a teenager all the while you're getting older and wrinklier. Unsettled, very unsettled. Martha, my girl, the state of being settled doesn't exist. It's a myth. Accept the truth.'

Martha held her breath, waiting for more. Once her mother got going, expounding, dishing out opinions, she was hard to stop.

'I blame the fairy tales. All that once upon a time and happily ever after. It's implanted early and people believe it. And it's nonsense,' Sophie continued.

Martha sighed. 'Still, I think about Jamie. I wonder about him. We were childhood sweethearts.'

Sophie snorted. 'Exactly. He'd only had one girlfriend, who became his wife. Not enough getting to know the opposite sex. He should have played the field when he was young. But he didn't, he followed you around like a love-struck puppy.'

'He didn't,' said Martha. Wind from the sea swept the hair from her face, pushed round her. She gripped her coat and huddled into it.

'He did, too. That boy was born forty. He was too sensible. I knew he'd end up working back to sixteen and start being silly. Unlike you. You were silly at seventeen, and did the stupidest thing of your life.'

'I don't think it was that stupid,' said Martha.

'No doubt you had your fun, got up to all the mischief Jamie went off to find. I think he was jealous of your naughty past.'

Martha thought about that. 'Maybe he was.'

'You should move on with your life, you should stop all the wondering and accept what happened.'

But Martha couldn't stop wondering. In her head she visited the awful time daily. She was sure Jamie's disappearance was her fault. She'd been hard to live with, demanded too much, hadn't shown him enough love. And she couldn't stop looking for him. On buses she stared at crowds in the street searching for that one familiar face in the sea of faces. She regularly walked the length of Princes Street scanning the people she passed. She stared at the crowd while watching football matches on television, always hoping that the assembly of familiar features she was endlessly looking for would suddenly appear and she might shout, 'That's him. I saw him.' She often imagined what she'd do if she came across him in a pub or making his way along the same street as she was making her way along. 'Oh, there you are,' she might say casually. Or, 'Where the hell have you been?' They might kiss. He might come back to her and things would be as they'd been before. This, she knew, couldn't happen. He'd walked out on her without telling her where he was going, indeed, without telling her he was going. After such a thing, it would never be the same again.

Sophie patted her arm. 'You should put all the hurt behind you.'

Martha looked out at the sea, huge waves galloping in, white horses and the wind slicing spray off their crests. She set her face against the chilly blast, a grimace. 'I like watching the waves. All the shapes they make, there's a rhythm to it. It's endless.' She put her arm round Sophie. 'You're wrong about the job. Working at the insurance office, I'm a dogsbody. My only prospect is the chance to become a slightly more important dogsbody. I could even rise to be the most important dogsbody. But if I stay there it's a dogsbody's life for me. Besides . . .'

She wanted to say she thought it time to join the world again. She'd been numb for so long. And there was a lot going on – music, men in purple shirts and velvet jackets, long-legged girls in short skirts, people crying out for peace and love, protests, films. Oh, everything was happening and passing her by. In this new job she might see a bit of life.

'Besides?' said Sophie.

'Besides, I'm getting a headache. I think it's this wind. It's cold.'

'In which case, we better get you home. If that's true. I don't think it is. I think your besides is something else that you don't want to talk about.' She waved away whatever it was Martha was about to say. 'Don't argue. I'm right. I'm always right. I don't get pleasure from this. In fact being constantly right is a burden.'

6

All the Missing People

Nine o'clock Monday morning Martha stood at the door of Charlie Gavin's office wearing her best work outfit: a slim black skirt, crisp white high-collar shirt and black stiletto heels. She fancied she looked like the perfect efficient secretary. The office, however, was locked. She wrestled with the door handle. She knocked. Nothing. She looked up and down the street. No Charlie.

Ten minutes went by, twenty, thirty. She looked at her watch, paced, stared up and down the street. No Charlie.

It started to rain. Pulling up her coat collar, Martha ran to the café across the road and ordered a cup of coffee. She sat watching the doorway to the office through the rivulets streaming down the window, debating if she should give up and go home. In the end, she decided against it. Turning up, disappointed and damp, so soon after leaving would give her mother an opportunity to launch into her I-told-you-so routine.

Sophie wouldn't say the actual words. She'd express her smugness in the way she moved, put on the kettle, stood waiting for it to boil with her back to Martha. Her silences were always more crushing than anything she might say. No, thought Martha, I'm not going home. She'd wait in this café, and if Charlie Gavin didn't show up, she'd spend the day wandering the streets till five o'clock. Then she'd return to the flat and tell Sophie she'd had a wonderful day and the new job was fascinating.

She clasped her cup in both hands, eyes fixed on the door across the road. Of course, if this continued, she'd have to wander the streets every day. She planned to take the bus to Princes Street, find a murky backstreet café and sit drinking coffee while writing job applications. That would be the thing to do. Sophie need never know her shame.

The girl who'd served her traipsed from behind the counter to the jukebox and put on Martha and the Vandellas' 'Dancing In The Street'. It was the third time she'd played it. 'I love that song,' she shouted to someone who was working in the kitchen. 'It's wild and free, just like me.' She jiggled in time to the music, waved her arms over her head and sang along. Martha cringed. The record stopped. The girl put it on again. Martha's shoulders tensed and rose in horror. There was nothing like loud music and a young girl shouting, 'Wild and free, just like me,' to make a tense nervous woman tenser and more nervous.

A man, short, middle-aged and paunchy, definitely not Charlie Gavin, stopped outside the office door. He tried opening it, twisting the handle this way and that. He banged furiously with his fist. Peered through the letterbox. Finally kicked the door a couple of times before walking off.

Martha thought, Goodness, perhaps my mother was right and I will be dealing with lonely hearts and losers. Sometimes very angry losers. She wondered if she should have gone across to the man and explained in her best secretarial tone that Mr Gavin had been delayed and could she take his telephone number so Mr Gavin could get in touch? But considering the force of the two kicks, she thought not. So far, this had not been a good day.

At last, at ten-fifteen on the dot, Charlie Gavin slid into view. He was on a red bicycle with a deep wicker basket attached to the handlebars. His trousers were neatly tucked into bicycle clips. He rode slowly and appeared to be talking to himself. Murphy, the cocker spaniel, trotted along the edge of the pavement, looking up at him from time to time. Perhaps adoringly, or perhaps, like Martha, he thought Charlie Gavin a little bit outré.

Martha heaved her coat from where she'd draped it over the back of her chair, went to the counter and paid for her coffee and all the while watched Charlie as he got off his bike, removed the clips from his trousers, propped the bike against the wall and searched his pockets for his keys. All this was mundane. But the meticulously precise way he conducted the routine held Martha's interest. Meanwhile, the dog waited, eager no doubt to get on with his busy day of snoring and farting on the sofa.

Halfway across the road, Martha's relief turned to rage. When she finally stood beside Charlie, she didn't say a polite good morning as she'd planned. Instead she snapped, 'Where the hell have you been?'

Charlie turned, slapped his forehead. 'Oh, Christ. I forgot.'

'You forgot I was coming?'

'No. I forgot to tell you I don't get to work till quarter past ten. Sorry.'

Tapping his nameplate as he passed, he wheeled his bike into the corridor, propped it against the wall and, once again, rummaged through his pockets for the key to the inner door. 'They're not in my key pocket.' He patted his left-hand jacket pocket. 'I always keep my keys in here.' He gave her a pocket review. Patting a pocket and telling her what he kept in it. 'Keys, wallet, comb, notebook, pen, dog biscuits, hanky, loose change and various sundry things not listed but sometimes necessary. A pen knife, for example.'

Martha said, 'It's good to be organised.'

He nodded. Pulled the key from the back pocket of his trousers, announcing, 'Wrong pocket.' And opened the door.

They tumbled into the office, dog first. It barged towards the sofa, leapt up and twirled, pummelling the cushions preparing for a day's hard snoozing. Charlie looked round, checking that everything was as it had been when he'd left the place on Friday evening. Martha went to her desk, removed the cover from the typewriter and started to look through her desk drawers.

There were the usual things – typewriter ribbons, a couple of erasers, a stack of headed notepaper. In one drawer was a small book *A History of Jazz* and inside was a note: *You will need this*. In another drawer was a half-finished report with another note: *You will have to complete this. I'm off*. Other drawers contained books, knitting patterns and a selection of chocolate bars.

'Did Mrs Florey give you much notice when she left?' Martha asked.

'God, no. She came in one morning and said she was done working here. She was off. And that was that. Whoosh, she was gone.' He spread his arms and shrugged. 'Who knows the workings of the Florey mind?'

Another drawer contained a harmonica.

'Was Mrs Florey musical?'

'Yes,' said Charlie. 'I'd say she was.'

There was a letter in the bottom drawer. The envelope was addressed to *Whoever gets my job*. The note inside was brief:

Please take care of Charlie. I love him, I really do. But I've had enough of lonely hearts and lost souls. I've paid my dues and now I'm off to see a bit of the world. It's been out there waiting for me for a long time.

Charlie has his little idiosyncrasies but he's not as daft as he looks or acts. And please forgive Murphy his indiscretions.

Sincerely
Rosa Florey.

PS I hope you find your lost one. I know you must be looking, otherwise you wouldn't be sitting at this desk working for the kind of pay he'll be offering.

Martha looked up at Charlie. He was carefully slipping an LP out of its sleeve, finger in the hole in the middle, thumb on the edge, and putting it onto a small record player on the shelf beside his desk. Louis Armstrong burst into the room, a joyous sound. 'Louis in the mornings,' Charlie said. 'It's too early in the day for Dizzy Gillespie. Might do some Rolling Stones later.' He started to bop in the small space between his desk and the window, moving his head in time to the music. He stopped. Whirled round. Pointed at Martha with both hands, two fingers outstretched. A gunfighter's pose. 'My God, we forgot the bacon rolls. It's ten to eleven. We're five minutes late. You get them. Money in the petty cash box. I'll make the coffee.'

Ten minutes later, they were in the kitchen, a small, snug space, painted pale green and immaculately clean. Charlie had laid out two blue-and-white patterned plates and matching cups. The place was filled with the thick dark aroma of fresh coffee. He poured.

'Good coffee is the stuff of life. I have to go to the Italian deli up Leith Walk for this.' He bit into his bacon roll. 'Perfect. You have to get the right balance of tastes in your mouth. Roll, bacon and coffee.'

Martha agreed. Noticed it was after eleven o'clock and, so far, no work had been done.

'Do you know,' said Charlie, 'I had to go across to that café and show them how to make the perfect bacon roll. They used to undercook the bacon. It was flaccid. Bacon crispy, bread soft and a small amount of slightly melting butter, what's so hard about that?'

'Nothing,' said Martha. She wrestled with the mental image of him behind the counter wearing a large apron, waving a spatula and pronouncing on the importance of crispy bacon. 'Actually, while I was waiting for you, a man came to your door. I was going to speak to him, but when he started kicking the door, I changed my mind.'

'Good thinking,' said Charlie. 'What did he look like?'

Martha shrugged. 'Middle-aged, smallish, dark hair, a bit of a pot belly, cheap suit.'

Charlie said, 'You could be describing anybody. In fact, if it wasn't for the dark hair and cheap suit, you could be describing me. I don't have a pot belly either, come to that.'

Martha said, 'Nor are you smallish. So it couldn't have been you.'

'No. But when observing people, you've got to look closely. It's all in the details.'

Martha said she wasn't a detective. 'I wasn't aware I should be looking for details.'

'You have to be careful,' said Charlie. 'Sometimes people get upset. You know, when they've been happily missing and I find them and bring them back to the world they thought they'd left behind.' He sipped his coffee contemplating this. 'So,' he turned to Martha, 'who is missing with you?'

'I don't know what you mean,' Martha answered too quickly. And flushed.

'Yes, you do.'

'How do you know?'

'You kind of twitched when you asked me about my work. And, you've left a well-paid job to come and work for me for buttons. A bit like Mrs Florey. Except she worked for nothing.'

'She did?' said Martha. 'Why?'

'I found her sister and she couldn't afford my fee. After she'd paid it off, she just kept turning up for work. Said it was somewhere to go.' He put down his cup and pulled a hanky from the appropriate pocket to wipe his hands. 'So, it's not your mother, you live with her. It's not your daughter. Your father's dead. You've no sisters or brothers, so who is missing? Your husband?'

Martha was shocked. 'How do you know all that about me?'

'I checked up on you.' He was lying. Sheena at the newsagent's had updated him on Martha's life.

'That's not very nice. In fact, that's horrible. Why did you do that?'

'I needed to know who was coming to work with me. Checking up on people is what I do.'

'It's my husband. He ran away. I don't know why for sure. It's a bit of a mystery.'

Charlie finished his coffee and carried the cups to the sink. 'I don't believe in mysteries. I don't do mysteries. I gather facts and present them to my clients. They decide what to do with them. Your husband probably got scared.'

'What of?'

'Living the life he was living and never doing the things he dreamed about – going to California, riding a camel across a desert, seeing the sun come up over the Taj Mahal. Making love to a beautiful woman with the surf crashing over him. Becoming a cowboy. That sort of stuff. He got to the point where, yes, it was scary to go but even scarier to stay.' He sniffed. 'Unless, there is another reason and you know what it is, but you're keeping it to yourself because you're ashamed.'

Charlie said she should get on with the report Mrs Florey had left in her desk.

'Just write it up from my notes,' he told her. 'Then, perhaps, you could take a look at the filing cabinets. Mrs Florey had her own system. She put everything under degrees of tragedy.'

Martha spent the rest of the morning typing the report. Charlie set and lit the fire before running a carpet sweeper over the rug and dusting his desk and shelves. After that, he put on another Louis Armstrong LP, carefully removing the first one and replacing it in its sleeve. He took off his jacket, draped it over the back of his chair and settled down to work, scribbling furiously in his notebook.

Every time the phone rang, Charlie would look at Martha. 'Who's that on the phone?'

Before picking up the receiver, Martha would say she didn't

know. Then she'd slip into her perfect secretary routine. 'Good morning, Charlie Gavin's office, who is calling?'

The caller would tell her their name. Martha would repeat it and glance at Charlie. He'd wave his arms in the air, shaking his head and mouthing no, no, no. Unless it was Brenda or Art, in which case he'd pick up and say, 'What now?' He'd listen then give appropriate instructions. 'The plunger is under my kitchen sink.' Or, 'No, you fry the onions first.'

'Who are Brenda and Art?' Martha asked.

'They stay at my place.'

'Lodgers?'

Charlie shook his head. 'Nah. They just stay.'

When Martha asked Charlie why he didn't take his work calls, he told her, 'Not on a Monday morning. It's too early in the week for dealing with broken lives. I need to warm up to get ready to cope with life's absurdities. Anyway, I was working yesterday. I work most days. So Monday is sort of my Sunday.'

'What are you doing at the moment?'

'Making my weekly list. Records to be played on different days. Beatles tomorrow and a bit of Van Morrison, Miles Davis on Wednesday, then as we approach the weekend Nina Simone and a splash of Ella Fitzgerald finishing with Charlie Parker and Billie Holiday on Friday. What d'you think?'

'Sounds fine,' said Martha. What else could she say? Matching music with the days of the week was new to her.

'Good. Now I'll get on with the sandwiches. A list of the week's fillings. What's your favourite sandwich?'

She stopped typing and considered the question. 'Roast chicken. I like it when the chicken's still warm, with just a touch of mayonnaise and some lettuce. Or just plain tomato, thinly sliced with a dribble of olive oil and pepper.'

He frowned, thinking about this. 'Good sandwiches. Of course, it all depends on the bread.'

'Absolutely,' Martha agreed and continued typing. *Thomas*

Markham (75) disappeared 20th March 1967. Found 28th February 1969.

'Could you take a letter to go with that?' said Charlie. 'It'd be good if we could get it in the post tonight along with an invoice.' He coughed. 'It's to Mrs Patterson, Thomas Markham's daughter. Just say, here's my report and invoice and I hope she finds everything satisfactory. And tell her not to worry, and her father is well and would like to hear from her. Yours sincerely, Charlie Gavin.'

'You want me to write the letter, then?' said Martha.

'Well, put all that stuff in, but nicely. Remember you are writing to someone who has been confused, worried and probably guilty.' He got up, whistled and jerked his head towards the door. 'C'mon, Murphy. Time for a walk.'

He leaned on the doorpost. 'Lives in suspension. People going through their daily routine, work, meals, sleeping, and all the time they're waiting. And they don't always know why this happened. Why the person they're waiting for went away. So be kindly.' He left.

Came back again. 'Just write the letter you'd like to get from someone like me.'

Martha waited. Called out, 'Remember to tap the nameplate.'

'Tapping has been done,' Charlie replied.

She went out into the passage. 'Why do you do that?'

'It's lucky.'

'You're superstitious?'

'Only slightly. But why risk the wrath of the unlucky gods when a tap will keep them at bay. To tap or not to tap. I choose to tap.'

Martha shrugged and went back to her desk.

She pulled some files from the filing cabinet hoping to get an idea of Mrs Florey's kindly writing style. To Mrs Hutchinson whose husband, a bank manager, missing for four years and found living in a cave on a remote Scottish peninsula, she wrote:

Please don't worry about him, he is warm and quite comfortable. He has built some amazing furniture from driftwood. He claims to have found peace watching the sky and combing the beach at low tide. I know you must be puzzled by how he has chosen to live. But, please, when you think of him, think of him kindly.

There was an escapee teenager, a serial runaway who'd regularly been brought home, drunk and shouting abuse, by the police. Her final bid for freedom had been successful. She'd disappeared. Charlie had found her in a convent training to be a nun. Mrs Florey had written to her parents: *Your daughter has found her soul and is serene in her new vocation. You must be proud. Hold her kindly in your thoughts.*

On and on it went. In file after file there were people whose friend, husband, wife, lover, mother or father had either turned up in the oddest of places or had swapped one ordinary suburban life for another ordinary suburban life. Mrs Florey told them all to be kindly when thinking of or contacting their lost ones.

Martha closed the files and sat, hands folded on the top of her desk, wondering. How had Charlie done that? How had he traced a wild child to a convent? What made him suspect a bank manager might be living in a remote cave? He'd said people left trails, there were clues to their present in their past.

She visited long gone conversations she'd had with Jamie. And found them to be empty. They'd spoken about what was on television tonight. What had been on television last night. The neighbours. Evie. They'd talked a lot about their daughter. But before she'd come along, had they had deep conversations? Martha didn't think so. Now she thought about it, Jamie had never revealed any secret longings and ambitions. In fact, he hadn't spoken much at all. She'd done all the talking. She'd prattled. He'd flicked through a newspaper saying, 'Oh,' and 'Right,' and 'Hmm.'

Jamie had spent his free time in the garden shed. At the time Martha had thought that's what men, well, married men, did. They also did manly chores like unblocking the sink, mending fuses and anything that required going up a ladder. She, being a woman, cooked, did the washing, ironed, and chose the curtains. The more she thought about it, the more she doubted her marriage.

They'd both been role-playing, an easy, unexciting husband-and-wife routine they'd picked up from magazines and sitcoms. They'd hardly communicated. They'd become boring. Not even halfway through their twenties they'd embraced being Darby and Joan. They could have sported matching beige cardies and fleecy-lined slippers.

Martha put her hand to her mouth. My God, if she'd realised all that at the time, she'd have run away, too. Of course, she'd have taken Evie with her.

She typed out the letter telling Mrs Patterson that her father was now living in Manchester with his new love, Eleanor Harris. She'd been a barmaid at the pub where Tom drank and played dominoes. *Your father claims to have found domestic bliss* Martha wrote. She looked at the photo Charlie had taken of the couple. They were sitting on a green-and-gold striped sofa. He wore pale trousers with a green shirt and yellow tie and seemed to blend in with his background. Why, he was almost camouflaged. He was smiling a small smile. He looked a little tired. Eleanor Harris, face heftily made up, thighs bulging from a red mini skirt, beamed and glowed. Martha thought, Oh well, good luck to them.

She wondered if Jamie had found bliss with a similar woman. A floozie, her mother would call her. She sighed. All this wondering was getting hard to bear. She was beginning to understand what her mother meant about thinking. It wasn't worth the pain.

Thomas has instructed us to tell you that he'll be in touch when he is ready to talk.

We hope you are pleased with our work in finding your father. And please, when you think of him, be kindly.

Yours sincerely

Charlie Gavin.

She put the letter on Charlie's desk for him to sign. Paused and looked at his lists. Along with the lists of music and sandwiches for the week, there was a list of shirts he might wear, a list of possible suppers, a list of chores, a list of people to meet and phone calls to make and a final list: *Things I dread: weak milky coffee, not having clean socks, the small man, people reading my lists, stop it, Martha.* She blushed. He'd doodled squiggles and odd comments down the side of the page: *What if . . . could be. Ah, Jesus wept. Sore days and sorry days. The things people do. Of course I couldn't take the small man – he is too bitter, too disappointed. But we're all disappointed one way or another. People have to forget themselves and then become the person they wanted to be all along. Except me, I have to forget myself in order to become the person I ought to have been. It's hard.*

Still blushing from having been caught out snooping, Martha returned to her desk and was sitting upright, typing furiously, when Charlie returned with the dog. It took up its place on the sofa. He smiled to her, said nothing about his lists, signed the letter and told her he was going out for the rest of the day. 'Stuff to do.'

On Mondays he shopped for groceries and visited his aunt's grave. He couldn't break his routine. He was a man of habit. He just didn't want Martha to know that.

Two minutes after leaving, he was back standing in the doorway patting his pockets, mumbling, 'Keys, notebook, pen, cash, hanky. Yes. OK. Right. I'm off.'

Seconds later, he stuck his head round the door. 'Put the guard in front of the fire if you go out.'

Martha said she would. He shut the door. Opened it again. 'Is the gas off?' Martha said it was. He told her once more he was going and shut the door. Martha waited. But no, this time Charlie seemed to have made it to the street and was finally on his way.

She spent the afternoon sorting out the filing cabinets. There were three of them, all stuffed with files labelled by Mrs Florey. She'd had her own take on filing, proving to Martha that Mrs Florey had her own take on life. Cases were placed in alphabetical order. But it was an alphabetical order based not on the names of the people Charlie had been looking for, but on Mrs Florey's opinion of them and their tragedies – A for awful, agonising and adorable. B for boring and beautiful. On it went through D for disastrous, H for hippies, I for I can't believe how stupid people can be, J for jolly nice outcome. Among the files labelled S were stupid people, sorrowful people, sweetie pies and stinkers. T was divided into sub-sections of tragedy – abominable tragedy to unbelievable tragedy and weepy tragedy and wince-making tragedy. The stories the files revealed were of people who had run away because of debt or some kind of shame. And escapees who felt driven to slip away from unhappiness and start a new life.

At the back of the final file, at the bottom of the third cabinet, after Z for zealot (there was only one, a man who'd taken to living on the streets and spent his days standing on corners shouting about the end of the world, which he claimed was nigh), was a huge bundle tied with dark blue ribbon and labelled Nope Not Telling. These files, as far as Martha could tell, were details of searches that had been successful. But Charlie was keeping the results to himself. For the record, these people were still missing.

It took Martha all afternoon to empty the cabinets and sort the files into alphabetical piles on the floor. Every so often, she'd open a file and sit on the rug reading it. It was strange comfort to find people who, like her, were struggling with rejection, loss, upset. And were walking through a new silence, staring at the phone, watching for the mail, caught in a time of waiting.

By four o'clock her back ached. She sweated and cursed and told the dog how awful this was. He looked doleful, but interested. Three times Charlie phoned. Was the gas definitely off? Would she remember to post the report and the invoice? Would she please take the record off the turntable and put it back in its sleeve. Carefully.

The man was a worrier.

7

The Smell of a Mother

By half-past five she was done. In her last job she'd have been entitled to overtime. She doubted that would happen at the Be Kindly Missing Persons Bureau. She didn't think she deserved any extra cash. She'd done an awful thing – turned a gentle and whimsical filing system into something ordinary and boring.

'That's what I did with the songs,' she told Murphy. 'I took the sting out of them. I have a sweet voice. My "Away In A Manger" made 'em weep at the Sunday school nativity play. But it did nothing for "Great Balls Of Fire". I wasn't cool. No soul. I wanted to be a wild-haired boogie queen, a woman whose voice could make grown men weep. But there's nothing rock'n'roll about me.' She sighed, put on her coat. 'My old friend Grace, now.' She nodded to Murphy. 'She was in the band. She could belt out a song. She'd shut her eyes and tell the world about love, loss and loneliness like she'd been there and back many times. What the hell was that about? She was good-looking and rich. She had it all. Where did that pain come from? God, she could sing the blues.'

She checked the gas was off, made sure the guard was firmly fixed in front of the fire, took the record from the turntable and, without touching the grooves, put it in its sleeve. Then she switched off the lights and stood at the door patting her pockets. 'Keys, gas off, fire guard on, record player off, record put away. I'm turning into Charlie.'

She locked the door and out in the street tapped the nameplate. Walking home she scolded herself for being boring.

She'd been a boring leader of a rock'n'roll band. Nothing original. No wild clothes. Didn't write our own songs. Couldn't even play our instruments very well. Except Grace. Then I got married and I was a boring wife. Keep your marriage alive, it says in magazines, by wearing nothing but a suspender belt and black stockings when your husband gets home. I never did that. And if I had, I doubt Jamie would have noticed. Or he'd have asked me if I wasn't a bit chilly with no frock on.'

She stopped. 'Murphy.'

The dog. She couldn't leave it there alone. How could a man so concerned about checking the gas was off forget about his dog? Cursing, 'Bloody man, bloody filing cabinets, bloody dog, bloody, bloody, bloody,' she stamped back to fetch Murphy.

The dog looked unsurprised to see her. He lifted his head, yawned and settled back to sleep. Martha found a leash in one of the kitchen drawers, clipped it on Murphy's collar and said, 'C'mon then, let's go home.' Murphy jumped from the sofa and trotted out the door at her side. She stopped, patted her pockets. 'Keys. Gas off. Fireguard on. Record player off.' Out in the street she tapped the nameplate and set off once again for home.

They'd gone a few yards when Martha became aware of a squeak of unpolished shoe, the soft squish of thick rubber sole on pavement, steady steps behind her. She was being followed. It didn't bother the dog much, but it bothered her. Ignore it, she told herself, walk on, don't turn round.

But she did turn round. Persistent footfalls behind her were annoying and frightening. 'Are you following me?'

'Yes.' It was the small man. The one she'd seen this morning banging and kicking Charlie's door. The one who was listed among Charlie's dreads.

'Well, stop it.'

'No.' Up close he didn't look so small. He reminded Martha of a bull – densely muscled. He was unkempt, his trousers crumpled, his tie stained. Here was a man who cared nothing for himself. And nothing for other people. 'I know who you are.'

'No, you don't.'

'You work for him. I saw you going in there with him. And,' pointing at Murphy, 'that's his dog.'

Murphy growled. A deep throaty rumble that took him by surprise. He looked up at Martha. Was that me? Did I do that? He sat down to consider the matter.

'He found me,' the small man said. 'I was happy where I was with the life I had. Nobody knew me. I was a constant stranger.'

'And that made you happy?' Martha thought this an odd admission. Surely it was better to be among friends, familiar faces – people who knew you and forgave your quirks, absurdities and faults, people who may even love you.

'Of course it did. Nobody criticised me or looked down at me. They didn't know who I was and they didn't care. Then Charlie found me and told my wife where I was. She dragged me back home.'

'Why don't you just disappear again?'

'As if. My wife won't let me out of her sight. She phones my work every morning checking I'm there. My boss thinks it's hilarious. Everyone's laughing at me. I can't go to the pub without her. I can't go anywhere without her. Except work. All the neighbours know what I did. I ran away. They're talking about me. Charlie Gavin did that.'

Martha said, 'Goodness.' She looked round. 'So where's your wife now?'

'At home, looking at the clock, wondering where I am.' He dug into his pocket and brought out a small handful of change. 'That's my money. That's what I get every day for fares and lunch. It's like being at school again. She's got nothing to worry about. I'm not going anywhere. How far would I get with this money?'

Martha surveyed the coins and said, 'Not far.' She turned and walked away. He followed.

'Go away,' Martha shouted.

He kept on walking behind her, shoes squeaking.

'Go away or I'll call the police.'

Still he followed. 'Charlie didn't take me. He takes others. But not me. I was left to cope on my own.'

Martha turned. 'What do you mean?'

'Rooms and silences. Her and me staring at one another. She hates me for going and not saying I was going or where I was going to. Just upping and leaving. I hate being there in that house. She feels rejected. She'll never forgive me.'

'I'm sorry.'

'Charlie Gavin's not sorry. If he was he'd take me. What's wrong with me that he won't take me? Tell me that.'

'I don't know what you're talking about.'

'You people, you think you're doing good. But you're not. You're ruining people's lives.' He jabbed his finger at her, shouted, 'Bastards.'

Martha walked on. Didn't turn, didn't reply. She rounded the corner, and ran. Handbag banging on her hip, heels clicking on the pavement, the dog pounding along beside her, ears flapping. He was enjoying this. She didn't stop till she reached home. She burst in, slammed the door and leaned against it, panting.

After she'd recovered, she opened the door, stuck her head out and surveyed the street. Nobody.

She went upstairs, took off her coat and draped it on the post and went into the kitchen.

Sophie was at the cooker, working on her latest Elizabeth David recipe. 'Where the hell have you been? It's after six.'

'Working,' said Martha.

'You're all hot and sweaty.'

'I ran home.'

'Why?'

'I was late.'

Sophie spotted the dog. 'What's that?'

'Murphy. He's a dog.'

'Where did you get it?'

'He's Charlie's.'

'And what's he doing with you?'

'I brought him home rather than leave him at the office. I thought he'd be lonely.'

'So, on your first day you work till after six and you take pity on your boss's abandoned dog and bring it home. What sort of job is that?'

Martha shrugged. 'One that pays?'

'You're being taken advantage of.'

'What else was I to do? I couldn't just leave him there.'

'Of course you could. He's not your responsibility.' She took a bowl from the cupboard, and spooned some of the stew she was cooking into it. 'Does he eat boeuf bourguignon? It's got wine in.'

Martha said she'd no idea what the dog ate, 'But judging from his digestive indiscretions, he eats anything.'

'Digestive indiscretions?'

'He farts.'

'Not after my food, nobody farts over my cooking. I wouldn't let them. It's just not polite.'

Sophie put the food on the floor and invited the dog to eat. He did, following the bowl as the force of his enthusiastic eating and licking sent it scudding across the floor.

The noise brought Evie to the room. 'A dog. I've always wanted a dog.' She flung her arms around him. Held him to her.

'Hello, Mum.' There was cynicism and disappointment in Martha's voice. 'How are you? Did your first day go well? It's nice to see you.'

Evie stared at her and said, 'Hello, Mum. How are you? Did your first day go well? It's nice to see you.'

'Thank you,' said Martha. 'The day was good. Busy but I coped.' She was still cynical.

Evie tired of the joke, turned to Murphy. 'Coming to play?' She headed for the living room. The dog followed.

'Perhaps,' Martha sighed, 'if I had a thick coat and long silky ears my daughter would adore me.'

'Not if you farted,' said Sophie. 'You can set the table. And wash your hands first. And tell me about your day.'

Martha sighed. 'I arrived early. I typed a report. I sorted out the filing cabinet. Had a good bacon roll in the morning. That was it.'

'No adventures, then? No tracking down a missing person and bringing happiness to lost souls?'

Martha shook her head and mentally revised her report. I wasn't told the proper starting time, I sat in a café listening to a song that upsets me, I ruined a sensitive and genuinely interesting filing system, I got chased by an embittered scary man and I learned my daughter prefers slightly smelly cocker spaniels to me. This day so far hadn't been enthralling.

Charlie arrived as they were sitting down to eat. Sophie let him in. Martha heard him take the stairs two at a time, asking if the dog was here. He burst into the kitchen, spotted Murphy lying at Evie's feet and sighed. 'There you are.'

The dog came to him, leaned on his leg and sighed in return.

'You should have left him in the office,' Charlie said to Martha. 'He doesn't mind. He knows I'll come for him.'

'She should do no such thing. A dog doesn't like to be left alone in the dark. He worries.' Sophie pointed towards the sink. 'Well, wash your hands. You can't eat after you've been touching an animal.'

Charlie said he was fine.

Sophie said, 'We can't eat with you looking on. Murphy's had his share, now it's your turn. Martha, fetch Mr Gavin a plate and a knife and fork.' Turning to Charlie, she said, 'Sit down and eat. You look like you need feeding.'

Charlie obeyed.

'So,' said Sophie, 'tell us about yourself, Mr Gavin.'

'Charlie, I prefer that name.'

Sophie asked, 'You find people?'

Charlie took a forkful of food and nodded.

'And how do you do that?'

'Follow the trail.'

Sophie told him to help himself to veg and asked what sort of trail missing people left.

'They leave hopes and daydreams and wishes with the people left behind. They have old haunts I can visit. It's interesting the paths people follow.'

'I suppose it is,' said Sophie. She concentrated on her food for a while before saying, 'You're not married Martha tells me.'

'No,' said Charlie.

'Have you ever been?'

'No. It's a huge step getting married. I don't know if I could do it. It's so final, a big commitment. There'd be someone else constantly in my life. I wouldn't be free. I like to know I can do what I want when I want.'

Sophie said, 'You're sounding just like a man.'

'I am a man.'

'No reason to sound like one. Marriage is lovely. It's warm and comfortable. And it's wonderful to have someone next to you in bed every night. Someone you can heat your cold feet on. You should try it.'

Charlie shook his head, smiled and told Sophie he didn't believe her.

'Oh, marriage is a good thing,' said Sophie. 'I enjoyed the companionship. But I'll admit it is messy. You become entwined with your spouse. Close, sometimes too close. There are stains you wish you didn't know about and gurgling noises from the bathroom. But these things can be endearing in one you love. Still, there is a certain loss of identity. You become a couple; suddenly you are two people instead of one. I found I had

"Martin and" in front of my name. I was *Martin and* Sophie on Christmas cards and invitations. It takes getting used to.'

Charlie said it was definitely not for him.

'Will you stop asking questions?' said Martha. 'This isn't the Spanish Inquisition. Evie, stop giving the dog your food.'

'He's hungry,' said Evie. 'He just told me.'

Charlie smiled to her and started playing his finger and thumb drum solo on the table, chewing in time to the music in his head.

'That's a fine bit of drumming,' said Sophie. 'Do you play?'

'No, I wish I did. I love music. Do you play?'

'No,' said Sophie. She pointed at Martha. 'She does – very well, in fact. The piano.'

'And the guitar,' said Evie.

Charlie knew this, but didn't want Martha to know he knew. 'You didn't mention that.'

Martha shook her head. 'I didn't think it relevant.'

'Oh,' said Charlie, 'everything is relevant.'

'Yes,' said Evie, forking food into her mouth, 'it was the guitar that led my mother to doing the stupidest thing she ever done.'

'That's enough,' said Martha. 'Charlie doesn't want to know about all this.'

'Yes, I do,' said Charlie.

'See,' said Evie, 'my gran says working for you is the second-stupidest thing my mum done. On account of the bad pay and such like. But the stupidest thing she ever done was when she went to play in the band.'

'Band?' said Charlie. He acted interested. He knew all about the band.

Martha said, 'Evie, that's enough.'

'Yes,' said Evie. 'She got a place at university to study chemistry but she never done that, she went off with the band instead. They were rubbish and they all argued all the time. That was the stupidest thing she ever done.'

Martha blushed and groaned. She stared down at her food, too embarrassed to bother correcting her daughter's grammar. She was aware of Charlie staring at her, aware, too, of the silence at the table. She rummaged through her mind, searching for something to say. The subject needed changing.

Evie came to her rescue. 'What's the Spanish Inquisition, anyway?'

Another thing that happened today, Martha thought. I discovered that no matter how old you get, your mother and also your child can always embarrass you.

All this passed by Charlie. He barely noticed the undercurrents and unspoken fears and doubts going on at the table. He was dining with two mothers and mothers fascinated him. He wondered about them. In the street and in cafés and shops he watched them. He longed to be on the receiving end of their kindness, toughness and caring. He'd never been part of a family. He didn't know the smell of a mother, hadn't been held close. There had been a time when he'd answered a horse or a puppy or a red bike when asked what he'd like more than anything in the world. The real answer had been a mother. He wanted one. He knew he had one. Ella had told him she was dead. But he'd discovered she was out there in the world somewhere leading her life. It didn't include him.

At this table there were two whole mothers eating and laughing and bickering and they didn't know how special they were. They had changed nappies, baked scones, bathed cuts, clapped at first steps, taught an infant to speak, picked up toys, washed clothes, played games, sung lullabies. How amazing that was. Oh, how he wanted one for himself. If he'd had one he'd have led a different life. He'd be a different person, with friends and someone to love and maybe a child of his own. He ate his beef and marvelled.

8

The Ukulele

Sophie always claimed that if she hadn't bought that bloody ukulele the stupidity would never have happened. It hadn't even been a proper ukulele. It had been a plastic toy – beige at the front, pale blue at the back.

It arrived in Martha's life in 1956 when she was fourteen. Two huge things happened then: her father, Martin, died and she heard Gene Vincent singing 'Be-Bop-A-Lula'. Everything changed. Martin, a carpenter by trade, had fallen from a roof, broken his spine and neck, and died instantly.

Sophie stopped communicating with everyone she knew. She was bent double with grief and shock. Her eyes sank into her head and dark rings developed round them. Sometimes she'd open her mouth to speak and nothing would come out. She moved slowly, going through her daily routine. Get up, make breakfast, see Martha off to school. And after it all was done, she couldn't remember doing it. She'd go back to bed and lie looking at the ceiling, empty of thought, empty of feeling. Numb. The truth of her situation was too grim to face. She'd lie until Martha was due home from school, then she'd will herself to get up and clean a little and prepare supper. It was months before she emerged from her grief. By then she was sure her daughter was lost to her. She didn't recognise Martha's ordinary teenage behaviour.

Martha was lonely, monosyllabic and angry. Only Gene understood. He was out there in the world, singing songs just for her. She knew this from the way he gazed at her from his picture on her bedroom wall.

'Where are you going?' Sophie would ask.

'Out,' Martha would reply.

Their conversations rarely amounted to more than this, till the night Martha spotted the guitar hanging in a shop window. After that it was all she could talk about. It was the first object of lust in her life.

At school Martha belonged to a small group of friends – Patricia, Laura and Grace. In fact, Grace was, in Martha's opinion, a hanger on, always slightly apart, listening to rather than joining the ardent conversations about Gene Vincent and Elvis Presley. They also discussed classmates they hated, boys they fancied, their mutual loathing of physics, films they wanted to see, and Jamie Walters, who had a crush on Martha. Gene was their passion, though. Patricia wanted to meet him and chat about important things like did he believe in God? Laura wanted to be held in his arms and feel the warmth of his lips as he whispered undying love to her. Not Martha. She wanted to *be* Gene Vincent. She wanted to strut about a stage, a guitar slung round her neck as she sang moody songs about loneliness, love and death.

The night of the red guitar was bitterly cold, early December. Martha and her mother were returning home after visiting Sophie's sister, Lou. Nine-thirty in the evening, they were at the bus stop in Haymarket waiting for the number twelve bus. The music shop was behind them. Martha turned, saw the beautiful thing – dark red and glistening – hanging in a rack of guitars in the window and was filled with instant longing. It was the answer to her prayers. It could make her life complete. This was exactly the kind of guitar Gene would play.

At the time she was wearing a green tweed coat with a velvet collar, shiny black shoes and white ankle socks. On her head a green pixie hat with a pom-pom – clothes chosen as suitable for a fourteen-year-old by her mother. But in her heart Martha wore blue jeans, white T-shirt and beaten-up leather jacket.

She'd clutched her mother's arm, pointed at the object of lust in the window and said, 'That's what I want for Christmas.'

Sophie laughed. 'That's not the sort of thing a girl should have. Guitars are for boys.'

'Why?'

'Because they just are.'

The bus arrived. Sophie and Martha climbed aboard, found their seats and travelled in silence. Sophie worried about money. Martha dreamed of the red guitar.

Of course, at the time Martha had no idea of the serious dip in her family's finances since her father's death. He'd been a respected craftsman, but not well paid. The family got by. Any spare money they'd had was spent on Martha. It bought her clothes, paid for her trips to the swimming pool and her weekly piano lessons. Martin and Sophie had great plans for their daughter. She was quiet, studious, did well at school. They planned for her to be the first in the family to go to university. She'd be a doctor, a lawyer, a professor. Who knew? But whatever it was, it would be well paid and important. She'd have letters after her name.

Now, there was no money for luxuries, certainly not for a gleamy red guitar. So, not wanting to disappoint her daughter, Sophie bought the ukulele. Well, it was guitar-shaped. It would have to do. Having to do was how things were.

On Christmas morning, Martha hid her feelings. She didn't cry. She didn't throw the hideous toy across the room. She smiled at her mother and thanked her. But oh, the disappointment. It swamped her, gripped her throat and the pit of her stomach. She'd hoped, wished and prayed that the red guitar would be waiting for her, glinting in the Christmas tree lights. Well, this was rock'n'roll for you. A lot of woes and tears before you hit the top. How was Sophie to know a plastic ukulele was not the sort of thing an aspirant rocker could be seen carrying around? It did nothing for Martha's rendition of 'Be-Bop-A-Lula'.

Still, by the end of Christmas Day, Martha had mastered several chords and could accompany herself as she sang a rather sweet and tinkly version of 'Heartbreak Hotel'.

Sophie knew that this rock'n'roll thing would not go away. Her daughter was hooked. She cursed the ukulele, wishing she'd bought Martha her first proper lipstick and a copy of *Catcher in the Rye*. All she'd done was fan the flames of Martha's longing to play the music she loved. 'Bloody ukulele,' Sophie thought.

Martha now knew that she'd have to buy the guitar herself. She supposed Gene and Elvis did the same. She took a paper round. Up at six in the morning, out into the dawn facing biting winds, rain and, from time to time, fresh, glistening air and a watery sun sparkling on the sea. Jaw set, Martha would stride up and down garden paths, ramming papers through letterboxes, thinking red guitar, red guitar.

She'd been a sickly child, prone to colds and flu. As winter deepened and February with its thick sea mists and drenching rain rolled round, Martha was regularly laid low. She ignored her health. Sophie could not. Unable to watch her daughter, sweating, fevered and coughing, go out into the pouring weather, Sophie would say, 'Go back to bed. I'll do your round for you.' She'd stamp the streets, cursing with every step, 'Bloody ukulele. Bloody ukulele.'

Nine months later, Martha had fifteen pounds, an accumulation of earned money, pocket money, birthday money and money she'd cadged from her mother and various relatives. This was a huge amount, enough, Martha was sure, to buy the red guitar, extra strings and all sorts of guitar accessories. She left her job and took the bus to Haymarket.

In the shop she slapped her savings on the counter, pointed to the guitar and told the man she'd have it. He looked at the small pile of notes and change, then at her, shook his head and told her the object of her desire cost seventy-five pounds. 'But I have got a beauty, just the thing for you. Fourteen pounds.' He disappeared into the back shop and returned with an old, battered yellow guitar. 'I'll be sorry to see this go. But I know you'll give it a good home.'

She took the guitar, held it. Glanced up at the beauty she'd fallen in love with, then at the scratched and worn instrument she'd been offered. This was a bitter blow. But holding the guitar, knowing she could have it, take it home, was a little bit thrilling.

'Been around the block a bit,' said the salesman, nodding at the guitar, 'but that's what you want. It's been played. Lovely tone to it. And it came all the way from Memphis. Bluesman touring the country brought it in. He needed a bit of cash for whisky. Almost wept when he parted with it. The sound you'll get from that guitar will lift your heart. You could say it's run in, playing smoothly.'

Martha said, 'Gosh.' This was her first encounter with salesmanship and she was overwhelmed.

'I've been saving it for the right person. That's you.'

She took it.

Over the next few weeks Martha's life centred round the guitar. It was her only topic of conversation. She mastered three chords. Flickering her fingers to her friends, she demonstrated them. Her real talent wasn't making music; it was talking about making music. She enthused so much it wasn't long before it became the thing in her small clique to own a guitar. Laura was first to get one for her Christmas. Patricia pleaded with her folks to buy her one. But they refused on account of having bought a drum kit for her brother. He'd bashed at it for several weeks then abandoned it. Patricia's new passion was, they said, a passing phase. She'd get over it. She didn't. She took up the drums and spent her evenings battering them in the garage where they'd been put out of the way.

Two guitar players and a drummer – why, it was the beginning of a band. The three practised in Patricia's parents' garage on

Tuesday, Thursday and Friday nights. They strummed, bickered and made a dreadful noise, but, as Sophie said, they were out of the way, she didn't have to listen to the din, and the new passion was keeping them away from boys. They called themselves Vinnie (after Gene Vincent) and the Vixens. They were sure they were cool.

Grace had joined the group at school break-times, but never went out with them on their trips to the cinema or the local chip shop. She was the child of affluent parents who kept her busy with after-school activities – riding lessons, swimming lessons, dancing class and classical guitar tutoring.

It was this last that interested Vinnie and the Vixens. They cultivated Grace, offered her swigs of their Vimto and bites of their Mars bars. She was welcomed into their break-time discussions about rock'n'roll, if fat chips were tastier than small crispy ones, and the general loveliness of Gene Vincent. Being in a band, they told her, was the best thing in the world. Vinnie and the Vixens were going to be famous one day. 'Of course,' Martha said, 'we are playing the stuff we want to play. We'd never sell out and become commercial.'

Grace said, 'Surely if you're commercial you'll make money. You'll be singing songs people like.'

Martha said, 'Yeah, but you have to be true to yourself.'

Grace shrugged and reluctantly agreed. She joined the band. She turned up to rehearsals in the garage, bringing her brand new guitar. 'My dad bought it for me. He got it in a shop in Haymarket.' She opened the case and brought it out.

It was beautiful. Gleamy. Dark red. Martha's heart skipped a beat. That was her guitar. It wouldn't have been so heartbreaking if Grace hadn't been able to play the thing. But she could, very well indeed.

Spotty, dumpy Grace with her thick wiry hair, squint teeth and glasses could riff, improvise and run easily through chords. Her music soared. Martha almost wept. Oh, the jealousy.

9

A Man of Instincts

'I was followed last night,' said Martha. 'That man I saw kicking your door was waiting outside when I left.'

She and Charlie were in the office. It was morning bacon roll time. He'd made the coffee; she'd fetched the rolls. The fire was lit, Miles Davis on the turntable.

Charlie said, 'Did he bother you?'

'He shouted at me. You should have a word with him. You can't have someone standing outside your office doing that. What's up with him?'

'He hates me for finding him and telling his wife where he was. He was very happy with his new life. He's miserable now and he thinks it's all my fault.'

'It is your fault.'

'No, it isn't. It's his fault. If he's miserable he should do something about it, not shout at me or you.'

'So tell him that.'

'He won't listen.'

Martha asked the shouter's name.

'Marvin,' said Charlie. 'Marvin Hay. I found him five years ago. He's been furious ever since. Every so often it gets too much for him and he comes here and shouts.'

'Shout back,' said Martha.

'Well, Mrs Florey always sorted him out. She'd shout back sometimes. Then again sometimes she'd bring him in, sit him down and talk to him over a cup of tea.'

'Why can't you do that?'

'I'm useless. I hate confrontation.'

'I think a little confrontation is necessary.'

'Well, you do it.'

'No. I'm paid to type and answer the phone, not to shout at people.'

He sighed, chewed his roll and stared into the fire. 'Vinnie and the Vixens, eh?'

'Don't change the subject.'

'When you're uncomfortable with the subject, changing it is what you do. So, Vinnie and the Vixens.'

Martha told him to shut up. 'People shouldn't have their adolescent dreams cast up to them and mocked.'

'Oh,' he said, 'I think a little gentle mocking is in order.'

'We had principles. We weren't going to taint our artistic integrity by playing commercial rubbish. We wouldn't be corrupted.'

'Of course not.' He smirked.

'Oh, smirking, how cruel. Didn't you want to be cool in your youth?'

'Oh, God, yes.' He stared into the distance, remembering. 'However, I have to say, when you think of your youth, there's a lot to be said for amnesia.' He slapped his hands on his knees. 'Enough of this looking back.'

'You're changing the subject again. Not fair, you know all about my silliness but you won't confess yours to me.'

'It's a secret.' He took a pound from his wallet, waved it at her. 'If you ever get anything about my young days out of me, this is yours.' He put it on the table.

Martha matched the pound. 'I bet I get it out of you. I bet you tell me.'

He shook his head, gathered the cups and plates. 'Never.'

'You've a lot to be ashamed of, then.'

He made his way to the kitchen. 'I'll never tell.'

They were both working, heads down. The clatter of Martha's

typing, the burble of the fire, Murphy snoring and Charlie writing a list – the atmosphere was verging on companionable. Someone tapped on the door.

Charlie looked up. 'Who's that?'

'I don't know,' said Martha. 'Are you expecting somebody?'

Charlie said he wasn't.

Mesmerised, they both stared at the door.

'I think you should answer it,' said Charlie.

Martha said, 'Oh, of course. It's such a surprise. I forgot that people would come and ask us to find someone.'

Charlie said, 'That's the way of things. We find people. We get paid.'

The tapping stopped. Charlie and Martha watched as the door opened slowly. A woman peered in. She coughed, raised anxious eyebrows and asked, 'Is this the Be Kindly Missing Persons Bureau?'

Charlie said, 'It is.'

She shut the door, walked awkwardly across the room. All the while, moving through that long space between door and desk, she stared fixedly at Charlie. Sizing him up, taking him in.

She stopped. Turned to Martha and said, 'I came yesterday. But there was a small man in the street outside who said, "Don't go in there. They'll ruin your life."'

'I don't think we'd do that,' said Charlie. He held out his hand. 'Charlie Gavin.'

'Bernice,' said the woman, shaking the proffered hand. 'Bernice Stokes. Well, Bernice definitely.' She sat opposite Charlie. 'I'm looking for my husband. Brendan. I've written down my details.' She handed a sheet of paper to Charlie. 'I think I've noted everything you might need to know. My name, age, address and telephone number along with Brendan's details.'

Charlie asked how long he'd been missing.

'I'm not sure,' Bernice told him. 'Thing is, I'm beginning to think he doesn't exist.'

Charlie said, 'Really?' Not existing interested him.

Bernice turned to face Martha. A woman would understand. 'And he was the perfect husband. Hardly ever there. Turned up on Tuesday evenings, left Thursday afternoon. Came back Saturday. Stayed till Sunday evening then he was off again. Never got under my feet.'

Martha was fascinated. Here was a woman whose husband had disappeared with no explanation. She, too, would run to the phone each time it rang, thinking, this will be him. She'd wait for the mail to arrive, hoping for a letter. She'd wonder what she'd done wrong. There was a hole in her life, too.

Charlie stood up, walked over to her, leaned on her desk and whispered, 'You are getting this? You are taking notes, aren't you?'

'Absolutely,' said Martha. But she blushed. She'd been too absorbed to remember to take notes. She opened her notepad. Took up her pencil and started.

'A lovely man,' said Bernice. 'Always had presents. Laughed. Brought me breakfast in bed. Then he'd be off. Couldn't have had a better arrangement.'

'What does he do?' Charlie asked.

'Travelling salesman. On the road a lot. That's how I didn't know he was missing. First he didn't turn up one Tuesday. Well, I thought he might just have been busy. Then come Saturday and Sunday, still no sign of him. Come the next Tuesday and nothing, so I started to get worried. Then the weekend and he's still away and I was really worried. The next Tuesday he's still away, I thought it was time to do something. So I phoned his work. They'd never heard of him. Said no Brendan Stokes ever worked there.' She pursed her lips, exhaled, story finished.

'Has this happened before? Him not coming home for a while?' Charlie asked.

'Yes. That's why I wasn't too worried at first. But he'd usually phone.'

Head down, Martha scribbled. Charlie leaned back, put his hands on his head. 'How long have you been together?'

Martha wrote, *Charlie puts hands on head. Bernice twists the handle of her handbag. She frowns, bites her lower lip. She's very uncomfortable about this. She is good-looking, though. At first I thought she was mid-forties. But now, with the light from the window behind Charlie hitting her face, I see she's late fifties.*

'Six years. Seven this September. Anyway, I was shocked. Stunned. Could hardly breathe. He'd said he came from Manchester. So I go to the post office, get phone directory and look up all the Stokeses. That night I sit and phone all the numbers. Nobody's heard of a Brendan Stokes.'

'Did he leave anything behind?' Charlie wanted to know.

'Some clothes. But his bits and bobs, driving licence that sort of thing, are all gone.'

'Passport?'

Bernice shrugged. 'Don't know if he had one. If he did, it's gone.'

'I'm wondering,' said Charlie, 'if this isn't a matter for the police.'

'Oh, no,' said Bernice. 'You find my Brendan; tell me what he's been up to. Besides, I don't know if the police could do anything. We're not actually married. I just took his name.'

Charlie said, 'Ah. But a missing person is a missing person. The police would look for him no matter what.'

Bernice shook her head. 'No police. Not yet, anyway. There's a bit of money missing.'

'How much?'

'Six thousand pounds.'

Charlie whistled. 'Six thousand.' He looked at Martha. 'You could buy a bungalow for that.'

'You could,' said Bernice. 'If you wanted one.'

'Had you argued?'

Bernice shook her head. 'No.'

'Was he in any sort of trouble? Did he seem worried or distracted?'

Bernice shook her head again. 'He was normal. If he was in trouble, he never mentioned it to me.'

Charlie asked how she'd met Brendan.

'At a friend's house. Jean Peters. Anyway, her husband had mates round to watch football on television. Brendan was one of them. Jean and I went to see a film, don't like football. When we got back, he was still there. We got chatting and,' she shrugged, 'that was us. We dated a bit. Drinks. Meals. Eventually he just came to the house and we'd sit in, just like an old married couple. It was comfortable.'

'Then?'

'He suggested we move in together. I was so pleased. Couldn't believe my luck. He is the handsomest man I ever clapped eyes on.'

'So, he moved into your house?'

'No, I sold my house and bought a bigger one. He moved in then. That's when I changed my name to his.' She turned to Martha. 'It's easier. I was Bernice Maguire before that.'

'Maguire?' said Charlie. 'Was that your married name?'

'Yes. My husband died twelve years ago. He left me a bit of money.'

Martha quietly considered Bernice Stokes. An expensively dressed, slightly nervous woman, she thought. But the nerves could just be from the situation she was in, for there was an assuredness to her. She was a woman who knew her mind, got her own way. No doubt about it, Bernice Stokes had been beautiful in her day. She was a grown-up. If such a thing existed.

Still, Martha thought, Bernice Stokes couldn't be as assured as she appeared. She had, after all, fallen for a man who seemed to have given her a false name, and who'd taken some money. She'd been duped.

Charlie asked Bernice his usual questions. Did Brendan have

any haunts – pubs he visited, a hairdresser, perhaps? Did he have friends Bernice had met? Had she ever met any sisters or brothers?

'He said his sister lived in Australia. Don't think he mentioned her name. Don't know where he got his hair cut. The only friends I ever met were that night at Jean's house.' She stared ahead, thinking. 'He did mention a pub in Leith. The Bull something. Dunno. I'm not being very helpful.'

'The Bull and Barnacle,' asked Charlie.

'Yes,' said Bernice. She turned to Martha again. 'I feel so stupid. He never said exactly where he was going. He'd say he was headed north this week, or south. He was so cheery I never doubted him. I'd just tell him to drive safely.'

Charlie asked what Brendan sold.

'Jewellery. Not that I ever saw any rings or anything. He said he dropped his stock off at head office before coming home.'

'Do you have a photo?'

'Oh, yes.' She fished in her handbag and handed a pile of photographs to Charlie.

'He was cheery as ever when I last saw him. Waving and tooting the car horn as he drove off. He always phoned when he was away, except for this last time. But he never said where he was. He was so chatty you couldn't get a word in. Now he's gone. Just gone. And I don't know who he was.'

Martha offered her a cup of tea. But Bernice refused. 'I must be going.' She sighed. 'I suppose you must think I'm a fool. A handsome man comes after me and I fall hook, line and sinker. I suppose you come across stuff like this every day.'

Charlie shook his head. 'No. But don't jump to conclusions. You don't know the truth.'

'The house is mine, you know. He said he'd take care of the bills, but he didn't often do that.' She turned to Martha. 'Of course, I didn't always look like this. I used to be a looker. Used to take better care of myself. I suppose I've let time, vodka and chocolate eclairs get to me.' She got up, draped her handbag over her arm. 'How long does this sort of thing take?'

'Days, sometimes,' said Charlie. 'Then again it could be weeks. I have had cases where it took months.'

'I'm not keen on paying for months.'

'We only charge for work done. Time and expenses.'

'I want you to find him quickly. I've quite a lot I want to say to him.' She held out her hand to shake Charlie's. 'I'm looking forward to hearing from you.'

Charlie walked her to the door. 'I'll need your friend Jean's address.'

'She used to be my next-door neighbour before I moved. I wrote the address down for you.'

Bernice walked up the passage to the street. Charlie followed. Martha heard him ask, 'What sort of car did Brendan drive?'

'A green one. Don't know what kind. I'm not interested in cars.'

'So you wouldn't know its number.'

'No.'

Martha stopped taking notes and listened. They'd be in the street now. Charlie would be tapping the nameplate. Bernice would be wondering what that was about. Now, Charlie would be shouting out last-minute questions as Bernice tried to walk away.

He returned, sat at his desk drumming his fingers. 'What do you think?'

Martha shrugged. 'I think she seems like a nice woman. A bit nervy. But underneath that, quite sure of herself. Still, if I was putting myself up for adoption, I'm not sure I'd want her to take me home with her.'

Charlie did his double point, using a finger on each hand. 'That's right. That's what I thought. If you were looking for someone who offered shelter from the storm for a few nights every week, she'd be quite far down the list. Not a nurturing type.'

'No. Do you think Brendan was after her money?'

'Could be. She's not happy with her appearance. Thought she'd let herself go. But she looked good to me. Perhaps he undermined her confidence. Perhaps her fear of ageing was what he exploited.'

'Exploited?'

He scratched his chest. 'Yes. Don't you feel it? Can't you smell it? Doesn't the business of someone using someone creep under your skin?'

'A little, but not as much as it creeps under yours. I'm not scratching.'

'Once you've worked here for a while, you will be. It gets into your blood.' He spread his arms. 'You have to wonder what gets into people.'

'Then you start scratching. Then again,' said Martha, 'Bernice did take up with Brendan because she thought he was handsome. And she did seem happy that he was away a lot. Also, she didn't know what sort of car he drove or where he was going. Maybe she was doing a little bit of exploiting herself.' She scratched her shoulder.

Charlie nodded. 'Good point. Anyway, we'll start at the pub.'

'We?'

'Yes. You don't want to spend all your time at a desk, do you?'

'I'm quite happy getting on with things here.'

'Please come with me. It's rough I don't want to go in there alone.' He pressed his palms together, pleading.

'So, how are we going to get there? By bus? Or are you going to give me a ride on the back of your bike?'

'I'll bring the car.'

'You have a car?'

'Oh, yes. Do you drive? Only I hate it. It's fine when it's late and there's not much traffic about. But if the roads are busy and other cars are coming at me, I sort of panic.'

'So you don't like going into rough pubs alone and you hate driving. What sort of detective are you?'

'Pretty dire. Though I don't think of myself as a detective. I'm a follower of trails. A listener to dreams. A man of instincts.'

'The itchiness you experience when you wonder what gets into people and you start scratching. Is that your instinct?'

'Exactly. The itchiness serves me well. We'll go tomorrow.'

'Why tomorrow? Why not today?'

'I like a bit of procrastination. Gives me time to ponder.'

'And work up your courage,' said Martha.

10

Pleasurable Fumbling

Sophie wasn't having the best of days. She'd been woken by bad dreams and had lain awake worrying. At first she'd worried about Martha. She should have a proper job, one with prospects of promotion and decent pay. And, it was time she had a man in her life. In fact Sophie thought it was time Martha had a life. It didn't do for a woman to sit in night after night watching television with her mother. Sophie knew she would never have done such a thing. But then, back when Sophie was Martha's age nobody had a television set.

That bit of worrying done with, fretted over, Sophie moved on to worrying about Evie. The girl was seven going on fifty. Too mature by far. She'd overheard Martha and Sophie talking about the menopause, absent fathers, death and goodness only knew what else. She was being denied her innocence. 'Why, I knew nothing of these things at her age,' Sophie said out loud. 'I certainly didn't know about sex. I never even knew we all had genitals.'

After that, Sophie worried about worrying. It could cause headaches, ulcers and heart problems. She clasped her forehead and took her pulse, checking it wasn't racing. Feeling assured she wasn't about to die, she arranged herself into her usual sleeping position and tried to drop off. Instead she worried about her newly commissioned cakes. One was for an astronomer's sixtieth birthday and was to be iced with an accurate depiction of the night sky. The other was for a retiring professor. This cake was to be in the shape of an open book with a Burns poem iced on top.

Knowing nothing about astronomy and having forgotten every poem she'd ever learned, she'd have to go to the library tomorrow for the relevant books.

At half-past seven the alarm roused her from a perfect sleep. 'Bugger,' she said. She lay a while wishing she wasn't awake. Hearing Evie stumble from bed and run to the bathroom – she always liked to get there before anyone else – Sophie heaved back her blankets and shoved on her beloved dark green dressing gown. It was ancient but a constant source of comfort. She padded to the kitchen, put on the kettle and set the table for breakfast.

By the time Evie appeared in the kitchen, Sophie had boiled a couple of eggs, made a pile of toast and brewed a pot of coffee. Evie sat down to eat.

'What's a genital?'

'I beg your pardon,' said Sophie.

'You shouted it in the middle of the night. I heard you. Something about not knowing people had genitals.'

'I did nothing of the sort.'

'Yes, you did. You woke me up.'

Martha came to the kitchen door. Paused, listened in.

'Well,' said Sophie. She took a deep breath. This was not the sort of thing she wanted to talk about first thing in the morning. This was a serious evening discussion topic. 'It's a two-handled jug. In the olden days people used it to carry water. They put it on their heads.'

Martha sat down, took a slice of toast, poured coffee and silently stared at her mother. Sophie turned to face the cooker and stood with her back to her.

When Evie had finished eating, she went to her bedroom to pack her school bag and put on her shoes. Alone with Sophie, Martha hissed, 'Why did you say that? It's nonsense.'

'I do not want to talk about such things in the morning. My brain isn't functioning. I wouldn't know what to say.'

'You told Evie a lie. I vowed I'd never lie to her. I want to be honest with her at all times. I want her to grow up trusting us and developing into the person she is meant to be and not some screwed-up neurotic who doesn't know who she is and what she wants to be because she was lied to as a child.'

'Well, I lied,' said Sophie. 'It was just something that popped into my head. And that's a bit over the top as a bit of criticism especially at this time in the morning.'

'What if she's asked to write an essay about olden days at school and she says they used to carry water in genitals?'

'Well, we'll cross that bridge when we come to it. I'd better get ready to walk Evie to school or she'll be late.'

Surveying her limited wardrobe, Sophie opted for a pair of lime green bell-bottom trousers Martha had bought at a sale, deeply regretted and rejected, a pink blouse that was old but too beloved to throw out and a voluminous red cardigan that hid her gathering layers and rolls of fat. She claimed she wasn't naturally this size. The shape everyone saw was her body's response to the many nibbles of marzipan, icing and melted chocolate she indulged in while baking. 'My body doesn't like me,' she claimed. 'It doesn't like the way I earn my living. So, this is what it does to me. In some ways you could say that being a baker is a much more dangerous occupation than being a stuntman.'

Martha gave her a swift head-to-toe sweep of a look and told her she was looking a bit gaudy today.

'I'm comfortable,' said Sophie. 'As you know, I'm happy with me. It's the casing I hate, the thing me is packaged in – my body. I don't care what I put on it.'

Just after nine, Sophie left Evie at school and headed for the library. She walked quickly. She thought that if she moved at speed, she might outpace her thoughts. She could leave them behind. It didn't work. Her doubts, fears and embarrassment kept up with her. She cursed herself. Why hadn't she answered Evie's question truthfully? 'They are our bits,' she could have said.

'Down there,' pointing to the relevant area, 'but we don't talk about them.' That's what she should have said. Damn. Now she was upset. Damn again. Soon, she'd be visited by visions of the falling man. It always happened when she was unnerved.

The man was Martin, her husband. He'd been working for a building contractor at the time and had died after falling from a roof. Had Martin known that he was going to tumble to the ground when he slipped? What had he said? Had he sworn? What did he think on his way down? Had he time to think?

She'd seen people falling from buildings in films. It had always been spectacular. The faller would have his arms spread wide, hair flying behind him. His wild screaming would diminish in volume as he went down. She knew it wasn't like that. The fall would have lasted seconds. Martin would have looked like a large tumbling bundle. There would have been a thud as he landed. That was all. He'd died instantly. Nothing spectacular about it. Still, when the vision of a tumbling bundle that was her husband, the man she loved, came to her she wanted to be in the picture. She wanted to rush forward and catch him.

The vision had been with her for months and months after it happened. Now it came when she was nervous or upset. Walking towards the library she shut her eyes and shook her head, willing it to go away.

In the library she quickly found a book of Burns poems. Finding a celestial view that could be copied in icing took a while. As she thumbed through books looking for a simple image she became aware of a man staring at her. She slipped round to the other side of the bookshelf, removed three books and stared into the gap. He appeared, or at least his eyes and nose did, staring back.

'Are you looking at me?' asked Sophie. She was whispering. A loud harsh whisper.

'Yes.'

'Why?'

'I thought I recognised you.'

'Well, you didn't. Can't a woman visit the library without being harassed by men?'

'I wasn't harassing you. I was wondering if you are Sophie.'

'What's it to you if I am? Mind your own bloody business.' She regretted this. She hadn't spoken to anyone in such a manner since she was a teenager. God, she'd been rude then.

'My goodness, you *are* Sophie. You haven't changed a bit.' He disappeared. Then reappeared peering through the gap. 'Wait there.'

He came to her, beaming, holding out his hands to grasp hers. 'Sophie Snow. This is wonderful.'

He was tall, greying at the temples, wore a grey jacket with leather patches on the elbows and a pink shirt, open at the neck. Stylishly scruffy, she thought. He did seem awfully familiar. But she couldn't place him.

He leaned towards her. 'Duncan. Duncan Henderson.'

She almost swooned. 'Duncan, oh my goodness, Duncan. How are you?'

This man had been the love of her young life. She'd written his name all over her schoolbooks. *Duncan and Sophie. Sophie loves Duncan. Sophie Henderson.* That last was the signature she'd practised a lot in the days when she practised signatures. Sophie Henderson was who she wanted to be.

The romance had started when she was thirteen and ended five years later when Duncan had left to go to university. He'd won a place at Oxford studying history. They'd vowed to write to one another every day. They'd exchanged parting gifts, tokens of their love. She'd given him cufflinks. He'd given her a charm bracelet. It was still tucked at the bottom of her jewellery box.

In time their long passionate letters became shorter and more sporadic. Caught up in his new life he'd tell Sophie about people she didn't know, pubs she'd never visit and books she imagined she wouldn't understand. She told him about her life in the place he'd left behind – her work at the local library, what her colleagues were up to, films she'd seen, shoes she was planning to buy when she got paid. She thought she sounded dull, trivial even. Their exchanges trailed off. They lost touch. Years later she heard that he'd graduated, married an American and moved to Boston. It hadn't bothered her, though. She'd met Martin and was in love once more.

Yet, with Duncan Henderson she'd shared her first kiss. Experienced the thrill of holding hands. He'd filled her thoughts. She hadn't much cared about passing school exams, because she was going to marry him, live in a house overlooking the sea and care for the two children they were going to have. At fifteen, she'd had it all planned. In the back of her geography jotter, she'd drawn a plan of the living room she imagined them sharing. She thumbed through magazines looking longingly at bright modern kitchens where she dreamed of cooking Duncan's meals. She was going to be the perfect wife. Remembering all this now, she was almost too embarrassed to look at him.

But she did look at him. She gazed at that once familiar face with a mix of shock and delight. Delight at seeing him again. Shock at what time and experience had done to him. For years Duncan had remained in her head exactly as he had been when she last saw him. He'd been fresh-faced, barely needing to shave, floppy-haired and young. Now look at him. Skin tired and with wrinkles on his brow and round his lips. His chin bristled with greying stubble. Small creases spread from his pouchy eyes. He was old. If this was what life had done to Duncan, had it done the same to her? Did she look old?

'I haven't been Sophie Snow for an awfully long time,' she said. 'It's Sophie Campbell now.'

'I'd heard you married.'

'Well, so did you.'

'I've been single for years. Divorced.' He held her at arm's length. 'Still the same old colourful Sophie.'

It was a horrible reminder of how she was dressed. It wasn't so much that she displayed a cacophony of colours, more that the ones she did display clashed. She was regretting the lime green trousers and couldn't think of anything to say in their defence. But she smiled and decided the comment wasn't a criticism of the collection of garments she was wearing. It was a compliment.

He followed as she went to the desk to have her selection stamped. When she reached the street he was still with her.

'What about we go for coffee and a catch up? You can tell me what you've been up to all those years.' He took her arm and led her to the café opposite the bureau where Martha worked. 'It's a bit basic. But the coffee's good. I like to sit here and watch the world go by.'

Sophie chose a table by the window as Duncan went to the counter and ordered. The lights were on at the Be Kindly Missing Persons Bureau; Sophie imagined Martha sitting neatly at a desk furiously typing. She saw Charlie slowly cycling into view, the dog trotting alongside him. She watched him remove his bike clips and wheel his bike inside, tapping the nameplate on the wall as he went. A superstitious man, she thought. She approved. Superstitious, too, she was relieved to discover her daughter was working for a man who believed in keeping on the right side of the lucky gods.

Duncan joined her at the table carrying a tray filled with mugs of coffee, two bacon sandwiches and doughnuts. 'We're celebrating,' he said.

Sophie said, 'Splendid. Bacon sandwiches, so much better than champagne.'

Duncan agreed. 'So tell me everything. Your life. What have you been doing for the past forty years?'

Sophie said, 'Goodness, not much. I got married, had a daughter, became a widow and now I bake cakes for a living. I'm a bit boring, I'm afraid.' Was that it? Was that all she'd done? Her life in three sentences. She hadn't travelled the globe.

In fact, she hadn't even been on an airplane. She hadn't become an actress, as had been her ambition in the days when he was her love. She was disappointed in herself. 'What about you?'

'Oh, not much. I graduated. Married an American. Went to the States with her. Lectured in history. Divorced. Went to pieces. Drank too much. Lost my job. Well, I resigned but they were very happy to see me go. Travelled a bit, you know, India, Japan, China, South America sort of thing. A few affairs here and there. Nothing lasting, but sweet romances. Stayed in Puerto Rico for a couple of years, propped up one or two bars, wrote a novel while I was there. It didn't do much, sold a few hundred copies and disappeared. Gave up drinking. Came back to Edinburgh and now I write school textbooks. Simple accessible things, but they give me pleasure. And that's me. No children, though. I envy you that.'

'Well,' said Sophie, 'you've certainly got a lot more sentences in your biography than I have. You've done things, been places.'

'I've drifted,' he said. 'I've done a lot and achieved little. You, on the other hand, married and raised a child. That's a huge achievement. You must be proud.'

'Well, I am. But having a child doesn't excuse my humdrum life. I haven't done anything. I just sat back and let life happen to me. You've done things, been places. You've written books.' Sophie bit into her bacon sandwich and considered her life. She sipped her coffee and declared herself a failure. 'I've done nothing. I have waddled through my life living from day to day, washing, ironing, baking cakes, watching too much television. I have never reached out for glory.'

'Why would you want to do that? Glory is transient and, in the end, empty. You have everything you could want. You seem content.'

She shrugged. 'Perhaps. But I'm not happy being content. I'd like to have had more adventure in my life.'

He told her he'd frittered away his life looking for adventure and being disappointed. 'I wish I'd settled down again after my divorce. I wish I'd lived a smaller life – a home, a wife and children. There's happiness there.'

She smiled. Finished her bacon sandwich and started on a doughnut. 'Good,' she said, waving it at him. Her upper lip was encrusted with sugar. 'I wrote your name all over my geography jotter. I was crazy about you. First love should come with a health warning. It takes your breath away.'

She became aware, as she spoke, of someone standing at her side, looking down at her. It was bacon sandwich time at the Be Kindly bureau and Martha had come to collect them. 'Mum?'

Sophie had a turn-around moment. She was the foolish one sitting in a café talking, flirting almost, with a strange man, eating sugary food. Martha was the grown-up. This happened often these days. She looked at Martha and then at Duncan, waving her hand, still clutching the doughnut, between the two as she introduced them. 'Martha, Duncan. Duncan, Martha.'

Duncan pulled a large red handkerchief from his pocket and wiped his hands before shaking the hand Martha held out to him.

'Martha's my daughter,' Sophie said to Duncan.

To Martha, she said, 'Duncan's an old friend. We were at school together.'

'We were sweethearts,' said Duncan. 'Haven't seen one another in forty years.'

'And we met today at the library,' Sophie added. 'Wasn't that lovely?'

Martha took a handkerchief from her pocket and wiped the layer of sugar from her mother's mouth. 'Yes, it was. There, I've got rid of your moustache. I better collect my bacon rolls, Charlie's making the coffee.'

On her way out she waved.

'Lovely girl,' said Duncan.

'Yes,' said Sophie. 'Though she's gone the way of all children. She's ended up older than me. That's what happens. They get more sophisticated than you ever were and understand the world we live in now better.'

Duncan smiled. 'But you have experience on your side. You've lived.'

'That's the problem, I don't think I have. Take this hippie thing going on. If I were alive today that's what I'd be – a hippie. I'd have flowers in my hair and I'd dance barefoot.'

Duncan frowned. He didn't understand, thought she was being absurd. 'But you are alive today.'

'Yes, but I'm too old to join in. There's all sorts of exciting stuff going on to the soundtrack of wonderful music, and I'm not part of it. I'm doing what I've always done. Sort of trudging along doing my regular day-to-day things. Things that I have always believed I ought to do.' She bit into a second doughnut, considering this. 'Do you think that for most of us life is but a theory?'

'I have no idea what you're talking about,' said Duncan. 'I just wanted to have a cup of coffee and something nice to eat while we talked about old times.'

Sophie said she was sorry. She wanted to reminisce, too. 'But things are coming to me. I'm beginning to think I've been duped. Did I need to live the life I've lived? Where did I get the idea I needed to get married and have a child before travelling the globe? Why do I think I have to work to earn money?'

'You need money for food.'

'I could grow my own.'

'Gas. Electricity. Insurance.'

'If I didn't have possessions I wouldn't have anything to insure. I suspect there's some sort of con going on here. It's the work of the government, teachers, parents, all sorts of authority figures. They put notions of security and respectability into your head.'

Duncan sighed. 'You were always like this. Questioning everything.'

Sophie said, 'I always thought I knew why Jamie did what he

did. But now I feel a little sympathy. I understand. Which is better, deeper than just knowing, don't you think?'

Duncan said, 'Who's Jamie?'

'Never mind,' said Sophie. 'I'll tell you one day.' She reached over and patted his hand. 'Do you remember that time we were meant to be doing our homework together in your back room and your mother burst in and caught us kissing? Well, we were doing a little more than kissing. We were getting fresh. I think that's the term. I have to say I was enjoying it. But your mother was so shocked she sent me packing. Said she'd tell my mother what we'd been up to. And I was so scared of what my mother would say. Actually, I got a stern lecture on not letting boys having their way with me and the horrors of becoming an unmarried mother.'

'Yes, I remember. Only a kiss. But what a kiss. Best of my life. If you'd become pregnant, I'd have stood by you.'

'I don't think I could have got pregnant doing what we were doing. It was pleasurable fumbling.'

'Yes,' Duncan agreed. 'Didn't we have fun, though?'

Now he was remembering how Sophie delighted him. The pleasure he'd had just talking to her. She blurted out ideas as they popped into her head, never pausing to consider that they might be nonsense or even offensive. Still, her notions were always new to him and took him by surprise. He'd never known what she was going to say next. She was never dull. Perhaps he ought to have married her.

11

Something Was Happening Here

Six o'clock in the evening Martha parked opposite the Bull and Barnacle.

'You're facing the wrong way,' Charlie told her. 'If we have to make a quick getaway we'd be better facing the main road.'

'Why would we have to make a quick getaway?'

'You never know. That's a mean pub. People go there to drink.'

'Why else would anyone go there?'

'To chat, to socialise. But that's not a chatting pub. It's a hard drinkers' place.' He drummed on the dashboard. 'People in there don't take kindly to questions. They might think we're the police.'

'We don't look like the police. You're hair's too long and I'm only five foot two. You're being ridiculous.'

Martha pulled out of their parking place, drove to the end of the street, did a clumsy three-point turn and parked once more across from the pub. Charlie got out and stood looking anxious. 'Do you think we should lock the car?'

'If we don't someone might steal it.'

'Who'd want to steal it? It's a heap of junk.' He waved his hand at the car, a rusting ten-year-old Saab that took its time to start and lumbered along making worrying clanking noises. It wasn't pretty.

'Murphy's in the back. We wouldn't want him stolen despite his digestive problems.'

Charlie shrugged. 'OK, lock the car.'

Martha surveyed the street. Nobody about. A thick layer of

gravel lay along the side of the road. Several discarded crisp bags and sweet wrappers scraped the pavement, pushed by a slight wind. Even street sweepers avoided this place. It was early evening, chill, and though darkness was descending the street-lights were not yet on. Silent here. Menacing.

'I don't like it here,' she said.

'Neither do I,' said Charlie. 'Neither does anybody who's sane.'

The pub had no allure whatsoever. There was peeling paint and letters missing from the sign above the door – the ull and Ba na le it read. Blinds pulled down over the windows and the pane of frosted glass on the door. Inside, Martha found the lack of charm scary. It was murky, a smell of stale booze and cigarettes. The ceiling was low and had a dense nicotine-yellow coating. There was a scattering of wooden tables each with an ashtray dead centre. The few drinkers were at the bar, hunched over, exchanging the odd monosyllable. One couple sat at a table in the corner, both nursing a beer and sucking a cigarette. They didn't speak but stared into the distance lost in regrets and fallen dreams. Martha thought, Oh, please don't let me end up like that.

She whispered that she didn't like it here and sat at the table closest to the door. Charlie sat across from her, saying, 'I don't like it either.' He took a five-pound note from his pocket. 'You get the drinks. A pint for me. I'd rather have a half, but I don't think that's manly enough for this place. And while you're at it, show the woman at the bar this and ask if she knows him.' He gave her the photo of Brendan Stokes.

'Why should I do it? It's your job. I'm only here to make us look like real people.'

'You're a woman. It's easier for a woman to ask questions.'

'I've never heard anything so ridiculous in my life.'

'It's true. Women like other women. Men like women. Life's a breeze for women.'

They were leaning towards one another, hissing hoarse whispers.

Charlie gave Martha a pleading look. 'Please.'

'Oh, all right. I'll do it. But I want you to know this is not what I signed up for. And don't give me the puppyish look. I may be a woman, but I'm also a mother. Puppyish looks cut no ice with me.' By now, she wasn't far from shouting. Everyone in the room turned to stare. She snatched up the money, marched to the bar and slapped the money down. 'A vodka and tonic and a pint, please.'

'Giving you trouble, is he?' said the barmaid. A small elderly woman with thick glasses in bamboo frames. Her face was generously powdered so she looked as dusty and crumbling as her surroundings. She fitted in.

Martha said he was.

'That's the problem with men. They have minds. I sometimes think if their mothers didn't teach them to speak the world would be a better place.'

Martha agreed. 'There'd be no wars for a start.' This was good. She and the barmaid were exchanging a bit of banter. Perhaps Charlie was right. It was easier for women to ask questions.

The barmaid poured a measure of vodka into a warm and suspiciously greasy glass and dumped a small bottle of tonic alongside it. Martha asked for ice and lemon. 'No ice,' said the barmaid, 'we don't do it. If you want lemon you can buy one from the shop round the corner. I'll slice it for you.'

Martha declined the offer and waited while Charlie's pint was pulled. The barmaid put it down beside the glass of vodka, lifted the five-pound note and stared at the photo of Brendan Stokes that was underneath it.

'You know Bill Simpson?'

'Yes,' said Martha. She was proud of herself. She hadn't questioned the new name or shown the slightest sign of surprise when she'd heard it. She was good at this – a natural. 'His photo was in my wallet. I must have pulled it out with the money. Does he come in here?'

'Yes. Though these days he's busy with Belinda and the little one.'

‘Of course,’ said Martha. ‘The baby. I’d forgotten he’s a father now. So is Bill still living at the old place?’ Martha asked. She was very proud of this last remark. Casual but informed.

‘Corstorphine, I think so.’

‘I must give him a call. You don’t have his number, do you?’

‘As a matter of fact, I think I do. He was in the darts team.’

This was going very well. Martha was pleased with herself. A little bit smug. Brendan Stokes also known as Bill Simpson lived in Corstorphine and soon she’d have his phone number. Job done. Easy. Nothing to it.

A man standing a few feet along the bar turned and stared at Martha. ‘Who are you, anyway? Why are you asking questions?’

Martha reddened. Who was she? She didn’t know. She couldn’t think. Her mind emptied. ‘Martha,’ she said, ‘Martha Walters.’ Damn, she should have given a false name. Harriet McGregor would have been good. Picking up the drinks she turned to head back to the table, noting as she did that Charlie was wiping it with his handkerchief.

The barmaid, who’d ducked below the counter looking for the phone number, reappeared. ‘Where did you meet Bill?’

‘Oh, it was years and years ago. I was in a band and he came along to a gig. It was an all-girl band. We got a lot of blokes. It wasn’t the music that interested them.’

The barmaid smiled. ‘I’ll bet it wasn’t.’

The man gave Martha a disbelieving look. He reached over and took the photo. ‘Martha Walters. Never heard of you.’

Martha shrugged, ‘Bill and me were mates. We weren’t . . . you know . . . intimate.’

The man, small, stocky, muscled and wedged into an ill-fitting suit, took another step towards Martha. ‘I asked what’re you asking questions for?’ He jabbed the air with his finger.

Martha took the photo and put it in her pocket. She looked round at Charlie. He was still wiping the table top, paying no attention.

'I'm not asking questions. I'm just wondering how my old pal Bill is doing. Haven't seen him in years.'

'But that's a recent photo. He only shaved off his beard a couple of weeks ago,' said the barmaid.

Martha said, 'Ah . . .' She was standing holding a couple of drinks with her mouth open as she rummaged through her mind searching for something to say. She felt alone. The room was suddenly big. She was small. And scared. The man was standing horribly close, finger still in jabbing position. She could see sweat on his brow and the open pores on his face. Things were out of control. Something mean was happening here.

Then Charlie was beside her, taking the drinks from her, putting them onto the bar. He took her elbow. 'Time to go, darling. We promised the babysitter.'

Martha looked blank. 'What babysitter?'

He hustled her across the room, feet tripping on the sticky floor.

Pointing at Charlie, the barmaid shouted, 'You. I know you. You were barred years ago.'

He hauled Martha out the door and across to the car. 'I said you shouldn't lock it. Where are the keys?'

'In my bag.'

'What are they doing there? You should keep them in your hand.'

Opening her bag, peering into it, shifting things about looking for the keys, Martha said, 'You never mentioned keeping them in my hand. Why did you yank me out of there anyway?'

'It was turning nasty.'

She opened the car, they both got in, slammed the doors. 'I can deal with nasty. I can cope.'

'No, you can't. Please start the car and get going.'

Martha put the key in the ignition, then leaned back, folded her arms and said, 'No. I want to know why you dragged me out of there.'

'Didn't you feel it? Didn't you see it in that guy's face? There was menace. There was about to be shouting, insults, threats and maybe even some punching. And you were scared. Admit it.'

'I may have been unnerved, but I was fine. I am . . .' She was about to say she was a mother and he had no idea of the many things that role prepared her for, but the banging on the car window distracted her.

The man from the bar was thumping the side of the car, shouting, 'I want a word.'

'Just drive,' said Charlie.

Martha waved to the man to step aside, started the car, signalled, looked over her shoulder, checked the mirror and slowly moved off.

'What the hell are you doing?' Charlie stamped his feet on the floor.

'Moving away from the kerb in the correct fashion as described in the Highway Code.'

'Jesus, just go. Use the Getaway Highway Code. Put your foot down.'

Martha cruised the car along the road, stopped at the end, signalled, looked right, left and right again before sliding onto the main road. 'We are slipping away in the correct fashion. This is what responsible people do.'

Charlie shoved his fingers through his hair and shouted that they were not responsible people. 'We are fools. Go faster.'

Tootling at a gentle twenty-five miles an hour, Martha said, 'No.'

'Stop the car. Stop the car. Let me out.' Charlie was waving his arms and stamping on an imaginary brake pedal.

Martha stopped the car. Charlie jumped out, slammed the door and started to run along the pavement. Head down, arms pumping, he steamed past pedestrians who turned to watch him go. Martha drove beside him, doing less than ten miles an hour now. She wound down the window, shouting, 'What are you doing? Stop this. You're being silly.'

But Charlie ran.

'For God's sake. This is absurd. Get back in the car,' Martha yelled.

And Charlie ran.

A few hundred yards later, he stopped, bent double and hands on knees, heaving for breath. Red-faced, sweat-soaked and panting, he looked up and walked back to the car.

'What was that about?' said Martha.

'Just had to run. Had to feel I was moving at speed. Had to get that business at the pub out of my system.' He waved his hand, pointing up the road. 'There's a place nearby where we can go.'

She stopped outside a small Italian restaurant. Inside was crowded. Charlie waved to a tall, dark-haired woman in a long white apron who looked to be presiding over all the eating and chatting that was going on.

'Charlie,' she called, waving back. 'Table for two?' She led them to a table at the back. 'This do? It's all we got.'

'It's fine,' said Charlie. 'A bottle of house white and two plates of carbonara.'

The woman gave him the thumbs up and disappeared.

'You ordered for me,' said Martha. 'What if I don't like carbonara?'

'It's comfort food. It's what we need right now.'

'To calm you down?' She watched as he aligned his knife and fork and then moved the small vase containing a single plastic rose from the centre of the table to nearer the edge.

'Yes.'

'That woman at the bar shouted that she knew you.'

'Did she?' He moved the vase slightly to the left.

'Yes, you know she did. She said you were barred.'

'I used to go to that pub.'

'You went *there*? It's awful.' She stared at him. This was hard to believe. 'That's why you wanted me to come with you and ask about Brendan Stokes. You thought the barmaid would recognise you.'

He nodded. 'It was years and years ago when I went there. I was a kid. I didn't think the barmaid would still be there. She was old back then. I thought she'd be dead by now.' He moved the vase back to the centre of the table, sat back considering this positioning. 'I got into a fight. Didn't start it. Just got caught up in it. She said I was a troublemaker and barred me.'

'Were you?'

He realigned his knife and fork. 'No. I was sort of quiet. But places like that fascinated me.'

'What was the fight about?'

'A woman. Well, a woman I thought was a woman. But when she turned round and I saw her, I realised she was a man and I said she was ugly. Which, by the way, she was. Anyway, she punched me and so did the bloke she was talking to. I got beaten up and barred.'

The waitress brought the wine. He told her to fill the glasses when she offered to go through the tasting routine. 'It'll be fine.'

He took a large swig.

'So you had a wild and turbulent youth?' said Martha.

He scratched his head. 'I had a mixed-up, lonely youth.'

Martha leaned back, slapped the table with the palm of her hand. 'You owe me a pound. You said you'd never tell me about your past. You bet me a pound.'

'Well, you can take it out of the change from the fiver I gave you for the drinks. You never got it from the barmaid.'

12

The Lives We Didn't Have

Sophie was upset. Duncan had promised her he'd call, and he hadn't. She lingered by the phone every time she passed it. She lifted the receiver, checking for the dialling tone. When she was in the kitchen, she left the door open in case she didn't hear the ring.

There had been times when she'd been wistful about her youth, remembering it as a sunny time filled with movement and laughter. Now she thought she was too old for young things – romance, longing, sighing and daydreaming. A woman was better on her own, making her own decisions, keeping her feet on the ground and not being prey to other people's promises. Especially if the other person was a man.

So, when Duncan turned up on her doorstep, she had worked herself into a state of passionate disinterest. 'Oh, hello,' she spoke flatly. 'What brings you here?'

'I wanted to see you. I want to apologise for not phoning.'

She shrugged. Put on her best who-gives-a-damn face, as if she hadn't noticed the silent phone.

'Only I've been busy. I had last-minute edits on my book. Deadlines and all that, you know.'

She remained impassive. Oh, she knew about deadlines. Cakes wanted on a certain date and no other, but she rarely let a deadline interfere with her life. She always walked Evie to school and picked her up again at half-past three. She always put food on the table at suppertime and she always phoned friends when she said she would. Anything less would be bad manners.

Crumbling under her stare, Duncan said, 'That's not totally true. I did have a sudden deadline, but that's not why I didn't phone. I tried. I dialled your number, but I was afraid to speak to you. I kept thinking you might say no to a dinner date. I couldn't stand it. So, I put the receiver down. It was just like being a teenager again. Lost for words and scared of rejection.'

Sophie invited him in. Led the way up the stairs to the kitchen. 'You can't feel like a teenager again. You never were a teenager. We didn't have them in our day.'

'That's true,' he said. 'We were children one day, next day we were grown-ups.' She was aware he was desperately trying to take in the flat as he went, staring at the pictures and the heaps of shoes and coats on the landing. 'Youth wasn't invented when we were young,' she said.

'I suppose it wasn't.'

'My daughter had it. Wasted it.'

He sat at the kitchen table as she made coffee.

'This place in wonderful. All the pictures on the wall. It's lived in, homey. It smells marvellous.'

'It's the cake in the oven. I still love that smell even though I've been baking every day for years and years.'

'It's welcoming.'

Sophie agreed.

'Don't you get fed up of all the baking? All the butter and sugar and mixing?' Duncan asked.

'Yes, I do. But that's the way of it. Everybody gets fed up. Then again, I never know what I'm going to be making next. People ask for the oddest things. I've even been asked to make, you know, rude cakes.'

'Rude cakes?'

'Cakes in naughty shapes. Pornographic cakes.' She brought two cups of coffee to the table. 'It's a cup. Can't be doing with this new mug thing. I like a cup.'

'Oh, my goodness me,' said Duncan. 'Whatever next? I mean the naughty cakes.'

'I know,' said Sophie. 'The cheek of some people. I'd never have the nerve to ask for such a thing.'

He leaned towards her, lowered his voice. 'What sort of cake did they want? I mean was it a shape of cake or just some rude words on the top?'

'Both. I was asked to do one in the shape of boobs. And one in the shape of a man's . . . you know.'

'Did you do it?'

'No. Couldn't. I'd be embarrassed. And what if I'd got it wrong? It's years since I've seen one.'

Duncan dismissed that. 'Once seen never forgotten.'

Sophie supposed that was true. 'Still, I like my work. I enjoy working out how to shape sponge or fruitcake into various shapes. I've done galleons, trains, telephones, tractors, dogs, elephants, all sorts. And once I get going I can muse while I do it.'

He asked what she mused about.

'My life. How I ended up here, doing this. Things I've done. Things I haven't done and would like to do. Things I should've said. I remember some insult from years ago and suddenly what I should have replied pops into my head. Of course, it's too late,' she told him.

'That's musing for you. I mull over regrets. Opportunities missed, people I've let go. I wonder what might have been. What if I hadn't married Lisa, stunning though she was, and come back here and married you. I think I would have been happy.'

'Perhaps,' said Sophie. 'But I'm not sure about childhood sweethearts marrying. I think we might have regretted not playing the field before tying the knot.'

'Nonsense, I'd never have regretted marrying you. It would have been marvellous. We'd have had a big flat in town, or perhaps a large house somewhere with a garden. It would be full of delphiniums and roses and we'd have had a vegetable patch that I'd have looked after. The house would have been filled with music, books, laughter and children. Lots of children – William, Alexander, Matthew and little Hannah.'

'Goodness, you have a very detailed list of regrets. I'm not sure about Alexander. I knew an Alexander and we didn't get on. I prefer Peter. And, I think this is unfair to Martha. I can't write her out of my life, even my pretend life.'

'Yes, Peter. I like that. I understand about Martha.'

They smiled to one another. This was silly. And this was wistful and rather lovely.

'I feel disloyal to Martin, thinking all this,' said Sophie. 'But tell me about our house. What would it be like?'

'Big.' He put down his cup and held his arms wide demonstrating the bigness of the house. 'Victorian, probably, with bay windows. Big sitting room with matching sofas, an open fire and French windows leading to the garden.'

'Ooh, I love it,' said Sophie. She got up to take her cakes out of the oven. He watched as she slid them from their baking tins onto a wire rack to cool. 'Perfect,' she said. 'This is my astronomy cake. I have to put the planets on it and the Milky Way, I should think.'

'Tricky,' he said. 'You might have to carry on with the baking in the big house. They take a lot of upkeep. But you'd have a good-sized kitchen. It would be the heart of the house.'

'Yes, kitchens should be. We'd need quite a few bedrooms with all these children. But then they'd all grow up and move out. We'd be rattling around on our own.'

'There'd be the grandchildren, and think about Christmas with everyone home and gathered at the table. Big golden turkey, candles and the tree in the window.'

'Lovely,' said Sophie. She returned to the table, sipped her coffee, looked at Duncan and suffered a twinge of sorrow. 'You really imagined all this? I'm thinking it's sad to have an imaginary life rather than a real one.'

'I got a bit carried away. I do sometimes wonder what my life would have been like if I had married you.'

'We'd have bickered and worried about money like most couples. And you'd probably have wondered what life would have been like if you hadn't married me.'

He told her she was wise. 'But a little gentle bickering can be fun. It can relieve the tension. It's better than yelling insults and throwing crockery.'

'Is that what your wife did?'

He nodded.

'Goodness me. Not my style. Well, I don't have enough plates.' She gazed out of the window. 'It's turned sunny. I should be out walking. It's good for me.'

Duncan stood up and offered to go with her. 'A breath of fresh air is just what I need.'

It was cool; a watery sun glinted on the sea. Small waves rolled in. Duncan heaved in a deep gulp of ozone and sighed. 'I love being by the sea. Don't know why I ever left.' An ice cream van was parked at the end of the street. 'Not many tourists about to buy his wares this time of year.'

'He has hopes,' said Sophie. 'People like an ice cream when they're walking by the shore.'

He offered to buy her one. She shook her head. 'It would rather negate the walk. I'm meant to be losing weight.'

'Why? There's nothing wrong with you. You're fine just the way you are.'

'That's not what the doctor thinks. He says I'm overweight and have to lose a stone. It's a thin world we live in, I'm afraid.' She set off at a brisk pace, arms swinging. Duncan struggled to keep up. 'Don't worry, I only do brisk for a little bit, then I slow down. By the end I'm dawdling. I'm not keen on walking.'

He puffed. 'That's a relief.'

Sophie said, 'So, why did your wife throw crockery?'

'She was passionate and spoiled. When she didn't get her own way, things flew. It wasn't just plates and cups, she threw shoes and just about anything that came to hand.'

Sophie sighed. How marvellous to be wild and thin and passionate, to just let go and hurl things when you felt the need. So much more interesting than being dumpy and placid and a cake-baker.

'My wife found me to be a plodder when she wanted a high-flyer. She knew I'd never be anything much.'

Sophie imagined a tall, willowy woman in a long mink coat with two Afghan hounds by her side. This woman never baked, wouldn't know a fruitcake from a Victoria sponge. Her lips were painted scarlet, her hair swept back. She was terrifying, haughty. So were the dogs.

'I hate arguments,' said Duncan.

Years ago, Sophie had come up with her idea of the perfect husband. He'd hate arguing, wear a soft jersey she could snuggle into, be jovial, gentle and tender and have a working knowledge of plumbing.

'Do you know anything about plumbing?' she asked Duncan.

'I can change a washer in a tap. Why, is there something you need doing?'

'No. Just wondered.'

Sometimes Martin had been jovial. He'd risen from his pessimism and gloom. He'd joked and laughed and gently teased her. She couldn't fault him there. He'd been tender in his way. Often he'd bring her flowers. He'd carry them awkwardly and thrust them into her hand. 'There,' he'd say, 'bought you these.' He'd walk away before she could thank him. 'Don't get all tearful on me. It's just a bloody bunch of roses.'

Soft jerseys she could snuggle into had not been a success. Once she'd saved in secret for almost a year to buy him a pale blue cashmere sweater for his birthday. He'd considered it. Held it against his chest and gazed into the mirror. 'Nice jumper.' He laid it carefully on the chair in the bedroom and ignored it. A couple of days later Sophie had found it folded in the bottom of a drawer.

It took her a while to mention it. 'What happened to that cashmere jersey I bought you?' she asked, though she knew perfectly well.

'It's pale blue,' he'd said. 'A bit girly.'

'I like it,' she'd told him. 'The colour suits you. It's so soft, I rather fancied snuggling into you when you were wearing it.'

'I'm not the snuggling sort,' he'd said.

She'd sniffed and walked from the room, head high. Hurt and misunderstood, she'd shed a few tears. She never mentioned the jumper again.

Frank Sinatra saved the day. Two years later he appeared in a magazine spread looking suave, debonair yet masculine wearing an identical pale blue sweater. Martin had obviously seen this and appeared in the kitchen patting his chest, displaying his pride in what he now called the jumper he'd forgotten he had. 'It's grand.' He spread his arms. 'So soft, you can snuggle into me if you like.' Sophie hadn't taken up this offer. She was a proud woman.

Walking with Duncan, she sneaked a peek at him. Plainly, he was a man who thought about his clothes. Today he wore black trousers, grey herringbone tweed jacket and a dark blue shirt with a red silk tie. He had a black scarf casually slung round his neck. He looked interesting and academic. In fact, she had to wonder what such a man was doing with her. Today she wasn't looking too bad. She wasn't, thank heavens, wearing the lime green trousers. Instead, she sported grey ones, a red shirt and black shoes with a black coat. She thought she looked smart, but not as eye-catching as he did.

'You like clothes, don't you?' she said.

'I try to look smart,' he replied. 'I put a bit of thought into my appearance.'

She supposed that when a chap lived alone, and had responsibilities only to himself, he had time for such things. She, on the other hand, had a daughter and granddaughter to think about and look after. So no time for self-pampering.

She puffed and said, 'This walking makes me all sweaty.'

He told her she looked wonderful. 'You're glowing.'

She smiled, thought that a nice thing to say. He was a nice man. Of course, Martin had also been a nice man. Nice, but annoying and argumentative.

He'd argued about everything – what was for supper, why fish when he fancied a thick hearty stew? Her make-up – you're beautiful without it – the news, the books she read, the way the furniture was arranged. 'I'm taking an interest,' he'd say. 'I will not be forced into being one of these silent husbands who agree to anything to avoid a scene.'

All that was bad enough, but Christmas was awful. Martin objected to having goodwill to all men thrust upon him. Why do I have to be jolly? Why do I have to send cards to people I never see and don't like? Is there anything more absurd than having an actual tree in the living room? Why turkey? Who says we have to eat it? On and on it went. 'Tradition is only an excuse for lack of innovation and imagination.' In time Sophie began to dread Christmas. Though, she had to admit, Martin was always in a good mood on the day and gave the impression of enjoying it by doing the expected things – looking delighted at his presents, eating too much and falling asleep on the sofa.

Duncan was strolling by Sophie's side, hands in pockets and looking out to sea. He looked happy. She had no doubts that he would throw himself into the Christmas spirit. After all, he'd just enjoyed telling her about their imaginary festive time in their imaginary house with their imaginary children. It sounded like everything she longed for, a glistening time of wine, laughter and love.

She supposed that passers-by would think them a couple and wondered if that was his motive in coming to see her. They might start dating. She shook her head at that thought. Dating was a young thing. She was too old for such nonsense. Dating meant lingering looks, holding hands, kissing.

Oh, kissing. I can't do that. She was shocked and frightened at the idea. Kissing was not what it had been when she was young. It was complicated nowadays. She'd seen an article in one of Martha's magazines. *Give him long, sizzling, sumptuous kisses.* She didn't think she could do that. There must be more to modern kissing than just pressing your lips together. It was a worry.

And, if there was kissing, it would lead to sex. Sophie stopped walking, put her hand to her mouth. 'Oh, no.'

Duncan turned, put his hand on her shoulder. 'Is something wrong? Are you in pain?'

'No. No pain. Just a sudden thought. I couldn't remember taking my cakes out of the oven.'

'But you did, I saw you.'

'I know, silly me. I'm getting old.'

He gave her a fleeting hug. 'Never.'

They ambled side-by-side, smiling, each acknowledging the other's enjoyment of the day. But inside Sophie was awash with a new dread – sex. I just can't do that. I can't slip into bed with a man that isn't Martin. I can't take my clothes off in front of someone else. I can't be naked with Duncan looking on. The shame. The horror. My thighs are a mess; my knees crumbly and wrinkled and my other bits are beyond redemption. No sex. No kissing, no dating.

He moved in front of her, starting walking backwards so he could look at her. 'I don't suppose you'd like to come out to dinner with me? I know a lovely little Italian place that does wonderful mushroom risotto.'

'Well . . .'

He pressed his palms together. 'Please.'

'Oh, all right. I'd love to,' she said. Well, she loved risotto. But no kissing and no sex, she vowed, but didn't say.

13

Mothers Don't Sing 'Be-Bop-A-Lula'

Martha rolled a sheet of headed notepaper into her machine and started typing today's letters. The first was to a couple that had written asking if the agency looked for missing dogs. No. 'Where would I start? It could be anywhere. Someone could have taken it in,' Charlie had said. 'Tell them to go to the dog home.'

The next was to Mr Lewis. He'd written in a tentative, almost apologetic scrawl about his wife who'd walked out of his life twelve years ago. In his late seventies now, he said he was nearing the end of his time and wanted to see his lost love before death came for him.

Charlie examined the letter. 'Strange loopy writing. He's nervous. Guilty about something.'

'Maybe he's just got shaky hands.'

'Maybe. Sometimes people drift apart. Sometimes there's been an argument and one person has stomped out of another's life. I have a feeling this is a stomping scenario.'

'His wife could be anywhere,' said Martha.

'Yes, but she can speak. She can tell people where she's going and where she's been. That's the difference. There will be a trail. Tell him we'll come and see him. He'll be more relaxed in his own home. Might make it easier to find out if this is a drifting case or a stomping out one. And tell him to look out a photo of his wife.'

'It'll be an old photo. She may be totally different now.'

Charlie shrugged. 'An old photo is better than no photo.'

Martha told Mr Lewis to get in touch and arrange a suitable time for a visit, and to please have a photograph on hand. She also told him to rake through his memories so he could tell Mr Gavin everything he knew about the missing one and asked him to please be kindly when he did.

After that she took Murphy for his lunchtime stroll. As she walked she did her usual scanning of on-coming faces looking for one familiar missing face. It had become a habit. She had mastered the art of scrutinising a face before its owner noticed and retaliated with a what-are-you-staring-at glare. Still, there weren't many people about – a few fellow dog walkers, a family on holiday ambling, chatting, eating ice creams and staring at nothing in particular as tourists did, a solitary bearded hippie in wide-bottomed jeans, floral shirt and Afghan coat leaning on the rail gazing out at the water.

The tide was out, the sea pewter grey. She debated taking Murphy down onto the sand to let him run along the shore, but decided her shoes weren't up to it. Murphy didn't mind. He trotted along, looking up at her from time to time. He seemed to be smiling. Though he was a dog. Only a dog, she thought, but companionable, friendly, did what he was told, never complained. And, judging by the number of dog walkers who greeted him by name, he had a lot more friends than she did. She thought that if he didn't have certain problems with his digestive system, he'd make an ideal husband.

An interesting thing happened this morning. She'd woken, yawned, stretched and lain a moment contemplating the day ahead feeling relaxed. She hadn't thought about Jamie. This had been a first. In the years since he'd gone from her, he'd been in her thoughts as she drifted to sleep at night and was still there when she moved out of it in the morning.

Today she'd thought about Charlie and the Be Kindly bureau. She'd been almost happy. She rather enjoyed her new job – Charlie's company, the music, the excellent coffee and the bacon sandwich ritual. All that, and she found some solace in the files of people who had gone through the same emotional turmoil she'd endured. She was not alone in her guilt, shame and constant wondering. Other people were, as Sophie put it, walking with the void. She was not alone. It made her feel better.

Charlie was there when she got back to the office. He'd bought a new LP that was playing on the turntable. 'The Grateful Dead,' he said. 'I made you a sandwich. Ham. It's a ham sort of day.'

She asked what made a day a ham day.

'It's sunny but blustery. It needs to be warmer for chicken and it's not cold enough for roast beef.'

'I could eat chicken any time. But it's interesting to note you're so concerned about sandwiches.' Martha went to the kitchen and returned pointing to her sandwich. 'Good.'

'It's more than good. It's excellent. I am the sandwich king.'

'But are you the missing person king? How did you get on this morning?'

'Good.'

'Not excellent, then.'

'Just good. Of the four B. Simpsons, one's a Barry, one's a Brian and one's a Bradley. The five W. Simpsons include a Walter, a Wilfred and a Warren. So, I've got two William Simpsons and one Bill.' He took the needle off his new album. 'Need quiet. I had a thought. If I was a con man extracting money from ladies with my wit and charm, I wouldn't be registered to vote. I don't even think I'd be in the phone book.'

Martha said, 'I can see that.'

He gave her the double finger gunfighter pistol point. 'Another thought. The woman in the pub said Bill was busy with Belinda and the little one. There is a Belinda Simpson in the phone book. I took a trip to her house to see what she's about. Large terraced house, lawn scattered with plastic toys, pushchair at the front door. So, a child. Nobody about so we'll check up on her tomorrow.'

'Will we? And how do we do that?'

'The house across the road is up for sale. We'll wander along and pretend to look at it.'

'We? Why do I have to come?'

'It looks more real. A man and a woman walking along the street is less suspicious than just a man.'

Martha thought about this. 'What makes you think that?'

'If you see a man on his own you think he might be a burglar or a murderer. You're wary. But a man with a woman is fine. You think he'll be normal. A woman comes in handy sometimes.'

'That's good to know.'

Charlie nodded. 'Yes, you can't beat a woman at your side when it comes to walking down a street looking natural. So, I need to know if Bill Simpson lives in that house.'

'Why don't you just knock on the door when it's obvious someone's in? Or show the photo to one of the neighbours? Then you tell Bernice where her husband is, invoice her and that's that. Anything else is up to her.'

'Because I need to know what's going on. I can't just drop a client in it. I have to prepare them for what they might encounter.'

'So we're going to look at the house across the road?'

'Yes. I'll ask about the neighbours, especially about the people with the messy garden. We'll be a married couple, the Monroes. I'm a doctor, you're my wife.'

'Why do you get to be the doctor? I want to be something more than just the wife. I'll be an architect. We'll be a professional couple.'

'You can't be an architect. You don't look like one. You're not arty enough.'

'I'm arty. I'm just not arty when I come here. Besides, architects look business-like. OK, if I'm not arty enough, I'll be a lawyer. Why should you be the only one to have a make-believe identity?'

He sighed, agreed, and put the needle back on his new LP. 'What do you think of it?'

'I like it. I always liked rock'n'roll. But that's bluesy and sort of jazzy, too. Reminds me of Jamie. He played Grateful Dead all the time.'

'Didn't you play any music?'

'I just listened to the radio when he wasn't about. I was caught up with baby stuff and absolutely knackered. You know.'

He shook his head. 'No. I've never had a baby.'

'I don't think Jamie and I talked much after Evie was born. Well, we spoke about her.'

'Before that?'

'We didn't speak much. We watched television. We played records. We'd put on our favourite tracks and listen to them over and over. He read the newspaper, did things in his shed.'

'What was in the shed?'

Martha shrugged. 'Tools. A radio. My old guitar.'

'What happened to Vinnie and the Vixens?'

'It was Grace. Bloody Grace. Not only did she turn up with the guitar that was meant to be my guitar, and she could play it, but also she could sing. She sounded a bit like Aretha Franklin. Then we got discovered. Every wannabe's dream. An agent, Roger Seaton, signed us. He made me and the others play in the background wearing jeans and leather jackets. Grace was in front in gorgeous frocks. Slinky silk and lace. We got reviewed in the music press – rag-tag leather-clad wild girls fronted by an angel. We thought we were on our way.'

Roger Seaton looked like a rock'n'roll agent – leather jacket, jeans, cowboy boots, pink shirt and sunglasses. He smoked cigars and drove an Alfa Romeo convertible. He had business cards.

Martha treasured the one he'd given her. It was precious, a sign she was a real, live actual rock musician who was going places. She kept it in her favourite book, *Catcher in the Rye*, and took it out nightly to turn it over in her hands, to stroke the embossed gold lettering, ROGER SEATON, ARTISTS' AGENT. How wonderful. That he wanted fifty per cent of their earnings didn't bother her. After all, he'd be getting fifty per cent of nothing. And if they hit the big time, they'd still be filthy rich after handing over half their money. Besides, it wasn't about money, was it? It was about the music.

'Well, it turned out bloody Grace was also writing her own songs. They were seriously good. Bitch that she was. We recorded one. Roger took the demo to London and got a contract. Only the record company didn't want us. They wanted bloody Grace. That was it for Vinnie and the Vixens. We never played again.'

Charlie said, 'That's sad.'

'Well, my mother put it very succinctly. Because by then I was throwing up every morning. She heard. She knew what was going on. "You and Jamie will have to get married," she said. "And you'll have to give up all the Vinnie and the Vixens nonsense. Mothers don't have time for rock'n'roll. Mothers don't sing "Be-Bop-A-Lula".'

Charlie smiled and patted her hand. 'Of course they do.'

Martha thought it was the nicest thing anyone had said to her in a long time.

14

Do Lawyers Hug Strangers?

Charlie walked, hands in pockets, head up and looking about. Martha trotted at his side, heels clicking on the pavement. The street was suburban sleepy. Rows of semi-detached Victorian houses snoozing in the spring sunshine, blackbirds hopping on lawns, sparrows bickering in clipped hedges. It was soporific. Anyone could be forgiven for thinking nothing ever happened here. Nothing nasty anyway.

They'd parked the car a few doors away from Belinda Simpson's house after making sure it was facing the right way for a quick exit.

Charlie said, 'Take my arm. We'll look more like a couple. Like we're real people.'

'As opposed to pretend people?'

'As opposed to a pretend couple. It's what couples do, link arms.'

Martha took his arm, matched his stride and was hit by a sudden, long-buried memory.

She and Jamie were on their first night out together since Evie was born. Sophie was babysitting. Martha had wanted to go to a restaurant. 'Somewhere where we can relax and chat,' she'd said. 'It's been ages since we just chatted.' Jamie wanted to go to the cinema. 'I do enough chatting at work.' He won.

When they'd emerged into the night after the film ended it was raining. Wet pavements shimmering under streetlights, the rush and bustle of traffic, aromas drifting from restaurants, voices, singing from a pub nearby – it was magic. Martha had long forgotten the thrill of a city at night. All this had been going on while she was behind drawn curtains at home busy with baby things. Her heart skipped a beat. She wanted romance. She slipped her arm into Jamie's and pressed her cheek to his shoulder as they headed to the bus stop. 'Let's see if there's somewhere open for a late meal.'

Jamie shook his head. 'Nah. I've got work tomorrow.' He pulled himself free of her grip. 'Don't. I don't like linking arms.'

'Why not? It's nice. We're a couple.'

'Hate it. I'm walking funny being pulled to one side.' He'd shaken his arm free of her grip. 'Can't we just walk normally? We don't have to declare our married state to the world. This linking arms stuff is so Darby and Joan.'

She stopped. It wasn't a good memory.

Charlie said, 'Anything wrong? You look pained.'

'No. I'm fine. I just remembered something, that's all.'

'What?'

'Oh, nothing really. Just Jamie used to hate linking arms.'

'It's a bloke thing. I quite like it though. For a brief walking moment you're not alone.'

They reached the house for sale and stopped. Martha stared at it. Charlie stared at the one across the road.

'The front garden's pretty. I love these old houses with bay windows, don't you?'

Charlie glared at her and pointed at the house opposite. The windows were open. Inside a radio played and a child on a tricycle hurtled up and down the driveway making siren sounds. He was being a police tricyclist.

'I don't know why you don't just go and knock on the door and ask who lives there,' said Martha.

Charlie shook his head. 'Nah. Not yet.'

A voice from behind. 'Oh, it's all right. People do it all the time. Just turn up and ask if they can see round. I don't mind. I rather enjoy the company.'

She must have been in her early fifties, Martha reckoned. Dressed in a pink jumper and forlorn grey tweed skirt. Her hair was tightly permed; the cauliflower look, Sophie called it. She wore large blue gardening gloves and waved a muddied trowel.

Charlie said, 'We don't want to bother you.'

'Oh, it's no bother.' She opened the garden gate. 'Come in. I insist.'

Charlie looked briefly over at the house he wanted to watch. He smiled, thanked the woman and stepped through the gate. Martha followed.

Inside the house smelled of lavender polish, vegetable soup and loneliness. The woman said she was Mrs Weatherfield. Martha didn't know what got into her. Maybe it was the rude way Charlie stood in the doorway looking across at the house over the road. Or maybe it was the atmosphere, the emptiness in the wood-panelled hallway where she now stood. But she held out her hand and announced herself, 'Avril Monroe. And this is my husband, Hamish.' The words just came out. She hadn't known she was going to say them. Horrified, Charlie turned and, behind Mrs Weatherfield's back, mouthed, 'Hamish?'

Mrs Weatherfield led the way into the living room. 'This place is too big for me these days. Just me rattling about like a single pea in a pod. So, why are you looking for a new house?'

Martha glanced at Charlie, but he was at the window looking over the road.

'We're moving to Edinburgh,' she said.

Charlie said, 'There's someone in over there. I think it's him.'

Mrs Weatherfield said, 'Where are you based at the moment?'

Charlie said, 'Manchester.'

Martha said, 'Birmingham.'

Mrs Weatherfield said, 'That's awkward.'

'Well,' said Martha, 'Hamish works in Manchester. I work in Birmingham. So, yes, it's awkward. But now we've both got new jobs up here.' She looked round at the room. It was painted a pale mushroom and the furniture didn't fit. The two armchairs and small sofa looked hopeless and out of their depth, dwarfed by the huge windows and high ceiling.

'The kitchen's through here,' said Mrs Weatherfield. 'We used to spend all our time in it. We were kitchen people.'

The kitchen was painted dark red with orange tiles behind the cooker.

'My husband, Stuart, did this room. He liked colour. I'm more neutral myself. But it was a happy room.' She turned to Martha, saw her enquiring look. 'He left me. Met someone else. That's the way of things, I suppose. I'll show you upstairs. We have four bedrooms. So, plenty room if you have children.'

'Two,' said Martha. 'Humphrey and Lauren.' Names that popped into her head. She wished she hadn't stayed up late last night watching an old film. Still, Mrs Weatherfield didn't seem to notice. 'Isn't your husband going to come and view the bedrooms?'

'He's more interested in the garden.'

'Is that what he does?'

'No, he's a doctor.'

'Very nice. Do you work?'

'I'm a lawyer.'

Mrs Weatherfield nodded and looked ashamed. 'How clever you are. I'm just a housewife, I'm afraid. I should've worked harder at school.'

'Nothing wrong with being a housewife. It's an under-valued job.'

Mrs Weatherfield snorted, 'That'll be why I'm alone, then.'

Martha noticed the marks on the walls, large squares and rectangles where pictures had been removed. There were several of them on the stairway and more on the landing. Stuart, the creator of the colourful kitchen, must have taken his favourite paintings when he left.

'All those years cooking, cleaning, ironing and this happens.

My husband falls for a younger woman. My children off to university. And me walking from room to room with my memories.'

Unable to think of some comforting words, and ashamed of her lies, Martha said it was a lovely light landing. It was a relief to hear Charlie coming up the stairs to join them as they viewed three bland bedrooms. He had his camera dangling round his neck. Tapping it, he said, 'Like to keep a reminder of what I've seen. Nice house, though. Love the garden.'

'It's my pride and joy.' Mrs Weatherfield glowed.

'I'll bet,' Charlie agreed. 'What are the neighbours like?'

'Lovely,' Mrs Weatherfield smiled, nodded, agreeing with herself, 'very quiet. But if anything went wrong they'd help.' She moved to the door of the fourth bedroom.

'What about the folks across the road? They have young children.'

'The Simpsons? Belinda and Bill, I don't see much of them. He's away a lot. She was on her own for a long time. He's quite new.'

Martha said, 'Ah.'

Mrs Weatherfield opened the door to a bedroom. Purple. Everything was purple. 'This is my daughter's room. She's at Oxford now. Economics and history. She doesn't come home much.'

'Students,' said Martha. 'It's how they are. And fares are expensive.' She was trying not to gasp.

Purple walls, purple ceiling, purple curtains, purple bedspread – it was overwhelming. One wall was decorated, over the purple, with a collage of Jimi Hendrix posters, album sleeves and photographs interspersed here and there with the words Purple Haze written in purple ink.

Mrs Weatherfield took in Martha and Charlie's awe. 'I know,' she said. 'My daughter's a Jimi Hendrix fan. This is how she wanted to decorate her room. All the magazines I was reading at the time said it was important to let your children have free expression. I'm not sure about that now.'

Charlie gazed round. 'You have to admit your daughter's made a statement about what she likes. You have to admire that.'

'I suppose,' agreed Mrs Weatherfield. 'But she's gone and she'll grow out of all this and I'm left to clean up the statement. She's crazy about this Jimi person and his music. She's in a band.'

'Really.' Martha was interested. 'What's it called?'

'Mistral Annie and the End of Time.' Mrs Weatherfield sounded glum. 'Susie likes the names of winds.'

'Good name, though,' said Charlie. 'I like it.'

'It doesn't mean anything,' said Mrs Weatherfield. 'There is no Annie. Susie says that's the point. There's no bandleader. They're a democratic group and all profits will be divided equally. Though, there are no profits. They're an all-girl group. Susie says there's never been one before. Well, there have been singing ones, but they all play guitars and drums. This is a first.'

Martha opened her mouth to protest. But thought, Oh well, let Susie dream. I did.

Mrs Weatherfield looked bewildered. 'Susie says rock'n'roll belongs to the universe. Everyone owns it. Why should men make all the noise?' She spread her arms, taking in the room. 'What is this all about? What is going on? I don't understand anything any more. I hear strange music on the radio. People are wearing clothes I wouldn't be seen dead in. Everyone's talking about free love. I've been tucked away in this house cooking, cleaning, ironing, thinking I'm doing fine, and the world has gone whizzing past me. I've been left behind.'

She stood, head bowed, arm dangling by her sides. Martha thought she might cry and wondered if she ought to hug her. She wasn't the hugging sort. Avril Monroe might be, though. She wondered, do lawyers hug strangers?

Charlie looked out of the window. At the house across the road a man and a woman were kissing, and a small child was clinging to the man's leg. Charlie lifted his camera to his eye, focused and snapped. 'It's him. Definitely him.'

Martha and Mrs Weatherfield joined him. The three stood fascinated by the farewell scene below.

Bill Simpson lifted the child, kissed him. Then kissed the woman once more. Charlie snapped them.

Mrs Weatherfield asked what the hell he was doing.

'I'm a bit of an amateur photographer. The people down there make a good composition – the way they're standing, their expressions, the light.'

Charlie put his arm round Martha. 'Time for us to be getting along, darling.' He turned to Mrs Weatherfield. 'Thank you for showing us round.'

As Charlie and Martha clattered down the stairs, Mrs Weatherfield ran behind them. 'There's plenty of cupboard space in the house, and you haven't seen the back garden.'

Charlie said he'd seen it from the window, 'It's lovely.' Arm firmly round Martha's shoulders he hustled her towards the front door. 'We really do have to go.'

As they barged up the front path, Mrs Weatherfield shouted, 'You can't judge the neighbourhood on these people. They're only renting.'

At the gate, Martha looked back; Mrs Weatherfield was at her front-room window looking small and mystified. Martha waved. If anyone anywhere needed a friendly gesture it was Mrs Weatherfield.

They walked to the car. Arms linked. Behind them, the fond farewell ended. They heard Bill Simpson shut his car door, shout a final goodbye and drive off. He passed them as they climbed into the Saab.

Charlie got into the driver's seat. Switched on the engine and roared off. A screech of tyres and swirls of dust shifting in the air.

'Very Clint Eastwood,' said Martha.

Charlie didn't answer. He was going too fast, and when the car in front stopped at the end of the road, he almost rammed the back of it. Bill Simpson glared into his rear-view mirror. Charlie gave him a weak apologetic wave.

When Bill Simpson moved off into the stream of traffic on the main road, Charlie waited.

'What are you doing? Follow him.' Martha was pressing an imaginary accelerator on the passenger-side floor.

'I want to wait for a couple of cars to pass so we won't be directly behind him.'

'There are no cars coming.'

'I know. I'll have to go.'

He pulled out and drew up behind Bill Simpson who, once more, glared at them in his rear-view mirror.

'He's giving us a filthy look,' said Charlie.

'There's an idiot driver behind him. He's worried about his car.'

'If you think I'm an idiot driver, you drive.'

The lights ahead changed to green and the traffic trickled forward. When it stopped once more, Charlie stopped several feet behind Bill Simpson's car and saw he was still on the receiving end of a filthy look. When the cars once again started to move, he stalled.

'God's sake,' he said. 'This is your fault. You're all tense and shouty. You're making me nervous.' Infuriated, he watched the tail-lights of Bill Simpson's car disappear round the corner. He started the car, accelerated, shot through the lights as they turned from amber to red and caused cars crossing his path to brake. A cacophony of tooting, a flare of lights being flashed.

Martha shouted, 'You're not safe. You're driving like a . . . like a . . .' She couldn't think of an insult dire enough to express her fear and rage. '. . . man.'

'I am a man.'

'That's no excuse.'

He sighed a huge indignant sigh. Drove on, gripping the steering wheel, lips tight. At the next set of lights Charlie stalled again. Cars behind honked. He slapped the steering wheel and turned on Martha. 'This is no use. Why did you let me drive? You know I hate it.' He got out of the car. Drivers in cars behind leaned out of their vehicles and yelled at him. 'Moron.' 'Idiot.' And worse.

He walked round to the passenger door, opened it and told Martha to shove over to the driver's seat. 'You drive.'

They followed Bill Simpson to Princes Street, then down to the New Town, Heriot Row, and parked several yards behind him. They watched as he got out of his car, pulled a jacket from the back seat and walked up the steps to the glossy black door of a large terraced building. He paused, turned to look at them and waved. Charlie took a new photograph of him. 'He certainly knows we're here.'

Martha said, 'He's coming over. I think I should drive off.'

'Yes, definitely, drive off.'

But by the time Martha turned on the engine and reversed, Bill Simpson was knocking on the window. Charlie rolled it open and said, 'Yes?'

'Are you following me?'

Charlie said, 'No. What makes you think that?'

'The way you're following me and taking photos.'

Charlie said, 'Ah. Well . . .'

Martha leaned over. 'We're moving up to Edinburgh from Manchester and taking photos of where we might like to live so we can look at them when we get back.'

Bill Simpson said, 'That'll be right.' He stepped back. 'Doesn't matter who you are or what you're up to. Whatever it is, you're not very good at it.' He walked away. Slowly, hands in pockets.

By now a young woman in a long skirt and loose gypsy top had appeared at the glossy black door. Bill took the steps two at a time to get to her. He slipped his arms round her, lifted her, whirled her round and kissed her.

'The full smackeroo,' said Martha. 'Tongues and everything.'

'Cheeky shite,' said Charlie.

Driving back to the office Martha said, 'I think it's fair to say that didn't go well.'

'You lied,' said Charlie. 'You lied and lied to that woman. Avril and Hamish. Humphrey and Lauren.'

'If I remember correctly, you said we were the Monroes.'

'Oh, probably. Still, don't like to be lumbered with a false name. Too much baggage.'

But then, he knew about baggage. He was a man with two names. He used Charlie Gavin because that was the one that was not registered, and that was the one he'd grown up with. The other he tried to forget.

15

An Evening with Duncan

Sophie was ten minutes late, fashionably late she told herself as she walked from her car to the restaurant. She had the evening planned. She'd taken care over her appearance. She looked good. She wore a black low-cut top under a blue velvet jacket and black velvet pants. She'd considered a skirt, but full length was too dressy and anything shorter was out. She might reveal her knees 'My knees let me down,' she told Martha. 'They don't like me. They creak and ache and they're fat and creased with wrinkles. It's revenge for the years of strain they've suffered.'

Knees covered, she thought she looked like a respectable woman out for a pleasant evening with an old friend. She'd enjoy a bit of chat, some laughter, food and a couple of glasses of wine – no more than that, she was driving. Refusing Duncan's offer to pick her up in a taxi was a masterstroke. She could limit her alcohol intake and thus avoid making rash decisions. She would decline any invitations to go back to his place, for example. Anything that might lead to complicated modern kissing or nudity was to be avoided.

As she walked from the car to the restaurant, she imagined the evening ahead. He'd be at the table when she arrived. He'd wave, stand up as she approached and reach out to greet her. She'd kiss his cheek. He'd tell her she looked lovely. They'd order. She was planning to have the risotto and hoped there would be a tempting selection of puddings. She'd ask him about his travels and confess with a small smile that she'd never been out of the country.

'I always wanted to visit Paris,' she'd say. He might put his hand over hers and tell her that one day they would do that together. Oh, it was going to be wonderful. A date, she thought, fancy that. Me on a date. Heady stuff.

He wasn't there. Sophie stood at the door scanning the faces, but there was no Duncan. She couldn't believe it.

A waiter approached and asked if he could help. She told him she was here to meet a Mr Henderson. 'He doesn't seem to have arrived yet. I'll wait at his table.'

The waiter crossed the room to the reception area, opened a large book and peered at it. 'Henderson,' he said. 'Our usual Mr Henderson hasn't reserved a table tonight.'

'I'm sure he must have. He said he'd meet me here at half-past seven.'

The waiter shook his head and said, 'Sorry.'

Unnerved, Sophie scanned the restaurant once more. Duncan must be here. This was definitely the place and she was sure she'd got the time right. What, she wondered, would a woman of wit and sophistication do? Someone who wasn't on her first date in well over thirty years. 'Well, is there a table for two available? I'll wait there.'

She was shown to a small table in a cramped corner next to the lavatories.

'It's all we have at the moment. We're very busy.'

It would do. She sat facing the door, watching for Duncan. When the waiter asked if she'd like to order a drink, she asked for a glass of the house white. Never before in her life had she sat alone in a restaurant drinking. This was what sassy women in the movies did, not her. Still, she was sure that this was how the woman she was pretending to be would behave.

The kitchen was across the aisle; waiters breezed past and always glanced at her, sometimes shooting her a small smile. This made her feel worse. She sipped her wine and stared at the door, willing Duncan to walk through it. He didn't. People sitting at other tables gave her interested but sympathetic looks. Her predicament was a talking point. Here was a middle-aged woman who'd been stood up. She imagined they were laughing at her.

She stared at the door till her eyes hurt and wished it could be Martin that came through it. He'd burst into the room, see her, spread his arms wide and shout, 'There you are,' as if he'd been looking for her for ages. He'd come to her, press his cold hands on her cheeks, say, 'Feel the chill. I've been out in freezing temperatures making my way to you.' He didn't own a car. Never had. The Beetle, though old, was relatively new to her.

A year or two ago Martha had brought home a new LP, *Blonde On Blonde*. Sophie had gasped when she saw on the cover an intense young man with tousled hair in jacket and scarf. Not that Martin resembled Bob Dylan, but he'd been slightly built and even in deepest winter he'd rarely worn a coat. He'd staved off the chill with a jacket, scarf and a scowl. His hair, curly and usually out of control, caused annoyance. The more he was told to get it cut, the less likely he was to do it. He was ahead of his time, Sophie thought. These days he'd have fitted in. He'd have loved all the stuff going on now. She pictured him coming along the street to meet her on their early dates. He'd have his hands deep in his pockets, a scarf wrapped against his throat and he'd be looking intense. But his face always lit up when he saw her. 'Hey,' he'd say. 'My heroine.' When their relationship deepened and Martin came to her home to collect her, Sophie's mother would say, 'Here he is at last. Martin in his jacket and curls.' He always was late. Even now Sophie could never quite accept that he would never again come to her.

An hour later, she'd finished her drink and didn't want to order another. She wanted to be out of here and at home, back in her comfort zone. She planned never to leave it again. The waiter and a man in a suit – the manager, Sophie thought – were talking, and every few moments they'd turn to look at her. Soon, they'd ask her to either order a meal or leave.

She signalled the waiter over, told him her friend must have mistaken the day and paid for her drink. Now came the humiliating trek to the door. Head up, eyes on the world beyond the window, she made her way past the other diners – shamed woman passing.

Outside, she stopped looked up at the sky and welcomed the chill night air on her face. 'Car and home,' she said. 'And don't tell anyone about this.' She thought Martha might laugh, or, even worse, be overly sympathetic. Such treatment usually made her cry.

On the other side of the road a group of girls were surging along the pavement arm in arm singing 'Satisfaction'. And just above that noise, she heard someone calling her name. She turned; saw Duncan running towards her, waving. 'Bastard,' she said and started to run for her car.

She was aware of being, yet again, the object of derision. People were stopping to stare. It wasn't often two people of a certain age were seen hurtling along the pavement, the one behind shouting, 'Stop, Sophie. I can explain.' The one in front shouting back, 'Leave me alone. I never want to see you again. Bastard.' But she ran. Not very quickly, though. Her knees were no longer built for speed and her shoes made walking tricky. So running in them was dangerous. From the other side of the road came the sound of clapping and cheering. The teenage girls stopped their chorus to cheer her on, chanting, 'Sophie. Sophie.'

Well, she supposed she did look comical. She was teetering as fast as she could, handbag banging against her thigh, puffing and wheezing. She stopped, leant against a shop door and fought for breath. She glanced back at her tormentor. He was a few yards behind her, bent double, also gasping for breath. He looked up at her, held out his hand. 'Please, Sophie. I need to talk to you.'

The teenage girls switched allegiance, 'Give him a break, Sophie. Be a pal, Sophie,' they hollered. The cry was rolling along the street, lights went on at windows, people came to the window of the restaurant Sophie had just fled to see what was going on.

'All right,' she called, 'I'll talk to you.' She waited till Duncan reached her and they both stood, facing one another, panting.

'I need to get to my car,' said Sophie. 'I need to sit down.'

'Good idea,' Duncan agreed.

They walked slowly together. Lights in the flats above them went out. They didn't speak. Right now speaking wasn't easy.

At last Duncan, patting his heaving chest, said he was sorry. 'I got caught up. I didn't realise the time. I ran all the way here.'

Sophie snorted, 'Huh.' She was angry with him for keeping her waiting, and even angrier with him for not being Martin. 'I have never been so embarrassed in my life,' she said. 'I was sitting there alone waiting for you and everyone was looking at me. They all thought I'd been stood up.'

'Well, you weren't. I'm here.' He smiled a reassuring smile and patted her hand. A small patronising gesture that enraged her.

'You're too late. I waited and waited. It was awful. It was lonely sitting there by myself surrounded by couples smiling and laughing. Even the couples who were eating in complete silence were having a better time than me.' Words were not enough; she had to let him know the depth of her fury and punched him on the shoulder. 'You didn't even book.'

Frowning, but not really in pain – it had been an ineffectual punch – he told her he didn't always book. 'I eat there regularly. At least once a week. Let's go back. We'll order risotto and have a lovely time.'

'No. I'm never going into that place again. Never.'

'Well, let's go somewhere else. I know some fabulous places.'

She was tempted. She didn't want to go home early. Martha would comment on it and ask questions. Sophie knew the truth would come out. She was a terrible liar. She avoided eye contact. She squirmed, coughed and sometimes even blushed. Her voice went slightly out of control, going up an octave, as the lies got deeper and thicker. No, she couldn't face Martha's interrogation. She'd go somewhere fabulous with Duncan. 'OK.' She started the car. 'Tell me where to go.'

He directed her through a maze of dark canyon streets she didn't know and thought she wouldn't want to know. 'Where are we?'

'This is my world. I'm a wanderer. This is where I roam at nights.'

'Why on earth do you do that?'

'There are all kinds here. Life in the raw. This is where the drunkards roll. I am a watcher in the wings.'

'Romantic drivel,' scoffed Sophie. She was hunched over the steering wheel peering ahead and battling her rattling emotions – fury over her long wait in the restaurant, fear, curiosity and a deep longing to be at safe at home.

'No, really,' said Duncan. 'Thieves, whores and students live here.'

'And a fair amount of normal ordinary folk living decent lives,' said Sophie. And, reflecting on what Duncan had just said, 'Students? You class students alongside thieves and whores?'

'Well, in time they'll be doctors, lawyers, teachers, historians, whatever. But for the moment, they're poor, living far from home, sometimes in dubious localities and seeing life from a new angle. So, they can count as outsiders.'

Sophie said, 'Rubbish.'

Duncan didn't say anything. He shifted in his seat and sulked. Here was a man who didn't like to be contradicted. Shame on you, Sophie thought, a bit of argument is good for the soul.

She thought herself to be an expert arguer. A master, Martin, had taught her. In the first months of their marriage all their arguments had been about arguing. He loved the verbal wrestling. She hated it. 'Argue with me,' Martin would say. 'Fight for your point of view. Don't just stand there nodding your head and looking bovine.'

They'd been debating the colour of new curtains at the time. He'd wanted plain. She fancied striped.

'Bovine. How dare you. I'm not bovine. What a thing to say just because I disagree with you about curtains. You're the rudest man in the world.'

'That's the way. Go for it. Disagree with me. Say what you think.'

'I think the striped would set off the room wonderfully. The plain is boring.'

She'd won. Two years later Martin had admitted she was right. The blue and grey stripes were subtle and, dammit, tasteful. By then they had turned their arguments into an art form. They disagreed about politics, films, books, where to put up shelves, how to cook an omelette and how to bring up their daughter. Sometimes Sophie worried they argued too much, enjoyed it too much. It could replace sex. But it didn't. It usually led to sex. They didn't settle their differences in bed. They celebrated them.

Duncan told her to turn left and park where she could find a space. 'We're here.'

She found a space behind a row of taxis and looked around. The street was narrow, badly lit and busy. People, shapeless bundles wrapped against the night, moved to and from a small restaurant across the road.

'I'm looking forward to this,' said Duncan. 'I hope you're hungry because the portions here are huge.' He spread his arms, this huge.

The air was heavy with kitchen smells – hot fat, vinegar, a thick hint of garlic and onions. Chuck Berry boomed. When Sophie spoke she had to shout. 'This place is intriguing. But it must be awful to live in this street.'

'Oh, don't worry about the residents. They're all . . .'

'Thieves, junkies, whores, drunkards and students,' said Sophie.

'Exactly.'

Tonight's menu was scrawled on a blackboard in the window

– spag bol, salt in bocca, fish and chips, pie and chips. No salad. Puddings of the night – bread and butter, vanilla ice with amaretto.

'No salad,' said Sophie. 'What does that mean?'

'They don't do salad.'

'I don't think that's anything to crow about.'

'It's reassuring. It's good to know you won't find any unwanted greenery on your plate. It's what makes this place such a delight.'

'It's men who come here, then?'

'Yes. How did you know?'

'Men don't get lettuce.'

'What is there to get about lettuce? What's the point of it? But yes, it's mostly men who eat here – taxi drivers, truckers, off-duty police, that sort of thing.'

'This is where you've brought me? I don't think I want to go in. It'll be noisy and probably filthy.'

'Oh, come on. It'll be fun. You'll love it.' He barged ahead of her and into the restaurant.

Alone in the street Sophie considered what to do. She wanted to go home but had no idea of the way back. Besides there was a large group of men all in dark clothing and bawling incomprehensibly to one another coming towards her. She followed Duncan inside.

It was noisy; wreaths of cigarette smoke swirled blue over the heads of the diners who at first glance seemed to be all male. The clamour came to Sophie in layers of shouting; people had to bawl at one another to be heard. To be heard over one table's bawling people nearby had to bawl louder. So the cacophony swelled.

Duncan was already at a table in the corner. He waved to Sophie and pointed to the empty chair across from him indicating that she should hurry before it was snatched away.

He rubbed his hands together as she sat down. 'Isn't this grand? Don't you love it?'

She pointed to her ears, shouted that she couldn't hear him.

He leaned over the table and said, 'The food here is to die for.'

'It had better be to make up for the noise.'

'It's passion,' said Duncan. 'This place has it in spade-loads. What do you fancy?'

'Salt in bocca. Is that saltimbocca?'

'Yes. Great choice. I'm having a pie. The pies here are splendid.'

He picked up a grease-splattered card with the number eighteen on it. 'I have to go to the counter with this and make the order. They don't wait on tables. That's part of the appeal. You feel involved.'

The kitchen was behind the counter, open to the diners' view. Five people clattered about, yelling at one another as they chopped, rattled pans on flaming cookers and skilfully slid food onto plates. A thin, grey-haired woman shook huge wire baskets about in a large deep-fat fryer. Every so often she'd yell a number, 'Twenty-two,' and someone would get up from the relevant table, go to the counter and collect their meal. It was pandemonium.

While Duncan was at the counter ordering their food Sophie gazed round the room. She guessed this was where people came to eat rather than dine. There were no trimmings here. The eaters looked like they had just finished work or were on their way to start a night shift. They ate quickly and left.

In the far corner, near the window, sat a large group of young people. Hippies, Sophie supposed. They were flamboyantly dressed and spoke very loudly. One man, bearded with a thick mane of dark hair, kept glancing across at her. He was flicking his cigarette ash into an ashtray, and then he'd quickly look at her. She couldn't imagine why. Perhaps he wondered why she was here. She certainly didn't belong.

Duncan returned. 'Ordered. Got you vanilla ice with amaretto for pudding.'

'Excellent,' she said. 'I never knew this place existed. What's it called?'

'Jelly's. The owners are Jessie and Louis. She's Scottish, he's Italian – it's a combination of their names. They split the cooking.

She does the deep-fried things. He does the Italian stuff. It's all very good. We'll come again when it's risotto.' He put his thumb and finger into a circle and raised it to her, making a kissing sound. 'The risotto is to die for.'

Not wanting to say she wasn't sure if she wanted to come again, and start a discussion as to why not – the racket was too loud for discussion – she smiled.

'Didn't order coffee,' said Duncan. 'Thought we might go to my place for that. It's quieter there.'

No, no, no, she thought. Can't do that. There might be an attempt at modern kissing. He might want to get me into bed. She squirmed at the idea. It was too embarrassing to contemplate. She shook her head. 'I have to get home. Early night and all that. I have a busy day tomorrow.'

'Oh well, another time,' said Duncan.

Sophie nodded but thought, never.

The flamboyant people were leaving. A scraping of chairs on wooden floor, heaving on of coats and laughter. They moved to the door. The man who'd been sneaking peeks at her opened it and held it as the crowd went out, all of them talking loudly, too lost in the important business of being young to notice any of the other people here. The man who held the door open didn't join in with the laughter. He seemed weary. Aware, perhaps, of being a little too old to even play at being young, he looked down at his feet as his friends bustled past him into the night. Then, he looked over to Sophie. He didn't glance. He stared.

Sophie stared back. Looked hard at the face beneath the beard.

The man joined his friends outside. Sophie saw him jerk his thumb in the opposite direction from the one they were taking. 'Think I'll split,' she heard him say. He walked off, hands deep in his pockets, head bowed.

And something stirred in Sophie's memory. Slowly the features of the face beneath the beard slipped into place. She stood, pointed and shouted, 'My God. That was Jamie.'

16

This Is No Time for Stew

Bacon roll time, Charlie stared into the middle distance and played a slow finger-drum solo on his knee.

'You're very quiet,' said Martha.

'Thinking,' Charlie told her. 'Raking through the dark muddle in my brain, looking for decisions.'

'About?'

'Everything. My life. You. Bernice Stokes. Like the outfit, by the way.'

'I'm going for arty. What have you decided about me?'

'Don't know, haven't decided. It suits you, the red shirt thing and black T-shirt. Better than the lies you tell with the Miss Perfect Secretary clothes.'

'Lies?'

'Yes, lies.'

'You mean I'm masquerading as a perfect efficient secretary by wearing a smart, clean outfit.'

'You are presenting yourself to the world as a calm, organised, efficient human being when you are as bewildered, upset and disappointed as the rest of us. Of course, people wear disguises these days.'

He chewed his bacon roll, musing about modern disguises. 'You get dyed-blonde women who wear skimpy clothes and sunglasses and pretend they're mysterious and vulnerable because they think that will win them fabulous friends. Or maybe they're just hiding the fact that they think they're stupid. And men in suits who want to look high-powered and affluent when they're not. And there are weekend hippies who dress to look young and free from Friday night till Sunday evening. On Monday they go back to their safe nine-to-five office job.' He turned to Martha. 'Everyone's at it, dressing to fool.'

'My efficient clothes are to tell the world I'm managing. What do your clothes say about you? You mostly wear black and grey.'

'That says I'm coming to terms with who I am and who I'm not.'

'You have settled for not being a famous jazz trumpeter.'

'No. That would be abandoning a daydream. Not doing that. I have settled for being someone who is unsettled about reaching forty.' He finished his coffee. 'I think we better go and show Bernice yesterday's photos.'

He gathered the cups and plates and took them to the kitchen. Martha put the guard in front of the fire before joining Charlie in the kitchen to dry the dishes. 'How do you mean we? I wasn't hired to go out and see people. I'm the secretary, I answer the phone and type stuff.'

'I've been thinking of promoting you. You're to be my assistant.'

'Does that mean I get a rise?'

'Don't be silly.'

'Better hours? More holidays? An office of my own?'

'No. No. And there's no room for a separate office. So no to that, too.'

She finished drying the cups and stood back as Charlie put them away in the cupboard. 'So what's the point of my promotion? What's in it for me?'

'You get to come with me out into the world to meet the worried and lonely people I deal with. It will make you compassionate, and hearing other people's stories will take your mind off your own story.' He took the dishtowel from her hand, folded it and placed it neatly on the counter beside his coffee machine. 'Let's go. We'll take Murphy. You drive.'

'That's it, isn't it? You only promoted me so I'd drive you about.'

'How shrewd you are.'

He went into the kitchen, checked the gas was off. That done, he made sure his record player was off and then went back to the kitchen to check, once more, that the gas was off. 'Right, let's go.' He patted his pockets. 'Office keys, car keys, house keys.' He nodded to Martha. 'All set?'

'I've been set for the last ten minutes.'

'Right, photos, keys, dog, gas off, fireguard on. Let's go.'

In the car he patted his pockets once more, fussing and mumbling, 'Keys in correct pocket. OK.'

Martha started the car, signalled and started to move off.

'No, wait,' Charlie put his hand on her arm. 'Did I turn the gas off?'

'Yes, and you checked it after you'd done it.'

'Sure?'

'Positive. Relax. It's fine. The gas is off. The fireguard is on. All shall be well, and all shall be well and all manner of thing shall be well.'

'That's good. Did you just make that up?'

'No. It's very old. My mother had to ice it onto a cake a few years ago. Funny what you can learn from cakes. Julian of Norwich said it.'

'Wise chap.'

They were moving along Portobello High Street and Martha was congratulating herself on having distracted Charlie from his checking the gas was off routine. 'Actually, Julian of Norwich was a woman.'

'Really? She doesn't sound like a woman. Julian is a bloke's name.'

'I suppose,' said Martha. 'But it's a woman's quote all the same. My mother liked it so much she put it into one of her collage things along with a toffee wrapper, a scattering of lettuce seeds and a letter I sent to Santa when I was six. She called it Optimists and Heroes.'

'Excellent.' He shifted in his seat, and sighed, 'Are you sure we turned the gas off?'

'Yes. Did you remember to tap the nameplate?'

'Yes.'

'Then we are safe. We travel forth guarded by your lucky gesture. All shall be well.'

Bernice stared at the photographs, put them down on the coffee table in front of her, stared at Charlie and Martha, picked up the photos again and stared at them. 'That's him. That's definitely him.' She ran her fingers over his Kodak face. 'Who's the woman?'

'Belinda. He calls himself Bill Simpson,' said Charlie.

The room was tidy, almost unlived in. But the house was filled with the smell of stew simmering in the kitchen.

'Simpson? Bill and Belinda Simpson?'

He nodded.

'So they're married.'

'No,' said Martha. 'I don't think so.'

'You just don't *think* they are. You don't know.'

Martha said, 'No, I don't know. Just, the way they were behaving, they didn't look married.'

'What do you mean by that?' Bernice peered at her, eyebrows raised. 'Oh, don't tell me they were kissing and cuddling in public.' She sighed. 'You stop doing that after a while. After you've shared a bathroom, seen each other's old underwear and dirty socks.'

'I know,' said Martha.

'But you didn't find out for sure,' said Bernice. 'And the child, his?'

'Probably not,' said Martha. 'It seems he turned up in her life relatively recently. The child is at least three.'

Bernice's face hardened. 'I see. This isn't good.'

'And what's he doing in this last photo? Who is that woman in Heriot Row?'

Charlie shrugged. 'Not sure. He was going into her flat when we last saw him. We came to give you an update. Actually, we've found Brendan. It's up to you what you do now.'

Bernice reached over, switched off the electric fire. She stared at the photographs on the table. 'I've been waiting and waiting. Now this.'

'I know,' said Martha. 'It's awful.'

Bernice said, 'I can't take this in. Maybe I did something wrong and he ran off to another woman. I thought he loved me.' She stood up. 'I'm all confused.'

'Guilt. Shame. Disbelief. Anger,' said Martha.

Bernice said right now she thought anger was winning. 'All the time when I thought he was on the road working, he was with another woman, well, two other women. Maybe more. Where did he get his money?' She looked at Martha and Charlie, and then answered herself. 'From us. From the women. We've all been subsidising him. Roof over his head, food on his plate, comfort in bed.'

She disappeared into the hall. 'I have to switch off the stew.' She returned heaving on her coat. 'Life goes on. I have a hairdresser's appointment. Can't have him waiting for me. Waiting's hell. I know about waiting.'

They left the house, walked up the path to the gate. Charlie offered Bernice a lift. 'Martha could easily drive you.'

Bernice said, 'No. I'll walk. Walking's good. I can think. I might have calmed down a bit when I get there.' She stomped off. Turned and stomped back to them. 'I'll bet the other women all think he's wonderful, mostly because he's not there all that much. It's all tender hellos and goodbyes with him. It's easy.'

She stomped away. Stopped. Turned and came back.

'I sort of knew it. I just didn't let the wondering about him rise to the top of my brain. He swaggered. I watched him once coming down the street and he was moving the way cocky teenagers do. Pushing himself forward with his shoulders. I thought it was sort of cute. But really, I don't trust men who do that.'

Martha said, 'It's upsetting. An insecure man with too much testosterone, strutting.'

'Exactly,' said Bernice. 'Most men leave the strutting and swaggering behind. It just fades away with time and a mortgage and children. But Brendan still swaggered at forty-eight. I should've thought about that. You can tell a lot about people from the way they walk.'

She stomped off once more.

'The walk of an angry woman,' Charlie said.

Bernice turned and once more came back to them.

'Right now, I'm so shocked, I think my heart can't cope. I hardly trust it to keep beating. I'd cry, but I don't cry any more. I'd scream, but what good would that do. I'd throw things, but I can't afford to replace anything I broke.' She poked Charlie. 'You find out everything about him. All the women he sees, all the names he uses, all the children, all the lies. Then I'll confront him. I want to see his face when he finds out I know all about him. I want to see him squirm. I'll see him in hell.'

Charlie reached out, took her hand, patted it. 'We'll do that. We'll report back as soon as possible. Don't worry, all shall be well, and all shall be well and all manner of thing shall be well.'

Bernice yanked her hand away. 'What a stupid thing to say. That's the daftest thing I've ever heard.' She stomped off.

Charlie looked hurt. 'Well, I think it's cool.'

Martha sneered. 'Stew? A woman on her own worrying over a missing man doing a stew? Chopping veg? Onions? Carrots? Garlic? I don't think so. She'd not be eating much. Just a bit cheese straight from the fridge or a bite of fruit or a small carton of yoghurt. Never stew. And it smelled like she put it on a while ago.' She pointed at Bernice marching away from them. 'Something's not right.'

17

Drinkin' with Charlie

'I saw Jamie,' said Sophie.

Evening, two days after Sophie's sighting. Evie was in bed. Sophie and Martha were washing up. Martha washed, Sophie dried. The radio played. It was late. Supper had been delayed because halfway through cooking it Sophie had read the recipe properly and discovered the meat had to be marinated for two hours. She'd given it thirty minutes; people were hungry.

'When?' said Martha.

'A couple of nights ago.'

'And you only tell me now?'

To avoid looking at Martha, Sophie gazed at the painting on the wall. It showed two large elderly women in bulky coats dancing at a bus stop. It had cost a pound at a jumble sale, and originally she'd bought it for the frame, but the more she'd looked at it, the more she'd loved it.

'I was wondering if I should tell you. You seem happy. I thought my seeing him might upset you.'

'Of course it upsets me. But I'm more upset by your not mentioning it. Why didn't you tell me right away?'

'You should let him go. Forget about him and get on with your life.'

'Get on with my life? How can I do that? My husband disappeared. He just walked out and never said where he was going. What if I wanted a divorce? What if I wanted to move to Australia and take Evie with me, how could I do that? He wouldn't know where to find me.' She vigorously wiped a plate, plunged it back into the soapy water and wiped it again.

Sophie looked shocked. 'You're not, are you? Thinking of going to Australia?'

'No,' said Martha. 'But I should be able to if I wanted. Right now, I'm stuck. What if I died? He could claim guardianship of Evie and take her away so you'd never see her again.' She put the plate in the dish rack and started on another.

'I never thought of that. You're not stuck. Not if you don't want to be. If you met another man you don't have to get married. You could live in sin. It's quite the fashionable thing these days,' said Sophie.

'I don't want to live in sin with anybody. I've gone off all that relationship stuff.'

'You might meet someone,' said Sophie. 'You don't know what will happen.'

Martha lifted a dripping hand from the water and pointed at her mother. 'You're not going to change the subject. Where did you see Jamie? Did he see you? Did you talk to him?'

'Jelly's. I saw him at this place called Jelly's. Yes, he saw me. He kept glancing at me. In fact that's what made me notice him. No, I didn't talk to him because I didn't recognise him. He's gone all hairy. A beard and a moustache and he was wearing shaggy clothes. One of those Afghan coat things. It was only when he was leaving that it clicked who he was.'

'You could've run after him.'

'With my knees. I don't think so.'

'You could've shouted out. You could've done something.'

'My food had just arrived. I was distracted.' She dried the plate Martha had just put on the rack. 'It was surprisingly good. Better than I expected.' She put down the plate, stared at Martha. 'You're not going to die, are you? There's nothing wrong with you, is there?'

Martha said she was fine.

'Good,' said Sophie, 'I hate death. It's sneaky. It creeps up on people you love and takes them when you're not looking.'

'I'm not going to die. Just, if I did, it could be awkward.' Martha stared into the dishwater, floated a saucer on the surface, prodded it and watched it slowly sink. 'What were you doing in Jelly's?'

'Duncan took me there on our date.'

'Hardly a romantic venue. He's a cheapskate. I don't think I like him very much. Still, you saw Jamie. But you did nothing about it.'

Sophie looked at the two women dancing and said nothing. Remembering the Jamie moment embarrassed her. She *had* done something. She'd stood up and pointed, arm stretched out, finger rigid. 'My God. That was Jamie,' she'd cried.

People around her looked at her mildly, followed the direction of her point, stared with slight interest at Jamie and resumed eating. Duncan turned, watched Jamie set off along the street, and asked, 'Who is Jamie?'

Sophie sat down, said, 'Oh, nobody really. Never mind.' She'd taken a mouthful of her food. 'This is very good.' For the rest of the evening she'd tried to look inconspicuous.

Martha stepped back from the sink and dried her hands. 'I'm going out. I need to think. I can't believe you saw Jamie and didn't tell me till now.'

'I didn't want to upset you. And look – you're upset.'

Martha didn't answer. She fetched her coat, took the car keys and headed for the door.

'Where are you going?' Sophie shouted.

'Out,' Martha shouted back.

She drove to the Be Kindly Missing Persons Bureau, stopped the car and looked across at the building. For a while she considered going in. It would be quiet there. She could light the fire and think. But no, she wouldn't do that. It would be odd to be in there at this time of night, and besides, she'd miss Charlie.

She'd even miss Murphy. All that, and she had somewhere she had to go.

She drove on, joining the traffic heading into town. Ten minutes later she was in Princes Street heading for the West End and looking at the people walking the pavement. Scanning faces, she was always scanning faces. Couldn't help it.

At the West End, she turned onto Lothian Road and, still watching passing faces, drove to Tollcross. Then left into a maze of narrow, badly lit streets. She knew the area well. Once, it had been her stamping ground. She'd played youth clubs and a church hall here when she'd dreamed of girl-band glory. She parked across from Jelly's.

She hadn't been here in years. But there had been a time when she'd come often. It was where the band headed after a gig. Too broke to order a meal, they'd shared a couple of Cokes and a plate of chips. Back then poverty had been part of their lives. It had been exciting. In fact, they hadn't expected anything else. Hitting the big time without the struggle would have been a disappointment. Only Grace had money. But she'd pretended she hadn't and joined the others complaining about her empty pockets. It had been a bonding thing, Martha supposed. It hadn't worked. Grace never had been convincing as a penniless musician. When the chip-eating and Coke-sharing were over she'd climbed into her father's Jaguar and swished off.

Martha got out of the car and caught her breath. She'd forgotten what this place did to her senses. The air was heavy with the thick fat reek of heavy-duty cooking. Marvin Gaye's 'I Heard It Through The Grapevine' shrilled out. It was all smells and sounds here. For a moment she was seventeen again. Broke, alive with hope, passionate about Gene Vincent and with a digestive system that could cope with chips and swiftly swigged Coka-Cola.

She opened the door and looked round. Nobody looked at her. It wasn't the way of things at Jelly's to be interested in other people.

The face Martha was searching for wasn't there. A man at a table nearby said, 'Hello, darlin'. Been stood up? Come here.' He patted the seat next to him. 'I'll buy you a coffee.' She shot him a filthy glance and left.

Back in the car, she sat mesmerised, watching people. How busy it was here. Every night all this went on while she sat at home in front of the television hoping for easy-viewing sitcoms. Oh, the joys of an evening's numbness. If only for a moment, she could forget.

By half-past ten the theatre set were arriving. Dressed to the nines, and carrying their own champagne, theatre-goers would eat fish and chips, swig their wine and bray loudly about the show they'd seen and what fun it was to slum it. These days she thought them tiresome. Back in her days of trying to be Gene Vincent, she'd been more blunt. 'Wankers,' she'd said not quite loud enough to be heard. She'd been a rebel, but a whispering one.

It started to rain. People emerging from the café pulled up their collars, stared skywards in surprise and ran. Martha wondered if everybody in Edinburgh had eaten here at some time. All sorts were here tonight, students, taxi drivers, policemen, villains, rich, poor, revellers, one or two women of dubious occupation and Brendan Stokes. Or maybe it was Bill Simpson.

She sat up, stared. Yes, it was definitely him. Brendan Stokes tonight, she thought. Bill Simpson had been scruffy. This man wore a dark blue suit, pink shirt and ostentatiously patterned tie. A taxi stopped and he climbed into it.

Martha started the car and followed. No point in hanging about hoping Jamie might turn up. After being spotted here he wouldn't return for a while.

A second taxi pulled out behind the one Martha wanted to follow. She thought this excellent. She wouldn't be so obvious.

The three cars moved through the streets away from Jelly's and stopped at the junction that would lead them into the thrum of late evening traffic. The taxi carrying Brendan Stokes turned left, the next one turned right. The rain got heavier, drumming on the car roof, the windscreen steamed. Martha signalled left and moved up to join the stream of cars on the main road. Looking round she was surprised to note there were taxis everywhere. She counted three before there was a gap in the traffic. Well, taxi drivers always got busy when it rained. She was sure the taxi she was following was the fourth one ahead. She gripped the wheel, craned forward and peered into the rain. The windscreen wipers squeaked and struggled with the deluge. If she'd been a real detective, if she'd been using her brains, she'd have thought to take the number of the taxi Brendan Stokes had got into.

One taxi turned off to the right, another pulled over to drop off a passenger. So, two ahead. The one directly in front of Martha's car was hailed by someone on the other side of the street and did a swift U-turn. Now she was behind the remaining taxi. She followed it into Morningside, where it turned into Comiston Drive and stopped outside a large house. Martha drove past it and pulled up so she could see Brendan Stokes get out. This was the sort of thing they did on American cop shows. She was proud of herself. A natural detective, she thought, imagining how impressed Charlie would be in the morning when she crowed about her triumph.

She adjusted her rear-view mirror to watch what was going on behind her. And waited. And waited. Perhaps Brendan Stokes was rummaging through his pockets for change to pay the driver, or then again, they might be having an engrossing chat about football or some other manly thing.

It took ten minutes before the taxi door opened. Martha thought, here we go. But a tall woman in a long red coat climbed out. She spoke briefly to the driver then hurried up the path to her front door. The taxi drove off. Martha ducked as it passed. She didn't know why. It was a reaction. She was embarrassed and she was stupid. She'd just followed a complete stranger home.

Somewhere between Jelly's and here Brendan Stoke's taxi had given her the slip. Maybe that was why detectives went about in pairs. One to drive, the other to keep an eye on what was going on.

She headed home. The streets were empty now, hardly anything on the road. She drove slowly, giving herself a ticking off for her absurdity. That, and the car wasn't up to being driven at speed. It grumbled along noisily and made odd complaining grunts when she changed gear. The wipers squeaked, the rain got heavier, bounced off the pavements, rivers down the sides of the road. There was nobody about.

So the lone figure, plodding head down, drenched dog at his side, was a surprise. He looked resigned, walking towards Portobello as if he'd be walking for ever, as if it would be raining for the rest of his life, and the dog didn't look happy either.

Martha drove past, slowed down. She studied the man in her rear-view mirror, stopped and got out of the car. 'Charlie?'

He paused, squinted through the downpour and then ran towards her, waving, 'Oh, thank God. Wonderful.' He didn't wait for an invitation; he pulled back the passenger seat and shoved Murphy into the back, then got in himself, sitting at the front beside Martha.

The dog shook himself violently, splattering Martha and Charlie.

Charlie said, 'Sorry. He does that. All dogs do. Can't help it.'

Martha reached into the glove box for a tissue and wiped her face. 'No excuse.'

She handed the tissue to Charlie. He dabbed his face and handed it back. 'Don't think that will do the job.'

She agreed. Water was dripping down the back of his neck and running down his face. His hair was plastered to his head. His raincoat sodden. Really, she wanted to tell him and Murphy to get out of the car. They'd soak the seats. And, if she thought about it, what difference would it make to them being out in this downpour? They couldn't get any wetter. But she pulled away from the kerb. 'I'll take you home. What were you doing out in this weather?'

'Getting wet. Wasn't raining when I started out. It just suddenly came on.'

'You must have noticed it getting darker. You must have seen clouds gathering.'

'I'm not one for looking up. I'm a pavement plodder. I watch my feet.'

'Sometimes looking up can be your salvation. Where were you going?'

'Home.'

'Well, where have you been?'

'Walking. Took Murphy for a walk and kept on walking and walking. And thinking.'

'My mother thinks that's not very good for you.'

'Your mother is right.'

'I know. Annoying, isn't it?' They reached Portobello. 'I don't know where you live.'

'Bath Street.'

'Bath Street! That's yards from the office and you cycle. You'd be quicker walking.'

'I like cycling. You don't have to look at the people you pass. It's slow and gentle and solitary.'

She turned into Bath Street and stopped outside the building he pointed to.

'You want to come in for a drink? I could do with some whisky.'

'I don't drink whisky.'

'You should. This is a whisky moment.'

She followed him into the building, into a large open hallway. She noticed a small table with a pot plant and an upended top hat. He led her past the wide staircase to a room on the ground floor.

He took off his shoes and raincoat, and padded ahead of her into an adjoining room – the living room. 'Could you dry the dog?

His towel's hanging on the back of the kitchen door. I need to get out of these wet clothes.'

Alone, Martha looked round. It was a good room. She liked it. One wall was taken up with bookshelves, the others painted pale grey, dark green curtains, a leather sofa, an old armchair. A bit masculine, perhaps, but comfortable; could do with a few pot plants, she thought.

'Kitchen?' She pointed to a door leading off from the room, noting that the dog seemed happy with the suggestion.

It was long and narrow. And immaculate. A row of potted fresh herbs on the windowsill, a selection of olive oils on the shelf, gleaming copper pots hanging beside the cooker, a pile of cookbooks next to the breadbin; gleaming surfaces – not a crumb in sight. Martha said, 'Goodness. This puts my mother to shame.'

She took the towel from the hook on the back of the door, dried the dog and wiped the puddles of murky water that had gathered at his feet. Putting the mud-stained towel back on its hook, she looked round the spotless kitchen once more, then sighed to Murphy, 'I think we lower the tone here. Perhaps it is a whisky moment.'

Back in the living room Charlie was pouring drinks. He wore pale trousers and a blue sweater, no shoes or socks. Martha thought this was how film stars dressed when lounging at the pool drinking martinis. Except Charlie didn't look like a film star. He wasn't cool. He slouched. He frowned. He stared in dismay at his bare feet. 'No clean socks.'

'I thought you'd have your sock situation well organised.'

'I do. I have tomorrow's socks lined up. But if I put them on now they won't be fresh in the morning.'

Martha said, 'Ah. Life can be tricky.'

She sipped her whisky. Felt it burn the back of her throat. But it was a welcome heat.

'Where had you been?' asked Charlie.

'Just driving. Had an argument with my mother. She saw my husband at Jelly's the other night and only just told me about it.'

'So you weren't just driving, you'd been to Jelly's to look for him.'

'Yes. Didn't see him. I saw Brendan Stokes.'

Charlie raised his eyebrows. 'Really? What was he doing?'

'Wearing a suit. Looking pleased with himself.'

'Sounds about right. Did you follow him?'

'I thought I did. He got into a taxi and I followed it up to Morningside. But when it stopped a woman in a red coat got out. I followed the wrong taxi. Sorry.'

'Happens. Taxis all look the same.'

'Why were you walking in all that weather? Why didn't you get on a bus or something?' Martha wanted to know.

'A bit of discomfort helps with the guilt.'

'What have you got to be guilty about?'

Someone in the depths of the house went into the bathroom. Martha said, 'Who's that?'

'Art probably.'

'Who's Art?'

'Lives upstairs.'

The shower started.

'Art probably? It might be someone else?'

'Dave or Brenda. But they don't usually shower this late.'

'You said they weren't lodgers or relatives. Who are they?'

'Just people.'

'So,' Martha went on, 'what have you got to be guilty about?'

'Us. What we do.'

'We find people.'

A small woman in her sixties wearing a lavender-coloured dressing gown came into the room, waved, and went into the kitchen. Minutes later she reappeared. 'Needed an onion, darling. Soup for tomorrow.' She paused, considered Martha. 'You'll be Martha.'

'Yes.'

'Thought so.' She nodded to Charlie, 'Drinkin' with Martha.'

He raised his glass.

The woman pattered back up the hall.

'Lives upstairs?' said Martha.

'Brenda. She needed an onion.'

'I gathered that. Like I said, we find people.'

'Yeah, but look what we've done so far. Found out that Brendan Stokes is also Bill Simpson and made arses of ourselves following him. Then we tell Bernice that her bloke is seeing other women and make her miserable. Now, tonight, you follow some poor innocent woman home. Not only are we not very kindly, we're crap.'

'I wouldn't say that. I think we're doing fine. Then again, I've never looked for a missing person before.'

The front door slammed shut. A male voice called, 'You want me to lock up?'

Charlie shouted, 'No.'

'Your home is open to everyone,' said Martha.

'It's friendly. I like it. It helps me cope with being a crap finder of people and a purveyor of doom.'

Murphy jumped on the sofa beside him, put his head in Charlie's lap and sighed. He stroked the dog's head.

'You shouldn't be so gloomy. It isn't good for you.'

He reached over, touched her cheek with the back of his hand. 'You have a good face. I like it. Bit hard round the eyes, though. You've been wounded. You no longer trust people.'

Martha ran her fingers over the cheek Charlie had stroked. 'Perhaps.'

'It's been a while since your cheek has been touched. Thought it needed a little appreciative gesture.'

'My cheek thanks you for that. Maybe you should stroke more cheeks. You could put cheek stroker on your nameplate. Missing Persons Bureau and Cheeks Stroked. You could start with Bernice Stokes. There's a face in need of comfort.'

Charlie said, 'It's odd. Brendan was so easy to find. One visit to a pub, one look at the electoral register and there he was.'

'He probably didn't think anyone was looking for him. And then, when he realised there was, he started showing off. Men do that.'

'So do women.' He refilled their glasses. Chinked his against hers. 'Drinkin' with Martha. It's pleasant. In here out of the rain, getting warm, sipping whisky. Soon we'll be sharing our secrets. It's what you do when you're drinking.'

'I don't have any secrets.'

'Sure you do. I'll tell you one of mine. I'm beginning to hate rummaging through unhappy lives. I should have been a train driver.'

'I thought you wanted to be a cowboy or a jazz trumpeter.'

'I did. And a train driver, too. I used to go and watch trains going by. I'd dream about the people on them and where they might be going. I'd wonder if they were running away.'

'Is that what you wanted to do – run away?'

'Yes.'

'Why? It would have made your mum and dad very unhappy.'

'Didn't have either of those. I just got bigger by myself. It was a surprise to me. There, I've told you one of my secrets. I've shown you mine. Show me yours.'

'I told you, I don't have any secrets.'

'You're a bad liar. I'll tell you one of your secrets. Well, a theory, based on my scant knowledge of the rock'n'roll lifestyle. You were naughty when you were on the road with your band. You had affairs. Just a couple of flings. The sort of thing you thought very rock'n'roll. But Jamie found out about them and he wasn't a happy bunny.'

Martha didn't answer.

'I'm only guessing,' said Charlie.

Martha reached over to the bottle, topped up their glasses.

'Guess away. I'm not owning up to anything.' She chinked his glass. 'Drinkin' with Charlie.'

A voice, Brenda's Martha supposed. 'Art, you could take off your shoes when you come in. You got weather all over the floor.'

Another voice, a man. 'It's only rain. We've both seen a lot of that in our time.'

Martha said, 'Charlie, who are these people?'

'Leftovers,' he said.

'Leftover people?'

Charlie nodded. 'Yes.'

18

Leftover People

There were two groups of residents in Charlie's house, the staging post people and the leftover people. The staging post people stayed for a week or so while they sorted themselves out. They'd meet with family and friends to discuss their disappearance and negotiate their return. The lost and the left behind would gather round the big table in Charlie's house and battle out their grievances. There would be shouting and tears and long silences, sometimes begrudging, sometimes sorrowful. Charlie never attended these meetings. They were chaired, or rather umpired, by Art and Brenda. They were leftover people.

'There are three of them,' Charlie told Martha. 'Art, Dave and Brenda. I found them and they didn't want to be found. I didn't know what to do with them.'

'So they came here to your home and stayed.'

'Yes.'

'You let complete strangers stay in your home?'

'By the time I realised they were going to stay they were no longer strangers.'

Art's wife had asked Charlie to find him. He'd been missing for three weeks. No, she hadn't been to the police. She was sure he was out there watching her.

Even before he found him, Charlie liked Art. People smiled when looking at Art's photograph. 'Nah,' they'd say. 'Never seen him before.' Charlie could tell they were lying. Art was popular. Art had obviously asked everyone he knew to deny the relationship. Charlie decided on a New Town bar that was likely to be Art's favourite. It was snug, friendly and temptingly boozy. He stood across the road waiting for Art to turn up. On the third evening Charlie got lucky. Art shambled down the road, spotted him leaning on the wall, decided against running away and waved.

'Charlie Gavin, we meet at last.'

'So, you know who I am?'

'Oh, yes. I've been watching you watching me. I knew you'd catch up soon enough.'

They drank beer for most of the evening, but ended with a glass of single malt apiece. Charlie paid.

'It was bloody love did it,' Art said. 'I didn't just love that woman I married, I idolised her. Couldn't believe someone like that would as much as look at me. I bought her the house she wanted and then a bigger version of that house. A car and a better car, carpets, curtains, a huge fridge, landscaped garden, holidays, shoes, anything, anything. If she looked at something, I'd get it for her. I needed her. Every love song ever written – that's what I felt for her. I worked seventeen, eighteen hours a day to get money to buy her stuff. I hardly saw her, now I think about it. One day I was walking along the street and I saw this old man coming towards me. He was walking slowly. He was needing a haircut. There was a soup stain on his tie and his suit was shiny with wear. I stopped. Christ, it was me reflected in a shop window. I'm forty-two. I looked about seventy.' He looked shocked at his own admission. 'So I gave her everything. I sold every single thing I had – clothes, watch, books, car. I sold my share in the legal firm where I worked and I put it in her bank account. When I had nothing, I was free.' He drained his glass. 'Don't idolise anyone, Charlie. It's exhausting.'

After hearing that Art would spend the night at the railway station, Charlie had taken him home. 'He's still here,' he told Martha. 'He keeps me right on legal matters and travels to London,

Manchester or wherever for me when I don't want to go, which is most of the time.'

'Does he work? How does he pay for things?'

'He gives advice down the pub for drinks. He guided our local builder through a messy divorce and we got paid in new floors upstairs. It's fine.'

'What about Art's wife?'

'She's lovely. Sweet. She paid my bill after a year. She found someone new who didn't idolise her. Ordinary love was what she wanted. She said being idolised was exhausting.'

'What about Dave? How did he end up here?'

'He needed to lay low for a while.'

When it came to the matter of finding Dave, Charlie had always been thankful he hadn't accepted his client's offer of an upfront payment. He hadn't liked or trusted him. 'Just not the sort of chap you'd like to live next door to,' he'd said to Mrs Florey. The client, a builder called Frank Jeffrey, told Charlie to find Dave and say where he was. Dave was a financial whizz kid who'd stolen thousands of pounds of Frank's money. Charlie had doubts about taking on the case. But business was slow and money tight. Dave was elusive. He'd given up his flat, left his girlfriend and obviously told his mother not to talk to anyone. 'You leave my boy alone,' she told Charlie.

A Tuesday night, August, the air was soft and warm. Charlie had been drinking in a West End bar and decided to walk home to clear his head. It would take about an hour. He'd left the noise and bustle of Princes Street behind and was heading along London Road when he became aware of footsteps behind him. They fell into a rhythm with his. For a while they walked one behind the other. Charlie considered running, but he'd had a few pints and didn't trust his legs. 'Are you following me?' he shouted.

The voice behind said, 'Yes.'

'Why?'

'Frank asked you to look for me. So I started to follow you to make sure you couldn't find me.'

Christ, thought Charlie. I've been tramping all over the place looking for him and all I had to do was turn round. 'Are you Dave?'

'Yes.'

They walked on, one behind the other.

'Grand night,' said Charlie.

'It is indeed,' said Dave.

Charlie stopped walking. Dave caught up with him and they continued on down the road discussing many things – jazz, recent films, favourite sausages, cars, and the terrible things Frank Jeffrey would do to Dave if he got hold of him.

'Why did you do it?' said Charlie.

'I took his money and sent it to the people he'd cheated. You know, shoddy repair jobs, dubious plumbing, leaky roofs, that sort of thing.'

'Excellent,' said Charlie. When they reached home he invited Dave in. The offer was accepted. Dave came in and stayed.

'Well,' said Charlie, 'it wasn't safe for him out on the streets. Though Frank Jeffrey died of a heart attack a year after Dave moved in. I guess he likes it here.'

'But what about money. Do you feed them all? And bills and all that?'

'The top hat. I found it in a junk shop and took a shine to it. No idea what to do with it when I got home. So I put it on the table by the front door. If anybody has a bit of money they put it in the hat. Then again often someone takes some out. Dave puts in most cash. He bets. When he wins he puts in quite a bit. When he loses, they manage.'

'Does Brenda chip in?'

'Hell, no. Brenda has no money. But I love her. She made me a hero.'

Brenda's daughter had come to him. Her mother was missing

and had to be found right away. 'She's old, sick, has red hair and likes to sing. And yes, I have informed the police. But they have crimes to solve and traffic to control and so forth. You drop all your other work and look for Brenda.'

Charlie agreed to this. It was an easy decision; he had no other work to drop at the time. It was difficult, though. There wasn't a trail. Brenda had only ever left the house to shop at her local butcher's and to pick up her pension at the post office. She had few friends. The only thing anyone knew about her was she was small and liked to sing. She had apparently left the house after an argument and hadn't been seen again. She'd no money and had been wearing a floral apron. Where the hell was she?

He phoned the daughter to ask how long Brenda had been missing. Six years. 'What?' he said. 'Six years. She could be anywhere. Puerto Rico. Honolulu. Milwaukee.'

'She's in town. I know it. I know her. She wouldn't leave.'

So Charlie checked with homeless shelters and at night walked the streets looking for an old woman with red hair in all the places he knew where the dispossessed slept. He was hearing tales about a woman who sang for her supper but nobody knew much about her. She didn't have a fixed spot. She turned up, sang and disappeared.

He was walking through the Grassmarket one evening. It was cold, raw and threatening rain. A small crowd was gathered round a woman singing Mozart, 'Porgi Amor' from *The Marriage of Figaro*. The voice was pure and beautiful and achingly sad. It echoed in the damp air. Charlie pushed to the edge of the audience to see the owner of the voice. It was Brenda. Older than the photo he'd been given. But definitely her. Charlie smiled. He'd thought perhaps she sang Doris Day golden oldies. Opera hadn't occurred to him.

When the aria was over the crowd drifted away and Charlie went forward to speak. 'Brenda?' He showed her the photograph.

She glared at him. Picked up the hat containing her evening's takings, pushed him hard in the stomach and ran. He followed and caught up with her in a doorway.

'You nearly made me lose my place,' she hissed. Very angry.

He was shamed and suddenly polite. 'I'm awfully sorry.' He stood, arms dangling by his side, watching her prepare her bed. Plastic sheet, newspapers and then blankets. 'I've come for you. Your daughter wants you back home.'

She continued to glare.

Charlie went on. 'I could get a taxi. You don't have to sleep here.' He pointed to the bedding. 'This can't be good for you. You'd be warm and safe. We could go now.'

She shooed him away, flapping her hands at him. 'Get away from me. This is my place now. I'd rather sleep here than go back home. I'll never go back.' She nodded to a group of homeless men standing on the edge of the pavement watching him. He gave up and went home.

Three o'clock in the morning, the weather woke him. Rain was hissing down, wind rattling the windows. It was hell out there. He pulled his blankets over his head and luxuriated in his warmth and comfort. And then he remembered Brenda. 'Bugger.' He thought about an old, sick lady curled up on a cold, hard concrete floor, thin blankets soaked by sheeting rain. 'Bugger. Bugger. Bugger.' He wouldn't sleep now. His conscience wouldn't allow it.

Dressed in everything waterproof that he owned, and two jumpers underneath the long raincoat, he rode out into the wild night. It took him over an hour to reach Brenda's doorway. There she was, a sleeping bundle. Not nearly as soaked as he'd thought she'd be. She'd pinned a large plastic sheet over the bottom half of the entrance and pulled another plastic sheet over her blankets. She looked almost cosy. He made the mistake of waking her.

He clambered over the plastic sheet, noticing more plastic sheeting spread over the floor of the doorway. One of Brenda's plastic bags must contain more plastic bags, he thought. He crouched beside her and said, 'Brenda. Hello, Brenda. I've come for you.'

She opened one eye, threw back her blankets and flashed a knife at him. 'You bugger off. I'll use this.'

He held up his hands, 'No, please. I've come to get you out of here. I can't sleep for worrying about you.'

She glared.

'It's really bothering me,' Charlie told her. 'It's keeping me awake. You're cold and wet and I'm warm and snug. Come with me. I can give you a hot bath, food and a bed with clean sheets.'

'Why would you do that?'

'I told you. Thinking of you out here is keeping me awake.'

In the end, he thought it was the clean sheets that swung it. Who could resist clean, fresh sheets? At first they walked side-by-side. He draped her bags over the handlebars of the bike and they headed home. But she tired. Her steps got slower, smaller. She shuffled and stopped. 'Arthritis,' she said. 'Can't go on.' And it rained and rained. Water ran down the back of Charlie's collar, flattened his hair, seeped over his scalp, blurred his vision and soaked through his raincoat, through his jumpers to his skin. Wind whipped round him. He looked at Brenda standing glaring at him in disdain. 'I was daft to come with you.' They both knew the hopelessness of their situation. But they wouldn't give up. 'Get on the bike,' said Charlie. 'I'll push you.'

It took a couple of hours. They moved in silence. He could feel her body pressed against his, her arm hooked round his neck yanking him to the left. For days after he would ache.

When they got home, Charlie ran Brenda a bath. He dried himself, made bacon and eggs, tea and toast for two and showed Brenda to her room. In the morning she nodded to him. 'Thank you. I'm feeling better.' It was the only thanks he ever got from her. Later in the day she said, 'The room's good. Big and light. I'd prefer it to be white, though. I like white.'

He knew then he'd never get rid of her. She was here to stay. He bought white paint.

'You're kind,' said Martha. 'Too kind, perhaps. Does Brenda actually do anything?'

'She helps with the painting and fixing of things,' Charlie said.

'She paints, she does plumbing?'

'No, but she's good at bossing people who do.'

'How many bedrooms do you have?'

'Six.'

'And three of them are occupied by people you were asked to find. But when you found them you didn't tell those who asked you to find them. You kept them to yourself.'

'Well, sort of. If you put it like that.'

'Do you know what I think, Charlie?'

'No.'

'I think you better get a bigger top hat.'

19

Trailing Jamie

Recently Martha had taken over delivering Evie to school, leaving Sophie free to follow Jamie's trail. Every morning she caught the bus he'd got on, using the same stop he'd used. She sat watching the world he'd travelled through on his way to work.

She was sure this was the sort of thing Charlie did when he followed someone's trail. She would slot herself into Jamie's routine and hope to come across something that would shine a light on why he left. Something he'd seen, something that had troubled him and made him leave. She made notes as she went.

Today was to be her last day on the trail. It was beginning to be embarrassing. People were talking about her. And staring. Nobody wanted to sit next to her. With sinking heart she realised she'd become the passenger other passengers avoided – the old woman who muttered and scribbled odd jottings in a notebook.

Today a man, middle-aged and slightly paunchy, sat beside her and loomed over her, reading what she'd written. He asked if she worked for the council.

'Me?' said Sophie. 'Good heavens, no. What makes you think that?'

'You're making notes on the passengers. You're spying. You'll report back to the council that we don't need this bus and it'll be removed. Council's always making cuts.'

'No, I'm not a spy. I'm following a trail. My son-in-law used to get this bus every morning. Then years ago he disappeared. Just up and left. He sent my daughter a short letter telling her not to look for him. So, I'm digging into his life. Trying to see something that might have triggered this strange thing.' She fished in her handbag, pulled out a photo of Jamie and handed it over.

The man scrutinised it. 'Yes. He used to get on this bus every morning. Haven't seen him in ages, right enough.' He handed the photo back. 'Didn't know he was married. All he spoke about was music.'

'You knew him?'

The man nodded. 'Just saw him most mornings. We didn't say much. He was the only music type I ever met. I said to him I thought it odd he was doing what he did and yet he wore a suit and seemed to start at nine in the morning. I thought he was a bit of a liar. That's why I remember him, the rubbish he spoke.'

'What did he say he did?'

'He was in the music business. Not playing or anything. Something to do with management, arranging gigs, driving bands about and setting up equipment.'

Sophie nodded, said, 'Right.' She imagined Jamie standing at the bus stop, hands in pockets, quietly telling lies. He'd be matter-of-fact about this fantasy job. Probably even managing to look slightly bored about it. She was hurt that he hadn't mentioned Martha or Evie. She'd thought they were as important to him as they were to her.

The man leaned over. 'If you're following your son-in-law's trail, why are you still on the bus?'

'I'm going up to Princes Street. That's where he worked.'

'He may have worked there, but he always got off at the top of Leith Walk.'

'He did? Why did he do that?'

'How the hell do I know? He just did.'

'Damn,' said Sophie. 'Now I'll have to get off and walk back. Hate walking.' She brightened, turned to the man. 'This might be a clue. Thank you.' She bundled down the aisle and got off the bus at the next stop.

Walking back to where Jamie had always got off the bus, she stared about wondering what he'd done every morning. Most of the shops were still shut. She looked up at the flats above the shops. Perhaps Jamie had been seeing someone who lived in one of them. He could have been having an affair – an hour's passion before work.

She doubted that. Jamie had never seemed passionate. In fact, he'd been distant. Rarely speaking when she was about. He'd spent a deal of time in the shed at the bottom of the garden, she remembered. He'd come into the house, take a handful of biscuits from the tin in the kitchen and go and sit sideways on a chair in the living room listening to music.

'Is he thinking?' she'd asked Martha.

'Yep,' Martha had replied. 'Planning our future.'

No, Sophie decided, Jamie hadn't been passing passionate mornings with a lady friend. Perhaps he'd been buying something special for his lunch from the delicatessen in Elm Row. But he'd never been that interested in food. She'd seen him hack a huge slice of bread from a loaf. But that was a matter of urgency. 'I have to have something now.' He certainly never seemed to mind what it was. No, selecting a delicacy or two for his lunch wasn't Jamie's style.

She was caught standing still in the swirl of the morning – traffic and people on the move. Not knowing what to do, she looked up and down the street deciding which way to go.

It wasn't a part of town she visited much. But it was interesting to look round. She gazed longingly into the window of a shop selling kitchen equipment – glossy copper pans, mixers and French coffee makers. Oh, the life she could have if she was rich. After that she spent a while reading the menu posted in a glass case outside an Italian restaurant. It was a mystery, all in Italian. How did people know what to order? People were so sophisticated these days.

There was a lot going on that she didn't understand. Why

did young folk dress the way they did? They seemed to say everything they thought about the world through their clothes. Especially their trousers. You could see someone who looked barely old enough to be out on their own and you'd know they'd disapprove of the way you voted, the things you ate and every record in your collection – small though it was – and all because they wore velvet bell-bottoms and a T-shirt with a cannabis leaf printed on it.

Like that couple across the road. Him in purple trousers so tight at the crotch they were almost indecent and then so wide at the ankles they were ridiculous. And her in a shaggy coat, a headband and swathes of beads. She tinkled as she walked. Bells on her belt, Sophie noted. At this time in the morning, it just wasn't right.

The couple went into a record shop Sophie hadn't noticed until now. It was open. Well, there were lights on and one or two people milling about. She crossed the road to look at what was going on.

There were about five people in the shop. Mostly what Sophie saw was a lot of hair. The girl from a few moments ago was sitting on a chair by the window rolling a cigarette. The man she was with was flicking through records. The others were just lounging, talking, listening to the music that was booming out.

There was a copy of *Sgt. Pepper's Lonely Hearts Club Band* in the window. It was marked, *Second hand, cheapo, in good nick*. Sophie decided to buy it. She'd heard it on the radio and liked it. Besides, Evie wanted it. She went into the shop.

'We're closed,' said the man behind the counter.

'You don't look closed. What are all these people doing here?'

'We work here,' said a man with long hair, jeans and a T-shirt that read *I'm Far From Normal*.

'I doubt that,' said Sophie. Pointing at the T-shirt, 'I believe that, though.' She turned to the man behind the counter. 'I want to buy the record in the window.' She put her handbag on the counter while she fished inside for her purse. And was aware that her sudden arrival had caused an adolescent silence.

She remembered such moments. Years ago when Martha was a teenager, Sophie's appearance in a room where Martha was holding court with her pals always caused a deep awkward silence. Martha and friends would clam up. Here she felt the same pressure; people wanted her to go so they could resume their interesting chat. She wondered what they'd been talking about. Sex, probably. They'd think that an unsuitable subject for a woman of her years. As if she'd never engaged in that activity herself. As if she didn't know more about it than any of them. Still, this silence was impatient. And standing amid these colourfully clad youngsters made her feel frumpy. She'd committed the sin of ageing.

The behind-the-counter man fetched the record from the window and put it in a red carrier bag. 'Enjoy.'

'I will. And so will my granddaughter.'

'Everybody loves the Beatles.' He took Sophie's money. Put it in the till.

Taking her change, Sophie handed him her photo of Jamie. 'Do you know him?'

He examined the face in front of him, shook his head. 'Nope.'

But there was a flicker. Sophie swore she saw a flash of recognition.

'Why?' he asked.

'He's married to my daughter. He loves this music you're playing. Just wondered.'

The photo went round the shop. Everyone took it, gazed at it and shook their head.

'Nope.'

They were lying. Sophie knew their mutual expression well. She called it the it-wasn't-me look, or the don't-know-what you're-talking-about look. It was very familiar. She figured all mothers knew it. Everyone was staring at her, wide-eyed and mildly baffled. 'Never seen that guy before.' They were all lying.

'Just thought I'd ask,' she said, taking the photo back and slipping it into her pocket. She took the bag containing her record from the counter, thanked everyone and headed for the door. They were mocking her. Oh well, such things happened. Silly, really, for one day they'd all be her age and ripe for mocking, too. Behind her a small ripple of sniggers. She turned. 'Oh, stop being so young. It's annoying.'

Out in the street, she made her way to the bus stop. But changed her mind, and went back to the shop. Through the window she saw the man who'd served her talking on the phone. He was talking to Jamie, telling him an old lady in a frumpy outfit was looking for him. Sophie was sure of it.

On the bus home, she took her new record out of its bag. Turning it over she noticed the price label stuck on the back. It was the same label that was on many of the records Martha had brought to the flat when she moved in. 'Records Jamie left behind,' she'd said. 'Obscure bands I've never heard of. He gets them second-hand from somewhere or other. Don't know what to do with them. I'll never play them.' They'd put them in the attic.

She held the record to her face and sniffed. Opened the red bag that the record had been in and stuck her head inside, sniffing and sniffing. The smell was familiar. It was dense, slightly spicy and herby. It was the scent that sometimes hung about Jamie. It was the scent that had greeted her on the few times she'd gone into the garden shed where he'd spent so much of his time. Once, she'd been searching for a trowel to weed Martha's small garden and the place had reeked. She put the bag on her knee and stared ahead contemplating this.

'Marijuana,' she said. 'That's the smell.'

Of course marijuana hadn't been part of her youth. She hadn't even known it existed till some film star or other had been arrested for smoking it.

So that's what Jamie had been up to. Smoking dope and staying young. Dreaming of being a dropout with a droopy moustache who went around saying things like right on, cool, man, and make love not war.

'He should have been helping with the baby,' she said. 'Giving Martha a little rest.'

People on seats nearby stared.

Sophie looked out of the window and tried to settle her mind. 'Too much to think about.'

People shifted in their seats, looked uncomfortable.

A memory swirled into her brain. The arrival of a long-buried snippet of information startled her. 'Robert Mitchum,' she said. 'That's who it was. Did time for drugs.'

Nobody looked at her. They turned away, pretended she wasn't there.

Sophie scolded herself. Be quiet, stop talking. You have become the dreaded one, the nutter on the bus.

20

Not Sure About This

Ted Lewis's flat was in Great King Street, two floors up, with views across the city towards the river. The man matched his handwriting. He was elegant, well mannered and old-fashioned. Not a shirtsleeves man. Even at home alone in the afternoon, he wore a jacket and tie. He showed Martha and Charlie into a large room, invited them to sit on the polished leather sofa by the fire and brought them tea served in fine china cups on a large tray. He handed round delicate shrimp paste sandwiches, macaroons and sponge cake. It looked like he'd spent some time preparing for this visit. Perhaps people didn't come round much any more.

He interrupted his story by making regular trips bearing plates of goodies from his armchair to the sofa where Martha and Charlie sat, urging them to help themselves. 'Eat up. Too much for me to finish after you've gone.' His voice, large, rounded vowels, belied his age. Martha put him somewhere in his seventies.

'Chrissie dropped out of my life years ago. I came home from work and she was gone.' He addressed Charlie. A man would understand this. 'I confess I didn't notice at first. I thought she'd popped out to visit a friend to go to one of her committee meetings. I was just annoyed she hadn't left me any supper. Had to make it myself. Scrambled eggs.' He paused, drifted off a moment, gazing towards the window. Remembering. 'Yes, definitely, scrambled eggs.'

Martha said, 'Scrambled eggs.'

'Yes. Haven't eaten them since.'

Martha felt the same about lamb chops, the meal she'd cooked on the night Jamie didn't come home. The very smell of them brought rushing back the gnawing anxiety she'd felt. 'So,' she said, 'how long were you married?'

'Twenty-five years when she went away. Birthdays, anniversaries missed.' He leaned forward. 'It worries me. I might not recognise her now. She could have dyed her hair. She'd be wearing clothes I haven't seen before. I might walk past her in the street and never know. She'll be sixty-five. Twelve years younger than me. It seemed a lot at the time. But we were happy.' He scratched his chin. 'I thought we were happy.'

'Police?' said Martha. 'Have you been to them?'

'Yes. They have a record of my wife going missing. They checked. Looked for unidentified bodies most likely. I used to go to the station once a week. Then once a month. Now I go on her birthday, once a year. They found nothing.'

'Do you have children?' Charlie asked.

'No. We never got round to it.' He poured everyone a second cup of tea and handed round the macaroons. 'I've made a list of all her friends. All that I know of. And of the committees she sat on.'

'Do you think she was having an affair?' Charlie raised his eyebrows. 'Sorry, I have to ask.'

'I don't think so.'

'Had you argued?'

'Yes. She'd run up a bit of debt. Very angry about that. But she never could resist pretty things. New dresses. Cushions. Perfume.' He looked at Martha. 'You women, you're too easily tempted.'

Martha opened her mouth to object. Charlie silenced her with a nudge.

'Well,' Mr Lewis slapped his knees. 'Time for my nap. I think you've got all the information you need. Go out and do some sleuthing. Find my wife and bring her back to me. I've got a few things I'd like to say to her before I depart this planet and, to tell the truth, I miss her.'

'There are a few more things I'd like to ask,' said Charlie. 'Had your wife any dreams or aspirations? Did she have a driving licence and a passport?'

'No dreams that I knew of. No driving licence. I don't approve of women driving cars. It's beyond them. They are not safe on the road. Can't focus on more than one thing at a time. And she didn't have her own passport; she was on mine as my wife. Anyway, she hated travelling. She hated abroad. We used to go to the south of France every year and she complained the whole time about the heat. Said the place was not suited to her pale Scottish blood.' He started to usher them out of the room, thanking them for coming. Halfway along the hall, he stopped. 'She used to sit in the shade drinking Pernod. I hated that. Hate Pernod. Hate scrambled eggs.' He resumed hustling Charlie and Martha towards the front door.

Charlie protested, 'I have more questions. What was your wife's maiden name?'

Mr Lewis picked up a folder from a small table by the front door. 'Everything I know about Chrissie is here. I've written it all down. An honest account, no detail left out, no lies.'

'We'll keep in touch,' Charlie said.

Mr Lewis raised his hand, a slight protest. 'Don't bother. Just let me know when you've found her.' He shut the door.

Out in the street, wind whipping round them, Martha said, 'He's brokenhearted.'

'He's furious,' said Charlie. 'He doesn't like to be made a fool of. Not sure about this.'

21

It Takes One to Know One

The letter said *Stop it*. That was all. No signature. But Sophie was well acquainted with Jamie's hand. She knew it was from him. And she knew what he wanted her to stop.

'Won't,' she said, stuffing the letter into her apron pocket. She was on to something. 'I'm hot on the trail.'

She'd been back to the record shop several times since her first visit. She didn't go in but observed from a distance, sitting in her car, often using binoculars. They didn't make a lot of difference. All she saw was people looking through racks of LPs and people buying LPs. No sign of suspicious goings-on and no sign of Jamie. This was probably because her stake-out time was restricted to the hours Evie was at school. She was sure Jamie was more likely to appear later in the day when the pubs were open.

She wasn't sure what she'd do if she spotted him. She imagined herself confronting him, slapping his face perhaps. 'That's for seriously upsetting my daughter,' she might say. That seemed feeble in the light of the hurt he'd caused. But she couldn't call the police; he hadn't really done anything that was against the law. Still, one good hard smack across his face at least would let him know he hadn't got away with leaving his wife and child. He'd know there was someone in the world that loathed him and his cheek might smart for an hour or two. Jamie would also know you do not fool with Sophie and get away with it.

Meantime, when she wasn't spying on the record shop, she was making a Mona Lisa cake. Taking this on had been a mistake.

She now knew it was impossible to copy a masterpiece painting in seven days using icing. An approximation would be the best she could do, she'd finally told the man who'd made the order. 'I'm no da Vinci. And I believe he took years. You've given me a week.'

'An approximation is fine,' the man agreed. 'After all, we're not putting it on the wall. We're eating it.'

She was working on the background, leaning close to the cake shaping fuzzy trees in blues and greens with a palate knife, when the idea struck her. She could flush Jamie out. It was the sort of thing New York cops did in the movies. They frightened suspects into making a dangerous move that would be their undoing.

She went to the phone.

A young female voice answered.

'Is Jamie there?' asked Sophie.

'Jamie?'

'Jamie Walters.' Sophie could hear music in the background. The Rolling Stones, she thought.

'He doesn't work here. He just comes in sometimes.'

'Oh.' Sophie heard someone in the background asking the girl who she was speaking to.

A man's voice. 'Who's this?'

'A friend,' she said. 'I want to speak to Jamie.'

'There's no Jamie here.' The line went dead.

Sophie replaced the receiver. 'He's definitely there, then. Or they know where he is.' She spoke to the cake. She'd fallen in love with it. The classiest thing she'd ever done. 'He'll be up to no good. Dealing drugs. That's the sort of thing hippies do, along with calling the police the fuzz and protesting about wars. And him so quiet, too. It's the quiet ones you have to watch.'

Just before one o'clock Duncan turned up. This happened often these days. Sophie suspected the man only wanted to be fed. She was happy to oblige with a plate of homemade soup, a hunk of bread and some cheese. He repaid her with his company on a walk. She enjoyed the chat. It helped her to avoid thinking, a habit she deplored in herself.

At first she had been sceptical about Duncan's tales. His past life seemed like something out of a novel. But then as he elaborated about lonely nights in foreign bars and lost loves, women who'd abandoned him and jobs that had turned out to be dead ends, she decided that if Duncan's life had been gleaned from a novel, it hadn't been a very good one. In fact, it would be meaningless and not exactly a page-turner.

It wasn't hard to unravel the truth of Duncan's past. He'd married the wrong woman, taken to drink and lost his job. After that, down on his luck, he'd got by using his charms. He flattered women into feeding him. He was masterly at turning up at mealtimes, looking surprised and a bit embarrassed to see a table being set and food being brought out of the oven. But it never took a lot of persuading to make him sit down and join in the eating.

He wouldn't have much money, Sophie supposed. And she was sure that Duncan spent a lot of what he did have in pubs and on clothes. Well, a charmer needed to be well turned out.

It didn't really bother Sophie that she was being charmed for a bowl of soup. In fact she was rather flattered. A man with Duncan's looks and wardrobe could surely have found a more sophisticated and wealthier woman to flatter. She imagined herself to be on a long list of fascinating females. This might have been flattering if she didn't think that Duncan was getting old and losing his powers. Captivating young, rich and beautiful women was getting beyond him. If he'd been a woman, he'd have been called a gold digger. But he wasn't interested in money, really. He certainly wasn't a sugar daddy. Men had to be rich to merit that title. After careful consideration, Sophie concluded he was a soup digger. He was after a warm kitchen and comfort food.

He never patronised her. He never overly praised the meals he ate. He was kind and considerate. And Sophie was glad of his company. It was good for her morale to be seen out and about with a nattily dressed man.

Today she offered him tomato and leek soup and toasted cheese. She reckoned the vegetables would do him good. Plus there was fibre in the wholemeal bread and protein in the cheese. 'Ach,' she scolded herself, 'why should I care if the man lives on take-aways. All this nurturing has to stop. Too much thinking and worrying about others and forgetting about myself.' But she couldn't help it. She imagined the poor man's arteries clogging, his heart struggling as he sat at her table. Cholesterol was having its way with him.

He told her the food was wonderful, raised his hands in awe at the Mona Lisa cake and said he was looking forward to their walk. It was a lovely day out. After their initial spurt, when they'd slowed to an amble, Sophie asked Duncan why he thought Jamie had left Martha so abruptly.

'Ah,' he said, 'there could be many reasons. Boredom. Fear. Curiosity.'

'Curiosity?'

'If Martha had been his childhood sweetheart, he probably had started to wonder what other women were like. To kiss, to hold, to have in his bed.'

'You think he left her for another woman?'

'It's a possibility. If he's still in town it could be he simply traded one married life for another. Maybe the other woman offered him something Martha didn't.'

'Careful what you say about my Martha.'

'Oh, I didn't mean anything sexual. I didn't mean to imply your daughter isn't a lusty and willing lover.'

'Please, we'll have none of that talk. A parent doesn't like to think of their child doing naughty sexy things. Though I suppose they must.'

'I was thinking maybe Jamie hooked up with someone who offered him a way out of the job he hated. Offered him a more glamorous life.'

'You think he met a rich woman.'

'Something like that. He met someone who woke him up to his dreams. After all, he'd had an exciting time being on the road with Martha's band. Then suddenly he was a father living in a small rented house working at something that didn't interest him. I think someone turned his head.'

'He thought he'd found something better than life with my Martha and my Evie.'

'Some men are like that,' said Duncan. 'Always on the look-out for the main chance. Always hoping for a cheap ticket to easy street.'

'The bastard,' said Sophie. 'They could have worked it out. People do. Everybody knows that it can be awful being newly married with a child. Suddenly you're not young and free any more. And you've hardly any money. It can be a shock.'

Duncan supposed it could be.

'It certainly was for Martin and me. The whole baby business took us by storm. It was nappies and feeds and washing and sterilising bottles and making more feeds and washing more nappies and never getting enough sleep. Stumbling about in grubby clothes, living on bacon sandwiches while the baby lies in a pristine cot wearing pristine clothes. Then there was the crying. We dreaded that. We loved Martha, adored her, boasted about her, doted and wept with joy over her. But we had a running-away rota to get away from her. One week it was me. Next it was him.'

'That sounds awful. It's a wonder the human race survives.'

'I've wondered about that, too. Still, it bonded Martin and me. We took comfort from knowing that if one ran away, the other understood.'

'Did you do it?'

'Of course not,' said Sophie. 'I couldn't have done that. Neither could Martin.'

But Jamie had. Sophie always wondered how Martha coped with it. How did it feel to see your husband actually taking flight and hurtling away from you? She'd just told him they were expecting a second child and he didn't take her in his arms and kiss her and tell her how wonderful, clever and precious she was. Oh no, he fled. Sophie pictured him waving his arms as he sprinted away, screaming, 'Nooo.'

'Yes, Jamie was a bit of a bastard in the end,' she said.

Duncan agreed. 'A bit of a rogue. One of those people who don't think twice about using others to get what they want. Or even what they think they want. Oh yes, there are rogues about.'

Sophie rammed her hands into her pockets, scowled out to sea and thought, it takes one to know one.

22

She'll Always Remember You

Martha knew that in life good things and bad things come in clusters. A person went humming along doing their day-to-day things – going to work, coming home again, eating, watching television, bed, sleep and then up again and work again. Something wonderful would happen – they'd fall in love or win a prize or spot a bargain in a sale. It wouldn't be an isolated splash of fortune, other good things would come along before life's routine hum returned.

It was the same with terrible things; disasters arrived in a series of black days. Horrible thing followed by horrible thing, like Jamie suddenly leaving and then a miscarriage. So, when one relatively small catastrophe happened, Martha prepared herself for the worst.

Charlie was somewhere in town following Brendan Stokes. He'd complained about this. It wasn't the sort of thing he did. 'I don't follow people about. It isn't polite. It's not the sort of detecting I do. I think. I muse. I use my instincts. I'm good at musing.'

'I noticed,' said Martha.

He was wearing a grey collarless shirt and a darker grey jacket. 'Do I look inconspicuous?'

'Only slightly.' There was something about him that drew the eye.

'Only, I don't want to be noticed. If someone notices you following them they're going to get upset. They could punch you. I hate getting punched. It hurts.'

'Have you been punched often?'

'I've been punched. Not often. But enough to know I don't want to get punched again.'

'Understandable,' said Martha.

'You are sounding flippant. You have no idea about being punched. It can leave you reeling, gasping with pain and shock. You just stand hurting so much you can't think, mouth open as you try to remember how to breathe and work at not vomiting.'

Martha nodded. In fact she knew a little about being punched. There had been catfights on the road. They erupted, swift and vicious and noisy. Martha had found them ugly and the sudden fierce bodily contact embarrassing. She winced, remembering. She'd spent about eighteen months on the road, hardly any time at all. Now she felt sure she'd spend the rest of her life squirming at her memories.

'Well, I'm off then,' said Charlie. 'Take Murphy out at lunch-time, will you? And check the gas is off and the fireguard is up.'

'Will do.'

He left. Martha sat, waiting. Charlie returned. 'You will remember about the gas?'

'And the fireguard. Of course.' Martha nodded.

Charlie lingered at the door. 'Promise.'

'I promise.' She listened to him walk down the corridor and out into the street.

'He's gone,' she told Murphy. 'Didn't keep coming back to check that I'd check the gas and fireguard. He must be pre-occupied. Dreading doing a bit of shadowing, or tailing as proper detectives say.'

She spent her morning chasing Chrissie Lewis. She phoned all the numbers on Ted's list. Chrissie, she discovered, was an intriguing and elusive woman. All these years after her disappearance rumours about what had happened to her still flew. One or two of the people Martha got in touch with thought that Chrissie had run off with Ted's money; a few were surprised she hadn't run off sooner than she did. One woman thought Chrissie was in London, another thought she'd taken up doing something somewhere in South America. Others thought Ted should forget about Chrissie and get on with his life. At least what was left of it.

Martha's tenth call was to Wendy Jenkins, who was marked on Ted's list as a friend. *But one I disapproved of, a bad influence* he'd written. Martha thought this hopeful. She approved of people who were disapproved of. Being a bad influence was to be admired, she thought. Once she'd been considered to be a bad influence. Grace's father had loudly declared Martha an appalling young woman who looked like a female thug in her leather jacket and jeans. She punched the air. She was rather proud of that.

Good times bumping along in the back of the van, singing Gene Vincent, Eddie Cochran and Buddy Holly. It had been grand to swagger into a pub, girls in blue jeans and leather jackets, and demand pints in straight glasses. They'd revelled in the stiff disapproving silence they'd always provoked. Grace never joined in. She was a gin and tonic girl. 'C'mon,' Martha would say, 'have a pint. Join the lads.'

'I'm not a lad,' Grace would reply, 'and I never will be.'

Martha sniffed and wondered if Grace had not in fact been right.

Wendy Jenkins wasn't like the other women Martha had spoken to. Her voice was softer. It lacked the hard edge of a woman who was sure of herself. Wendy Jenkins didn't hide behind an accent. Her guard wasn't up. 'The what?' she said.

'The Be Kindly Missing Persons Bureau. We're looking for Chrissie Lewis.'

'Oooh, Chrissie. Funny you should phone about her, I saw her the other day. I thought she was missing.'

'As far as I know, she is. Where did you see her?'

'She was in the Grassmarket. Just walking along. I was in the car. I tooted and waved. She waved back. I tried to stop, but by the time I found a parking place and walked back to talk to her she was gone. No sign of her.'

'Are you sure it was her?'

'Oh, yes. I'd recognise her anywhere. We were best friends.'

'Have you any idea where she might be staying?'

'Not a clue. She's hardly likely to be with Ted, though. Not after what she did.'

'What did she do?'

'Well, Chrissie fell in love with some diplomat or minor foreign aristocrat she met at a reception. She was smitten. Said she didn't know she could feel the way she did. Love was new to her.'

'Really?'

'Yes. I was dubious. I mean, he was quite a bit younger than her. Anyway, the rumour was she emptied Ted's bank account and ran off with her new love.'

'Goodness.' Martha noted Ted hadn't mentioned this. 'What was the diplomat's name?'

'Paul.'

'Paul what?'

'Don't know. Chrissie never said. I have to go. I'm due at work in half an hour.' She hung up.

Quarter to two, Martha slipped on Murphy's lead. Time for a late lunchtime walk. It was a perfect day. Sun on water, sand warm under her feet when she pulled off her shoes to walk along the shore. She threw sticks and watched Murphy plunge after them. She stared out at the horizon – waves and sparkle, ships silhouetted black slipping by. A light wind drifted against her face, lifted her hair. She smiled.

She lingered. Her mind emptied. She relaxed. Maybe for a whole two minutes before her pleasantly vacant head filled with all the questions she should have asked. What sort of minor aristocracy? A prince? A count? And where from? Where did Chrissie and the minor aristocrat run off to? And what time of day did Wendy see Chrissie in the Grassmarket? It was humming with tourists in daylight hours, but at night it was no place for a woman alone. It wasn't safe. Had Chrissie been alone?

She considered Murphy pattering beside a retrieved stick, eager for it to be thrown again. He was soaked. He'd dashed out of the sea and shaken himself – a vibrant silvery spray, sea and sand, had splattered her. She put her hand to her mouth. She hadn't been clever. 'So much I didn't say. Things I didn't ask. God, I'm a seriously lousy detective. And look at me, a lousy dog walker, too.'

The best plan was to take Murphy back to her home, dry them both before returning to work.

The house was empty. Martha found an old towel and dried the dog. She changed into a pair of jeans and a shirt, the only clean clothes she could find. Everything else was heaped in the laundry basket. Sophie had abandoned all household duties while she perfected her masterpiece Mona Lisa cake. Martha looked at her watch. Half-past two, the cake would now be delivered and swooned over. Sophie would have been congratulated, praised and, Martha hoped, paid. Now she'd be on her way home, in time to collect Evie from school.

In fact Sophie was on her knees on the pavement. The cake was splattered in ruins before her. She was bleeding and weeping. A small crowd had gathered round her. Nose running, mascara seeping down her cheeks, she pointed at the smeared mess of icing spread before her. 'The cake, my cake,' was all she could say.

Carefully carrying the cardboard box, she'd been walking towards the house where the cake was expected. She was taking her time, moving carefully, watching where she placed her feet. She didn't want to trip. She was moments from what she imagined would be her finest hour.

The thugs, as she would describe them later, came up from behind her. Suddenly they were walking one each side of her, moving quickly, making her move quickly too. 'What's in the box, missus?'

'A cake. I'm delivering it to a house along here.'

'Sort of cake?'

'A very special one.'

'Chocolate?'

'Yes. But that's not what's special about it.'

They started to jostle her, pushing her from side to side between them. 'Let's see, then.'

'No.' She was getting scared. She didn't like this at all. Sweat pricked her face and chest. Breathing was hard. 'Please leave me alone.' She looked round. Was there somebody who could help? A man on the other side of the road was walking away from her.

The boys were about fifteen and both wore unwashed jeans and T-shirts. 'Give's a bit, then.'

'I can't. It's for someone.' This was awful. Sophie's heart thundered. Her knees shook. And the cake, nothing must happen to the cake. This cake was her pride. Her creation, more than just a cake – it was a thing of beauty. The boys had troublesome teenage skin. Smelled of a liberal dousing of cheap cologne. She was swamped by youth, testosterone and acne. Horrible. Horrible.

The afternoon was quiet, cars drifted past the end of the street. But no traffic turned into the crescent. Sophie's throat tightened. She felt her knees weaken and thought she might cry. One boy reached forward and bashed the top of the cake box, trying to knock it out of her hands. She held on. 'Hey, leave it alone.' He grabbed the box and yanked it. Sophie kicked him and pulled the precious cake back to her. The box wasn't up to rough handling and buckled. And Sophie suddenly got angry. 'You bloody thugs. Stop it. I'll call the police.' She flung back her head and shouted for help. Looked wildly around. Yelled once more. Nothing happened.

There was a swift, sweaty skirmish, Sophie whirling this way and that, trying to keep the cake box away from their grasping hands.

She lashed out with her foot and caught the cake-grabber on

the knee. He howled and, in retaliation, punched her face. She reeled back, turned and crashed to the pavement. Not wanting to release the box, Sophie didn't put out her arms to break the fall. She hit the pavement head first, landing on the cake, demolishing it. The thugs each gave her a parting kick in the ribs before running off with her handbag.

The small crowd had gathered by the time she came round. She lay a moment, wondering why she was on the ground. Then, moaning and in pain, she heaved herself onto all fours. Blood poured from the side of her head. But all she could do was mourn her cake and worry about her grandchild, who would soon be waiting for her at the school gates.

The police arrived before the ambulance. They sat her by the edge of the pavement and asked her name.

'Evie,' said Sophie. And asked the time.

'Quarter to three,' said one of the policemen.

'My cake,' said Sophie. 'I have to deliver my cake.'

'It's all right, Evie. You can buy another one.'

'I don't think so. That was the cake of cakes. I made it.'

An ambulance arrived. Two men got out and leaned over Sophie, commenting on the gash on her head. 'Nasty.'

'Her name's Evie,' said one of the policemen. 'Couple of boys tried to grab the cake she was delivering.' He pointed to the mess of icing on the ground. 'Took her handbag.'

Sophie was helped to her feet. She felt dizzy. She ached. 'My sides hurt. I think I've broken a rib. They kicked me.' She was eased into the ambulance. 'Evie. I have to . . .'

She couldn't move through this misunderstanding. People were shifting round her, touching her, being kind to her and she was shaking. She was the centre of this drama, but other people, faces she hadn't seen before, were taking control. They were all younger than her, but confident. The words she needed to say wouldn't come out.

Martha and Murphy returned to the office and found Charlie sitting on the sofa holding an ice pack to his cheek, a glass of whisky on the table in front of him. 'I said I didn't do following people. Bastard punched me.' He took a slug from his glass. 'Don't blame him, really. I'd punch someone who followed me as obviously as I followed him. I was really annoying.'

Martha asked what happened.

'It was unfortunate. Didn't know which house to start at. So I hung about outside the Heriot Row flat. That's where he was. Tough luck.'

He'd waited a few doors along from the Heriot Row flat, on the opposite side of the road. 'Look casual, relaxed,' he'd told himself. And had gone through a pretence of a man who'd been stood up. He checked his watch, looked this way and that, gave a flamboyant shrug and, when Brendan Stokes emerged from the house, walked off.

Walking bothered him. He'd noticed there were various types of walk. The out-for-a-walk walk, the purposeful walk, the furtive walk and many more. Right now, he suspected he was doing a sneaky walk. He'd hunched, stuck his hands in his pockets and fallen into step behind his man. Thinking this suspicious, he'd straightened up and assumed a nonchalant air – strolling, enjoying the day.

At the end of the street Brendan Stokes turned right and headed for Princes Street.

Charlie followed. When they reached shops, Charlie gazed into windows pretending to be taken by some object on display. In fact, he'd spotted a rather natty shirt, navy and pale cream stripes. If he hadn't been involved in a spot of serious tailing a suspect he might have nipped in and bought it. But no, he was on the job. He crossed the road and kept an eye on his man from there.

Brendan Stokes went into Princes Street Gardens. Charlie did, too. At this time of day there were only a few tourists, a couple of mothers pushing prams and a man walking a dog. Charlie put on his best amble and looked about him, smiling at the small occupants of prams and leaning down to pat dog. He was a man enjoying the day. They walked to the West End. Brendan turned on his heel and headed back, passing Charlie on the way. And Charlie knew he'd been rumbled. Brendan left the Gardens, crossed the road and disappeared into a shop. Charlie did the same, but once inside he couldn't see Brendan. He went out the rear exit into Rose Street, but still no sign of his man. Charlie sighed, shrugged, decided he was useless at the proper private eye stuff and decided to go and buy the shirt he fancied.

He was grabbed from behind. Choked by an arm pressing hard against his windpipe, and with his right arm pushed up his back he was marched up an alley that led to a pub backyard. But nobody to help. He was slammed against a wall. His breath gushed out of him. His arm ached. The wall slam crunched his shoulder and the left side of his face.

'You following me?' said Brendan. His face was horribly close to Charlie's.

'No,' said Charlie.

Brendan pressed a knife against his throat. 'Follow me again and it'll be the last time you follow anybody. Right?'

'Right,' said Charlie. A thick sweat spread under his arms, across his chest. He was going to be sick. Fear churned in his gut. His legs shook. He couldn't breathe.

Brendan stepped back. Put the knife away. Charlie breathed. He wasn't going to die. Then Brendan punched him, a fierce blow to his stomach, and as he doubled over, gasping, retching, Brendan hit him on the face. The blow stunned him. A thick pain to his cheekbone, his head wrenched to one side and his face knocked momentarily out of shape. For a second he couldn't think what had happened. There was a sliver of darkness. He heard Brendan walk away. He stood wrestling with shock and fear. Stunned at the daylight and the nearness of voices and city sounds.

Then the pain started for real. A thick gnawing in his gut and eye socket. He stayed in the alley for a while, gathering himself. He threw up. Ran his tongue round his mouth, checking his teeth were still in place. Gingerly touched his bruised cheeks. Now all he had to do was put one foot in front of the other and make his way back to his car. It wasn't going to be easy.

'Jesus, he can pack a punch,' said Charlie. 'You wouldn't think it to look at him.'

'No,' said Martha. 'You wouldn't.'

'That's it. I'm not having this. This isn't what I do. I'm not a slick private eye, a lippy street-smart guy in a cool hat who solves murders. I just find people and bring them home. I don't get punched. I don't charge for stuff like that. Punching's extra.'

It was a picture he held in his head. It had been in a storybook. The only book in the flat he shared with Ella. A kindly shepherd, a tall and smiling man with a crook, was leading two tired and hungry children home. They were emerging from a dense and chilling wood walking towards a cottage where a plump woman wearing a floral apron was standing at the door, arms spread, welcoming them. Through the window, lit against the dark, the travellers could see a warm fire, a fat black pot on a stove, a table spread with a pristine cloth upon which were laid jars of jam and a warm brown loaf.

All this lingered in Charlie's mind. At his lowest ebb, when he longed to know who he was, where he belonged, this was what he imagined. And, when he couldn't get that for himself, he thought it a grand notion to do it for others. He would, he decided, always be kindly like the shepherd in the picture.

'We're going tomorrow to tell Bernice Stokes we no longer want to work for her. Buggered if I'm getting punched again.'

He asked how she'd got on. She told him about Wendy Jenkins seeing Chrissie in the Grassmarket. 'So she's back in town.'

'Yes. Perhaps we should get in touch with her husband and tell him.'

Charlie shook his head. 'Leave it till we find her and talk to her. We need to know why she left before we take her home. Going back after years away can be painful and awkward. People left behind have been hurt. And sometimes so have the ones who ran away.' He held his ice pack against his cheek and winced.

At five o'clock Martha went home and was surprised to find the flat empty. She went from room to room, shouting, 'Hello. Anyone in?'

She sat at the kitchen table frowning. This was odd. A small worm of worry started gnawing at her stomach. Where were they? Perhaps Sophie had been paid a huge amount of money for her masterpiece cake and had taken Evie out for a treat. But surely they'd have left a note. They were dead. There had been an accident and right now even as she sat here the police were on their way to give her the bad news. Martha got up and paced. She peered out of the window. She went out into the street, looked this way and that, praying for them to appear sauntering hand-in-hand, chatting. But no. Back inside she put on her coat. She'd walk up to the school, checking as she went for signs of a terrible accident on the road. She took her coat off. Perhaps it would be better to stay at home. She needed to be here when the police arrived. She paced some more.

At seven o'clock the phone rang. For a moment Martha couldn't place the familiar voice on the line. 'Missing a daughter?'

'Yes.' She gazed ahead. Rummaging through her brain. Who was that?

'Shame on you. What sort of mother are you? The poor child was at the school gates in floods of tears.'

'Sophie was due to collect her. Wasn't she there?'

'Nope.'

'Jamie, is that you? Do you have Evie?' Martha was shouting. She was furious and she was relieved. 'Where are you?

'It's me. And I have my daughter safe here with me.'

'Thank God. I'll come and get her. And where's my mum?'

'Don't think so. I think I'll keep her a while. No idea about your ma.' He hung up.

Martha slammed down the receiver and ran out of the house. She stormed up John Street and along the High Street, past the Be Kindly office and on to Bath Street.

She burst into Charlie's house shouting, 'Charlie. Charlie.'

He was standing in his living room and turned to her. His face was swollen, turning a blackish blue round his left eye. He swayed slightly. 'Martha.' He was drunk.

Martha stepped towards him. 'Evie's been kidnapped. My husband's taken her.'

Charlie put his hand to his aching face, trying to take this in. Alcohol didn't make it easy. 'At least she'll always remember you.'

23

Embroiled

Martha stood, mouth open. 'What the hell do you mean by that? At least she'll remember me?'

Charlie looked pained. He spread his palms and said nothing. Some things were hard to explain.

'I can't believe you said that.' Martha turned and stormed out of the door.

He caught up with her at the end of his street. Gripped her arm and stopped her running. 'Will you slow down. I can explain.'

Martha wouldn't slow down. 'Evie's been kidnapped and my mother's missing. I have to get back.'

Charlie galloped sideways, huge strides. 'Listen to me. I was missing. I was abducted. I don't remember my mother.' He was breathless. Jolted with each bouncing step, his bruised head hurt. 'Just stop.'

Martha stopped. 'You?'

'Me.' He tried to catch his breath. 'Jesus, you can move when you're angry.'

'I can't stay still. I'm out of my brain with worry. Running helps.'

'No, it doesn't. It makes you sweaty and out of breath and you can't think straight. Stop it.'

Martha slowed to a brisk walk. 'I don't believe you.'

Charlie trotted beside her. 'It's true. I'm not me. I'm someone else.'

'Don't be ridiculous.'

'I'm Norman McKenzie. Norman Harry McKenzie. That's the name my mother gave me. Ella carried me off when I was a baby. She thought my mother had abandoned me and she was saving me from the children's home. She called me Charlie Gavin.'

Martha stopped. 'You're kidding.'

'No. It's God's honest truth. Mrs Florey always thought her sister was the first person I ever found. But she was wrong. The first person I found was me.'

They walked on in silence, till Charlie said, 'Don't you believe me?'

'I'm wrestling with it. I'm finding it hard. Didn't your mother report you missing to the police? Didn't anybody look for you?'

'My mother didn't want me. At least she didn't want a baby. I was illegitimate, an inconvenience. Ella wanted me, well, a baby of her own. So she took me. My mother saw an opportunity to start afresh and took it. Everybody has a day when they do something they never thought they'd do when they woke up in the morning.'

'You think that's what happened with Evie? You think Jamie saw an opportunity and took it?'

'Yes.'

'Why wasn't my mother there to collect her?'

'We'll find out. And we'll find Evie.'

'How?' she snapped. She didn't believe him and hated his quiet, reassuring tone.

'I dunno. We'll follow the trail, that usually does it.' He said it slowly. The sharpness in her voice, her aggression – face craning towards him, jaw clenched – made him doubt himself.

They reached Martha's house. Charlie opened the gate and led the way to the front door. 'First, a cup of tea. Then we'll find your mother. She has to be somewhere. She hasn't run off. She's too happy for that.'

'How do you know? We argue a lot.'

'Exactly. Arguing in her safe place, her kitchen. Keeping her end up as a mother. Not the same as fighting or bottling up resentments.'

Inside, Martha sat at the kitchen table. Charlie filled the kettle. Made tea and put a cup in front of her. 'Drink.'

The phone rang.

Martha said, 'Who's that phoning us?'

'Answer it and find out.'

'I don't want to. It might be Jamie again.'

Charlie sighed, went to the small table in the hall and picked up the receiver. 'Yes.'

He returned, hands in pockets. 'You're not to worry. Sophie's in hospital. She's fine. She was set upon by a couple of kids trying to steal the cake she was delivering. Banged her head on the pavement.'

'What do you mean, banged her head on the pavement? What was she doing on the ground? She must have been knocked down.' Martha stood up. 'We have to go and see her.'

'Drink your tea.'

'It's got sugar in. I hate it.' She pulled her coat from where she'd draped it on the back of her chair. 'C'mon.'

She ran down the path, clambered into the Beetle, turned on the ignition. A feeble whine and a clunk. She tried again. Whine and clunk. She jumped out, slamming the door, and kicked the car. 'Fucking thing. It's always doing that. It dies when you need it.' By now, Charlie had caught up with her.

'Your car,' shouted Martha. 'We'll need your car.'

She took off down the street. Charlie was several yards behind her, protesting at every step. This hurt. His stomach ached where he'd been punched. His bruised face throbbed. He was sobering up. A hangover was nigh. 'For God's sake, wait.'

But slowing down wasn't for Martha. She hurtled on, reaching the car long before Charlie, and yanking the door, yelling, 'Keys, keys.'

From his distance away, Charlie shouted that they were inside. He was running and waving his arms, panicking because she was panicking and her condition was catching. Martha burst into the house, shouting, 'Keys. Keys. I need the keys to Charlie's car.' She reached out, making a desperate clasping motion with her hand.

Brenda appeared. She pointed to Charlie's living room. 'On a wooden tray on the bookshelves.'

In the car, Martha drove. 'We need to get there in one piece.' She gripped the wheel, leaned forward urging the car on.

Charlie said, 'Your mother was concussed. They're keeping her in overnight for observation. Apparently they thought she was called Evie. She kept saying it.'

'She'd have been worried about not picking her up.'

'So her brain's functioning.'

'Her brain constantly functions. Never stops. It keeps busy with recipes, speculations, gossip and the intricacies of the soap operas she watches. My brain isn't working. It's overloaded with worry and confusion.'

Charlie stared out of the window, watching people on their way to somewhere or standing in groups chatting, laughing, smoking. He imagined all the people he saw had families, mothers who bought them socks for Christmas and nagged them to eat some breakfast and wear a hat on chilly days. For a long time, he'd longed for a warm, boisterous, close family. Now that he'd seen families who bickered, held long petty grudges, fought over trivialities, insulted one another, he sometimes thought that maybe he was lucky to have nobody. He could live as he liked. He was relieved he wasn't embroiled in a family. Yet here he was in this car with Martha rushing to see her injured mother, worrying about her missing daughter. He was getting embroiled.

Sophie was sitting up in bed. She waved when she saw Martha and Charlie and looked pained at the effort this had taken. She was pale. Her head was bandaged.

'Six stitches,' she said. 'I'm lucky my nose wasn't broken. I held on to that cake.'

Martha leant over, kissed Sophie's cheek. 'But you're all right?'

'I'll live,' said Sophie. She shifted, heaved herself up the mattress. 'Can't get comfortable. Everything hurts.' She snorted, 'I was set upon. Mugged for a cake.'

'As cakes go, that one was very muggable.'

'Hoodlums,' said Sophie, 'vandals, thugs. I don't know what the world's coming to. What kind of parents do they have?' She stopped, looked round. 'Where's Evie?'

'She's not here,' said Martha.

'I can see that. Where is she?'

'I don't know.'

'What do you mean, you don't know? You have to know. She's your Evie, your daughter, you have to know where she is.'

'Jamie's got her,' said Charlie. 'I think he must have been watching the school for some time, waiting for his chance.' He stuck his hands in his pockets, stared at the ceiling. 'Do you think he knew? Do you think he set Sophie up so he could get a chance to talk to Evie and, you know, take her home with him?'

Martha looked at him. 'What are you saying?'

'I'm not saying anything. I'm just thinking out loud, speculating.'

'Well, stop it. You're scaring me.'

'Sorry.'

Sophie was shocked. 'Do you really think that? Jamie had me mugged so he could get hold of Evie? Bastard. I need to get up. I need to do something.' She reached out to grab Charlie. 'I need to go to the record shop. They know where Jamie lives.' She leaned back, stared at him. 'What the hell happened to you?'

'I got beaten up. A bloke took exception to me following him.'

'Too right. You shouldn't be following people. It's rude. Also, if you don't mind my saying so, you can't be very good at it if you were spotted.'

'I admit I'm not good at following people. And as a detective I should be expert at it. I worry about this.'

Sophie said, 'You think you're not a very good detective.'

'It has crossed my mind,' Charlie said. 'By the way, which record shop?'

'The seedy one at the top of Leith Walk.'

'What the hell were you doing there?'

'Tracing Jamie. I found out he went there in the mornings before work. I asked if they knew Jamie and they said they didn't. That's how I know they know Jamie. They were lying. I can tell when people aren't being truthful. Their faces go shiny and their voices go up. They look shifty.' Pointing at Martha, 'She was a dreadful liar when she was little. It was all "It wasn't me." And, "I didn't do that." And, "I've never been in a pub in my life." Even though she was reeking of booze.'

Martha flushed and looked down at her shoes.

'Look,' said Sophie, 'that's what she used to do. She couldn't lie. Even though she did all the time.'

Martha said, 'Sorry.'

Outside in the car park, grateful for fresh air, Charlie said, 'I don't understand. Why did your husband take Evie? Why didn't he just get in touch and ask to see her?'

'It's probably a power thing. He wants to show me he can hurt me. Or maybe he thinks I won't let him see Evie because he ran away.'

'So we're going to that shop?'

'Yes. It's all I've got. I need to find my daughter.' Her face crumpled, eyes glazed. Tears soon. 'I have to do something. I can't go home and just sit and wait.' She punched him with the side of her fist. 'You don't understand. I *have* to find Evie.'

Charlie rubbed his shoulder. 'Don't attack me. I haven't done anything. I've been punched enough today.'

'I feel like punching someone. And you're the only one here. I'm furious and worried sick and I want my little girl.'

He put his arm round her and said, 'I know. I know.' And thought, oh God. All this caring. All this love. It could stop you thinking straight.

24

You Were Wonderful

The shop was shut. Charlie and Martha sat in the car staring at its peeling purple paint and the arrangement of LPs, packets of joss sticks and T-shirts in the window.

'Looks interesting,' said Charlie.

Seedy, Martha thought.

'Is it the sort of place Jamie would hang out?'

'I don't know. I didn't know him. I was just married to him. I don't know what we were thinking. We were young and started to live a cliché. Like he'd go out to work and come home to slippers warmed by the fire and a plate of stew. Only he hated wearing slippers and I couldn't cook stew. We didn't discuss any of it.'

'Don't you think it's time to call the police?'

'I may not really have known Jamie. But I know this much, he won't harm Evie. Getting the police involved would make things worse. I'm sure he really wants to get to know his daughter. Hurting me is a bonus.'

The street was quiet, almost empty. A few cars and buses trundled past. The air smelled of early evening in the city – petrol, dust and the heavy tempting aroma of Italian food from the restaurant nearby. It was a time Charlie liked, when day was done and night hadn't arrived. It was a time when, in younger days, he'd be slipping into a clean shirt, slapping on some aftershave anticipating the evening ahead. There would be beer. There would be music, dancing and a woman, perhaps, if he was lucky. Luck didn't often smile on him, though.

He thought the thing to do now was eat. He liked eating and was of the opinion that food helped with most ailments and problems. He and Martha should have a meal. They could work through a plan and come back in the morning when the shop would be open. This was logical. But he could tell Martha was in no mood for logic. She needed to act.

'There might be someone in there,' she said. 'In the back counting the day's takings or whatever.'

She got out of the car and ran across the road. He watched as she rattled the door, knocked, thumped it with the side of her fist and, finally, crouching, shouted through the letterbox. She turned and shrugged to him, 'Nobody in.' He thought she'd come back to the car. But no, she pointed to the door next to the shop that led to the flat above. 'I'll try in here.'

Before he could say anything she disappeared inside. He got out of the car and leaned against it waiting for her to reappear. He breathed the evening air and remembered times when he'd gone out reeking of Old Spice hoping to find someone special and never did. He went to pubs and dancehalls with the men who worked at the same building site as he did. They were dandies. Dudes, he would call them now. After a couple of hours drinking they'd roll into the Palais to survey the talent and continue drinking. They'd stand at the edge of the dance floor eyeing the girls, nudging one another, making critical comments, 'What d'you think of that?' or 'It's got a good arse.'

What were they thinking? What a way to describe women. Had they been scared of them? Or did they have to assert their superiority by calling them it and that? He wondered what Martha would have said back then if she'd overheard. Quite a lot, he imagined.

Martha emerged from the doorway. 'I knocked. I shouted through the letterbox but nobody's answering.'

'Let's go home,' he shouted.

But Martha wasn't done yet. 'Trying the pub.' Pointing to the bar a couple of doors up from the shop.

He leaned on the car and returned to his reverie. There had been one bloke, Frankie, who'd had a way with women. He knew how to look at them – a lingering appreciative twinkling gaze. He'd been the king of chatting up. 'I work on a building site. The money's great. One day I'm gonna have my own business and I'll make a million and buy you a car.'

Girls had giggled. Surely they hadn't believed him? Christ, they'd only just met. How could they think he'd buy them a car? But Frankie never left the dancehall alone. He'd flag down a cab and disappear into the night with this week's pick-up and always looked smug on Monday mornings. Charlie always walked home alone. He wondered if Frankie of the dapper suits and shiny shoes ever did make a million and buy a girl a car. Probably not.

He stared across at Martha going into the pub. Came to his senses and shouted, 'No. Don't go in there.' She didn't hear.

He started to run across the road but had to stop as a bus and two taxis rattled past. By the time he got into the pub Martha was holding court. A space had cleared round her, mostly so drinkers could stand back and get a good look at her.

Charlie surveyed the faces. Expressions were mostly surprise. But there was some puzzlement, amusement and a little anger. Drinkers in here didn't like distractions or interruptions. There was alcohol to consume, badinage to indulge in and fellow consumers to size up.

'Jamie Walters,' Martha shouted. 'Is Jamie Walters here?'

There were mumblings and a babble of voices as people looked round to see if this Jamie Walters fellow would come forward. He didn't.

'Does anybody know Jamie Walters?' Martha sounded desperate. 'I need to find him. He's stolen my daughter.' She turned to Charlie. Her fists were clenched. 'Please,' she shouted.

Martha didn't notice the faces looking at her. There were men in business suits and shy men looking away from her, shrinking back not wanting to be noticed. There was a couple of bikers leaning back on the bar smirking slightly. All the while Martha stood, red of face, teary-eyed, shouting, 'Jamie Walters. Jamie Walters.'

Later, and for the rest of his life, Charlie thought this was the moment he truly fell in love with Martha. She was vulnerable and so very fierce. She was that young girl at the bus stop again. The kid in blue jeans clutching an old guitar, glaring at the world, daring anyone to disapprove, that had so intrigued him years ago. But what he was seeing now was love. He hadn't realised love could take you by storm, whoosh through you, make you weak at the back of the knees and doubt your ability to breathe. Love was chaos.

It occurred to him that his mother hadn't done this for him. Stepped up and yelled to get him back, ready to wrestle the world to keep him safe. Now he knew he wanted what he was seeing. That passion, that fierceness, that love.

Martha turned to him. She was crying. Her voice was reduced to a rasping croak from the strain of shouting. 'Somebody here must know Jamie.' He could see her panic. She was frantic. Nobody was answering her. They just stared.

He went to her, put his arm round her. Felt her lean into him. That's right, he thought, lean; you need to lean right now. He saw the barman move to the other side of the counter. He knew the sign. They were about to be asked to leave. They were bothering the customers. People in here didn't want to be bothered. Many didn't want to be noticed. They liked to slip in and work at being inconspicuous.

'Time to go home,' Charlie said and led Martha to the door. Outside, evening was slipping into night. Streetlights flickering on and people moving towards the restaurants across the road. Martha turned on him. 'You should've let me be.'

'I don't think so. It's not the sort of pub a woman goes into. It's more of a man's place.'

'Someone in there might know Jamie. He goes into men's pubs.'

'Not that one.'

'Why not?'

'Men go there to meet men. You won't find any women in there.'

'I saw two women sitting near the bar.'

Charlie sighed, 'They weren't women.'

Martha was silent for a long, long minute and finally said, 'Oh, you might have said.'

'You were in there before I could stop you.' He took her arm and led her to the car.

'So it's unlikely Jamie would drink in that pub.'

'Yes. Mostly the men in there go because it's safe. Not that they wouldn't care about you looking for your daughter. They just wouldn't want to get involved.'

'I've made a fool of myself.'

'You were wonderful.'

25

Stay With Me

Something inside of him had shifted. He wanted to protect her, keep her safe, make her happy. He wanted to come to her smiling and carrying her lost child. He wanted her to see him punch Jamie on the jaw. He wanted to be her hero. 'Let's go home.'

'I don't want to go home. Evie's not there.'

'What do you want to do?'

'Find Evie.'

'How are you going to do that? Knock on every door in the city?'

She sat clutching the steering wheel in the perfect ten-to-two position, head up. 'If that's what it takes.'

'Home,' he said. 'A bath, food and bed. You'll feel better in the morning.'

'I'm not moving. I'm staying here to see if someone comes to that flat above the shop.'

They sat. Charlie worried they'd be here all night. It would be uncomfortable and cold. He thought of his bed. His favourite place, if he was honest. Sleeping was his second-favourite thing to do after eating. His heart sank at the prospect of missing out on both.

Martha stared across at the flat above the shop, shoulders tense, white-knuckling the steering wheel, willing a light to go on. Nothing happened. After twenty minutes she sighed, switched on the engine and admitted they might as well go home. 'I'll be back tomorrow at dawn.'

She put her foot down and hurtled along London Road. Charlie gripped his seat. 'I think you're going too fast.'

'Evie might be at the house. Jamie might have brought her back. She could be sitting on the doorstep waiting for me.'

But she wasn't. Martha walked to the front door, stuck her key in the lock while Charlie hung back by the gate. 'I'll be getting home, then.'

'Don't go. Don't leave me. I can't be alone in the house. I'll just walk from room to room thinking about Evie. She might be terrified.'

'Would Jamie scare her?'

'Probably not.'

'You'll have told her about him. So he's not a complete stranger.'

'Yes.'

'He'll be talking to her. And he'll be getting her stories about her life. That's what will be happening.'

He followed her in through the door, up the stairs into the kitchen and stood looking slightly vacant as she put on the kettle. He didn't know what to do. He didn't want a cup of tea. He wanted food. 'I think you should eat something.'

'I don't feel like eating. I'm not hungry.'

'You'll feel better.'

'I don't want to feel better.'

'Have a bath. It'll help you to relax.'

'I don't want to relax. I'm on duty waiting for Evie to come home. I need to be ready for whatever happens. I won't relax. I refuse to relax.' She stood rigid, determined not to relax. There were tears in her eyes.

Charlie didn't know what to do. He considered himself one of life's onlookers. He frowned. This was a moment to be masterful. Only he didn't know how. He was standing with his helpless hands dangling by his sides and his mouth slightly open. He thought he must look like a scolded schoolboy.

The kettle boiled. Martha didn't notice and stood staring at him, fighting tears as clouds of steam billowed behind her. For a second or two Charlie was mesmerised before coming to his senses and moving round her to switch off the kettle. He took her by the shoulders and guided her to a chair and sat her down. She didn't object. Encouraged by this, he made a pot of tea and poured her a cup.

After that he raked in the fridge, took out eggs and cheese. He'd make an omelette. Quick, easy and nutritious, that would do the trick.

She looked uninterested as he set the table. Then, seemingly without taking in what was being put in front of her, vacantly surveyed the omelette before taking up her fork and starting to eat. He slid a second omelette from the pan onto a plate and took a place opposite her at the table. He vigorously sliced bread and heaped some sliced tomatoes onto both plates. This was better, food. After eating they could consider the Evie problem sensibly.

Martha stopped her fork on its journey from her plate to her mouth. 'You're kind.'

'You think?'

'You have leftover people staying in your house. Brenda was there when I went to get your car keys.'

'She is convinced she's doing me a favour by staying with me. She says I sleep better knowing she's safe. But I can't complain, she has more than doubled the value of my house and she cooks a mean curry. What more could you ask of a tenant?'

'You're kind,' said Martha a second time.

He made a harrumphing sound. He gathered the plates, took them to the sink and told her he'd wash up before going home.

'Don't go. I don't want to be alone. I'll start to think and my imagination will take over.'

'An on and off switch for the brain would be good.'

'Right now I'd like one of those. I could go dull and stare ahead with nothing on my mind.'

'Of course,' said Charlie, 'if you switched off your brain, you wouldn't be thinking and so wouldn't know to switch it on again. You'd just sort of sleep all the time.'

'Sounds good to me. Talking of sleep, I think I'll try and get some. We've got an early start tomorrow.'

'We?'

'You started the we thing. I want you to come along. I need you to come along.'

'OK.'

Charlie wondered if she wanted him to stay all night. In that case, where was he to sleep? He briefly fantasised about sharing her bed – the warmth of it, the feel of her skin, the softness of her breathing.

She rose from the table and left the room. Charlie took up a dishtowel and dried a plate. The problem with falling for somebody was doing something about it. You had to let the loved one know and risk pain and rejection.

Martha appeared in the kitchen doorway carrying a bundle of bedding. 'I hope you don't mind the sofa.'

He said he didn't. He carefully folded and hung up the dishtowel and followed Martha to the living room. He watched as she made up the sofa, smoothing the sheets, tucking in the blankets.

'This is good of you. I need someone here. If anything happens, it'll be good to have backup.' She sat on the made-up sofa. 'Do you suppose Evie's all right?'

'Yes. She's with her dad.'

'How do you know he'll be OK with her?'

'You chose him. You married him. I'm thinking he'll be OK. He wasn't violent, was he?'

'No. He was quiet.'

'There you go,' said Charlie. 'Evie will be fine.' He hoped this was true.

'She hasn't got a toothbrush. She needs to clean her teeth.'

'She'll be fine.'

'She has a bath every night before bed.'

'It won't hurt to miss it just once.'

'She doesn't like tomatoes.'

'So, she won't eat them. Tomatoes aren't ever the meal, only a bit of the meal.'

'I suppose.' She got up. Nodded, reassuring herself on the matter of her daughter and tomatoes. 'Thank you.'

'For what?'

'Staying with me. Comforting me.' She leaned over, kissed his cheek and bade him goodnight.

Alone, Charlie tested the sofa. It seemed large enough and soft enough for a reasonable night's sleep. He went into the hall, found the bathroom. He peed, washed his face and rubbed some toothpaste onto his teeth with his finger. Back in the living room he took off his clothes, folded them and laid them on an armchair before, still in his underpants, he slipped under the covers on the sofa. He sighed, stared up at the ceiling. He touched his cheek. He could still feel the kiss. He wished he'd kissed her back instead of standing stock still and looking sheepish. Damn. He doubted he'd sleep tonight.

It was a surprise, then, when he woke from a deep sleep at four in the morning. He'd been disturbed by something moving nearby. Martha was sitting at the end of the sofa staring at him. She was wearing a pair of men's striped pyjamas and thick green woolly socks and had her legs curled under her. 'Sorry. Did I wake you?'

'Yes,' he said. 'Has something happened?'

'No. I was watching you sleep. You're very good at it. You looked peaceful.'

'Thank you,' he said. Was that a compliment? Being told you were a good sleeper? Rather than, say, a good footballer, athlete or, something he would have liked, a good lover. That would be excellent.

'I've been thinking about your being abducted when you were little. I didn't take it in earlier. I was crazed with worry about Evie. What was it like?'

'I don't know. I was a baby. I didn't find out about it for over twenty years.'

'Didn't your mother look for you? Wasn't she frantic?'

'No. I think it suited her fine.'

'Didn't she love you?'

'In her way, perhaps. I think not, though. She was very young when she had me. I got the impression she thought it for the best. I only spoke to her once, on the phone. I never met her.'

Martha pulled back the bedclothes at the opposite end of the sofa. She shoved Charlie's feet aside and climbed in. 'Can't sleep,' she said, 'too worried about Evie. Tell me your story.'

26

Hating the Pink

He was Norman McKenzie. He'd found himself. The solution had sneaked into his brain when he wasn't using it for anything much. He was sure this was how it worked. Solutions to problems crept in when you weren't using it. He'd been in his new house, lying on a mattress on the floor, looking through the grubby window at a scrap of blue sky, wondering what life would have been like if he'd been born in New Orleans when it came to him.

'Mairi,' he said, 'Ella told me my mother was Mairi.'

There couldn't have been many women with that name giving birth in Glasgow on that day. It was a clue. Something to hang on to. Something that might lead to finding a family.

The next day he went back to Register House to check and there she was. Mairi McKenzie who'd given birth to Norman. Father unknown. But there was an address in Glasgow's Byres Road. He made a note of it and went home to lie on his mattress once more and think about this. Being Norman and not Charlie was hard to take. It was as if he was a whole different person. He'd grown up being someone he wasn't meant to be.

Norman would be practical. He would have fixed the creaking floorboards and anxiety-inducing plumbing in the house. It was likely that he would have worked hard at school and would now be a doctor or lawyer. Charlie was a dreamer. He was prone to melancholy. Life with its wonky floorboards, worrying plumbing and any other disturbing thing was to be fretted over briefly before being cast aside to deal with later. He decided he was a lot better at being Charlie than he was at being Norman. In fact, Norman rather scared him. He didn't think he was up to being Norman.

The emotional turmoil laid Charlie low. It was three weeks before he finally went to Glasgow to investigate his past. He had to know his history.

Byres Road was busy. A street of small shops, cafés and tenements. But it was moving with the times. It was getting arty. There was a lot of corduroy around. Charlie liked it. He found the building, went inside and breathed deeply. It smelled of disinfectant with an undertow of lentil soup. It unnerved him. His stomach was already in a turmoil of nervous apprehension.

He climbed to the top floor examining the nameplates on all the doors on the way up. There wasn't a McKenzie. On his way back down he met a woman coming up. He asked if she knew of anybody called McKenzie living here. She shook her head, told him she didn't think so but he should ask at the Thompsons on the ground floor. They had lived in the building for ever.

Mrs Thompson answered the door. There was a lot of her. She filled the doorway and considered him with mild interest. He smiled a nervous smile and told her he was Charlie. 'Charlie Parker,' he said. He hadn't wanted to mention his real name so picked one close to it and beloved. 'I'm looking for my aunt.'

Mrs Thompson raised her eyebrows.

'Yes,' said Charlie. 'Mairi McKenzie. I think she lived here some time ago.'

Mrs Thompson continued to look mildly interested.

'My mother is ill. She wanted to get in touch with her sister, Mairi.'

Mrs Thompson nodded and invited him in. She led him down a short hall into a small cluttered living room. 'This is Mr Parker,' she said to a small man seated on a large maroon chair. 'He's asking about Mairi McKenzie.'

Mr Thomson said, 'Well, that's going back a year or two.' He looked at his wife and added, 'Mairi. God, she was a beauty.'

Walking into the room was like walking into a wall of heat. It was airless in here. Mr Thompson gestured to the sofa and told Charlie to sit down. He lowered himself onto the seat and looked round. There was so much stuff in here there was hardly any room for people. There was a large collection of teapots displayed in the cabinet by the door, a writing bureau was wedged behind the sofa, a long coffee table was placed in front of it, and a small fire glowed in the grate. Mr Thompson had one foot placed on a stool by his chair. He looked to Charlie to be steeling himself for a long chat. Mrs Thompson leaned forward and said, 'Cup of tea.' Plainly this wasn't the offer of a refreshment but an announcement of what was about to happen next. She disappeared into the kitchen, keeping the door open so she could hear the conversation.

'She was a looker, your aunt,' said Mr Thompson. 'Never saw a woman as beautiful as she was. Film-star looks. If she stood in front of you, you couldn't believe what you were seeing. You couldn't believe that a creature like that was out and about walking down the street like an ordinary person.'

Charlie smiled. 'Beauty takes you like that.'

Mr Thompson agreed. 'And she was young. Eighteen. Nineteen. And expecting.'

'Four months gone,' Mrs Thomson shouted from the kitchen.

'Her man came three times a week. Mondays, Wednesdays and Fridays. He paid her rent. Never took her nowhere. He couldn't. Too well known about town to be seen with his bit on the side. Someone would have told his wife.'

Mrs Thompson bustled into the room carrying a large tray. 'Arrived at seven, went away half past ten. Never varied.' She put the tray on the coffee table. Set out three cups and saucers and poured tea from a huge brown teapot.

'Do you know the man's name?' asked Charlie.

'Ian Bain,' said Mrs Thompson, handing him a cup. 'Mr Three-Times-a-Week. Him and his hat.'

'He wore a hat?' said Charlie.

'One of them gangster ones you see in the films. He fancied himself.'

'He stopped coming just before the baby was born.'

'How do you know this?' asked Charlie.

'Steps outside,' said Mr Thompson. 'We hear it all. We know who's coming and going. We get to know the sound of feet.'

'He left Mairi to fend for herself. Put ten pounds in an envelope that he left on the table and walked away from her. Said he had a wife and two young daughters to care for. He didn't want to hurt them,' said Mrs Thompson. 'Ella told us that.'

'Ella?' said Charlie, though he knew who Ella was.

'Lived across the landing,' Mr Thompson said. 'It was the baby interested her. She always wanted one of her own but that wasn't going to happen. Her young man was killed in the war. The first war. Charlie Gavin he was. She never got over him.'

Charlie looked at his feet, said, 'Ah,' and prayed he wasn't turning red.

Mrs Thompson took over the story. 'She'd drop by for a cup of tea now and then. She'd had a hard life. Brought up in an orphanage. Half starved. She remembered being beaten for wetting the bed. Had to wash the sheets at three in the morning in cold water. She grew up afraid to fall asleep.'

'Afraid of everything,' said Mr Thompson. 'She was a wall walker.'

Charlie said, 'Huh?'

'She didn't like being outside on her own. She was scared of doing something wrong. She walked close to walls so as nobody would notice her. She wore grey clothes.'

Charlie knew this to be true.

'Soon as that baby was born Ella took to him. She prepared his bottles, changed his nappies, took him out in his pram. Mairi took a job at the grocer's across the way. Ella doted on the boy. She took in sewing, didn't go out to work. She worked when the baby slept. Mairi was too beautiful to work in a grocer's.'

Mr Thompson took over once more. 'Men stared at her. It just didn't seem right buying cheese or potatoes from someone who looked like that. Women didn't like her. She never took to being a mother. She started being young again. Out at nights dancing and going to see films. It worried Ella. She thought Mairi would meet somebody to marry and move away with the baby.'

Mrs Thompson handed Charlie a slice of fruitcake on a small plate. It was stale but he didn't mind. It was more than warm here. There was an aroma of soup cooking and the tea was good. The story was thrilling.

'It had to happen,' said Mrs Thompson. 'Mairi got home later and later till one night she didn't come back at all. What a night that was. Ella in a state going up and down the stairs, up and down every ten fifteen minutes looking out for her. Then later on it was leaning out the window staring down the road. But Mairi didn't come.'

Mr Thompson took over. 'Ella was out of her mind with worry. She came to our door and asked if we'd seen Mairi. She said if Mairi didn't come back the police would take the baby away. I think she'd decided then she'd take the boy. Save him from the children's home. And that's what she did. Took the boy and disappeared. Of course Mairi came home. Stayed for a couple of days then went off.'

Charlie said, 'That's quite a story.'

'Oh yes,' said Mrs Thompson. 'Ella abducted the baby and Mairi said nothing about it. Wasn't in the papers. No police came to enquire. Nothing.'

Charlie asked if she knew what happened to Mairi. Mr Thompson shook his head. 'There was gossip. Of course there was gossip. She took up with her man again. Didn't marry him. His wife wouldn't give him a divorce. Mairi and her man formed a company Bain and McKenzie. They did loans. Never heard anything about Ella.'

'I saw her go,' said Mrs Thomson. 'I'd been to the butcher's to get a pie. So it was a Friday when she took the little one. Butcher did good pies on a Friday. I was just down the street and there was Ella ahead of me striding out. She had the babe in one arm and was carrying a big suitcase. There she went. Walking down the middle of the pavement and not up by the wall. Big steps. She did a brave thing.'

Two years later, Charlie had set up his missing persons bureau and was happily going to his small office every morning, playing records and eating bacon rolls. He hadn't many clients and didn't mind at all. He felt he had a purpose in life that suited him as it took very little effort.

He read newspapers and magazines. He strolled the length of the prom. He went to the pub. He congratulated himself on being a businessman and sighed with pleasure that he didn't do much actual business. He was free to daydream.

Sitting at his desk he read the local paper from cover to cover. He loved the small ads. Among the adverts for laxatives, extra large shirts, second-hand ice skates and kittens free to a good home was one for Bain & McKenzie Loans – no amount too small. No questions asked.

Charlie knew who this was and for months did nothing. He finally phoned on a Monday morning, knowing this to be a mistake. He didn't trust Mondays. A woman answered, 'Yes?'

'Is that Mairi McKenzie?' said Charlie.

'Yes. Who is this?'

'Norman.'

There was a long silence. Then Mairi said, 'I wondered when you'd get in touch.'

Charlie said, 'I'd like to meet.'

'I suppose you would.'

'Was Ian Bain my father?'

'Yes. He died three years ago. Heart attack. I'm on my own now. I could fit you in today. Here at my office. Two o'clock.'

Charlie wasn't happy. 'That's a bit soon. What about tomorrow? I'd prefer that.'

'Today. Two o'clock,' said Mairi. She rang off.

He took the eleven o'clock train to Glasgow. A taxi to the office cost him five pounds though the journey was only two or three streets. His feeling of foreboding heightened. He knew doing things right away was wrong. A person needed to procrastinate, to think, mull the situation over and prepare for the worst. The office was in a faceless building in a street of faceless buildings. The main door was locked. Charlie had over an hour to wait.

He found a small café, ordered coffee and sat watching the world go by. He saw women pushing babies in prams, men in cheap, slightly shiny business suits, school girls giggling past the window, arms linked with pals, and a long pink limousine slipped along the road. Charlie thought it odd. A slick and garish thing in a grey landscape.

At ten to two he paid for his coffee and headed for Mairi's office. The main door was open and a hand-written cardboard sign pinned to the wall told him that Bain & McKenzie Loans was on the first floor. The stairs were covered in grubby red linoleum. Here and there well-trodden holes showed the planking beneath. There was a strong scent of floral perfume. Charlie's stomach flared nerves.

The office door was open. Charlie stepped into a pink room. Pink walls, pink floor, pink coat hooks on the wall. The floral perfume was overwhelming now. There was nobody here. He called out, 'Hello. Miss McKenzie. Mairi. Hello.' Nothing happened.

Bare wires hung from the wall where lights had been yanked away. A telephone line had been snipped and the phone removed. Outside, traffic swished past. But the silence in this place was frightening. Charlie turned to run and spotted a slip of pink paper on the pink windowsill. He picked it up.

Dear Norman,
Couldn't do it. Couldn't meet you. I'm not much of a mother, I'm afraid. Never was. All the feeding, nappy changing, responsibility and downright guilt of motherhood just wasn't for me. You should forget about me. Sorry.
I'll tell you this though. Ella loved you. Right from the first time she saw you she was smitten. She couldn't keep her eyes off you. She'd just sit, hands clasped in her lap looking at you and sighing. She thought you were gorgeous. Such love. You were a lucky boy.
Mairi

Charlie dropped the note and ran from the room. He had to get away. He had to breathe fresh air. He clattered down the stairs, threw open the main door and barged into daylight. As he stood on the pavement wondering which way to go the pink limousine slid past him. He caught a glimpse of a woman in the back seat. Her blonde hair tumbled over her face so he couldn't really see her. It was his mother. He absolutely knew it. She'd waited to watch him go into the building and in time come out again. She'd wanted to have a look at him, to judge him, and she'd decided against stopping to speak. She'd rejected him once more.

Charlie ran. He threw himself down this faceless street and into the busy traffic-filled, crowded places beyond. He ran till his sides ached and his breath hurt his throat. He ran till he thought he would throw up. Trembling, he leaned on a wall and wept. When he saw the train station he stopped. Time to get on a train and go home.

27

A Mother on the Rampage

The room was morning-grey, gloomy. Charlie had a fleeting moment of being disorientated. He slowly remembered the night before. Martha had come to him and, unable to sleep, had asked about his life. She'd slipped under the duvet at the opposite end of the sofa to keep warm. He'd moved his feet to accommodate her. Not wanting to disturb her, he'd slept sitting up, propped against a cushion with his feet hanging over the edge of the sofa. When his tale was done, she'd opened one sleepy eye and said, 'Oh my, you poor boy.'

He could hear her moving about the flat. Dressing, he thought. Then she walked down the hall to the kitchen and he heard the rush of water filling the kettle, cups clattering. He slid deeper under the duvet, warmth and comfort. He indulged in the small delight of listening to someone preparing coffee while he lay sweetly still and removed from the world. Martha ruined the moment. She came into the room, loomed over him and told him it was time to get up. 'We've got to get going soon.'

He gazed at her mournfully. 'It's only just after six. The shop won't be open for hours.'

'You don't know that. These hippy music-types live by their own hours. Nine to five doesn't occur to them.'

'Still, I don't think they'll be open at this time in the morning.'

'Doesn't matter. I want to be there when they open up so I can go in and take them by surprise. They won't have time to think up some story about where Jamie is. They'll be so off guard they'll just tell me. So get up.' She stood back, folded her arms and glared at him. 'I'm not leaving till I see you out of bed and standing up.'

He shoved back the duvet and slowly, stiffly, got to his feet. The room was cold. He shivered. He was wearing only his underpants. He cupped his hands over his private parts and said, 'Underpants.'

'So I see,' said Martha. 'Very natty.'

And so they were – neatly fitting, dark red with tiny black polka dots. Not his usual choice of undergarment, but a present from Brenda last Christmas that he had added to his underpants routine because he rather liked them. They made him feel a little bolder and more outré than he actually was. Now Martha had seen them and heard his story, she had too much information. She knew his life, his rejection and his underwear.

In the kitchen he asked if he had time to nip home and change into fresh clothes. 'And a cup of decent coffee wouldn't go amiss. This is instant.'

'Get over it. It's coffee.'

He took a sip. Made a face. 'This isn't right. A day needs to start with proper coffee. It's disturbing if it doesn't. Things can go wrong.'

Martha left the room, returned with her coat. 'What can go wrong?'

'Anything. Everything. Your average day needs a rhythm to it. A pattern to hang the hours round – up at quarter past seven, shower, shave, dress in the correct shirt, underpants, trousers and socks for the day. Then coffee carefully brewed at the right temperature, feed the dog while listening to the news, breakfast – toast and boiled egg. Bacon roll at bacon roll time and so on.'

Martha said, 'You'll be fine. To hell with your routine. My child is missing. C'mon, we have to go.'

They parked outside the shop and settled down to wait till it opened. Martha stared at the dusty doorway, the peeling paint and the darkened windows, willing lights to come on. Charlie slid down in his seat preparing for a long wait. He had passers-by to look at and speculate about and Martha was by his side. If he wasn't dreading what might happen when somebody turned up to start the day's business, this might almost be pleasant.

But it wasn't. Martha fidgeted, slapped the steering wheel, ran her fingers through her hair, cursed and sighed. She regularly saw movements inside the shop and she thumped his arm. 'There's someone in there. I saw them.'

'No, you didn't. You're imagining it.'

'I'm not. They'll be using the back door. They'll hang about smoking pot and discussing the prospect of nuclear meltdown. That's what these people do.'

'There's nobody there.'

'There is. You just don't see anything you don't want to see. It's all right for you. The person you love most in the world hasn't been abducted. You haven't worried and fretted all night. Evie's a child. She won't know what's happening. I have to get her back.' She thumped him again and then reached out, stroked the abused arm. 'Sorry.'

He told her that when he was a kid he punched people as a sign of affection. 'Didn't know any other way. Cuddling was cissy. I punched Sally Turner on the shoulder several times a day. God, she hated me. I had a crush on her. First one of my life and I didn't know to be kind or gentle or even buy her a Mars bar. I just punched her shoulder in a matey, blokey way. I was twelve.'

'When I was twelve I was desperately in love with Eric Watts. I let him know by totally ignoring him.'

'So neither of us quite had the hang of love, then.'

'Looks like it. I'm a failure at romantic love. Motherly love, though, that's different. When Evie was born I was swamped by it. Took me by storm. I'd never known such love. It was bigger than me. I loved holding that girl, her little body. Her determined breathing. And the smell of her. Oh God, the utterly perfect smell of babies. Don't you love the smell of babies?'

'I don't recall ever smelling one. I haven't had a lot to do with babies. I thought they'd reek of vomit and foul nappies. It has never occurred to me to seek a baby out, lift it up and smell it.'

'You're heartless. Babies smell of milk and vanilla and innocence.'

'Ah, I'll grab the next one I see and have a good sniff.'

Martha ignored this. 'I used to think the love would fade or I'd get used to it. But it hasn't. I want to know where she is all the time. I need her to be safe. I'd murder anyone who harmed her.' She shifted in her seat, put her head against the side window and peered ahead. 'There is someone in there. A man moving about.'

She swung open the car door, jumped out, ran to the shop and battered the door with clenched fists. 'Open up. Open up.'

Charlie watched. Should have discussed a plan, he thought.

The shopkeeper appeared at the other side of the door and waved Martha away, flapping his hand. 'We're closed.'

Martha carried on battering the door. 'Open up or I'll call the police.'

Charlie thought it should be the bloke who called the police. Martha was causing disruption and the door didn't look up to the abuse she was giving it. But the man slid back a couple of bolts and inched the door open a crack. It was enough. Martha hurled herself into the shop, got hold of the man and shoved and manhandled him to the counter at the back.

Mesmerised, Charlie watched. Goodness, she was fierce. From where he sat in the car, the two wrestling in the darkened shop looked as if they could have been embroiled in passion rather than fighting. He was flailing, arms waving. She was leaning over him, gripping the collar of his shirt and shaking him. Charlie couldn't hear what was being said. Shouted, more like. He slowly realised that he better get in there and put a stop to things before the woman he was beginning to love was arrested and charged with assault.

By the time he reached her, Martha had her victim bent backwards over the counter and was threatening him with a pen. 'If you don't tell me where Jamie Walters is, I'll poke your eye out with this biro.'

She was red with fury, shaking, and, it seemed to Charlie, had completely lost her senses. The man she was attacking with a yellow biro was about twenty, absurdly thin, long-haired and dressed in faded jeans and a green and yellow floral shirt. He was shouting at Martha to get off him. The poor boy had probably been in the back of the shop, relaxing, welcoming the day with a joint, and then been cruelly jolted from his mellow moment by this onslaught.

'Gayfield Square. He lives in Gayfield Square.'

Martha released her grip, stood back and exhaled. 'Gayfield Square, just across the road.' Her brow was sweat-beaded. There were tears in her eyes. 'I'm going to get Evie.'

Charlie took the defeated young man by the elbow. 'You all right?'

'Yeah. I'm a bit . . . you know . . . shaken up. Didn't expect that. Wow.' Gripping the counter, he made his way to a seat. 'I mean, wow. Christ. You her old man?'

'No. Jamie Walters is. He took their daughter without asking. You don't want to do that to Martha.'

'No. You have to watch out for mothers, I'm thinking.'

'Well, mothers on the rampage, anyway. They could take over the world.'

'Yeah.' He reached over and took the small remains of a joint from an ashtray. 'My body's OK. Just my mind's a little knocked about.' He lit up, inhaled and offered Charlie a puff.

'Nah, thanks. I better catch up with the crazed mother.' He turned to go. Turned back. 'Where in Gayfield Square?'

He met Martha at the corner of the square. She was weeping.

'I'll have to go back and ask that bloke the number. I don't know which house. And I can't face him. I was awful.'

'He's fine. A little shocked but he's taking something for it.' He led her along the street, a terraced row. 'Here we are. I remembered to ask.'

The main door was open. They climbed to the first floor and knew they'd arrived. The smell, a thick, herby, pungent mix of pot and patchouli joss sticks, hit them when they were halfway up the stairs. When they reached the landing, the door in front of them was alive with colour – psychedelic whorls of purple, green, turquoise, yellow and red so vibrant, so loud, that, looking at them, Charlie and Martha could almost feel their pupils dilate.

'This is it. Has to be,' said Martha. 'This is where my husband who used to be boring is finding his youth.' She took a deep breath. 'Keep calm,' she told herself, 'don't shout. Don't beat anybody up. Just find Evie and take her home.' She knocked. Waited. Knocked again. Jamie opened the door.

He stood staring at Martha. 'Hi.' He spoke quietly, not at all surprised to see her. He was barefoot, in jeans and a white T-shirt. 'You've come for Evie.'

'I have.' Martha stepped past him and disappeared down the hall, which was lined either side, floor to ceiling, with framed prints. The scent of patchouli was stronger now the door was open. Music was playing, jazz; Miles Davis, Charlie thought.

Minutes passed, Jamie didn't move. He looked at Charlie. Nodded, but said nothing. Martha came back up the hall, leading Evie by the hand and carrying her school bag.

'I was just going to take her to school,' said Jamie.

'I'll do that,' Martha told him.

Evie stopped beside Jamie. 'Bye, then. Thank you for having me. I had a nice time.' She didn't sound convincing.

'You're very welcome,' Jamie smiled. 'Come back and see us.'

'She won't be doing that,' said Martha.

Jamie stuck his hands in his pockets, looked assured. 'She's my daughter. If I want to see her, I will.'

Martha led Evie to the top of the stairs. She signalled Charlie to take the child out of the building and returned to Jamie. 'Don't you dare do that again. Don't you dare take my girl without telling me.'

'She's my girl, too.'

Charlie took Evie outside. But he hung back listening to what was being said one floor up.

Martha hissed, 'She's not yours.'

Down the stairs she thundered. Hands still plunged in his pockets, Jamie watched. Then he ran, tumbled after Martha, leaned over the banister and yelled, 'I always suspected that, you bitch.'

In the street, morning bustle starting, Evie trotted by Martha's side and said, 'That was my daddy. I remember him. There's a picture of him in the book at the bottom of your wardrobe.'

'You shouldn't go poking in other people's things.'

'But he's my daddy. What do you mean, I'm not his?'

Martha stopped, sighed, thought. 'I mean you're mine. You've always been mine. You always will be. No matter where you are or what you do, you'll be mine. And you shouldn't listen to other people's conversations.'

Evie said, 'I wasn't listening. I heard. You were sort of shouting. Like whispering but loudly.'

Martha caught Charlie's eye, offered a silent plea. Don't say anything, not right now.

Remembering his own mother telling him to forget about her, Charlie thought, mothers on the rampage – they could make you cry.

28

Catastrophe

'What did you have to eat?' Martha asked.

'Rice with bits in,' said Evie.

Martha said, 'What sort of bits?'

'Green bits and beany-looking things and tomatoes.'

'Was it tasty?'

'It looked yucky. But it tasted OK. I didn't eat all of it. The little boy didn't eat any of it.'

Martha said, 'Ah.' She changed gear. Tried to sound relaxed. 'What little boy?'

'The lady's little boy. Jason.'

Martha said, 'Ah,' again. She bit her lip.

Charlie put a comforting hand on her knee. A few minutes ago, after they'd put Evie in the back of the car, he'd held Martha by the shoulders. 'Calm. Don't sound upset. Don't quiz Evie. Let it all come out at her pace. Don't let her think she's done anything wrong.'

Martha agreed. 'Calm.'

But she wasn't calm. 'Lady, what lady? What was the lady called?'

'Dunno,' said Evie. 'She was Jason's mum. She wore a floaty dress thing and no shoes and beads and when I asked for a chocolate biscuit she said she didn't keep poison in the house.'

'Well, you can have a chocolate biscuit when we get home.'

'They didn't have a television either. When I said it was time for my programmes the lady said I'd have to miss them.

She wouldn't have a set because the stuff they put on corrupts people.'

'And what did you say to that?'

'I asked what corrupts meant.'

Martha said, 'Ah.' Again.

'Am I not going to school, then?' Evie noticed they'd driven past the road and were heading home.

'No. Not today, sweetie. I thought we'd have time together. Did you have breakfast?'

'Yes. It was chewy stuff like uncooked porridge with bits in. They eat a lot of things with bits in.'

'Ah,' said Martha. Trying to sound relaxed, casual. 'You know you shouldn't go off with strangers.'

'But he wasn't a stranger. He's my dad and I didn't go off with him. You phoned the school and said he was coming.'

Martha tensed. Her knuckles whitened, gripping the steering wheel, shoulders hunched. 'I did?'

'Yes,' said Evie. 'You phoned and said you'd been delayed and my dad would pick me up and take me home. You said he'd drive a Volkswagen and he had a beard and he'd be wearing a denim shirt. And he was and that's how I knew him.'

Martha said, 'Ah.'

They pulled up at the door. Evie jumped out and ran up the path. 'Is Murphy here? I want Murphy.'

Charlie said he was back at home. 'I'll get him later.' He turned to Martha. 'Give me the keys. I have to go and see Bernice Stokes and tell her I'm not working for her any more.'

'No,' said Martha. 'I need the car to go and get my mother. Then I'll need to shop. I don't think we've any food in the house. Then I'll need to cook. Or, I thought you could cook. You're better at it than me. Then, perhaps as you're cooking, you could shop, too, then you'd know what you have and could cook accordingly. Actually, I want to stay with Evie. So you could get my mother while you're out shopping.'

It was Charlie's turn to say, 'Ah.'

He paused, considered his day ahead, and said, 'Might I remind you that I'm your boss?'

'You're only my boss in the office. But right now we're not there, so I can tell you what to do.'

He picked the car keys from her hand and said, 'OK.' Today was not a day to argue.

He went home, showered, shaved, cleaned his teeth and made a decent cup of coffee. He was restarting his day, getting into his proper routine. It made him feel more optimistic that everything would go well. He took Murphy for a brief walk before dropping him off at Martha's. 'It'll do Evie good to have him to play with. He's a calm sort, soothing. He likes wildlife programmes on telly.'

He shopped not knowing what to buy. So he got too much. He decided the best celebratory meal for a family would be fish and chips with champagne. He went to the Italian deli to get bread and decent cheese. He debated pudding and decided something fruity would be healthier than something chocolate. He put his shopping in the back of his car and felt pleased. He was looking forward to unloading his goodies in Martha's kitchen. He hoped she'd smile and declare his purchases wonderful. She might even say, 'Well done.'

He got into the car, waggled the gear stick, frowned and thought about Martha, his love. He wanted her. But she came with baggage – a child, a mother, a tangle of guilt, memories and secrets. When it came to winning her heart he feared fish and chips, champagne and some sort of fruity pudding would not do the job. He needed to impress her with a grand gesture and wondered if the bookshop he frequented had a volume entitled How to Win a Woman's Heart Without Promising to Buy Her a Car.

Sophie was dressed and ready to go. She was sitting by the side of her bed looking agitated. 'Where the hell have you been? I've been waiting for hours. Did you find Evie?'

'Yes, Evie's at home. And I've been shopping. Martha told me to get some food.'

'Did you go to the shop I told you about?'

'Yes. You'll get the full story when you get home.'

She bade goodbye to her fellow patients and the nurses, and indicated to Charlie that he should take her arm. 'I'm stiff and sore.'

He drove slowly. Sophie complained. 'Can't you go any faster?'

'No.'

'Why not?'

'There are other cars about.'

'They are mostly on the other side of the road and nowhere near you.'

'You never know. One of the drivers coming towards me could suddenly sneeze or have a stroke or a heart attack and veer over and bang into me. I need to be going slowly to lessen the impact. You never know what's going to happen.'

This struck a chord with Sophie. She said nothing more. But bored with travelling at a snail's pace, she painfully twisted in her seat and examined the shopping bags in the back.

'What did you buy?'

'Food. Usual stuff. Milk, bread, potatoes, butter. I got fish. Thought we'd have fish and chips, everybody likes that.'

'You've got wine. Champagne. Three bottles.'

'We don't have to drink it all. You could keep a bottle for another day. It's a celebration. Evie's home and you'll be home. Catastrophe over. And Martha's been stressed. This will cheer her up. She might even be happy.'

'You want to make Martha happy?'

'Yes, of course I do. She's lovely when she's happy.'

'You like Martha, then.'

'Yes, I like Martha.'

They were driving along Portobello High Street. Sophie had her hands folded in her lap and was staring at Charlie. 'That's very posh champagne.'

'It's a special occasion.'

Sophie said, 'Hmm.' She sniffed. 'You don't just like Martha. You've fallen in love with her, haven't you? Oh, you silly boy. Now that's a catastrophe.'

'I suppose you heard what I said to Jamie,' said Martha.

'You were whispering awfully loudly and angrily,' Charlie told her.

It was nine in the evening and she and Charlie were alone on the sofa in front of the fire. She sat legs curled under her. She was barefoot. Sophie and Evie were in bed. Evie had school tomorrow and Sophie had declared herself exhausted. 'All I did was lie in bed. I don't know how hospital takes it out of you, but it does.' She'd shuffled from the room, giving Charlie a fierce behave-yourself look as she went.

They were finishing the second bottle of champagne. Martha looked into her glass. 'I shouldn't have said that. I was angry with him, really angry. I wanted to hurt him. It was wrong of me.' She blushed. 'I have no idea who Evie's father is.'

'None at all?'

'It could be one of three people.'

'Jamie's one of them?'

'Yes. I was pregnant. I was scared. I didn't know what to do. I thought he wanted me. So I asked him to marry me. I wasn't totally truthful about my motives, though.'

'He probably did want you.'

'He wouldn't have if he'd known what I got up to.'

'What did you get up to?'

Martha smiled. 'Everything our parents told us not to do. I keep remembering me swaggering about with my thumbs hooked over the back pockets of my jeans, boasting about us being the queens of rock'n'roll.'

'Good boast, I like it.'

'We wanted to be like the boys. It didn't occur to us to play on our femininity. Boys had the best toys. They had all the fun. They got to play guitars and sing while girls looked on and adored them. So we went all blokey. Except we had tits and squeakier voices.'

They joined a tour. The other bands amazed Martha. They were skinny-voiced youths offstage, and gods under the lights. They spoke Glasgow or Aberdeen and sang New York or San Francisco. They wore sunglasses indoors.

'Everyone could see Grace was going to be a star. And that was my downfall.'

'*Your* downfall? How come.'

'Well, all the boys wanted to screw her. Even if it was only to brag about it after she hit the big time. But she was way out of their league so they settled for her backing band.'

Charlie said, 'Hmm.'

'I loved the attention. Being wooed by boys who had their eye on the main chance was exciting. They had their lines all worked out and I fell for them. I thought I was cool. And I got my comeuppance. Didn't I?'

'You got Evie. You got something good.'

'I know that now. But back then being single and pregnant was a disgrace, a scandal. I was terrified. So I told Jamie he was the father. I hate myself for it. I mean, marriage is huge. It's meant to be for life. I cheated him of his freedom.'

'No. You just acted out of fear. And I'm sure Jamie wanted to marry you.'

'No, he didn't. He felt trapped. He buggered off. Can you blame him?'

Charlie thought that perhaps he couldn't. His best plan was to change the subject before Martha broke down. 'Did anybody become a rock god?'

'Nah. They're all accountants or plumbers, insurance agents or car salesmen now. But with interesting stories to tell.'

'So, who was Evie's father?'

'Jamie or Alan or Bernie. There were only three. I wasn't that bad.'

'Whoever it was must be OK. Evie's a joy. She's bright and funny and she's going to be a looker.'

'She brought my mother and me together. We drifted after Dad died. She went into this cocoon of grief and I was obsessed with death. I used to lie underwater in the bath hoping to drown. I'd hold my breath till my lungs felt they were bursting. But I always shot back up gasping for air. I'd cut myself too.' She rolled up her sleeve, showed Charlie a row of scars running between her wrist and her elbow. 'Mum caught me once with my head in the oven. I wasn't trying to kill myself. I didn't really want to die. I just needed to know what death was like, so I could tell her it wasn't that bad. I played rock'n'roll. I got battered and bruised in an old van, I changed into my stage clothes in the back rooms of pubs and youth club cloakrooms. I didn't wash enough. I ate junk food. The other girls thought maybe they'd get famous and if they didn't they'd go to university and have a good time before having a career. I just wanted to make a lot of noise.' She stared into her empty glass.

'Do you want me to open the last bottle?' Charlie offered.

'God, no. I can never decide if I like champagne. I like the thought of it, the anticipation of it, the sight of the bubbles. But then I drink it and burp.'

'You're meant to sip, not swig.'

'Ah. It's my misspent youth, downing pints of beer and showing off.' She put her glass on the floor. 'I think I'd prefer a cup of tea. I must be getting old.'

'Do you want tea?'

'Yes, why not. I'll make a cup.'

They moved to the kitchen. Charlie sat at the table while Martha filled the kettle. He asked what happened to Grace.

Martha shrugged. 'She got a recording contract. Made a single that got to number twelve in the charts. So the company spent money on her – clothes, photo shoots, interviews, that sort of thing. A tour. She did a tour with other bands. The Beatles were on it. She wasn't top of the bill. Then her next single only went to number twenty and her album flopped. So she got dropped. She didn't make much money. Rock stars who fade away never do.'

'I suppose they don't. So, you don't know where she is now?'

'I heard she went to LA, and then she lived in Thailand for a while. Moved to Paris. Just rumours. It's a pity because she was good. Bluesy. Two or three years later and she might have been big. Grace Slick, Janis Joplin came along, she was up there with them. I still hear her records now and then. They say she was the start of it all. When they heard her, people knew what was coming. But where is she now?' Martha shrugged.

She brought two mugs of tea to the table, sat opposite Charlie.

He smiled. Actually, he had a hunch he knew exactly where Grace was. But now was not the time to mention it.

'It was rough and grubby and all that. But being young was magical. Magical.' She said it twice, that's how magical it had been. 'I remember a night we slept in the van. Middle of nowhere. And the night was soft and warm. Millions of stars and we picked up some station on our radio. They were playing Ray Charles "The Night Time Is The Right Time". And I danced on my own. Twirling and twirling, watching the stars go round. I was utterly, joyously happy.'

'Where was that?'

'I've no idea. Somewhere between Plymouth and Inverness. I just remember the moment.'

29

Bellow

There were words Charlie did not include in his vocabulary. They included relax and enjoy. He didn't do either. He didn't know how. Relaxing was a mystery. How did you do that? Relax in the bath? He showered. Relax in front of the television? Usually when he sat down to watch it, something awful was on. Relax with a drink in front of the fire. He'd tried this but sitting still was a problem. He tended to drum his fingers and look round the room. This led to his spotting things that needed done. And he couldn't relax while staring at an untidy pile of books or a thin film of dust on the table. Relaxing was hard work.

He sighed considering this. It was the middle of the night, indigestion time. He'd known even as he ate the fish and chips and drank the champagne that his body would object to the over-indulgence. Right now he felt that his mouth was coated in grease and millions of gassy bubbles were coursing through his system. They would in a very short time arrive at their exit point and explode into the room. Murphy would raise his head, prick his ears and look at him with disdain. Charlie thought this unfair of him. He envied Murphy. The dog had enthusiasm. Everything he did, he did with zest as if it was his favourite thing to do. The dog enjoyed himself.

Enjoyment was elusive. Charlie wasn't sure about it. What did a person do when the enjoyment was over? Say, he ate a scone and liked it. Did he have a second scone to prolong the moment? The thing about enjoying yourself was that you didn't notice it when it was happening. So you didn't enjoy enjoying yourself, you enjoyed thinking about it afterwards.

He supposed that the onset of his inability to relax or enjoy himself had come at that moment in the pink room when he was reading the pink letter and breathing in the thick floral scent that lingered. He'd stepped outside his life and started living as an onlooker. Now he had to beware of pink. It was everywhere. There were thousands of pink things in the world that could remind him of his loneliness, uselessness and inadequacies. A chap couldn't relax or enjoy himself with a lurid scent and a vivid colour to avoid.

Martha was different. She'd faced her truth. She was never going to be Gene Vincent. She couldn't rock like Chuck Berry. She wasn't sexy like Elvis. She'd been a fool. It was time to quit.

'God, that must've been painful,' Charlie said to Murphy, who was lying on the rug beside his bed. 'Me, I've always accepted failure. Never expected anything else. I've had it easy.' He heaved himself onto his elbow and punched his pillow. 'Can't get comfy. Of course, being pregnant would have influenced her decision to quit. To be honest, I don't know if you can take a version of "Pistol Packin' Mama" seriously if it's sung by a woman heavy with child.' He paused, thought, 'Then again, why not? Maybe that's why you'd be packin' a pistol.'

He rolled onto his back, put his hands behind his head, stared into the gloom and started to idly sing the song. 'Bugger. This will be running round my head for days now.' He threw back his blankets. 'Can't sleep. Too much stodgy food, champagne and heavy confessional conversation.'

He dressed – jeans, shirt, thick jumper and running shoes. A swift getaway might be called for. He wheeled his bike outside and stood a moment appreciating the air and the silence and chided himself for not doing this more often. The world was perfect when there was nobody else about.

The song was still in his head as he cycled. Tyres humming over tarmac, hardly a car on the road – if only it was always like this. Night air on his face and a song he didn't totally dislike bouncing in his brain.

It was after four when he cruised into the Grassmarket. He wheeled his bike along the pavement, looking into doorways. He was checking the slumbering bundles. He knew not to shine the torch he'd brought into any faces. Sudden light woke doorway slumberers and he'd learned the hard way to let sleeping tramps lie when a man, taller and stronger that he was, had roared out of his wrappings, pinned him to the doorway wall and held a knife at his throat.

Now, he looked at feet. They were a good indicator of the sex of the sleeper. He was looking for a woman. Women tended not to be violent. But they had a huge and lively stock of swear words. Chrissie Lewis would be fine, though. She'd have a working knowledge of curses. But he doubted she'd use them.

It was just a hunch that Chrissie was living on the streets. He knew that destitute people often returned to their hometown. He supposed they found it easier to sleep in familiar doorways and parks. And, during waking hours, which alleyways to wander to keep safe and to avoid people who'd known you in better times.

He searched every doorway and back yard, where the entrance wasn't blocked with a locked gate. Then he moved on to the Royal Mile. He knew of neglected overgrown areas behind buildings where homeless people spent the night. But none of the breathing huddles was Chrissie.

He stood knee-deep in weeds. Behind him grey buildings, and only a few windows lit. It was mostly small flats up there. Some of the flats had been divided into several smaller flats. Charlie thought it inevitable that in time these buildings would become fashionable. They were in the heart of the tourist area between the castle and Holyrood Palace.

There were rustlings in the undergrowth. Mice, rats, he thought, and looked in dismay at his feet. Small furry things might scurry over them. Moving back to the street, he disturbed a flurry of pigeons that rattled and flapped into the air. He jumped, pressed his hand against his startled heart. It was coming up for six o'clock. Light now and more people about. He hadn't found Chrissie Lewis. He was tired and still sore from his set-to with Brendan Stokes. Time to go home. He freewheeled down the hill and into Queen's Park.

It was always the best part of an early morning journey home, to cycle here. Flat road and hill and gorse, wildness in the city. Arthur's Seat looming, often climbed but never really tamed. He pedalled slowly, contemplating that wonderful moment when he'd slip into bed and let go and sleep.

He wasn't looking ahead. Instead, with no other traffic about, he was watching the road skim below him as he gained speed. So he didn't see Bellow surging towards him. But he heard him.

'Charlie Gavin. There you go, Charlie Gavin.' The voice was huge. Filled the park. This man wasn't called Bellow for nothing. He walked the city shouting. He wore a lot of yellow – scarf, shirt and trousers – and had once been known as Yellow Bellow. But maybe that was too much to say. It might take too long to come out of your mouth before his great voice drowned you.

He didn't so much walk as thrust himself forward, wild hair flying, shouting as he went about God, impending misadventure, doom and the fickleness of friends. He always carried two overstuffed yellow shopping bags rumoured to be filled with priceless antiques, but Charlie suspected contained rubbish.

'What are you doing here?' he asked.

'Been up on the hill watching stars. Good stars up there. Thousands of them. You should turn your gaze upwards.'

Charlie said maybe he would some day.

'Look at you, Charlie Gavin. Your face is mush. Been fighting?'

'Somebody got into a fight with me. I didn't fight back.'

'Looks like it.' He boxed the air, pranced. 'Footwork.'

Charlie thought it was a wonder that a man could dance like that in boots with no laces. But watching the agile gallop of boot on tarmac made him contemplate the grime-encrusted, blistered state of the feet the boots contained. To chase the image from his mind he took out his photo of Chrissie and showed it to Bellow.

He stopped his boxing demonstration. 'The Duchess.'

'Duchess?'

'Yes. Tells everyone she's met the Queen. Used to mix with the aristocracy. Shy type, though. Hangs about the Grassmarket. Slips away if she sees someone she used to know. Thinks she's better than the rest of us. But that's the way of it when you've no roof over your head, no bed to lay that same head at night. You have to believe you're better than those who have.'

Charlie said he could see that. 'Do you know where she sleeps at night?'

'Somewhere safe she says. Don't know where. Women have to be safe. It's their weakness. Along with chocolate.'

Charlie said, 'It's my weakness, too.' He gave Bellow a couple of pounds, mounted his bike and pushed off. 'Safe with a bar of chocolate works for me.'

The great voice followed him. 'It will come to you, Charlie Gavin. It comes to us all. Misfortune, bad luck, wrong choices. You will be among us who have no roof and no bed and come to know the night. The homeless will watch for you, Charlie Gavin.'

Charlie sped away from the roar.

'It happened to me. It'll happen to you. The great misfortune will happen to everyone. It's coming for you all.'

Charlie cycled faster. Shot out of the park and into the morning traffic. He didn't look back. He feared he was hearing the truth.

At home he removed his shoes, placed them carefully side-by-side and flopped onto his bed. He'd planned to shower and brew a perfect cup of coffee, but didn't. He fell instantly into a deep sleep and dreamed he was walking barefoot across rubble trying to reach a woman dressed in yellow. He was calling to her, mincing gingerly over jagged ground. When she turned to face him, he saw it was Martha. He tried to go to her. Had something to give her – a bundle he was suddenly carrying. But he couldn't move and his jaw was weak. He couldn't speak.

He was shivering when he woke. The window was open. He'd been sweating after his frantic cycling when he'd thrown himself on the bed. He rose stiffly, hobbled to the shower and stood under the hot spray trying to wash away his dream. Dreams bothered him. They visited often. He felt dreaming was his mind out of control, thinking on its own when he wasn't around to stop it.

30

Safe

He dressed after carefully examining his mood – grey shirt with black jacket today, rather than black shirt with grey jacket – and selected socks of the day before brewing his perfect cup of coffee.

He walked along the beach to work. The day was warm and Murphy needed a run. It was almost half-past eleven when he arrived at the office, well after bacon roll time. This bothered him.

Martha was at her desk looking industrious. 'You're late.'

'I know. Have you had a bacon roll?'

'No, I waited for you.'

'Better get them now. My day is all out of kilter. But I might put it back the way it ought to be if I can pretend that it's three-quarters of an hour ago.'

Ten minutes later, sitting on the sofa with their rolls and coffee, trying to get their day back on track, Charlie said, 'Where's safe?'

Martha said, 'Home.'

'If you wanted somewhere safe to sleep, where would you go?'

'My bed at home.'

'But if you had no home. If you were living on the street.'

'I'd go to a hostel.'

'Yes, there's that. Where else?'

'Home. I'd slip into the back garden after dark. It's safe there. And I know it. I'd be close to people I love even if they were unaware of my being there. There's a little secret place behind the lilac tree, soft grass and shade. It's where I went when I ran away once. And where I hid if I was in disgrace or feeling sad.'

He reached out, put a hand on her shoulder. 'Why were you sad?'

'I was sad when my dad died. Sad when I got a bloody ukulele. I was so disappointed I went and stood in my secret spot for hours. I was freezing and missing Dad. It was our first Christmas without him. Lonely and heartbroken me, I wallowed in sorrow.'

'You sound like you enjoyed it.'

'I had a great wallow. Don't you ever wallow? Just let sadness take you over? Just gorge yourself in self-pity?'

'No. It must be a girl thing.' He was not about to admit to his wallowing. He did it often.

'Oh, you should do it. It's good for you.'

He squeezed her shoulder and said, 'I prefer a beer to a wallow.' He got up and gathered their plates and cups, wondered if he'd squeezed her shoulder too hard. He'd been on the verge of giving her a slap on the back and inviting her out for a pint later on. He'd nearly advised her to stop praising the joys of wallowing and be a man. 'Keep it to yourself and have a couple of beers.'

He washed the dishes, slowly turning over the business of embracing misery.

'Christ,' he said, coming from the kitchen with dripping hands, 'you stood behind a lilac tree in sub-zero temperatures because you got a ukulele?'

'I wanted a red guitar. I was in love with it.'

'If you'd got it you would have tried to play it. Failed and given up. That's what happens when you get something without working for it. But you worked for your guitar. Bought it. Started a band. Went on the road. Behaved like a prat. Got drunk. Got pregnant. Had Evie. That ukulele is the best thing that ever happened to you.'

Martha told Charlie that he was dripping onto the floor. She stared at him, debating her reply to his ukulele remark. She couldn't argue about a bloody ukulele with somebody who'd suffered as he had. Instead she said, 'By the way, I'll need your car today. The Beetle's still buggered and I have to take my mother to the doctor. They want to keep an eye on her, check her stitches, poke at her ribs and so forth. Then she has to go to the outpatients' next week to get her stitches out.'

'What time?'

'Three-fifteen. So I'll need you to pick up Evie from school and walk her home.'

Charlie said, 'Please.'

'Sorry, could you please pick up Evie. You could please take Murphy. She'd like that.'

He picked up his list for the day, held it up. 'I've things to do. I've written them down.'

'Just because you've written something down doesn't mean you absolutely have to stick to it. Things happen. Life sneaks up on you.'

'I work very hard at not letting life sneak up on me.' He made lists. He kept himself safe by tapping his nameplate, putting his pens in perfect order, wearing the correct socks on the correct day. He couldn't explain to her, or anyone, the importance of his rituals. He just knew that if he let them go, something awful would happen. Life would sneak up on him.

'OK, I'll do it. I'll see Bernice tomorrow and tell her the investigation is over. I was going to see Ted Lewis and give him an update. But I'll do that the day after.'

'Not today? You've got time.'

'No, I have to procrastinate. I have to think. I'll pick up Evie and bring her here.'

'Why do you procrastinate?'

'I think. I don't rush in. Putting things off till tomorrow is a good policy.' He drummed his fingers on his desk, relishing the delights of procrastination. 'And if you make a wrong decision, you're also delaying the regrets for a day or two.'

'Just don't procrastinate on picking Evie up. Be there on time.'

Charlie reckoned it was a twenty-minute walk to the school. He planned to leave at three. Evie would get out at half-past. This gave him a ten-minute leeway. He was prepared for unforeseen things that might happen on route.

Of course he hadn't thought about anything unforeseen that might happen before he set out. Ted Lewis phoned and delayed him.

'I was wondering how your investigation is getting along.'

'Very well,' said Charlie. 'We've spoken to all Chrissie's friends.'

'So you'll know she's back in Edinburgh.'

'Indeed.'

'She was spotted in the Grassmarket.'

'Yes.'

'Her friend phoned and told me,' said Ted.

'Yes. I spent quite a long time there yesterday looking for her.'

'Are you planning on going back today?'

Charlie looked at his watch. Ten past three. He should be on his way. 'I'm a bit tied up at the moment. I was going to go in the evening.'

'Well, I'm going now.'

'Please don't. If she sees a familiar face, she might move on. We have no idea where she'd go.'

'The familiar face she'd see would be mine, her husband's. I have a great deal to say to that woman.'

'I'm sure you do. But please let us find her. I don't want her frightened off.'

'Frightened off? What do you think I'm going to do? Wield an axe at her? I just want to talk to her. Why would she be frightened?'

'Guilt. Shame. She might not want to face you.'

'I don't care what she wants. I want to talk to her. I'm going to look for her now.'

He put down the phone. Charlie looked at his watch. 'Damn.' He was late.

He put on his jacket, checked the gas was off, put the guard in front of the fire, clipped on Murphy's leash and set off, tapping his nameplate as he went. He walked a few yards and stopped. He patted his pockets, making sure he had everything placed correctly. He stood staring ahead. Had he turned off the gas? He thought he had. He remembered doing it. But had he? It was so automatic he might just be thinking he had. Better go back and make sure.

In the office he stared at the oven. 'It's off.' The fireguard was in place, his pens in a perfect parallel row and his LPs all in their sleeves in alphabetised order on the shelf. 'Excellent.'

He checked his watch. Twenty past. 'Christ.' He locked up. Put his key in the correct pocket, tapped his nameplate and headed to the school. Stopped. Had he really made sure the gas was off? 'Damn,' he said out loud. 'I have. I have. I know I have. But it's so automatic I maybe just think I have.'

He turned back. Checked his watch. Twenty-five past. 'No time.'

He ran. It wasn't just because he was late; it was what he did when he was agitated. He tried to put as much distance between himself and his problem as quickly as he could. Daft, he thought, because his fretting was in his head and he was taking it with him. But movement helped. So, he pelted along the pavement, cheeks red, pockets jingling and Murphy running beside him, ears flapping. He was enjoying this.

School had been out for ten minutes when Charlie jogged towards the gates. A van covered with psychedelic patterns and CND stickers was parked across the road. A woman with long dark hair was leading Evie towards it. 'No,' he shouted. 'No, Evie, no.' Letting go of Murphy's leash, he waved his arms in the air as he ran. Evie turned, saw Murphy, wrenched her hand free from the woman's grip and ran towards the dog arms outstretched.

It was like the tear-jerking end of a French film when two long-parted lovers rushed towards one another. It could have only taken moments for the two to come together in the middle of the road, but to Charlie it seemed to take an age. Evie knelt and clutched the dog to her. Murphy wriggled, jumped and licked her face. The woman looked briefly at Charlie running towards the two reunited lovers. She was beautiful.

Charlie could hardly stop himself from staring her. She was perfect. She smiled. 'Jamie wanted to see her one more time before we leave. Going to Australia soon. He wanted to say goodbye.'

Charlie said, 'Understandable. But probably best to arrange something with Martha. You weren't planning to take Evie with you to Australia, were you?'

The woman smiled. Perfect teeth. She shook her head. 'No. I've got what I want from Martha's life. She can keep her child.' She climbed into her van and drove off.

Charlie swept the lovers from the road and led them to the pavement before giving in to his sweat, panic and exhaustion. Panting and working at not throwing up, he said, 'I thought I'd left the gas on.'

He took Evie's hand and they walked slowly down the road. She held Murphy's leash.

Charlie said, 'Ah. I don't think your mother wants you to go with that lady.'

'She said Mummy had sent her.'

'She sent me. I was late because I went back to the office to check I'd turned the gas off.'

'Grandma's always doing that. She gets to the front door and says, "Did I switch the gas off?" And she has to go back to check because she'll not be happy if she doesn't. It's really boring.'

Charlie was relieved to know he wasn't the only one so afflicted. He looked down at his hand linked with Evie's and smiled to her.

'The lady said she and Daddy were going to live in another country. I could go too if I wanted,' said Evie.

'And do you?'

'Nah. Mummy can't come. Murphy can't come. So I'm not going. She asked if I wanted to come for tea. But I didn't. They eat too many things with bits in.'

They walked in silence before Charlie asked, 'Where do you feel safe?'

'Home. In bed all toasty with the covers over my head. But I keep one ear out so I can hear Mum and Gran moving about and chatting and doing stuff in the kitchen. That's safe.'

'What if you didn't have a home or a bed?'

'I'd go behind the lilac tree in the garden. It's a hidey place nobody but me knows about. It's a secret. You mustn't tell.'

Charlie said, 'I won't, if you promise not to tell that I was late.'

31

Transference

Sophie shuffled to the door. Moving was painful and if whoever was ringing wasn't so persistent, she wouldn't have bothered going to answer it.

Duncan was on the doorstep smiling his delighted, but slightly sheepish, smile. 'I hadn't seen you in a while so I thought I'd drop by.' He didn't at first notice the state she was in.

He followed her up to the kitchen, took his usual seat at the table and only when she went to the sink to fill the kettle did he notice how stiffly she was moving. When she turned to fetch the cups, he saw the bruising on her face and her stitches.

'What happened to you?'

'Got set upon by a couple of lads after my cake.'

He stared at her, taking this in, then asked, 'What cake?'

'The da Vinci one.'

'No. That was a beauty. Did they get it?'

'It got smashed when I fell.'

'A tragedy,' said Duncan. 'An absolute tragedy.'

'I was very proud of that cake. Best I've ever done. But I'm fine, thanks for asking. A bit knocked about and bruised, broken ribs, stitches – but otherwise fine.'

'Sorry, that was thoughtless of me. It was just such a wonderful cake.'

Sophie sighed. 'You can make the tea. It hurts me too much.'

She watched as he fussed with teabags and cups and kettle of boiling water. He was an insensitive buffoon, she thought.

She wished Martin were here. He'd have cared for her. He'd have plumped her pillows and made her comfortable in bed. He'd have brought her tea. He'd have asked her several times a day if she was all right. He'd have asked so often she'd have been irritated. 'Of course I'm not all right. Stop asking,' she'd have said.

Oh, but she missed him. The longing for him still swept over her. It always came unexpectedly. She'd be peeling potatoes or dusting the living room or lying awake in bed waiting for sleep and she'd remember he was gone. She'd never see him again. She'd be filled with a long slow sadness. It had taken her a year after his death to know she'd never truly get over it. She'd quietly grieve for the rest of her life.

Duncan laid a cup of tea on the table in front of her. He stepped back proud of himself and waiting for her verdict. She took a sip, made a face and said, 'Horrible. Too strong. I like it weak.'

Duncan reeled back in shock. 'Oh, sorry. I always make it strong.' He lunged for the cup. 'I'll make you another.'

She flapped him away. 'Don't bother. I'll drink it anyway. I'm in a lot of pain, a little more won't hurt.'

He sat opposite her and apologised. 'I just never think. I'm so used to making it for myself.'

'Martin always thought of others. Martin made lovely tea. I miss him.'

'Of course you do.'

'You're not like him at all. He was thoughtful. He was kind. He cared about people. He wouldn't ever just have turned up on someone's doorstep when he fancied a cup of tea or a meal.'

Duncan reddened. Looked into his cup.

'And if he'd been around now he'd have worried about me and not a bloody cake.'

Duncan opened his mouth but no sound came out. He squirmed.

'Look at me, I'm all bashed up. Bruised and broken. Ribs, stitches,' she pointed to her forehead, 'I was unconscious. I was in hospital. And it won't go away. It keeps coming back to me, pictures – vivid pictures – in my head. I'm falling again. I'm hitting my head again. Lying on the ground again. But mostly it's falling. The ground coming up to meet me and me scared and helpless. And all you can think about is my ruined cake.'

He put his hands to his face, shook his head. 'Oh, you sound just like my wife. She used to say I was a clumsy oaf in delicate situations. I always said the wrong thing. I lacked empathy.' He put his hands on his cheeks. 'It's my face. It doesn't do what it's meant to do. It smiles when it should look sad. And it goes grumpy when it should be smiling. I have no control over it. It doesn't reflect what I'm thinking.'

'You witter on about a cake because you have no control of your face and can't say out loud what you are thinking?'

'Exactly. I thought you might not like me to mention the fact that you were shuffling about. So I spoke about the cake instead. I thought you might be lamenting its loss. It was a stunner of a cake. Best cake I've ever seen.'

'You're doing it again. Speaking about the cake. PLEASE stop.' She clutched her mouth. Felt her face going out of control. It crumpled. Tears. 'It was a beautiful cake. I loved it. I was so proud of it. And it's gone. Smashed to pieces. Like me.' She put her head on the table and sobbed.

Duncan went to her. He stood, his hand hovering over her heaving back. 'Don't cry. Please don't cry. I don't know what to do when people cry.'

But Sophie wept on.

Duncan sighed, finally placed a consoling hand on her back. 'I think this is called transference. You are transferring your grief and shock about your recent trauma to your loss of cake. You're not really weeping for your cake. You are grieving over your broken ribs and bashed head.'

Sophie sniffed, wiped her nose with the back of her hand. 'Please leave.'

32

The Lure of Clean Sheets

'I wish I could fart like a dog,' said Charlie.

Almost midnight, they were in Charlie's car watching the gate of the private gardens in Drummond Place. It was his theory that Chrissie Lewis thought this to be her safe place. He suspected she knew it well. Had probably spent sunny afternoons here, reading and sipping a G&T. He decided she'd been happy out here. Happier than she had been in the flat she'd shared with her husband.

'What an absurd thing to say. Dogs are foul farters. Is that why you wanted me to come along, so you could talk about farting?' said Martha.

'I wanted you here because you're a woman. If a man approaches Chrissie she might be frightened. She might call out. She might have a heart attack. A woman's better.'

'I can see that. How long do we have to wait?'

'Till the lights in the flats are out.'

'Well, can we change the subject?'

'No. Dogs are master farters. They do not move, look up or acknowledge what they've done in the slightest way. It's a natural thing to do and they do it. They don't squirm with embarrassment; they don't blush and pardon themselves. They have no guilt. I envy that. That's what I was really thinking. Wondering what it would be like to get by on instinct. To live in the moment. No guilt.'

'Zen farting.'

'Exactly. What were you thinking about?'

'I was feeling guilty.'

'What about?'

'Drugs.'

'Oh, right. When you said you hadn't done them I didn't believe you. You were a kid in a rock'n'roll band, away from home, away from your mum. Of course you smoked a joint or two.'

'I remember staring at ordinary things and saying, "Wow." As in, "Wow, a daisy." Or "Wow, a chip." And I giggled myself witless.'

'Sounds like just the thing for a young rebel to do.' He leaned forward and said, 'I'm going to kiss you.'

Surprised, she put a forbidding hand on his approaching face and said, 'Why?'

He put a finger on her lips. 'Ted Lewis, coming along the street. I don't want him to see us.'

'He'll see us kissing.'

'He won't see our faces. He won't know who we are.' He kissed her. He felt the softness of her lips against his, smelled her musky perfume, and was embarrassed at how much he liked it. 'Sorry.' He kissed her again.

Ted drew level with the car, stared in, leaned down to get a better view then walked on shaking his head and muttering.

Charlie freed himself from the kiss and watched him go. Removed from the safety of his living room, Ted Lewis seemed less confident – his shoulders sloped, his head was bowed. He shuffled.

'He seems lost and old when he's out in the world,' said Martha. 'Wonder where he's been.'

'Visiting friends? At his bridge club? Wandering the Grassmarket looking for his wife? He won't find her.'

'Why not?'

'She was spotted. She'll be keeping away from there.' He got out of the car.

Martha followed. 'Why did you kiss me?'

'I told you, I didn't want Ted Lewis to see us.'

'Why not?'

They walked to the gate of the private gardens.

'Questions, questions,' said Charlie.

'But why?'

'I want to talk to Chrissie first. I want to find out why she left before I tell her husband we've found her. So I don't want him to know we're looking here in the gardens opposite his house.' He slapped his hands on the gate of the gardens. It was high, too high to vault. 'Don't you think it's odd that someone would wander the streets and sleep in doorways or here outside in the cold when they have a home?' He bent down, cupped his hands together. 'Put your foot in there. I'll give you a shove over.'

'She walked out on him. Maybe she thinks it isn't her home any more.' Martha put her foot in his hands and he heaved her up so she easily cleared the gate. She turned, did a small jump of triumph. 'Now you.'

A tricky one. He slapped his hands on the top of the gate once more and felt shamed by his weaknesses. If he was lithe he could clear it in a single bound in the manner of Steve McQueen or Paul Newman. He was not like these screen gods. He was not a model of desirable maleness. Recently he'd noted a certain softening round his middle, a grey hair or two on his temples and a strange new longing to take a nap in the middle of the afternoon. He was not a virile leaper of gates. This bothered him because the woman he wanted to impress was standing on the other side of the gate waiting for him to join her. He could still feel the kiss on his lips, her scent lingering as did traces of the way her fingers touched the back of his neck.

He heaved himself up, aware that the effort was making his arms shake and his face turn a hearty shade of red. He got his leg onto the top spar, then his other leg and was now lying on top of the gate. He didn't look at Martha, didn't want to see her derision as he rolled off and tumbled to the ground.

'How are we going to get out?' asked Martha.

'With difficulty.'

'And how does Chrissie get in here?'

'Maybe she's athletic.'

'Maybe she isn't here.'

'She has to be. It's safe. A hostel wouldn't be. Not if she thinks someone is looking for her. But this is right under her husband's nose. She's thinking she's safe. Everybody needs to feel safe.'

He looked round, thinking about Evie and Martha's secret place. He imagined them hiding, standing perfectly still, breathing quietly, feeling safe. That spot behind the lilac tree would have been softly grassy and scented in spring. He couldn't see anything quite so alluring here. Yet, if he was right, this was where Chrissie Lewis hid.

In the end, though, he didn't find Chrissie. She found him. He and Martha were searching areas of shrubbery away from the surrounding railings; he straightened up, stretched, turned and saw the old lady coming towards him. She wore a red cloche hat, a long blue tweed coat, had a silk scarf draped round her neck and carried two old and battered leather bags. Everything was worn now, but they'd been stylish and very expensive in their day.

She was small and frail but still had large brown eyes, high cheekbones and full lips. Her skin looked old. She put her bags down, crossed her arms. 'Are you looking for me.' A soft voice, but assured, well-rounded vowels.

'Yes. Your husband asked us to find you. But he doesn't know I'm here.'

'But you'll tell him.'

'No. Not yet.'

She spread her arms. 'Here I am.'

'Here you are.' He stepped towards her, took her bags. 'I thought you might like a bath, a bed with clean sheets and some food perhaps.' He looked at the sky. Held out his hand, palm upwards. 'I think it's going to rain.'

'It is. I can smell it coming.'

Martha had been watching from the far side of the gardens. She held her breath and moved closer, one slow silent step at a time. She couldn't believe this. There in front of her was an escapee human being. A woman who'd dropped out of a normal regular life to sleep on the streets. How odd. How wonderful. It was as if she was observing some rare shy wild animal that would bolt the moment her suspicions were aroused.

Chrissie sensed Martha's stare, turned and saw her stealthy approach. 'It's all right. No need to sneak up on me. I'm hardly likely to flee. Where would I go?' She turned back to Charlie. 'Yes. A bath, a bed, clean sheets, a bit of privacy, food. Thank you. I don't mind if I do.'

They walked in a silent line, Charlie then Chrissie with Martha coming along behind. At the gate, Charlie put down the bags, smiled to Chrissie. 'The key?'

She handed it over. 'I was hoping to have some fun watching the pair of you struggling to get out the way you struggled to get in. Very entertaining. How did you know I had a key?'

'Seems logical. You don't seem the vaulting type,' said Charlie. He opened the gate and held it as the other two went through.

Chrissie settled in the back of the car. 'So good to sit down. So good not to have to walk.'

Martha sat in the driver's seat, started the engine and then turned and leaned over to Chrissie. 'You took the key to the private garden when you left your husband?'

'Good heavens, no. Why would I have done that? I took the key to the flat. Then when I got back to Edinburgh I went in and got the garden key when Ted was out.'

Charlie said, 'Thought so.'

Martha said, 'Cool.'

Charlie said, 'I'm Charlie Gavin and this is Martha, by the way.'

'I know,' said Chrissie. 'It's a small world out on the streets.

Us refugees from living rooms and nine-to-five routines have a busy grapevine.'

The warmth of the car, the movement, the low growl of the ageing engine had a soothing effect on Chrissie. Minutes into the journey to Charlie's, she fell asleep.

'We could have been anybody and she came with us. We could be serial killers. We could be going to murder her and cut up her body.'

'I know. I think it's the sheets that swing it. These people are bone tired, hungry, lonely and frightened. The offer of a bed with fresh, clean, crisp sheets is too much. They can break hearts, clean sheets.'

'The lack of them?'

'Finding them again. The comfort. Realising the small important things that have been missing. They remember what they've let go. Slipping between clean sheets is a returning-to-the-world moment.'

Behind them Chrissie shifted and snorted. 'I'll have scrambled eggs and toast, a deep, hot, scented bath and clean sheets. But I'm not returning to any lost world. Those I've let go can stay gone. And clean sheets remind you of simple needs. I'm getting back my dignity.'

33

The Stare

Charlie didn't like this house. He hadn't liked it the first time he came, and he liked it less now. The short path from the gate to the door was depressing. His heart sank as he passed the neat, clipped pristine lawn and the borders with their regimented rows of flowers placed an immaculate twelve inches apart. Nature disciplined and told to behave, stripped of its personality. A scattering of daisies on the grass would help, he thought. A dandelion, somewhere, perhaps. Something living and happy about it would be good.

Bernice answered the door and looked mildly surprised to see him. He hadn't told her he was coming. He hadn't dropped a client before and now he was here, he thought it would have been better to have sent a letter.

Inside, the house had an unpleasant stillness. There was a slight whiff of damp. The place felt as if nobody really lived here, nobody cooked, laughed, listened to the radio or did anything other than sit still and hope that nothing would happen. He wished Martha was with him. But she was taking her mother to the outpatients' clinic. Bernice led him into the living room. 'So, have you any news?'

'I followed your man, Brendan. He led me up and down Princes Street Gardens. Then he cornered me in Rose Street and did this.' Charlie put his hand to his face, traced the line of his pain. 'Still hurts.'

'But did you find out anything new?'

'No.' Wrong question, he thought. She should have asked if he was all right. A bit of compassion went a long way. He didn't like this woman. She wasn't interested in his welfare. In fact she seemed dismissive of it. She was sitting in the armchair across from the one he was using, hands folded on her lap, her face almost expressionless. Charlie thought the chair too big for her. This house didn't fit her. It was too old and dark for her. It wasn't her style. He couldn't imagine her buying any of the furniture here. It was all bulky, dark brown pre-war. She looked the modern Swedish sort. Her clothes and hairstyle didn't match her interior décor.

Hand still touching his pain, he said, 'There's nothing on your mantelpiece.'

Bernice said, 'Pardon?'

'I'd have thought a woman like you would have some ornaments or photographs or something on her mantelpiece.'

Bernice shook her head. 'No. I'm not a mantelpiece person. I like it unadorned.'

'You've no pictures. I'd have put you as a Renoir woman. Maybe a Monet. And I'm having problems with your wallpaper.' It was dark maroon with fat gold stripes, torn here and there where it met the skirting board. Bernice was immaculate. Eleven o'clock on a Thursday morning her hair and make-up were perfect, clothes crisply ironed. There was a gleam about her. She looked polished. It took time and money to look this poised. It occurred to Charlie that such a woman would be unlikely to have grubby wallpaper.

'Do you normally criticise your client's décor? Is this part of the service?'

Charlie shook his head. He didn't know what had got into him. He'd never spoken to anyone like this before. There was something about this woman with her expensive clothes and dowdy home that irritated him. He didn't trust her. He didn't like her. She was staring at him, scrutinising his face. Watching his lips as he spoke.

'If I'd wanted advice about my colour schemes and choice of art for the walls, I wouldn't have gone to a missing persons bureau,' she told him.

Charlie said he couldn't argue with that. He blamed Martha for this embarrassment. He thought about her too often. All the time, if he was honest. Images of her, wondering what she was doing, made him forget to mind his manners. He'd remember the way she fondled the dog's ears, or reached down to take Evie's hand, or burst into the office holding aloft a paper bag containing two bacon rolls and his heart would skip a beat. And he'd say something inappropriate because he only wanted to talk to Martha. Nobody else mattered.

'In fact,' said Bernice, 'the wallpaper was here when I moved in. I didn't choose it.'

'It doesn't look like your taste.'

She gave it a critical look and said, 'It isn't. I keep meaning to get round to it.'

'Yes,' said Charlie. 'Time passes. Plans slip away unfulfilled. Suddenly you're ten years older and you've stopped noticing the wallpaper.'

'How very profound. You're quite the philosopher, Mr Gavin.'

'Not really. I just know a thing or two about not getting round to things.' He looked up at the ceiling. Someone was walking across the room above. Soft footfalls. 'You've got guests. I should go.'

Bernice flapped her hand. 'Guest. Singular. Nobody important.'

Charlie said he really had to go. 'Things to do.' He wanted out of here. He was squirming about his wallpaper remarks and would, he knew, squirm for some time to come. Months probably, if not years. He got up. Started towards the door. Bernice followed.

'You will let me know of any developments.'

He said he would. Though he was pretty sure he wouldn't.

Outside he leaned against the wall and breathed. Only ten minutes he'd been in that house and he'd forgotten about daylight. He blinked against the brightness. Someone nearby was mowing a lawn. The air was scented sweet green with freshly cut grass. He could hear children playing. He felt better. He knew he hadn't told Bernice he'd no longer work on her case. But he'd get Martha to write a business-like letter of goodbye to the icy Bernice, making sure she enclosed an invoice. This was a much better plan.

He bent down to put on his bicycle clips and heard voices coming from the living room where he'd been sitting moments ago.

'He's gone.' Bernice talking.

'What did he want?' A familiar voice.

'Don't know. Don't think he knew what he wanted. Unless it was to tell me you punched him. Why did you do that?'

'He was following me. It was getting on my nerves. He's very punchable.'

Charlie stood up. 'Brendan bloody Stokes. Bastard.' He sneaked a peek in the window. Brendan was standing, arms round Bernice, kissing her neck. She was stroking his hair and staring at the wallpaper. She pressed her lips against the top of his head and, sensing she was being watched, turned and stared at Charlie.

The stare only lasted a few seconds. That was how long it took for Charlie to realise he was standing looking into someone's living room. Looking back he remembered himself as having his mouth open and a puzzled, slightly glazed expression on his face. It wasn't an image he was proud of.

He simply registered that this woman was holding, stroking, the very person she'd asked him to find. And wondered what the hell that was about. She was staring back at him. It was a pure stare, expressionless, blank, almost Zen-like. It was the sort of stare that usually ended with one of the parties involved shouting, 'What? What the hell are you staring at?'

But Charlie didn't shout. He didn't barge into the house and demand to know what was going on. He fled. But it wasn't the disturbing sight of Brendan in Bernice's arms he was running away from; it was the stare.

34

Cake and Hello

The mugging had left Sophie afraid to go out alone. She felt exposed and could only manage to walk a few yards beyond the garden gate before panicking. There would be a tingling in her chest, a tightening of her throat; she'd swallow hard, look round wild-eyed and scurry back home. 'Too much air round me,' she said. 'I need walls. Walls to cling to, slide along. Something reliable behind me so I know nobody can sneak up and take me unawares.' A routine was established. Martha took her to the hospital for check-ups and along the prom for her daily walk. Charlie picked up Evie from school and brought her home.

The Charlie bit pleased Sophie. She enjoyed his gentleness, plus he made an excellent cup of tea. His dog, despite its dubious digestive system, brought a certain energy and completeness to the household. In fact, Sophie had started to consider getting a puppy. But for the moment a grown-up, house-trained visiting pet fitted the bill.

She wished she hadn't sent Duncan packing. He was puppyish. If she wanted to walk, he'd happily amble along with her chatting about his work. He'd tell her obscure facts about Rasputin, Mary, Queen of Scots, Attila the Hun and other luminaries from the distant past. These facts would briefly fascinate her before vanishing from her brain for ever. But it had been fleetingly pleasant to dally with strange facts. And it would be a relief now to spend time with someone who wasn't Martha and who wouldn't loom over her, stare piercingly at her, searching her face for expressions of pain, and, gripping her elbow, asking for the umpteenth time if she was all right. It would be a step towards being normal again.

The business of returning to normal bothered her. When did it happen? How long did it take to get better? 'Because, quite frankly, I'm fed up of feeling like this.'

'Like what?' Charlie was sitting across from her at her kitchen table. He and Murphy had done their duty and brought Evie safely home and he had brewed a pot of tea and laid out a plate of biscuits. It was a ritual they enjoyed. He hoped they might continue with it after Sophie was fit enough to walk to school and his collecting Evie duties were over. He liked routines. Involving himself in them day in day out gave him quiet comfort that all was well in his world.

'What makes you think you'll suddenly get better?' he said, and took a caramel wafer.

'Won't I?'

'No. Physically you'll improve. You'll notice your aches and pains aren't so achy and painy and you'll move about more easily and that'll be fine. But emotionally, getting better's a whole different ball game.' He unwrapped the biscuit, took a bite, made a face and looked at it in disgust.

'They're not meant for you. I'd have thought you'd be more of a ginger snap man. What do you mean, a whole different ball game?' Sophie asked him.

'I mean emotional scars don't heal in the same way. You don't wake up and find you're better. I sometimes think you don't ever get better. You just add the emotional hurt to your emotional baggage and carry on with your life. You just get better at hiding the pain.'

'I don't like the thought of that at all. I just want to feel normal.'

'You'll have to redefine normal. Now normal for you will be not really enjoying walking but doing it anyway, having aches and pains, worrying about Martha, enjoying seeing Evie grow up, feeling a bit scared when you are out alone because you got attacked and other stuff I don't know about because it happened before I got to know you. Plus the fear of getting attacked again.'

'And what is normal for you?'

Charlie stared over the rim of his cup and said he didn't know. 'I've forgotten, or rather I've lost track of who I am. I had it going perfectly. A good solid routine. Coming and going at regular times. Bacon roll at quarter to eleven. Everything in the right pocket. Not thinking about upsetting stuff. But it's all beginning to fall apart.'

'Martha?'

'I think so.' Charlie sighed.

Sophie watched him cross to the cooker, fill the kettle and put it on to boil. She knew he wasn't a man who was comfortable in other people's homes and certainly would never put on the kettle without being invited to do so. Even then he'd feel like an interloper. But he was relaxed here. Boiling Sophie's kettle and making a fresh pot of tea without being asked was all right. In fact it was expected of him. It was a small rite of passage that marked him as accepted in the household. She suspected he enjoyed it.

'Perhaps you shouldn't have hired her,' said Sophie.

'Oh, no. I like having her around. I like watching her work. She bites the inside of her cheek when she's concentrating. She's got dimples when she smiles. I like the one on the left. She's bossy, though.'

'Oh, for heavens' sake Charlie. You've really fallen for her.'

He didn't deny it. He made the tea and brought the pot to the table. 'Is it obvious?'

Sophie poured. 'You have just gone misty-eyed talking about my daughter's dimples. And you're her boss and you have for the past couple of weeks left your work to go and collect her daughter from school. Not many bosses do that. They have a business to run.'

'There's that. So it's really obvious then?'

'Not to Martha. She's the one you have to worry about.'

'I know. If she finds out, she may leave her job and I'll never see her again. But if she doesn't find out, she'll never know and she could meet someone else. Or she might feel the same and not tell me. And I wouldn't know how she felt. It's just awful.'

'You're not very good at this, are you?'

'No. Never done it before.'

'Never courted a woman? Done a bit of wooing?'

'There have been women. But no wooing. They were just there then not there.'

'You had crushes, though. Crushes are universal and they've been happening since the beginning of time. I had a crush.'

'You did?'

'There was a time when I was young and fell in love with inappropriate people. I didn't realise it at the time, but it was lovely. I can say that I thoroughly enjoyed being miserable. I wallowed in sorrow.'

'What came of it?'

'Nothing. I fell in love with Martin in the end and I was happy. Most of the time, anyway.'

'That's probably as good as it gets.'

Sophie cupped her chin in her palm and considered him. 'You know nothing about love, do you?'

He shrugged.

'Martha told me about your mother. She rejected you. It might have broken her heart.'

'No. I don't think so. I was roundly rejected. I've got used to the idea. I just have to make sure it doesn't happen again. No more pain.'

A voice from the living room, Evie teaching Murphy to speak French. 'Gâteau,' she said. 'Can you say that?'

Charlie said, 'Evie knows French?'

'Gâteau and bonjour. That's it.'

'It's almost enough.'

A string of gulls floated past the window. The sky was late afternoon blue, barely a cloud. Four-thirty, a time of day he loved. There was the promise of evening. The world would shut down for the day. He could go home and forget about Bernice Stokes and other worries such as being in love with Martha. He'd cook a meal – something simple tonight, he thought, pasta with clams – then he'd settle on the sofa with Murphy and imagine what it would be like to be happy.

Sophie said, 'You could just about get by with those two words. Cake and hello. The world would be pleasant enough if that's all we had to say to one another.'

They smiled, considering the possibilities of getting by in the world using only two words. 'It'd just be a matter of how you said them,' Charlie said.

He loved these afternoon chats. And felt guilty that he was glad Sophie had been attacked. If she hadn't she'd be able to collect Evie and he wouldn't ever have come to sit in this kitchen drinking tea. Was this what it was like to have a family? To just be with someone and feel relaxed enough to talk about anything? It was simpler than that. To just be, that was it. All a person had to do was just be who they were. It sounded so easy. But he found it incredibly hard. Verging on impossible.

'You suit your life,' he said to Sophie.

'What an odd thing to say. Of course I suit my life. I live it.'

'I know. But I deal with people who didn't have a life that fitted them, so they went off looking for one that did.'

Sophie was intrigued that Charlie thought of life as a coat, something that people put on, something that ought to fit. Life was something that happened to him, a surprise. She supposed Charlie thought his life was like a wrong coat he'd picked up in a cloakroom by mistake.

'This morning I spent time talking to a woman, a client, who really didn't fit her life,' he told her. 'I realised she didn't suit her house. She didn't look as if she belonged in it. There was nothing.

No pictures on the walls. No knick-knacks or photographs. No books.' He shook his head. 'Nothing.'

'I suppose that is odd. Most people have something on a shelf or hanging on a wall.'

'Something to remind them who they are and what they want to be or that they were happy once,' said Charlie. 'I've noticed that.' He leaned forward. 'There's more. After I left, as I was collecting my bike, I peeked through the window into the living room. There was my client in the arms of the man she asked me to find.'

Sophie said, 'Goodness. What did you do? Did you go back in and demand an explanation?'

'I ran away. I couldn't make sense of it. I thought they might be laughing at me. Or they might be duping me and I couldn't think why. So I got on my bike and cycled away as fast as I could. I can see myself flying down the street, jacket flapping behind me, and my face set with urgency.' He stuck out his jaw. 'Like this.'

'You should have confronted them both. There's something very strange going on.'

'I know. But I'm not good at confrontation. I'm beginning to realise I'm not good at anything that involves other people. I'm thinking I'm not very good at being me.'

Sophie snorted and told him not to talk nonsense. 'There's something going on and it's up to you to find out what.' She folded her arms and confirmed her instruction with a nod.

It wasn't what he wanted to hear. He wanted her to tenderly pat his arm and tell him not to bother. If there were nasty suspicious goings on, he was best out of it. But no, she was urging him on, keen for him to get wired in and solve the mystery.

'I was hoping you'd tell me to walk away.'

'Oh, you can't do that. You have to stand your ground. You can't let people use you. There's a piece of motherly advice.'

'Thank you. It wasn't really what I wanted to hear.'

'That's the snag about motherly advice. Nobody wants it.'

Charlie nodded.

'But of course,' said Sophie, 'as a mother I can't help dishing out advice. It's part of the job. And it doesn't stop. You don't retire from motherhood. You go on and on handing out advice nobody wants, can't help it.'

Charlie shrugged and said that he wouldn't know.

'I'll offer some more advice. I'd check up on the client who doesn't fit the life she lets you see.'

He stood. 'Yep. Good plan. I should do that.' He headed towards the door. 'See you tomorrow.'

'I'll have more advice for you. I can see you're keen. Unlike my daughter who stopped listening to me when she was thirteen. Mostly my advice is don't.'

'Don't what?'

'Just don't. Don't do anything you're tempted to do. It'll only lead to tears.'

'That's probably the best advice I've ever been given. So, I'll do what's expected and ignore it,' said Charlie. 'To use one of our acceptable two words, cake till I see you again.'

'Hello,' said Sophie. She flickered her fingers, a small goodbye wave.

He flickered back. Then felt a little embarrassed about it. Waving wasn't his thing. Even over small distances to someone he liked.

Still, he smiled as he walked to his office. It amused him to consider a world with only two words, cake and hello. And he felt comforted to be offered advice he knew he wouldn't take.

35

Optimism Never Occurred to Me

Charlie wondered what Martha would buy in the newsagent's. He reckoned chocolate and a magazine. She needed to make a reasonable couple of purchases as she quizzed the shopkeeper about the house Bernice claimed was hers. Then again, he thought, Martha might buy crisps. Crisps would be good.

A sadness had descended on him a couple of days ago. It was a fairly regular visitor. He imagined it as an external thing, a cloud that enveloped him from time to time. It blurred his thoughts, made him slow to react. He was viewing his world from behind a Perspex sheet, voices were muffled, and he was going through his day as if on autopilot. It tired him. He slept a lot.

He was sure he knew a lot about missing people, and was proud of this. He fancied he understood the human condition. People disappeared because of debt or because they found themselves living a life that had become unbearable or they had become convinced their family and friends would be happier without them. They ran away. And often he would find them. He raked through past lives. He followed trails. He realised that people didn't act randomly. They returned to where they had been happy or they moved to where they'd dreamed they'd be happy.

Of course, some people vanished. They walked out of their homes and were never seen again. They left behind grieving families gasping with pain, guilt and bewilderment. Then again, Charlie had discovered that some people wanted to be found.

They couldn't think of any other way of expressing their misery than disappearing for a while.

Martha slid into the seat beside him. 'Here.' She handed him a Mars bar.

'Chocolate,' he said. 'Thought so.'

'And two pens and a notebook. Can't resist stationery. You were right, the newsagent knows all about what's going on in the neighbourhood.'

'Newsagents know how you vote on account of the paper you take. They know if you're away and when you're coming back. They know stuff.'

It had taken Martha fifteen minutes to discover that the house Bernice claimed to be her own belonged to George Robertson, an accountant who'd been posted to India three months after moving in. He was due home in a few weeks and had hired an interior designer to tickle the house up before he moved back in. 'The designer's called Bernice Stokes.'

'She's using her own name?'

'It's a scam,' said Martha.

'I know that. But what has it got to do with me? Why get me to find someone who wasn't missing? What is it all about?'

'Dunno.'

'And I dunno.' He sighed. 'It's quiet here. Calm. You get the feeling nothing much happens.'

'It's the suburbs. Things happen. People just keep it under wraps.'

'I know. But looking around, it feels safe. It's light. There are trees and flowers and hedges.' He took a deep bite of his Mars bar.

'What brought this on?'

'I used to have a constant knot in the stomach. It faded as I got older. Now it's back. That feeling of dread. Something bad is going to happen.'

'You're being silly. Nothing bad is going to happen.'

'I feel it in my gut.'

'You're a doom-monger. How can you be like that? So positively, assertively negative?'

'You should talk, you're the most negative person I know.'

'Yes, but at least I'm not gloomy about it. Just certain events in my life have stripped me of my optimism.'

Charlie said, 'Optimism never occurred to me.'

They ate their chocolate, both thinking, but not saying, it was too sweet. Or maybe natural born pessimists grew out of confectionery. Silently wrestling with these gloomy thoughts they watched Bernice and Brendan Stokes walk past the car and on to the end of the street.

It took a moment or two for them to realise who they were looking at. 'Where are they going?' Martha wondered.

'Dunno.'

'We should follow them.'

'I think they'll know we're behind them.'

'So what do we do?'

'Go home. Make a cup of tea. Eat a bun.'

'But what if that pair are up to no good?'

'Let them be up to no good. What are we going to do about it? Rush to stop them? Get punched? No. Accept we are cowards. Feel the fear.'

'But . . .' said Martha.

'But nothing. You don't know where they might be going. To the library or perhaps one of them has a doctor's appointment or maybe they're off to the supermarket to buy toilet rolls. Even the vilest of criminals must take time off for ordinary things.'

'These two are not nice people. Who knows what nasty things they're doing. It is our duty to find out and put a stop to it.' Martha sounded righteous.

Charlie gave her a cold look. 'Get you. If you want to follow these two, do it. Me, I'm going home. I've had enough. This day, this place, this sunshine is making me sad.' He sighed. 'I grew up bored, scared and itchy.'

'Bored I understand,' said Martha. 'What were you scared of?'

'I don't know. My Aunt Ella was scared, she must have thought the police were going to come for her because she abducted me. She passed the fear on. And itchy was because of the woolly jumpers she knitted. I wore them winter and summer. Kids here are the colour of honey and cycling about in soft cotton T-shirts. They're happy, busy and comfortably clothed. It makes me want to cry. All the things I missed.'

'So cry,' Martha told him.

'I can't. I've told myself it's OK. But no tears come.'

She put her hand on his arm. 'You should let go and cry. Nothing beats a good cry. It's awfully good for you.'

He stared at the hand that was placed so gently on his arm. It was a lovely hand, pale, long fingers, nails painted a subtle pearlite. The colour reminded him of a Shell petrol pump. That hand had touched cheeks, stroked hair. It pained him to think of all the things that hand had done. But not to him. So he threw his Mars bar out of the car window. Well, a chap had to do something.

'Why the hell did you do that?' Martha glared at him.

'I was hoping for crisps. I like salty things.'

'Well, you go and pick it up. That's littering.' The hand was removed from his arm. A long pale finger pointed in the direction of the discarded Mars bar. 'Go on. You can't leave it there.'

Sheepishly Charlie got out of the car and retrieved the chocolate. It had a fine layer of grit on the bitten end. Back in the passenger seat, he wrapped it in his handkerchief and put it in his pocket. So, he'd had his first tiff with Martha. A tiff and he hadn't yet kissed her for real or held that lovely hand in his. Still, something had happened. The scolding, the finger wagging had stirred something inside him. It was as if a small wind had started up and shifted the black cloud. He thought it might drift away and leave him alone.

36

Good at Living

Sophie, thinking she ought to speed up her healing process by walking, risked going out. She hoped to bump into Charlie, who was fetching Evie from school. Martha had gone to the dentist. Finding the office locked, she'd gone to Charlie's house and knocked on the door.

Brenda answered. Sophie stared at her, taking in her ancient leathery face draped with a mane of dazzlingly shiny auburn hair, and said, 'I'm looking for Charlie.'

'Gone to the shops with the little one,' Brenda told her. 'Off to buy a card for Martha's birthday.'

'Oh, I usually do that. I leave it till the day before, though.'

'Oh, you don't want to do that. No pleasure in that. You want to have the card and the gift in plenty time so you can look at them and anticipate handing them over.'

Sophie said she hadn't thought of that, and felt a tad insensitive. This woman whose wildly coloured hair was at odds with her time-raddled face and saddened eyes went up in her estimation.

'Are you Charlie's lodger?'

'Nah,' said Brenda. 'I'm one of the found.'

It sounded religious. For a bewildered moment Sophie wondered if this woman and Charlie were part of a strange obscure sect. But no, that couldn't possibly be. Not Charlie.

'I was on the street. Missing. Well, missing from my family that I didn't want to know any more. But I wasn't missing from me.

I knew where I was. Charlie found me. Didn't tell my family. He brought me here when it was raining. And here I still am.'

'Well, that's lovely.' Sophie stared at Brenda's hair. It was so gloriously shiny. It was mesmerising.

Brenda said, 'No, it isn't.'

'Isn't what?'

'A wig. It's real. I'm letting my hair be outrageous. I'm giving it the youth I never had. Are you Martha's mother? You better come in.' She stepped back, held the door open.

Sophie was led into the communal kitchen. It was here the people Martha called Charlie's leftovers prepared their meals, did their laundry and chatted about their harsh past lives.

Charlie had his own small pristine private kitchen where he prepared gourmet meals and carefully brewed perfect coffee. This room, however, was bright, white walls covered with framed theatre posters, a large pine table, cream units and the usual washing machine, fridge and oven. A radio played pop songs. Brenda turned it off. 'You're shuffling well. Are you getting over being beaten up?'

'Slowly. Healing takes ages. I have to sleep sitting up.'

'I've done that often enough myself.' For a small moment Brenda drifted into memories. 'I won't say happy days. They weren't.'

'Do you do anything? Work?'

'Work? It's hard to get a job when you've been off the face of the earth for years. People ask what experience you have and you say, "I can survive sleeping in doorways and know which restaurants don't mind you picking food from their bins." Such an answer is unlikely to impress. But I pay my way. I clean. I know about plumbing and some carpentry. Mostly I tell Charlie when things need fixing and make sure he gets someone in to do the job. A man like Charlie needs nagged. Coffee?'

Sophie nodded. 'Thank you. Are you the only one?'

'Nah. There're others. They come and go. And there's Chrissie.

She's new. Charlie found her in the gardens near her house. She felt safe there. Safe's important.'

Sophie agreed. 'Oh, I like safe. There's nothing better than being snug and warm in bed when the wind is blasting and rain is crashing against the windowpane. That's safe at its best. And I always enjoy it more if I hear someone outside walking about in the weather.' She nodded, wistful for some fierce weather to make snuggling in bed a special treat, and caught Brenda's scathing stare.

Here was a woman who'd stood alone suffering whatever the elements threw at her. She did not appreciate being reminded of nights when cold had throbbed, aching in her joints, and the drumming icy rain had numbed her insensible. Brenda was unimpressed to hear someone coo that the delights of a cosy bed had been heightened by thinking about the misery of those who were out in the foul freezing weather. And suffering. 'No doubt when you're safe you can let go and really sleep knowing you won't wake up with someone with foul breath and a knife looming over you. Or peeing on you. You lose your social skills on the street.'

Sophie reddened and said, 'I understand about finding a place of safety. There's a secret spot in my garden, just behind the lilac tree. The grass is soft, in spring the air is scented and nobody can see you. You can gather your breath there. It's where I went all the time after my husband died. I could cry there.'

'Weep?' said Brenda. 'When you lose your keys you cry. When you lose the one you love most in the world, you weep.'

'I'll give you that,' said Sophie. 'I wept behind the lilac tree.' She sipped the coffee Brenda had put in front of her. Sniffed. Memories of time behind the lilac tree brought tears.

'There you go,' said Brenda. 'It's when you move on with your life the guilt sets in. Being happy, laughing, working, watching television without him. It's too bloody hard.' Brenda pointed upwards to the room above. 'Chrissie's mourning. She's staring into space, sleeping and eating.'

'Who is she mourning?'

'Herself. The life she missed on account of being battered and bullied by her husband, leaving him for a con man and ending up broke and homeless.' She leaned over, tapped Sophie's arm. 'You could do with Chrissie. When she's not eating or sleeping or staring into space she bakes.'

Sophie raised her eyebrows. 'Oh, yes? What does she bake?'

'Excellent cakes, scones, biscuits, other things. She could help you now that you're shuffling. She could beat mixtures and bend down to put things in the oven.'

'I do specialist cakes.'

'So? You could sit still and tell her what to do. Nothing better than sitting still and bossing folk about.'

Sophie stared, considering this. After all she hadn't met Chrissie, knew nothing about her.

'Don't sit there thinking. Say yes. It's your chance to help a sad and lonely woman. What right have you to deny her?'

'Well, none when you put it like that. Only I've no money to pay her.'

'Money, money – it's all you middle-class suburbanites think about. This isn't about money, it's about caring for another. Letting your compassion show. Animals show their feelings. Dogs wag their tails and leap about with joy when they see you. When emotions hit they howl, bark or whine. All sorts of animals just go with the flow. Not us people. We hide from our emotions. Sometimes I think us humans are not very good at living.'

'OK,' said Sophie, 'she can come and help me bake.'

Sophie walked slowly home. Trying not to shuffle was painful. Her mood was not lightened by the new worry that she was not very good at living. The more she thought about it the more she considered it to be true.

She'd asked Brenda, 'What do you mean us humans are not very good at living?'

Brenda had leaned over the table. 'I saw you people who had

all you could want and it seemed to me none of you appreciated it. How do you think I felt standing on the pavement watching you go by? Me standing there with all I owned in a couple of plastic bags.'

'I don't know.'

'I wasn't impressed.'

Later, bustling along the High Street, she spotted Charlie and Evie ahead of her and yelled, 'Hello there, you two.' And waved.

They turned. She could tell from their expressions that she was overdoing it. The wave was too flamboyant, the friendly greeting too loud, too enthusiastic. They were astonished and more than a little embarrassed. She couldn't stop. She kept waving as she approached them and was still waving when she was near enough to touch them. She pointed across to the café. 'Let's have milkshakes. I love a milkshake.' This was ridiculous. She didn't love a milkshake. She really wanted a cup of tea.

In the café, she examined the card and the silk scarf Evie had bought for Martha's birthday and knew that Charlie had chosen the scarf. She saw now that Charlie, afraid to let Martha know his feelings for her, would give her an expensive scarf through her daughter. He would give her something like a box of chocolates and say it was from Murphy. He'd hide his feelings. And if Martha cared for him, she'd hide that, too. They weren't good at living either. She looked at Evie, who was holding the scarf against her cheek. 'Can't wait to give this to Mum.'

Well, maybe the girl had the hang of showing her feelings. It would fade in time, no doubt. And here was she, Sophie, smiling too much at the prospect of a chocolate milkshake she didn't want. It was tiring. On the whole she decided melancholy was easier.

Afterwards they picked up Murphy from the office and walked home, Evie charging in front with the dog. She waltzed back and forth across the pavement. Sophie shouted, 'Careful. Keep away from the road.'

'She's fine,' Charlie said.

'She could get run over and die. I've had enough of death. It ought to be banned.'

'The world would be a little crowded if it was,' said Charlie. 'We need to make room for new young people.'

'People who are good at living.'

'Ah, Sophie. You've been talking to Brenda. She is obsessed with people being good at living. Or, actually, she's obsessed with people who aren't good at it. She doesn't understand them.'

'Not being good at being alive comes naturally.'

'Yes. I'm good at failing to be happy. In fact, Brenda gave me Murphy to cheer me up. She said I needed a friend.'

'Well, a puppy would help there.'

'He wasn't a puppy. He was like Brenda. He'd been abused. He was underfed and flea-bitten. But he loved me. Brenda told me he was willing to give human beings and life another go.'

'You've done a wonderful job with him. He's lovely except for the indiscretions.'

'Yes. I envy his lust for life. His lack of inhibitions.'

Sophie said, 'I think an inhibition or two is necessary. If only to ensure the enjoyment of life of innocent bystanders.'

Charlie said, 'I'm one of life's innocent bystanders. I never join in.'

Sophie agreed. 'Me too. Fun? Enjoyment? What, pray, are these things?'

Charlie blew out his cheeks, shook his head. 'A thought,' he said. 'The women Brendan visits. Innocent bystanders. I need to talk to them.'

37

The Exploding Suit

Martha was haunted by the moment her husband sprinted away from her. It played and replayed in her mind. The memory of him running would creep up on her if she was still, or doing some routine job that required no concentration, and make her shake her head and say no. In low moments she could visit it so she could dip even lower. Sometimes she needed as much pain as she could muster.

It was like crystal, that memory. She was standing holding the railings of Queen Street Gardens watching Jamie run. She held Evie's hand. The child was still peevish over the loss of her favourite chip. The floods of tears had taken their toll; her eyes were puffy and she was sniffing. Traffic rushed past. A blackbird hopped across the grass on the other side of the fence. Jamie ran and ran. He didn't look back.

She could see the colours of that day. The grass, a maroon bus trundling by, Evie's blue woollen mittens, her red duffel coat, Jamie's grey suit, her own black patent leather shoes. Whenever she thought about it, she cried. Back then it had been for herself, for Evie and later for the baby she'd lost. Now it was out of guilt. Jamie had fled the life she'd foisted on him. During her brief stint on the road she'd known cold, hunger, had worried about finding a place to sleep at night. She'd spent nights in the back of a van scared of noises – scrapings, rustlings – outside. She'd washed in public toilets.

When the band broke up she'd needed security. Every night

she'd slid into bed and thanked the manufacturer of her cotton sheets for their softness. For a while she'd bathed several times a day. Just being clean was a joy.

'A small home is all you need,' she'd once said to Jamie.

He'd made a funny noise and walked out of the room. Now she knew he'd snorted and put some small distance between them. He'd probably wanted to smack her. Oh, how he'd disagreed with her. And now, three years on, she didn't agree with herself either. Working for Charlie, living with her mother in that large tumbledown, frankly shabby flat, she was almost happy. She thought that was as good as it got.

She needed to know if Jamie was almost happy, too. Mornings, after she'd dropped Evie at school, she'd take a half-hour detour drive on the way to work. She'd park across the square from Jamie's flat and stare up at the windows. There were three. Blue blankets covered two; the third was draped with a Persian rug. As there was never any sign of life in the rooms behind the drapes Martha assumed that Jamie and his new love were late risers. Or maybe they didn't like the cruel blast of early sun and kept their living space dim. She imagined them moving quietly, drinking coffee, listening to music. She decided she wouldn't spot any goings-on at this time of day and should switch to night spying.

This was easier than morning snooping. On school nights Evie was in bed by eight o'clock and Sophie retired early because sitting up in bed reading was more comfortable than spending the evening on the sofa watching television. Just after nine Martha would drive up to Jamie's flat and spend a fretful couple of hours staring up at his windows. The curtains would be pulled back. Sometimes she'd see people up there – shapes drifting past the window. She fancied that from time to time they were dancing. She was sure the woman up there was wearing a long floaty thing and was swaying gracefully in time to music. She twirled, waved her arms above her head. But she was a shadow. Martha couldn't see her face.

Once she saw Jamie leave the building just after ten. He returned twenty minutes later with a take-away meal. He stood outside, whistled and held it aloft to a group gathered upstairs. They waved and whistled back and told him to hurry up with the food, man. It made Martha feel left out and lonely. She listened to Pink Floyd on the radio. It suited her mood.

From time to time Jamie would come to the window and gaze out at the night. Often he would sit on the windowsill, his back to her; he seemed to be talking at length, expounding, gesticulating. Martha hurt. He'd never done this with her.

She became obsessed. She was addicted to going to stare up at the flat imagining the lives of the people who lived there. The Jamie she observed from her car was nothing like the Jamie she'd known three years ago. That Jamie had been distant, withdrawn, had spent hours alone in his shed listening to his albums. This Jamie seemed to be friendly, relaxed, chatty. Martha winced to remember how unhappy the old Jamie had been. She was sure his misery was down to her.

It was Thursday, her favourite spying night. The night before the weekend started. Jamie might be relaxed and do something that made her surveillance worthwhile. At half-past nine she saw him at the window. He was leaning on the sill, head on the pane, staring out over the rooftops towards the river. He seemed to sigh and then turned and walked away. Martha waited for him to come back. But he didn't.

She listened to the radio. 'Mrs Robinson', a song she liked. She lingered, listening, tapping her fingers on the steering wheel, singing along. She was enjoying herself, didn't really register the thump on the car roof. The next thump shook the car. For a second or two Martha didn't know what was happening. She stared up at the roof. The pounding got louder, rhythmic. 'Open the window, Martha. Open the window, Martha.'

Jamie appeared at the window, banging the glass with the side of his fist. 'Bitch. Bitch.' Red with fury, spittle sparking from his mouth, he punched the glass so hard Martha thought it would smash. Shaking, fearful, she wound it down. 'Stop it.'

'You stop. You stop coming round here watching me. You stop spying.' He reached in, grabbed Martha's jacket and yanked her towards him. 'I've got something to show you, Martha.'

Behind Jamie a small crowd was gathering. She doubted anybody would come to her rescue. The crowd, hands in pockets, had settled down to watch. Joining in was not on the cards.

Jamie held up a suit on a hanger. She recognised it. His grey work suit. The only thing extraordinary about it was its ordinariness. Grey jacket, three buttons, grey trousers. Martha thought it smelled vaguely of petrol.

'See this, bitch. See this. It's what I wore when I was with you. You got me to marry you. You had a baby. You watched me go to work every day. To a job I hated in a suit I hated. I thought my life was over and I wasn't even twenty-four. You took my life. You turned me into a drab little nowhere man doing the nine-to-five. A man I hated. Then you tell me the baby isn't mine. My life. My life. That job. In this suit. You bitch.'

Martha noticed that a couple of men in the gathering crowd were cheering.

Jamie wept with fury. 'Things I wanted to do. My dreams. All lost because you lied to me.'

He took a Zippo lighter from his jeans pocket. Flicked it open, sparked a flame. 'This is what I think of you and this fucking suit.' He held the lighter to the trousers. The suit exploded. Fire shot up through the jacket, whooshed towards the sky. Leaping flames gushed and sparked. Jamie threw the hated burning thing to the ground and jumped back. A gust of wind caught it, set the flames searing hotter, wilder, and lifted the burning fabric towards the crowd. The onlookers scattered, pushing into one another. Running backwards, not wanting to miss the show, but fearful of getting burned. The street reeked of petrol and smouldering polyester. Jamie looked terrified. Horrified at what he'd just done.

'Jamie Walters, fucking stop it. What are you doing?'

'I'm burning my old life. I'm setting fire to this effigy of a time I hated.' He pointed at Martha. 'You know what she did. She lied. She fucked up my life.' His voice was raw, cracked, stretched beyond its normal range.

Martha was bent over the steering wheel, heaving in air. The smell was awful. She coughed. Heard sirens in the distance. She was dizzy, finding it hard to focus. She stared at the woman who had shouted at Jamie. She looked familiar. Martha lifted the hem of her T-shirt to wipe her face. Rubbed her eyes. 'Jesus. Grace. It's Grace.'

'It was always Grace,' shouted Jamie.

Martha wiped her face again, started the car revved wildly, and, tyres squealing, took off. She shot into the night-time traffic, no signalling, no pausing to check the road was clear. She hurtled forward, had to get away. Teary-eyed, sweaty, nostrils lined with the foul smell of smouldering polyester, she careened into a thick howl of blasting horns, slamming brakes and flashing lights. She whirled the car into the inside lane and battered away from the terrible scene. The enraged husband and his new love – her nemesis.

She thundered along London Road, staring ahead, white-knuckling the steering wheel. Then she pulled over and stopped. Scenes of moments ago played in her head. She couldn't believe it. Spread her hands before her, watched them trembling and swore quietly. She examined her face in the rear-view mirror. Her eyes were swollen. Her throat raw. She couldn't go home like this.

38

Cheers to All of Yez

Charlie opened the door and took in the state of her – shaking, tear-stained, mascara running. 'Jesus.' He noticed an odd reek of charred cloth and petrol. He put his arm round her and steered her indoors to his living room. 'What happened?'

'Jamie . . .'

He led her to the sofa, sat her down and stepped back to consider her. Tea? Brandy? Brandy, he decided. He opened a bottle, fetched ice from the kitchen and laid out two glasses. He was delaying the moment when he'd hear her story while he sorted out his feelings. Please don't let Jamie have hit her, he thought. He dreaded the idea of having to go and hit him back. That would lead to a fight which he'd inevitable lose and he'd end up face down in the street. Back in his fighting days he'd seen enough gutters close up and didn't want to visit any more. He wasn't keen on the pain either.

He gave Martha her drink and asked, 'What about Jamie?'

She told him.

He took Martha's hand, turned it over, drew his thumb across her palm. 'So what were you doing parked outside Jamie's flat?'

'Spying.'

'Why?'

'I needed to know all about him. Everything. What he was doing. Who he was with. Absolutely everything.'

'Isn't that snooping?'

'Of course it's bloody snooping. I'm a snoop. I'm a spy. I'm not very nice. Oh, look at me from the outside, my clothes are clean and ironed, my hair's brushed, I'm wearing lipstick, shoes polished – anyone would think I was a good, respectable, trustworthy woman. But I'm not.' She pointed to herself. 'In here I'm grubby. I have nasty thoughts. I want Jamie to be unhappy. I'm not very nice. I don't like me at all.'

'Know what you mean. I don't like me either.'

'You don't?'

'Nah. Not really. I haven't lived up to my expectations. Cowboy, trumpeter and generally cool dude. Still, I like you.'

'You do?'

Planning to pull her to him sometime soon, he slid his arm along the back of the sofa so it rested behind her head. 'Of course I like you. Even if your imaginary horse had a better name than mine. Durango. I could hate you for having such an excellent name.' They sat in silence staring ahead, sipping their drinks.

'It is a good name,' said Martha. 'I had a fertile mind back when I was a child. I had a keen imagination. Don't know what happened to it.'

'It probably got rusty after you stopped using it on account of growing up and starting to think about what to make for tea instead of enjoying yourself wallowing in your imaginings.'

'I was happy back then. It was before my life got complicated. Before I got pregnant and scared and duped a perfectly reasonable man into marrying me and making me respectable. I think about it and think about it. What was I scared of? People's opinion of me? I was a coward. I wasn't very rock'n'roll.'

Charlie said, 'Not many people are when it comes to telling their mother they're in the family way.'

Martha supposed this was true. 'Men,' she said. 'Why are they so butch? So blokey. I mean, burning a suit. Shouting. It wasn't necessary.'

'It was. He'd a lot of anger to get out into the world.'

'He didn't have to take it out on me.'

'Martha, I rather think he did.'

'He didn't need to be so shouty. I had no idea he was like that. The rage. The passion. When he lived with me he was mild, easygoing. He shrugged a lot.'

Charlie said, 'Ah.' As if the shrugging explained everything.

'Then he's suddenly like that. Yelling. Furious. Burning a suit for heavens' sake. I don't understand men. There's no let-up to their being men. Like if you ask a man what he wants to eat, he'll say steak. Never just a salad with a slice of wholemeal bread on the side. Or a cucumber sandwich.'

Charlie had been on the verge of slipping his arm round Martha's shoulders. But the steak accusation struck home. He was fond of a steak.

'It's all meat with men. Steak and chips. Steak and chips and sex,' said Martha.

Charlie withdrew his arm. He felt insensitive, boorish and blokey, obsessed with sex and large chunks of meat. So he politely asked Martha if she'd like a top-up.

She held out her glass. 'Then there's Grace.'

'Yes, there's Grace.'

'You knew about Grace? You knew she was here in town shacking up with my husband?'

'I had an inkling. I wondered about it. Then I saw her that day when I went to pick up Evie. She was beautiful. She was everything you said she was and I wondered some more.'

'She got my guitar and my husband.' Martha took a huge gulp of her brandy, coughed. Her eyes filled.

Charlie wondered if the tears were a result of the wild swig or was she suffering from shock and sorrow?

'I mean,' said Martha, 'that woman got everything I wanted. She got the manager, the recording contract, the hit song. She's got the amazing voice, the musical ability. She's beautiful. Beauty just suddenly happened to her. She had a father with a car. Bloody everything. Why did she come back for my husband?'

'Love?'

Martha put down her drink, turned to Charlie. 'Love? Love? She gets that, too?' She raised her hand, spread her fingers and counted Grace's blessings on them, 'Beauty, talent, a hit song, a manager, my guitar, my husband. And she's got a child, a son. And she gets love.'

Martha took up her drink, swigged, coughed again. 'It's really not fair. What do I get? Nothing. When do I get love? I want that. I want all of that.'

Her upper lip trembled. Her eyes glazed.

'There is no fair,' said Charlie. 'Fair doesn't exist.'

'It's my turn,' said Martha. 'She's got everything, now it's my turn to get something.'

Tears now. She swallowed, wiped her nose with the back of her hand. Charlie reached for her, took her to him.

'It'll be OK.'

'She's even got a bloody father. I want a home of my own. I want someone to love me. I want that red guitar. I want a father with a car. It's my turn.'

Charlie wanted to tell her life didn't work like that, but couldn't. Instead he stroked her back, felt her tears soak his shirt and said, 'It's your turn soon. Good things will come to you.'

He stroked Martha's back. Smelled her hair – a soft herby shampoo. He put his lips to the top of her head. He wasn't in luck tonight. The only thing that would happen would be his shirt getting damper and damper. Martha sobbed. He reached over and picked up her brandy. No sex for him, then. He raised the glass to the empty room, 'Cheers.' Cheers to all his ghosts. His mother who didn't want him, his father who also didn't want him, his aunt who wasn't his aunt and who had abducted him, 'Cheers to all of yez.' He drained the glass. And felt the seeping dampness of his shirt.

39

Bastards Bastards Bastards

'You need to be bolder. You need to be noticed. You need flashy cake boxes in bright colours. You need slogans. You need people to know that if it's not a Sophie cake then it's not a cake.'

'I don't think so,' said Sophie. 'I'm not that kind of person. I'm a woman of a certain undesirable age with large hips and a bit of an embarrassing bum. The only good thing about that is I don't see it. But it comes with me everywhere I go. And I fear that people might think it got the way it is through my having eaten too much of my own product.'

'So you should celebrate it.' Chrissie Lewis examined her fingernails as she spoke. The gesture made her seem superior. Sophie marvelled. Chrissie was small, had recently been rescued from living on the streets yet she was regal, proud and had the bearing of someone who was convinced she was right about everything. Brenda had sent her to Sophie's kitchen to demonstrate her baking expertise and she had whipped up a sponge.

'I do not feel like celebrating my body. It doesn't deserve it. I hate it,' said Sophie.

'Oh, you shouldn't do that. I love my body. I love being me.'

'You do?' This was fascinating. Until this moment Sophie had presumed nobody liked who they were. Everybody wanted to be someone else. She fancied being Katharine Hepburn.

Chrissie pointed to her face. 'Look at this face. My life is on this face. Look closely; you can see I once was beautiful. Silken creams were spread on this skin. Wonderful food slipped over these lips. Now this face tells of the times I overdid things, squandered a deal of money and ended on the streets. The face says it all. It isn't pretty any more and I wouldn't change it. I'm proud of this face.' She leaned forward, tapped the table with her finger. 'I worked hard for it.'

'I feel my face just happened to me when I wasn't looking.' Sophie touched her cheek. 'It takes me by surprise every time I look at it. I think, Goodness, is that me? In between glances and occasional stares in the mirror I forget about it.' She stared at Chrissie's face and had a fleeting glimpse of the life written on it. She saw sorrow, loneliness, hardship, worry and uncertainty round the eyes and, leaning closer, saw the remains of beauty, pride and mischief. 'You quite enjoyed yourself, didn't you?'

'I had a lovely time. Years of living with a mean, over-emotional thug of a man who stripped me of my self-respect made me shy, lonely, insecure. Then I came to my senses, fell in love with a man much younger than me and ran away taking a pile of the thug's money. Fifty thousand pounds. There is nothing more satisfying than squandering a nasty, miserly, bullying man's money. It's fun. Plain, simple, outrageously lavish fun.'

Sophie said, 'I don't think plain, simple and outrageously lavish belong in the same sentence.'

'Of course they do. I was lavish with my husband's money. It was delicious revenge for the years of misery he caused. I found it was very easy to be a wastrel. I hugely enjoyed it. Then it was over.' She shrugged. 'Money gone. Lover gone. Me on the streets feeling a bit cold, lonely and frightened, I must admit.' She sniffed, held her nose up to breathe in the cooking smells. 'The cake's ready.'

Sophie nodded towards the clock. 'It needs another few minutes.'

'Nonsense. The cake is ready now. I don't use clocks.' She tapped her nose. 'I use this. The smell turns, darkens and deepens when the cake is done. I have an affinity with cakes. Actually I have an affinity with all sorts of food since there were times when I didn't have any.' She opened the oven door and turned to Sophie. 'Perfect.'

This irritated Sophie. The cake was splendid, and better than any she'd made. Not that her cakes weren't excellent, just that as the creator of excellent cakes, she knew a cake that was more excellent than anything she produced. A pang of jealousy, then.

She felt inadequate in the presence of this woman. Chrissie had lived a full and tempestuous life. And what have I done? she asked herself. Stayed home and baked. Life was an adventure, a rollercoaster ride if you were bold. And she wasn't. A fire in the hearth, a warm bed, food on the table and the contented knowledge that her daughter and granddaughter were safe was all she asked. Well, more or less.

Chrissie eased the cakes from their tins onto a wire rack and left them to cool while she washed up. She dried spoons, spatula and whisk and put them away. Sophie noted that the baking bowl was being placed on the wrong shelf and grudgingly acknowledged that the new position was more convenient than the one she'd chosen. She thought it was probably acceptable to dislike someone who rearranged your kitchen, especially if they made a good job of it.

Yesterday, Duncan had phoned Sophie and asked if she was speaking to him.

'Of course I am,' Sophie had said. She was too proud to tell him she missed him. She found recovering to be a lonely business. Martha and Evie were out most of the day. She was stuck at home and still had to pluck up her courage to step outside. She told him to drop by any time he fancied.

So when the doorbell rang she knew who it was, and groaned. She didn't feel up to standing up and going down the stairs to open the door, and she didn't want to introduce Duncan to Chrissie. Sophie had a gut feeling about her. A notion that this small defiant woman, so firm about her beliefs and proud of how she lost her looks, who had survived life on the streets, would not have a conscience about stealing her man friend.

She gripped the table, rose stiffly and raised her hand to stop Chrissie from answering the door for her. 'I'll go. It'll do me good.'

By the time she got downstairs Duncan had rung the bell another couple of times, and when she opened the door he was at the end of the garden path heading home, having given up on her hospitality. When she called him back, he turned, smiled, and sheepishly retraced his steps. He apologised all the way up the stairs. He was sorry for just dropping in with no prior warning, he was sorry for forgetting to wipe his feet on the mat, he was sorry for not being sympathetic to the pain she must have been suffering the last time he called and for not appreciating the trauma she'd been through.

'Duncan,' said Sophie, 'do me a favour and shut up.'

And he did, but only after apologising for apologising too much. 'I know, I'm a fool. Sorry. Sorry. I can't help saying sorry. Sorry for that.'

He held his breath after that and only exhaled when they reached the kitchen. He stopped at the door, taking in Chrissie. He smiled and crossed the room, holding out his hand. 'Hello, I'm Duncan. Lovely to meet you.'

The man had completely changed. The humble apologetic Duncan disappeared and a lothario appeared in his place. He held Chrissie's hand fractionally longer than was polite. For a jealous moment Sophie thought he was going to press it to his lips. But no, he let her have it back as he gazed into her eyes. From Sophie's vantage point he seemed to be grinning dopily. He sat, spread his arms and said, 'I've got two lovely ladies. Lucky man, me.' He looked from one lovely lady to the other. A man expecting a cup of tea.

Chrissie obliged. Sophie watched. Chrissie filled the kettle, put it on to boil and quizzed Duncan. How long had he known Sophie?

'Years and years,' he told her. 'We were childhood sweethearts.'

'Lovely. Oh, I adore that. And what is it you do?'

'I write. History books. Textbooks, actually. But I enjoy it. Keeps me occupied.'

Chrissie threw back her head and laughed. Too much, Sophie thought. This woman is overdoing the mirth. Now she was making the simple question about what Duncan took in his tea sound nurturing and sexy. When Duncan replied a splash of milk and one spoon of sugar, Chrissie cooed. As if only a man of taste, wit and intelligence would drink his tea in such a way. Sophie took all this in and thought she might weep. It was lonely being in pain observing two people who were approaching old age playing at being sixteen. She wanted them both to go home.

She stood and announced that she was going for a walk, hoping her guests would take this as a hint to leave. But no, they decided to go with her. There was a bustle of coats being brought from the hallway, scarves being flapped, outdoor shoes being hauled on.

Sophie led the way to the front door, walking slowly, clutching the stair banister, a woman in pain. But too proud to let it show. Chrissie and Duncan followed. He was coughing from having hurriedly swigged his tea and its going down the wrong way.

This was Sophie's walk. She was in charge. She led for the first two or three hundred yards, pushing into the day, grimacing against the wind, fearing it might rain. The other two struggled to keep up. But when they got into their stride they walked at Sophie's pace. The three were abreast for a while, chatting about glorious cakes from their past. Then it became obvious that Sophie was out of breath and working hard at maintaining her set pace. She slowed up. Duncan and Chrissie slowed, too. But found this new snail's pace harder than the fierce stride and, without wanting to, moved ahead. Now Sophie was behind. She trailed the other two, listening to their laughter, watching them flirt, and felt forgotten and lonely.

She ached. Hugged herself, keeping the pain warm. She breathed heavily and stepped carefully watching her feet. She was afraid of falling. The loneliness deepened as her friends widened the gap, walking faster, enjoying the sea air. Chrissie linked arms with Duncan and leaned into him. Bitch, thought Sophie. A ripple of anger flashed through her. How dare they behave like that? This was her walk, her idea to come outside into the fresh air. If it hadn't been for her the two striding away from her would still be flirting in the kitchen. At least now they were flirting in a healthier environment.

She stood, breathing in the scents and sounds of the day; the tang of sea air, gulls laughing, a dog barking, children calling. A whole world of things going on and she was alone. And she was sick of it. She was furious with everything, everyone. She'd been alone too long. Cheek of Martin dying like that. Cheek of Chrissie and Duncan marching ahead not looking back. Cheek of people on the beach shouting and laughing and having fun when she was in pain. 'Bastards bastards bastards,' she said. She turned, stomped back home, clutching her coat round her. She heard Chrissie and Duncan call after her. No, she would not acknowledge them.

She marched into John Street, up the path to her door, slammed it behind her and locked it. To hell with them.

40

Mrs Simpson Who Isn't Mrs Simpson

Martha thought it was time to let the Stokes case go. 'Just send the bill and let's get on with other things.'

Charlie disagreed. 'I want to know what's going on. I need to know how it ends.'

'We found Brendan because he wasn't really missing in the first place.'

'We didn't know that when we were looking. I found Chrissie, didn't I?'

'I'll give you that. However, we won't make any money from that case as you haven't told the man who was looking for her that she's been found and therefore can't bill him.'

They were sitting in the car outside the house they'd spied on some weeks ago. They'd come to see Mrs Simpson, the woman they'd started with. They were arguing. The windows were getting steamed. Martha didn't want to be here. Charlie did. Martha was embarrassed by the memory of being shown round a house they had no interest in buying. 'We took advantage of that woman.'

Charlie shrugged and said, 'She was glad of the company. She invited us in.'

'It was a sad, lonely, empty house. Not a home. Pale gaps on the walls where pictures once hung. And a teenager's purple bedroom with no teenager. I hated being in there.'

'Can't say I enjoyed it much. But that's part of the job. We have to do things we don't like in pursuit of the truth.' He opened the car door and climbed out. Leaning down to continue the conversation with Martha, who was still sitting in the driver's seat, he said, 'Someone is taking the piss out of me, using me, and I want to know why.'

Martha got out of the car, leaned on the roof to answer him. 'It's because you're there to be taken the piss out of. That's all. People do things like that.' She had been going to say it was because he was a crap detective, but stopped herself. It was a bit cruel and not entirely true.

Charlie slammed the car door and set off along the pavement. Martha followed. 'Charlie, this isn't necessary. Let's bill Bernice and look for new clients. You haven't made any money since I came to work for you. Not good.'

'Money? There's more to life than that.'

'You might think so. I don't. I'm fond of paying my bills so I can have heat and light. And I'm rather partial to eating, too.'

'Don't worry about it. You'll have food on your plate and light to see what it is.' He swung through the gate and down the path and pressed the doorbell. 'I'm going to get to the bottom of this.'

'Are you wagging your finger at me?'

He looked in surprise at the offending digit. 'Only because you're standing where the finger is pointing. It isn't deliberate.' He shoved his hand into his pocket. Turned to speak to the woman who opened the door. And dried. Couldn't think what to say. 'Um, Mrs Simpson?'

She said, 'Yes.'

She was smaller than she'd seemed from the window of the house across the road. Her face was pale, free of make-up. It was a face used to revealing emotions, and it seemed there had been a lot of emotion.

Charlie looked helpless. His mind was suddenly and embarrassingly empty. And the longer he searched for something to say, the emptier his mind became.

Martha took over. She held out her hand for Mrs Simpson to

shake. 'We're from the Be Kindly Missing Persons Bureau. We wondered if we could talk to you about your husband.'

'Oh, Bernice said you might call. You better come in, then.' Mrs Simpson stepped back to open the door wider and let the two in. 'Excuse the mess,' she said as she led them down the hall to the living room. 'I haven't cleaned up today.' She sniffed. 'But then I don't clean up any day ever.'

The room was large, light and neglected. The floor was strewn with toys, shoes and discarded items of clothing. A small plastic bean-stained plate lay on the floor by the sofa. It was very familiar to Martha. A distant life came to her – Martha Walters, the sticky years. It had been a time of endless wiping and long conversations about lollipops, lorries, princesses and an invisible friend called Lola. A time of watchfulness, guilt, loneliness and fun. Remembering all that, her heart went out to Mrs Simpson.

She watched Charlie pick up a small toy car and turn it over admiring it. 'I always wanted one of these,' he said.

'A Jaguar?' asked Mrs Simpson.

'Just the toy.' He ran the car along the arm of the sofa. A smile to Mrs Simpson, sharing this small pleasure, was not appreciated.

'You want to talk about Bill,' she said.

Martha said, 'Yes. Your husband.'

'He's not my husband. We're not married. I just took his name to look respectable to the neighbours. You know how people are.'

Martha nodded. 'Indeed I do.'

Charlie reluctantly put the toy car back on the floor and said, 'Bernice Stokes asked us to find out what Bill was up to. She calls him Brendan. She thought he'd gone missing.'

'I know,' said Mrs Simpson who was not Mrs Simpson. 'She told me. Until she got in touch I thought Brendan was Bill.'

Martha said, 'What else did she tell you?'

'Pretty much everything. You two spied on me from the house across the road. You followed Bill to the flat in Heriot Row where his lady love Lucy stays. You,' she pointed to Charlie, 'waited outside Lucy's house and when Bill came out you followed him until he caught up with you and, well, beat you up.'

Charlie agreed. 'Indeed he did.'

'You,' Mrs Simpson who was not Mrs Simpson nodded at Martha, 'followed Bill from Jelly's to Morningside and watched Sheila go into her house.'

'In her red coat,' said Martha.

'Did she have that on? I like that coat,' said Mrs Simpson.

Martha agreed, 'It's a lovely coat. Great cut.'

Charlie said, 'We came to talk about Brendan or Bill. Does he live here with you all the time?'

'No. In fact I've hardly seen him since the day you two came hurtling out of the house across the road and took off in your car following him.'

Charlie said, 'Oh, did you see us?'

'Everybody saw you. The whole neighbourhood. You don't often see people running about making fools of themselves round here. We had a laugh.'

'I'm glad we amused you.' Charlie shrugged. 'So you haven't seen him recently.'

'No. But don't worry, we've got him sorted.'

'Sorted?'

'He'll get what's coming to him.'

'You're not going to have him beaten up?'

'Of course not. Don't be ridiculous. We're going to hit him where it hurts most. The wallet.' Mrs Simpson who was not Mrs Simpson indicated the door with a swift wave of her hand. 'Our Brendan or Bill is wealthy. But not for long.' She hustled the pair out of the room, up the hall and out the front door.

Back in the car Charlie said, 'What was that about?'

'We got thrown out,' said Martha. 'I'm guessing she didn't like you playing with the toys.'

'I can't resist.'

'I know, you're making up for an impoverished childhood.' She started the car. 'Come to think of it, we were all abandoned. Mrs Simpson who isn't Mrs Simpson abandoned by Bill or Brendan. Me by Jamie who ran away from me. God, even the woman across the road has been abandoned to live alone in a house with patched walls where pictures once hung and a purple bedroom. Do you think Bernice or the woman in the red coat feel abandoned?'

'Well, I don't think Bernice does, but perhaps the woman in the red coat. Why did you mention her to Bernice?'

'I didn't. I thought you did.'

'Why would I mention that my assistant had followed the wrong taxi?'

'Why indeed?' said Martha. 'But it is now evident that I didn't follow the wrong taxi.'

'How do they know you followed the taxi?' Charlie wondered.

'Maybe Brendan spotted me. Then again, maybe someone is following us.'

'You mean all the time?' He turned and looked out the rear window.

'Perhaps. How did anyone know I was following the taxi? I was in my mother's Beetle. Not your car, which Bernice or Brendan might have recognised. Someone must have followed me home. We're being watched.'

'When Brendan punched me these women might have been watching.' He placed his palm on his stomach. 'It makes me queasy. I hate that thought. Why would they do that?'

'To find out if we're doing a proper job. To find out what we are finding out before we tell them, so they don't have to pay the bill. I don't know. We should go and chat to these other women straight away.'

'Yes. We should. Only not straight away. I want to go somewhere quiet to sit and eat and drink a glass of wine, maybe two. Mostly I want to think.'

'You're procrastinating, Charlie.'

'It's one thing I'm very good at. I enjoy it. It gives me a feeling of being removed from the world while considering my options. So, you can go and talk to some woman who might or might not be called what we think she's called. Me, I'm going for a plate of pasta and a glass of wine.'

'Are you paying?'

'Yes.'

'Well, I'll join you. Though I shouldn't.'

They sat at a table for two in the corner of Charlie's favourite Italian restaurant. He ordered spaghetti arrabiata, saying they didn't want anything creamy when they were a little bit shocked and plotting their next step. 'And we'll have Chianti to go with it. A reliable wine. We need reliable at the moment.'

He took his notebook from his jacket pocket and laid it on the table, placed his pen neatly next to it. 'We need to make a list.'

'Of course we do,' said Martha.

Bernice/Brendan Stokes, Charlie headed the page. 'Right.'

Bernice comes to the office. Wants us to find Brendan. Mentions pub.

We go to pub. Find Brendan is also known as Bill Simpson, screw up. Don't get change after paying for drinks. Get chased out. Carbonara.

We go to address for Bill Simpson. Check up from house across the road. Follow Bill/Brendan. He knows we're there.

He shut the book. Drummed his fingers on the cover. 'I'm a fool.'

'Why do you say that?'

'Look at this list. Three items. Two balls-ups. I'm an arse.' The wine arrived. He refused the offer of a trial taste, took the bottle, filled his glass and swigged deeply. 'I just went plunging ahead doing stuff. That's not me. I stop. I think. I muse. I ponder. I mull.'

'You procrastinate.'

'I move forward with caution. I never barge. What was I thinking?' He refilled their glasses. Cursed himself because he knew what he'd been thinking. He'd wanted to impress her. His falling for her had clouded his judgement. Oh, he hadn't fully realised this till he'd seen her standing alone, pale and fearless, yelling at a crowd of barely sober men in a gay pub. That was when he knew he truly loved her. Everything before that had been a prelude, the overture, the beginnings of it all. But her passion had taken his breath away.

'I find people, that's all. I always thought I was quite good at it. Not excellent, just quite good. I who found I had no identity discovered I could slip into other people's lives and understand them. I am a gifted listener. Sometimes I'd persuade people to come home. Sometimes not.'

Martha smiled at this. 'Sometimes you took them home with you.'

'It's hard sleeping when you know someone you've spoken to recently is out there in the rain and cold. But this thing now isn't like anything I've done before. I'm getting the feeling I'm the one being watched. I can't figure it out. I must have pissed someone off.'

'You have an enemy?'

Charlie took another swig of wine. 'I don't have enemies.' He considered this statement and added, 'But then I don't have friends either.'

Martha hated to admit the pasta was exactly the right dish for the moment. She pointed to it with her fork and nodded. 'Good.'

He nodded back. 'Good. Spicy, filling, tasty, comforting. Perfect for a man getting a talking to from his conscience as he lives through a moment of failure.'

41

A Spoon Situation

Sophie had abandoned the walk she'd been taking with Duncan and Chrissie to go home, lock the door and sulk. She'd heard the forsaken two come up the path; their voices drifting up sounded bemused and concerned. They rang the bell, knocked, shouted through the letterbox. Sophie ignored them. She sat, mug of tea clasped in cupped hands, feeling righteous and alone. When the knocking, ringing and yelling didn't stop, she went to the front door, opened the letterbox and firmly said, 'Go away.'

Next morning Chrissie came to help. Cheery as always, she baked a cake that Sophie found annoyingly excellent. Neither of them mentioned the doings of the previous afternoon.

Duncan stayed away. Sophie heard nothing from him and cursed herself. She missed him. He's an idiot, she thought, but a nice idiot.

She decided she'd like to go back to Jelly's with him. She now considered it a fun place, noisy, energetic, with excellent food. She could invite Duncan to join her in a glass or three of wine as they enjoyed the dish of the day. A friendship thing, she'd say. Why not? Women did that sort of thing these days. Yes, she'd do that as soon as she'd sorted out the spoon situation.

In the time Chrissie had been helping with the cake orders quite a lot of cutlery had gone missing. It wasn't just spoons of course – two packs of cheddar cheese, a pair of shoes, a necklace (cheap but beloved), a Frank Sinatra LP, a vegetable knife, a silver ladle and a pair of canvas shoes were also missing. In fact it had taken Sophie a while to realise that the items had been removed from the house. The spoons were from a cutlery set she kept for special visitors and rarely used. The LP was scratched and never played. The shoes were hardly ever worn. The necklace lived in a kitchen drawer along with a couple of clothes pegs, a ball of string and two ballpoint pens. The cheese was missed, but Sophie assumed Martha had taken a craving, had a cheese fest and ate it. Though two packs seemed excessive.

The truth had slowly dawned when a silver tray that sat on a chest of drawers at the top of the stairs disappeared. For years Sophie and Martha had dumped their keys and small change on that tray when they came home. It was so much part of the household nobody noticed it. And it was a couple of days before Sophie became aware of its absence. She stood staring at the space it had occupied, wondering what had changed about the top of the chest of drawers. 'Tray,' she said at last, 'where's the tray?' In the living room she asked Martha if she'd seen it. 'Did you take it to polish it?' This rarely happened. Martha shook her head. 'No.' Together they went to stare at the vacant space and speculate.

'Who would steal such a thing?' said Martha. 'It wasn't very nice. Was it valuable?'

'When did we ever have anything valuable?' said Sophie. 'I think it has been stolen.'

'Who the hell would steal that?'

Sophie said, 'Don't ask.'

Next day Sophie visited Brenda. She sat at the kitchen table, took a deep breath. 'Chrissie is a thief. She's been taking things from my home.'

Brenda said, 'Nothing valuable, though.'

'You knew?'

Brenda nodded and pointed to a plastic bag on the kitchen unit. 'Your stuff.'

Sophie fetched it, put it on the table and peered inside. 'The cheese is missing.'

'We ate it. Didn't know it was yours. Sorry. I made macaroni cheese.'

Sophie sighed. 'You'll have to tell Chrissie she can't come to my house any more.'

'Why?'

'She steals things.'

'Nothing very nice, though. Except for the spoons. The spoons are nice. Now you have them back. Everything is as it should be.'

'No, it's not. I don't want that woman in my house again.'

'That's not very nice of you. If Chrissie didn't come and steal from you, she'd go and steal from someone else. Probably a shop, and probably she'd take things of worth. She'd get reported to the police, prosecuted and sent to jail. Her husband would like as not hear about it and contact the court. He'd try to get her back in his care. He'd beat her. It's your responsibility to save her from all this by letting her steal from you.'

Sophie said, 'Huh?'

'You heard. You should let Chrissie come and steal from you. It's safer. Besides, she doesn't want your stuff. She just gets a kick from taking something of yours with her every time she leaves. You'll get it back. Just come by and I'll return your belongings.'

'I should let Chrissie come and help with my cake situation and turn a blind eye to her thieving problem?'

'Exactly, it's the kindly thing to do. That's the way to go. We must all be kindly.'

'I am kindly,' said Sophie. 'I treat people well and I have never stolen anything in my life.'

'You have stolen a little bit of your gentleman caller's heart and a deal of his self-esteem. You locked him out the other day. He was very hurt. Chrissie told me.' She lifted the plastic bag from the table, handed it to Sophie and ushered her to the door.

'You must be kindly to Chrissie, to Duncan, and mostly you should be kindly to yourself.'

At home Sophie put all her recovered goods back where they belonged. She made a cup of coffee and sat at the kitchen table slowly drinking it and visiting her recent past. She felt her life had moved out of control. Events had shoved her pleasant but rather drab routine aside. These days she was in pain a lot and now had a woman of dubious morals coming to her kitchen to assist in her cake business. Well, the pain was beginning to ease and the second bothersome thing she didn't really mind. She thought it might be amusing to fetch home her purloined belongings once a week. She might see her things anew, and besides, it would be good to sit and talk to Brenda on a regular basis. Sophie rather liked the woman.

What bothered her was her naivety. A male voice on the phone had flattered her. She'd lapped it up.

'Do you think you could do a Mona Lisa cake?' the voice had said.

Sophie said she could. She became so obsessed with proving she was up to the task she did not heed the warnings from her gut. That voice on the phone had been familiar, its tone slightly mocking. Now she thought about it, the owner of the voice had been taking the piss and enjoying doing it.

At first that afternoon, the afternoon of the decimated cake she called it, had come to her only in traumatic flashback. The moment of falling, seconds before that the moment of knowing she was going to fall and there was nothing she could do about it, hard pavement coming at her and she was helpless to stop landing on her face.

Now, however, she could recall details. When she was being attacked she'd looked about seeking help. There had been nobody around. But when she'd first entered the street there had been a man standing on the other side of the road, watching. As she'd walked towards the house she was delivering the cake to, the man had walked quickly away. Straining to bring him to mind, Sophie was beginning to think she knew who he was.

She phoned Duncan. 'I think we should go for a meal together. My treat. Jelly's. Now I think about it, it was fun. It just didn't seem it at the time because I was angry at you and I got a shock when I saw Jamie.'

Duncan said, 'Um . . . well . . .'

'Good. Come round at half-past five tomorrow. I've got somewhere to go first. I need you to come with me. You don't have to say or do anything. Just look positive and slightly menacing.'

'I'm not good at menacing. And I'm not sure about Jelly's.'

'Nonsense. I'm telling you what to do. I've decided to be bossy from now on.'

'When did this happen?'

'About five minutes ago. I'm feeling better already.'

42

A Woman Unworthy of Her Living Room

They procrastinated. Martha enjoyed it. She found it comforting and pleasantly naughty to put off something she ought to be doing and sit by the fire in the office drinking coffee instead.

'Why do you procrastinate, Charlie?'

'It's pleasant. It's a bit like playing truant. But you're skipping off from your own life. Hiding from responsibility. Then again, I may just enjoy being by the fire.' He leaned back, admired the back of Martha's neck and the line of her jaw. A good jaw, he thought, firm. It would be good to run a finger along it, noting her stubbornness and determination. He considered reaching for her, taking her hand perhaps. But he didn't. A rejection would ruin the warmth and comfort of the afternoon. Besides, when he turned to look at her she was sleeping.

Well, it was warm here, and she felt safe. Recently she'd spent her nights lying staring into the dark, worrying, imagining dire happenings. It had been this way since the burning of the suit. The reek of it, the thick black smoke; what had that suit been made of? The cheapest material in the universe, Martha decided. She remembered how cruelly synthetic it had felt. It must have been hell to wear, hot in summer, cold in winter. And the cut of it, so conservative, so middle-aged. Jamie must have hated it. That suit deserved to die.

It wasn't the crazed treatment of Jamie's work outfit that had scared Martha. It had been the look in his eyes. A hard bitter gleam. She'd shared a bed with this man, felt his body on top of hers, explored his lips and mouth with her tongue, stroked his hair, laughed with him, shared meals and jokes and memories. She'd been young with him. They'd marvelled at their child. And then he'd run away from her. He'd broken her heart. She thought she'd never trust another soul again.

Business was resumed next morning and the pair decided to start at Morningside and then move to the city centre to talk to Lucy at Heriot Row. Perhaps there would be somewhere new and interesting to eat on the way. Charlie wanted to turn up unannounced at Sheila's door. 'We'll catch her unawares. She'll be more likely to let something slip.' Martha thought this rude and pushed for making an appointment. Charlie won.

The street was quiet, a few cars parked by the kerb. Martha pointed to a gate. 'That's it. It was dark and raining, but I'm sure that's it.' They walked through the small neat garden and rang the doorbell. They waited.

'Nobody home,' said Charlie.

'If we made an appointment we could have saved ourselves a trip.'

'Nah,' said Charlie. 'It's interesting to snoop about when people aren't at home.' He peered through the downstairs window. 'Posh.'

Martha looked in, saw a large white sofa, thick white carpeting, a chrome floor lamp and a long, honeyed-wood coffee table. 'Expensive.'

Charlie rang the bell again and stood back, hands in pockets, looking at the upstairs windows. He was smiling.

'You're glad there's nobody in,' said Martha. 'You can go away and procrastinate for another day.'

The smile widened to a grin. 'You could be on to something.'

The door opened. A tall pale-faced woman with fiercely bobbed black hair and eyes lavishly dark with kohl stared out at them. Charlie's grin faded.

'Charlie Gavin and Martha,' the woman said. 'At last. I wondered how long it'd take you to come and see me.' She opened wide the front door and stepped aside to let them in. Talking as she went, she led the way down the hall and into her living room. Her voice was assured, metallic. She was a woman who believed she was right about everything. Charlie thought she probably was. Failure would not occur to her.

Martha, meantime, was looking at the red coat. It was a thing of beauty. Even hanging from the peg on the hallstand where it had been carelessly draped, it looked perfect, the ultimate garment. Martha noticed the cut and the slight sheen of the material. Is it silk? She leaned towards it, considered reaching out to stroke it. But Sheila turned and imperiously asked, 'Are you coming? Or are you planning to make love to my coat?'

Martha sighed and said, 'I'm coming.' She would have preferred to stay ogling the coat. Like that guitar in a shop window all those years ago, it was an object of lust.

The house smelled of new carpets and fresh paint. The living room was so frighteningly pristine both Martha and Charlie shoved their hands in their pockets and looked down at their shoes. Shod feet had no place on this deep-pile cream carpet. This room was waiting for a Sunday supplement style page to turn up and photograph it. Martha momentarily stopped breathing. This place was too precious. It needed Evie and Murphy to romp about in it, create a little havoc, make it less forbidding.

She didn't sit. She hovered by the window. Charlie stood by the fireplace and Sheila perched on the arm of the sofa. 'Well. You two are probably the worst detectives ever.'

'I'm not a detective. I just find people. I found Brendan. That was all I was asked to do,' Charlie told her.

'Not a great feat of detection I should say. The man was practically walking about town wearing a T-shirt saying "I am Brendan Stokes".'

'I admit he was suspiciously easy to find.'

Sheila turned on Martha. 'You followed us home. You just about tailed the taxi we were in. A little advice, if you are following somebody in your mother's car get the exhaust fixed before you start. The Beetle you drove farted and coughed and roared after us.'

Martha shrugged. 'I hadn't set out to look for Brendan. I was parked outside Jelly's hoping to see someone else.'

'Your husband?'

'Yes. How did you know that?'

'I know all about you and him.' She pointed to Charlie. 'Bernice checked up on you both.'

'Why would she do that?'

'I suppose she wanted to know who she was handing over money to. She certainly knows a lot about Charlie here.' She nodded to him. 'You've led a solitary life.'

'I wouldn't say that,' said Charlie. 'I have friends. Not many, I'll admit. I've had lovers. Not family so much. But them's the breaks.' He looked about. 'Nice room.'

Sheila nodded. 'I like it.'

'Does Brendan?'

'Of course.'

'How long have you known him?'

'A while.'

Charlie said, 'Ah.' As if that meant something to him. 'How did you meet?'

'At a party at Bernice's house. I went along with a friend. She didn't want to go to a party alone. Of course she abandoned me as soon as we arrived and I was left wallflowering it in the corner of the living room.'

Martha said, 'Your friend got a drink and wandered off to mingle and flirt. She just needed someone to enter the room with. I know the type.'

'Yeah,' Sheila nodded, 'doorway cheats. Anyway, Brendan rescued me. He came over to chat and top up my glass. He stayed with me all night and a couple of days later phoned me and asked me out.' She shrugged. 'I didn't know he was with Bernice. No idea.'

'When did you find out?' Charlie asked.

'When Bernice turned up at the door and told me. Brendan had long taken a place in my bed and in fact I'd asked him to marry me.' Her face twisted into a bitter smile. 'If you don't ask, you don't get. Anyway, he hadn't accepted – or refused, come to that. He said he'd have to think about it. When Bernice turned up and told me all, I was heartbroken. Humiliated. And absolutely bloody furious.' She smoothed the loose cover on the arm of her sofa, patted it into place. After that she glared down at Charlie's feet and said that really he ought not to be in this room without having removed his shoes first. 'I will get my revenge,' she said. 'We all will.'

'You've met the other women?' Charlie asked. For a horrible moment he'd thought she was seeking vengeance for his shoes on the perfect carpet. 'I'm sorry about the shoes. I didn't think.'

'Oh, yes, I've met the other women. We've had dinner. Drank champagne. Made plans. I think it's time you and your shoes left.'

'So,' said Martha, 'what do you make of that?'

They were back in the car, reviewing the situation. Looking across at the house they'd just left, thinking how chilly it was in there.

'I'm glad I'm not Brendan Stokes. Hell hath no fury like a woman who finds the man she has proposed to may have received similar invitations from quite a few other women.'

'I suppose. It'd be awful to discover you were not the only one to know the secret things he liked in bed. I'd mind the intimacies,' said Martha.

'I wouldn't really know about that. I just wonder what the other fiancées and lovers are planning,' said Charlie.

'A hitman?'

'They wouldn't want him dead. Alive and miserable and penniless and cold and homeless and unloved will be the plan I imagine. These women will shred him.'

'I suppose. Even so, I can't help thinking that each lover would secretly like to think they were his favourite. They were the best fiancée and best in bed. People can be competitive about anything and everything.'

Charlie nodded towards the house. 'That one in there has worn herself out being competitive and humiliated. She's tense, nervous, critical, did you notice? She was sitting there, fists clenched and working her jaw, grinding her teeth. She's going to need some serious dentistry soon.'

'I didn't notice. I was busy noticing you noticing her. God, that house is terrifyingly perfect. You wouldn't want to sneeze or fart in there.'

'She's given that living room all she's got and now she isn't comfortable sitting in it. She needs it to be pristine. Absolutely perfect in every way. And now Brendan has rejected her, he has also rejected that room. She feels bad. Unwanted. Unworthy. She feels unworthy of the room she's painstakingly created, her own living room.'

Martha said, 'Nothing's worse than being rejected by someone you loved and trusted. I wondered for years what would have happened if I'd run after Jamie. Thing is, he'd have left me anyway. He'd decided to do that. Same with Sheila and the others. Brendan has decided to cheat on them. It's not about them. It's about him and his ego.' She looked pleased with herself, took a packet of fruit gums from her pocket, popped one in her mouth and offered them to Charlie. 'Perhaps I ought to go back and tell her that.'

'Perhaps you better not. Perhaps we should go and talk to Lucy in Heriot Row.'

43

Two Bloody Pounds

Sophie and Duncan sat in the Beetle staring across at the entrance to Jamie's building. The evening was warm. People were sitting on doorsteps. 'Look at this,' said Sophie. 'People soaking up sun. Beer or wine trickling over the back of their throats, minds empty of worries and filled with music, feet tapping and small conversations. I'd forgotten about this sort of thing.'

Duncan looked surprised. 'Had you? An evening like this, doing this mindless stuff, is the reason I failed at everything. I lived like this even when it wasn't sunny. A bit of booze, some music and as few thoughts as I could get away with. Such indulgence was my downfall.'

'Well. Good way to go. I've spent the last years with my shoulders tense, busy baking and worrying and fussing. I could have been drifting along with Joni Mitchell. I'd have enjoyed that. I completely forgot about enjoying myself.'

'Funny that. For years I thought about nothing else. In fact, it never occurred to me to do or think about anything I didn't enjoy. Responsibility wasn't an issue. Sometimes I regret that.'

'That's silly. What's the point of regretting something you can't fix? Your past is over. Let it go.'

'Easily done. I barely remember it. Still, I think I could have achieved more. My mother would be disappointed in me.'

'Your mother was a hard woman. She was terrifying. I don't think a human being has lived who wouldn't have disappointed her. If Albert Einstein had been her son she'd have said, "Well, relativity, who needs it? He still doesn't put his dirty underpants in the laundry basket."'

Duncan shrugged. 'That's familiarity for you. Probably Galileo's mother and Churchill's mother and Kafka's mother were the same. In my opinion, anyone who had some kind of involvement with your teenage underpants would have no respect for the grown-up you.'

'I never liked your mother,' said Sophie.

'Can't say I was particularly keen on her myself. But she was my mother and I feel strangely bound to defend her. Are we bickering, by the way?'

'Yes.'

'Why?'

'I am planning to have words with my son-in-law. I need to be angry. I'm practising on you.' She leaned back and drummed on the steering wheel.

'How do you know he'll come along?' asked Duncan.

'His stomach. All his life he has eaten at half-past six. He may have changed. But his stomach hasn't. It'll still need filling up at the same time.'

'Mine, too,' said Duncan. 'I'm starved. How long do we have to wait here?'

'Till he comes along. Not long, I should think.' She shifted in her seat, pointed ahead. 'There he is. In that pink kaftan thing. He's wafting along the street. Looking smug. I didn't think men wafted.'

Clumsy and stiff, she clambered out of the car. 'Jamie,' she shouted, 'Jamie Walters. I want a word with you.' She advanced on him, angry finger pointing.

He looked at his building and for a moment seemed poised for flight.

'Don't you dare run away. You've done enough of that already.'

He turned to face Sophie, thumbs hooked over the back pockets of his jeans. He smirked as she lumbered closer. 'Hi, Sophie.'

The smirk faded as he saw how she moved. It was plain that every step hurt.

'Oh, yes, you did this. I'm bruised and battered and everything aches. It hurts to walk. It used to hurt to breathe, but that's getting better. I still have to sleep sitting up.'

'I had no idea. It was meant to be a joke.'

'It wasn't funny.'

'I just wanted to do a little damage. I wanted you and Martha to hurt. But not that much.'

'You wanted to abduct my grandchild. And I'm more than a little damaged.'

'I just wanted a little time with Evie. To talk to her.'

'You duped me into baking the cake of my life, delivering it personally. The cake was smashed and I got beat up. Nothing like having your stupidity pointed out to you to make you realise you're not invincible.' She pointed harder. 'You did it, didn't you? You ordered the cake.'

He shrugged. 'Sorry.'

Sophie wanted to hit him. She realised it would be foolish. Lashing out would be a source of derision. 'When it comes to being stupid, you score highly. Not quite stupid or plain stupid but off-the-scale seriously stupid,' she said.

'I don't know what you mean.'

'The damage you did to me. The damage you could have done to us all. Martha could have called the police. You could be facing charges. What if the police had come to your flat and found you smoking dope and an abducted child in the room?'

Jamie looked a little shocked. 'Never thought of that.'

'Of course you didn't. Now Evie's old enough to know what's going on, Martha isn't likely to let you near enough to hurt her.' Sophie's rage went on. 'You ran from your daughter. And you ran from your wife. On your legs. Top speed as they stood watching. What sort of husband and father does that?'

Jamie shrugged. 'Dunno.' He grinned, pleased at the adolescent nonchalance of his reply. 'Except, of course, Martha says Evie isn't mine. So yeah, I'm a husband. But I'm not her father.'

'That doesn't make it right to abduct her and have me mugged.' Sophie's anger was beginning to seethe.

Further along the street a group of men on their way to the pub called Jamie's name and waved. They were young, muscular, tight T-shirts tucked into jeans. 'Hey, Jamie.'

'Hey, guys,' he shouted back. 'See ya later.' He mimicked swigging a straight glass of beer.

Sophie watched and disapproved. 'Are those men friends of yours?'

'Yeah.'

'Are they friends of the two who bashed my cake and mugged me?'

Jamie grinned again. 'Nah. They were a couple of kids who come into the record shop.'

Sophie drew her breath, stepped closer to Jamie. 'And how much did you pay them?'

'Couple of pounds.'

'Two pounds. Two pounds! To beat me up. Is that all I am worth?'

'That was each.'

'Two pounds,' Sophie shouted. 'Two bloody pounds.' Her voice cut through the evening, slicing into the radio songs drifting from a doorway. Pavement people stopped walking and turned to stare. Faces appeared at windows. A woman holding a small child looked down. She turned the child away. There were things the little one wasn't ready to see.

'You bastard,' shouted Sophie. 'You cheap little bastard.' She shuffled to him and stamped on his toe. 'Arse.'

Jamie bent forward to clutch his ruined toe and Sophie walloped him on the cheek.

She heard the car door behind her slam shut as she raised her fist to land a second blow. Someone was shouting, 'Arse. Arse. Arse.' It dawned that it was her.

Someone took hold of her from behind. 'Time to go, Sophie.' Duncan, she'd forgotten about him. He pulled her away. 'Come on, before someone gets the police. You're assaulting a man.'

'Not a man, my son-in-law, the arse. I get to assault him. He deserves to be assaulted.'

She whacked him one more time. He squealed. But couldn't defend himself. That would have meant letting go of his toe. He hopped on the spot, red of face.

'You've broken my toe, you bitch.'

Duncan put his arms round her waist and pulled her back towards the car. She protested and wriggled and lashed out at him, trying to elbow him from behind. She panted and heaved, too caught up with breathing to shout out. She pulled at his hands, working at loosening his grip.

'Sophie, you're making a fool of yourself. Stop this.'

He lifted her feet off the ground and, wheezing with effort, staggered half-dragging her, half-carrying her, to the car. Sophie struggled to free herself, flailed her arms and screamed her protests. 'Put me down. Put me down.' He opened the driver's door and shoved her in.

'I'll kill him. Did you hear that? Two bloody pounds to mug me.' She beat the steering wheel. 'The pain I've been in. Forty pounds would have been more like it.'

'I know. Start the car, please. Go. We have to get away from here.'

Sophie calmed. She reviewed the situation. Perhaps Duncan was right. Perhaps he had saved her from an embarrassing encounter with the police. Stamping on your son-in-law's foot and whacking him on the cheek was as illegal as having her mugged. 'Duncan, I think you may be a hero. I didn't know you had it in you.'

He nodded and said, 'Neither did I.'

44

Emotional Camouflage

'That's her.' Charlie pointed to a woman leaving a building as he and Martha pulled up at the kerb. She was tall, immaculate and magazine up-to-the-minute. Lucy Moncrieff.

'Interesting,' said Martha. 'Slightly bohemian. Long blond hair. A black beret and dark green silk jacket. Cool. I'm jealous. It should be against the law to be that good-looking.'

'Legs,' said Charlie.

'Yes, I noticed,' said Martha. 'You're a leg man?'

'For the last two minutes.'

'She looks like a rock star. To be thought of as a rock star you don't have to sing or play guitar. You just have to look like a rock star.'

'You can easily hide who you are with clothes, lipstick and a haircut. Emotional camouflage. You can dress up as who you want to be and leave your actual self behind. How old do you think?'

'Twenty-four, twenty-five.'

'Why would Brendan take up with one so young? Surely that would infuriate the others?'

'I'd have thought so.'

'So, why?'

'How the hell should I know? You're the muser and ponderer; I'm just employed to type up the results of your thinking. How do you know that woman is her, anyway?'

'I saw her the first time we followed Brendan. I didn't realise she was so young and so gorgeous. We should follow her. She might be going somewhere interesting. We'll walk along a little bit behind her acting normally. Pretending we are real people.'

'Yet again.'

'It's a nice day for it.'

He was right. It was pleasantly liberating to be mindlessly following a woman while pretending to be a real person.

'I have a frisson of naughtiness. I am a voyeur. It's quite exciting,' said Martha.

'But slightly sleazy at the same time. I wonder what right have I to follow someone just because another someone asked me to and will pay me? And if I can follow someone, is someone following me?' Martha whirled round, walked backwards for a few steps and said, 'No.'

Pretending to be real people – something they found easier than actually being real people – they trailed behind Lucy, watching her duck through streaming traffic, nip gracefully up the street and disappear into a restaurant.

Charlie stood outside making a show of reading the menu as Martha cupped her hands against the window and peered in. 'It's lovely in there. Shimmering candles and beautiful people eating. I feel like a starving orphan spying on the king's feast.'

The restaurant was dimly lit, crisp white linen tablecloths, sparkling glasses and waiters in pristine white shirts and black waistcoats tenderly handing over plates of succulent food or carefully pouring wine. It was an ordinary grey day out in the street, but in that room it was a permanent romantic evening.

'I never knew about this place. Have you ever eaten here?' said Martha.

'No. Of course not. You don't come here to eat, you come to show off or celebrate your birthday or graduation or anniversary. I take eating too seriously to come here.'

'Ooh, there's Lucy. Blimey, she's sitting with a bunch of women. Bernice is there and Sheila. And Mrs Simpson. And quite a few others we've not seen before.'

Charlie joined her peering in. 'You're right. New faces. Who are they?'

'I don't know. Where did they come from?'

They faced one another, shrugged.

'I think Brendan has been naughtier than we thought,' said Martha. She pressed her nose to the glass once more. 'They're having champagne. Two bottles. They're laughing and holding their glasses high. They're celebrating something. They're waving fists in the air and shouting. People are staring at them.'

'What are they shouting?'

'I don't know. Can't hear.' She pressed her ear to the glass. 'L something. Can't make it out.'

'L,' said Charlie. 'Love? Life? Lemonade?'

'Linoleum. Lions. Laughing Cavalier. Who knows? What's it about?'

'Revenge,' said Charlie. 'They are anticipating the downfall of Brendan. Poor sod.'

'We should go in and eavesdrop.'

'I think they'd spot us. We should go back to the office and think about all this.'

On the drive back to the office, Charlie thought about appropriate food. He thought they needed something substantial but flavoursome. Thinking food rather than comfort food.

'Thinking food?' said Martha.

'Food to eat while thinking.'

He made roast beef and mustard sandwiches.

They sat on the sofa and thought. But not about what they should be thinking about. Martha thought about that restaurant and how she'd love to go there. She would for an hour or two feel special. She'd wear the blue dress she rarely wore because she kept it for good, and good never happened. It saddened her to realise she hadn't celebrated anything for a long long time.

Charlie thought about women. He often did. He hadn't had many relationships – certainly none that had lasted more than six months. A woman alone in a bar or restaurant mystified him in a pleasing way. He'd wonder about her, want to talk to her, but never did. He imagined such a being to be too sophisticated and too emancipated for him. Women en masse, sitting round a table celebrating, drinking and laughing, as they had been earlier today, terrified him.

'What were they talking about, these women sitting round a table looking at one another, drinking and smiling?'

'Brendan, I suppose.'

'What were they saying? Horrible things? Are they making bedroom comparisons? Mocking the size of his penis?'

'That will come later. Drunker. You don't want to think about that,' Martha said.

Charlie nodded. It was true he didn't want to think about the scathing conversation of drunken women. Then again, he didn't want to think about his present situation. He'd been hired to find someone who wasn't missing. He couldn't dismiss this as a mystery because somehow he was involved. It was a mess, a quagmire he was being sucked into.

45

A Gruncle

Jelly's wasn't busy. A bit of a disappointment for Sophie, she'd loved it noisy. Duncan had bought a bottle of wine from an off-licence on the way. Sophie smiled and said, 'Did you see that? I was splendid. I never knew I had such anger in me. I feel wonderful. Powerful.'

He didn't want Sophie to speak. His steak was the best he'd ever tasted and she was paying. He just wanted a little while alone with it.

Duncan reluctantly put down his fork. 'You're not going to turn bossy all the time, are you?' He sipped his wine. This place wasn't licensed but customers could bring their own bottle in with them. He'd chosen a bottle of Margaux.

'I am beginning to see the advantages of bossiness. I had an effect. I made my mark. I'm thrilled.' Sophie was high.

'You stamped on a man's toes.'

'I got mugged. He paid two pounds to have me mugged. I was furious at the mugging, then at the cheapness of the mugging. That's what he thought I was worth. I let him know what I felt. Once I would have bottled it up. I'd have been churning and seething inside about it for months. But today I just let rip. I let my anger flow. I feel marvellous.' She had chosen fish and chips. It seemed appropriate to celebrate her new-found aggression with something relatively unhealthy.

'You have found the advantages of screaming and shouting,' said Duncan.

'And kicking.' Sophie took a second generous swig of her wine.

'You better take it easy with the wine, Soph. You're driving.'

She swigged some more, grinned at him, glazed. 'You drive.'

'No. I can't. I can't drive. I never learned.'

'I don't believe you. You're a grown man. All grown men can drive.'

'Not this one. I've never owned a car. I live in a tiny flat. I don't have a lot of money.'

Sophie put down her fork. 'Really? And what brought this on? This sudden telling of your truth.'

'I told you I couldn't drive and thought I might as well tell you all my failings. Get them out in the open.'

'I think I must have known all along. After all, I never asked you where you live. After your wonderful description of the life we might have had, I sort of imagined you in a large comfortable city flat. Old sofas and modern prints, little-used kitchen because you ate out mostly. But somehow, back here,' she tapped the top of her head, 'I knew this wasn't true.'

'Do you care?'

'No. Though I had looked forward to tea in your splendidly comfy flat while secretly suspecting it wouldn't happen.'

'You are very welcome to visit my tiny uncomfortable flat.'

'I don't call upon men without a chaperone.'

'Very wise. I have always warmed to sensible women. You don't mind my motoring failing or my scant bank balance?'

'Your finances are yours alone. I'm a bit pissed off about the driving. I deserve wine after finding my aggressive side.'

'You don't mind that I'm not rich. I am getting on, thundering through middle age and I don't own a house. I am a non-achiever.'

'You fit the bill for me. You have excellent clothes. You are moderately handsome. All I want is someone to walk along the street with. You are extremely good at that. I see other women looking at me with envy.'

'You want me as an accessory? I'm up for that. I could do that.'

'Not an accessory. A companion. You've aged well, you bastard. It makes me think. You've done what you wanted, followed your fancies. You've been debauched at times. You look good on it. Me, I've been good. Done the right thing, worked hard, paid my way, fed and loved my child and grandchild, obeyed the law, stayed sober, kept a clean nose, and I'm bloody stiff and sore and old and wrinkled. It's plain not fair.'

'I suppose.'

'I should be wise round the eyes, but beautiful. You should be blotchy-cheeked with a pickled red misshapen nose.'

'I drink a glass of warm water with lemon juice every morning after I do fifty squats and sit-ups.'

'Goodness. I have a mug of coffee, toast and a stroll to school with Evie. Not energetic. Perhaps that explains the wrinkles.'

He reached over, placed his hand on hers. 'You're beautiful.'

'No, I'm not. But thanks for trying. Eat your steak.'

He did. It tasted even better now that he'd confessed his failings. All Sophie wanted was someone presentable to walk with her along the street. He could do that. No problem. There might even be tea and scones when they got home. And really, Sophie *was* beautiful despite her denial. She had a kindly face, thoughtful, a good face. He could look at that face, that collection of features, and wish some of that openness and honesty and humour would rub off on him. It would warm his heart to have someone in his life who wanted nothing more than his company. He would no longer be a failure. He'd become part of the Walters family.

He could sit in Sophie's kitchen slightly dizzy from the thick aroma of cake-baking. He loved being in that room, sitting back sipping tea as Sophie and Martha prepared food. Once, they'd hummed in harmony a tune he didn't recognise. He had asked what it was, but they didn't know either. 'Just a song,' Sophie said. He'd loved the closeness of two women who could harmonise a song neither of them knew.

He could watch little Evie grow up. Help her, advise her, give her the benefit of the knowledge he'd gained living his fancy-free, debauched (as Sophie would have it) life. He would be an unofficial uncle and the grandfather she didn't have. A gruncle.

It was a good family, he thought, if a little screwed up. They had misconceptions. They worried, but when the worrying got too much they buried their heads in the sand. For example, Martha's naughty youth – they didn't want to think of what she'd got up to and who with, so they hid from it. They assumed the worst. And the worst was that they hadn't a clue who Evie's father was. It was a sensitive and painful area. So naturally they wouldn't discuss it.

A couple of hours ago Jamie had complained that Evie wasn't his. How nonsensical they all were. Too caught up in grief and hurt. Couldn't they see? Hadn't they noticed Evie's eyes, the way her mouth moved when she smiled, the shape of her nose, her high cheekbones. The girl was developing into the spit of Jamie. The man was obviously her father. For heavens' sake, the girl looked so like him she could have been cloned.

46

Hello, Charlie, Welcome to Your Life

Charlie sat in Martha and Sophie's kitchen staring glumly at his notes. Across the room Martha chopped onions. Charlie noted she was doing it badly. 'What are you making?'

'A quick meaty thing.'

'What? Roast beef?'

'That takes ages. You're feeding a child. She doesn't just get hungry. She starves. So she'd fill up on biscuits and rubbish, then she wouldn't want her meal and she might get a sugar rush and not go to bed till late and she wouldn't sleep so she might not get up at the right time and she'd be late for school. You can't start a complicated meal after five. Not with children about. Also those are expensive things. We are your basic cheap eaters.'

'Plainly I have a lot to learn about parenting. I'll cook. I don't like figuring out my notes, trying to find motivations, delving into the murk of human emotions. You do it.' He pulled off his jacket, draped it on the back of his chair and rolled up his shirtsleeves.

Martha took his chair. 'It's about money.'

'You have no idea how to chop an onion. You cut it in half, put the flat side down. Now you can chop it without it sliding about. What makes you say it's about money?'

'Everything's about money if it isn't about love or jealousy. But mostly it's money. I have managed with onions all my life so far.'

'No, you haven't. You'll have cut your fingers, sworn at the slippiness of any onion you are dealing with and wept. How would they get money? Can't be from Brendan. He's dedicated to getting it from them.'

'You make him sound sleazy.'

'He punched me. I have nothing decent to say about him. Except I suspect he can charm women. He knows the right thing to say.' He spread mince into a thin layer.

'What are you doing?'

'Making burgers.'

'Are you serving them with chips? Evie is keen on chips. She eats them. I'm keen on her eating. I'm just a bit bothered about the money thing.'

'OK. Chips.'

'Bernice asked you to find someone who wasn't missing. A scam, definitely. I think she chose you because you are so far out of town. None of the women involved is likely to come and check you out.'

Charlie put the frying pan on the stove. 'That's true. Not these champagne women, anyway. But there's nothing to check out. I'm a nice enough guy.' He poured oil into the pan. 'They're the money, aren't they? I definitely think better when I'm cooking. It's doing something you don't have to think about, frees the mind.'

Martha read his notes. *Saw Bernice. The house smelled of nothing. Weird that. Houses smell of being clean or overly clean. Or coffee or polish or laundry. Ironing smells nice. Last time it smelled of stew. This new emptiness. Is she planning to move away? That woman looks at me strangely. Freaks me out. Heard someone moving upstairs. Left. Saw though window Bernice and Brendan embrace. She was holding the man she hired me to find. Freaked out. Ran away. Had disappointing herb omelette. Crap day. Depressed.*

He spread the chopped onions on his layer of mince. Martha looked at Charlie. He was seasoning his mince – salt, pepper, a touch of garlic and mustard. He divided the layer into balls which he flattened and put in the frying pan. A comforting sizzle. He peered into Sophie's cupboard. 'Ketchup. Ah, there you are.'

'You're not using up all our food, are you?'

'I'll replace things.'

'Maybe that's why she picked you. Out of town, nice enough guy. Not a world-weary cynic like Sam Spade.'

'How would she know that? Where's Evie? This will be ready soon. You won't be wanting any.'

'You bet I do. I'm starved. It's my food. And Evie's outside in the garden. She's teaching Murphy to jump through a hoop.'

'That could be handy in emergencies.'

'She thinks so. Murphy not so much.' She leafed back through his notes. 'Right at the beginning, when Bernice first turned up in the office she said she'd been put off by the man shouting outside. That man shouted at me. He seriously doesn't like you. You should go and talk to him.'

Charlie dropped sliced potatoes into hot fat. A wild sizzle. 'You go. I'm not going near him. Mostly I am not going near his wife. A terrifying woman. A zealous man-hater. A woman who peers at you, face in a permanent pre-formed dirty look.'

'You have to. It's your job.'

'Nah, it isn't. I won't have anything to do with scary women. I know nothing of women. I know one woman didn't want me and another gave up her life for me, but removed me from the life I should have had.'

Martha looked across at him. He was turning the burgers, then pressing them flat with his fish slice. Concentrating. Frowning. His hair had fallen over his forehead. A small splatter of escaped onion had landed on his shirt. He'd hate that he hadn't noticed. She thought him gentle and lonely and, though she wouldn't mention it to him, a little bit lovely. She shut his notebook and placed a determined palm on the kitchen table.

'Charlie, this is the life you should have had. This is the life you've got. This life you're living. What happened, happened. You were taken away. You lived with Auntie Ella. You found money in the biscuit tin. That's your life. The other life doesn't exist.' She waved. 'Hello, Charlie, welcome to your life.'

He stared at her, mouth agape. Of course she was right. He stared at his burgers. They were slightly burned at the edge. Good, he nodded. He knew that it was time to accept this life he led and to stop imagining the life he ought to have had. And really, this life, this time here in this kitchen with Martha, was pretty good. For a life, it would do.

Martha stood. 'Do you hear that?'

Charlie held his breath and listened. He shook his head. 'No. I don't hear anything.'

'Silence. I don't like the sound of it.' She stuck her head out of the window. 'Evie?'

A small voice from outside. 'Yes?'

'What are you doing?'

'Nothing.'

'What's that you're eating?'

'Nothing.'

'It's an ice cream. Where did you get that?'

'The lady gave it to me.'

'Lady? What lady? How often have I told you not to take sweets from strangers?'

The small voice from outside rose in protest. 'But she wasn't a stranger. She knew my name. And she knew Murphy's name. And she knows Charlie. She knows all about him. She said Charlie's auntie used to be her best friend. She lived across from her in Glasgow.'

47

Is She Watching Me?

Charlie clattered down the stairs, out the front door, up the path, out the gate and stood panting, looking up the road and down the road wondering which way to go. He looked up at Evie standing at the window. 'Which way?'

Evie shrugged, shouted that she didn't know. Realising before he started jogging up the street that he hadn't a clue what the woman he was after looked like, he ran indoors to quiz the child. 'What did she look like?'

'I don't know. I didn't look. She had a face.'

'Well, she would.' He gripped Evie's shoulders. 'Tell me about the face.'

'She had a nose. Lips. All that.'

'What colour were her eyes?' He knelt in front of her.

'Dunno, didn't look. I was looking at the ice cream.'

'Hair,' said Charlie, 'what was it like?'

'Sort of faded. Like something old left in the sun. It hung on her head past her ears and it was sort of tied up at the back.'

He turned to Martha. 'I think it might have been my mother.'

Evie put her hands on either side of his face and turned it to her. 'You don't remember what your mummy looks like? Everybody knows what their mummy looks like.' She pointed to Martha. 'See, there's my mummy. She's got wrinkly bits at her eyes and a scowly bit on her forehead. And some of her hairs are grey. Her eyes are brown. Mostly she's quite pretty.'

'Thank you,' said Martha. 'I'm glad I'm quite pretty despite everything.'

Evie ignored her. 'So why don't you know what your mummy looks like?'

Charlie sighed. He didn't want this conversation. 'We lost touch when I was little.'

'You lost touch?'

'I kind of got carried off by someone and I never saw her again. I was a baby. I don't remember any of it.'

Evie swooned. 'That's awful. That's just like a fairy tale. You might be a prince and you don't know it.' She hugged him.

Martha was sure she saw his eyes glaze. Of course, she thought, he wouldn't know about the power of hugs. Charlie's dilemma was too much for people to take in; they'd stare piercingly at him and ask painful questions, eager to know the intimacies of such a strange and isolating beginning to life, or they might back away as if misfortune was infectious. But probably nobody had ever reached out as Evie had.

Martha was sorry she hadn't put her arms round him and held him. But she hadn't. Maybe events in her life had eroded the knack of spontaneous compassion. Maybe you had to be seven and still believing in Santa Claus and fairy tales to take a sorry soul in your arms and say, as Evie had, 'Never mind, Charlie. Me and Murphy love you.' It was almost too much for Charlie to bear.

He might love, but being loved back hadn't really occurred to him.

After Evie released him, he went back to the meal he was about to serve. Stood clutching the fish slice. 'I'm sure it was my mother. Perhaps she's looking out for me. Watching over me. Maybe she's always been doing that.'

Martha put cutlery on the table. She glanced at Charlie. He was wrestling with his emotions. A mother, a secret guardian angel watching over him, obviously filled him with a strange new happiness that he didn't really trust. 'If she's out there, why hasn't she come and said hello? Is she watching me? D'you think she wants something? What?' He spread his palms. 'I haven't got anything. I've only got me and she didn't want that.'

And Martha thought, no good will come of this.

48

Emotional Exploitation

Charlie desperately wanted to sleep. He ached. He lay on his side, spread himself into his favourite sleeping position, closed his eyes and breathed. But thoughts of his mother plagued him. What if she was out there in the dark watching the house? She might be cold. Maybe she needed somewhere to stay. Twice he got out of bed and went to a window to look out onto the street and the empty night. Pools of streetlamp-yellow light and silence. Not a soul in sight.

Back in bed, sleep still slipped away from him. Imagined scenarios filled his mind. His mother would come to him, lightly tap his arm and say, 'Hello. I'm your mum.' And they'd hug. In fact, he doubted this would happen. There would be issues to be dealt with and, besides, he wasn't much of a hugger. He might be angry and demand to know if she had looked for him when he first went missing. And if she had, why had she given up? And if she hadn't, why not?

Mostly, though, he found the notion that his mother was watching him scary. She appeared to know all about him and he knew nothing about her. He imagined a small rosy-cheeked woman. When she saw him she raised one hand in a slow, unsure wave. He didn't know why this unnerved him. But it did.

Leaving the house in the morning he looked up and down the road checking for a small, rosy-cheeked woman before he set off to interview Lucy Moncrieff. Again, when he reached her flat, he stared up and down the road expecting to see the small frail figure watching him and cautiously waving. She didn't appear. He chained his bike to railings and walked backwards to the entrance of the building, keeping an eye out for the ghostly mother. Then he took the stairs two at a time and knocked on Lucy's door.

Though she was well into her twenties, Lucy Moncrieff's living room was teenage messy. There was a wide spill of LPs round the record player, discs long separated from sleeves. Two empty coffee mugs sat on the floor beside the sofa and six more lined the mantelpiece, a pair of shoes lay abandoned centre-carpet, a small pile of coats was heaped on a chair by the door; elsewhere in the room lay books, cards, assorted T-shirts and jerseys and a fat black cat.

'How long have you known Brendan?' he asked.

'Two years or so.'

'How did you meet?'

'A party at Bernice's.'

'She holds a lot of parties.'

'Yeah. They're boring, though. Just people standing around drinking wine and eating small nibbly things and chatting rubbish. It's all tinkling laughter, no dancing and no music and nobody gets pissed and throws up and goes off their head telling people the unbearable truth.'

'You have very clear ideas about parties.'

Lucy nodded. 'I do. A party is a party, fun. You should let yourself go. Shout and scream if you want to. You should leave yourself at the door with your coat. And pick yourself up with the coat when you leave. And when you're in the party room wearing your party clothes you should forget all about being you and drink and dance.'

This sounded excellent to Charlie. He knew, though, that he could never cope with such abandon. Not only would he fail to actually be abandoned during the party, he'd be sleepless with embarrassment for weeks afterwards. This notion bothered him. He wriggled in his chair, and then, unable to sit still for worrying about his inability to party, he stood up and strode to the window. Out in the street there was no sign of the woman he suspected of following him.

'Still,' Lucy went on, 'I met Brendan there. Then, couple of years later at another party I met the gang.' She spread her hands and examined her nails. Up close, in this light, she looked pale. Thin enough to be blown away in a strong wind. His Auntie Ella would have insisted she eat a bowl of her broth, a soup so thick a spoon could stand up in it. 'Meat on her bones is what she needs,' Ella would have said. 'Proper food that needs chewing. She needs anchoring.'

Lucy's clothes were expensive – loose silk trousers and a grey cashmere jersey. She sat on a red velvet sofa, legs tucked under her. She was barefoot. Toenails painted black.

'Gang?' asked Charlie.

'Yeah. The LKB club. We're mates. Course at first we hated one another. We were near to hissing. So angry. Blaming each other.'

'LKB?' said Charlie.

'Let's Kick Brendan.'

'I see. It's a club dedicated to kicking Brendan. Metaphorically?'

'Yes. He has used all of us. Cheated on us. Taken our money. Lied. Bastard. Now we're going to get him back. We'll all putting a couple of grand into the fund.'

'What's the fund for?' Charlie stared once more down into the street and still didn't believe that there was nobody there.

'Getting Brendan's money. We're going to sue him,' said Lucy.

Charlie returned to his seat. 'What for?'

'False pretences. Duping us out of cash. He's engaged to four of us.'

'Is that a crime?'

'It'll be a civil case. Bernice says it's emotional exploitation.'

'This is a thing?'

'Of course it's a thing. Using people, making them promises, taking their money, turning up drunk, shagging their friends, flirting with their mother, taking their wine to give to another woman, not turning up, phoning at three in the morning saying he's in bed and you can hear that other woman laughing. Oh, yes, that's emotional exploitation and he is going to get punished for it. He deserves all he gets. Us women are not to be tricked and used and fleeced and fucked and why, by the way, were you looking out of the window?'

Charlie said, 'Um.'

'Checking on your bike?'

'How did you know I have a bike?'

'I know all about you. Bernice checked you out before she hired you.'

'She did? What did she find out?'

'Stuff.' Lucy shrugged. 'You have a dog. Your house is full of strange people you found and didn't know what to do with. You're dreamy. You like to cook.'

'You know how to make a chap feel uncomfortable.'

'Do I? I didn't mean to. In fact the gang adores you.'

This made him even more uncomfortable. 'Who checked me out?'

Lucy shrugged. 'I never met him. I don't think Bernice said his name.'

Now Charlie was even more uncomfortable. This news was hard to believe. He looked round, and to lighten the stiff atmosphere said, 'Nice place you got here.'

She nodded.

'What do you do?' he asked.

'I design clothes for pop groups.'

'That pays? People fork out money for these weird multi-coloured things?'

'Yes. In fact they pay quite a lot of money for these weird multi-coloured things.'

She got up and walked to the door. She was telling him it was time to go. It struck him that she was a woman skilled in telling people to leave. He walked past her, out into the hall and headed for the front door. She followed, thanked him for coming and said it had been nice to meet him.

'Love to Martha.'

'You know Martha?'

'I know about her. I know everything. We all do.'

She shut the door. Alone on the stairs, Charlie remembered all the questions he'd come to ask.

How often had she seen Brendan? Had he asked her to marry him? Had she given him money? But going down the stairs, he wondered if any of it mattered. And he should have asked why the gang adored him.

This adoration bothered him. He didn't want it. A seething mass of women coming at him, reaching for him, calling his name, God almighty, no thanks. One at a time, he could handle that. But not all together. He should have asked how many women were actually in the gang. He would go back to the office, make a list of questions and come back and get answers.

He unchained his bike and wheeled it towards the main road. Then stopped. 'Bloody woman,' he shouted and slapped his forehead.

The rosy-cheeked woman he thought was watching him, the one he imagined to be his mother, had been a picture in the book he'd read all those long years ago when he'd been a child alone in the flat waiting for Ella to come home. She had been the woman waiting for her children to come home. The one the woodsman had brought the lost infants to. She'd had a fat teapot, a loaf of warm bread and a cosy fireside.

Christ, he thought, my life has been built round a cheap tattered book, second-hand no doubt and probably dire. I kind of thought all mothers of lost children looked like that. Mine, however, was living it up and loving her freedom.

49

Look Behind You

Remembering that Marvin Hay had told her he'd spoken to Bernice on the day she first came to the agency, Martha had come to talk to him or his wife. Well, Charlie wouldn't. He thought Marvin's wife scary. Marvin wasn't home. But Louise, his wife, was. This woman was born to be Mrs Hay. She was too tense, embittered and too downright scary to be given her first name. She sat across from Martha, hands folded on her knees, face muscles kept tight lest any emotion flit over it.

'You want to see Marvin. So would I. He buggered off. I have a feeling I won't be seeing him again.' She pulled in her lips, raised her eyes and glared.

'So you don't know where he might be?' said Martha.

Mrs Hay shook her head. 'No. It'll be a city. And he'll be in a small terraced house near a pub. He always liked the idea of drinking in a local where everyone knew him and shouted hello when he came through the door. He likes friendliness. Though he's not very good at it.'

Martha nodded.

'Friendliness doesn't interest me.' Mrs Hay waved her hand, dismissing the thought of many friends. 'People are nosy. They talk behind your back. Criticise. I like being with me. Well, me and him when he was here. Things I did for him – packed lunches to die for, ironed his shirts, starched the bed sheets, scrubbed, dusted and kept this place immaculate.' As she spoke she acted out the motions of ironing and scrubbing. Then she sat back, hands folded on the knees once more, performance over.

Martha was uncomfortable here. This house wasn't a home. It was an overly clean bubble where the world wasn't welcome. 'You sound angry,' she said.

'Course I'm angry. That woman did it. She gave him money. Bitch. I always got Charlie Gavin to fetch Marvin home when he went off. I always thought Marvin ran away because of some wanderlust. This time I realised he went because he doesn't want to be here.'

Martha said, 'Oh, surely not.'

'Oh, surely.' Mrs Hay's voice was flat and definite.

'Do you know who the woman who gave him the money was?'

'No.' Mrs Hay shrugged. 'But she employed him to follow you and Charlie.'

Martha shook her head. 'He didn't do that. Nobody followed us.'

'Oh, yes, he did. The two of you followed a woman from Heriot Row to a restaurant. You peered in and looked sad and envious. You,' Mrs Hay pointed at Martha, 'were parked outside your husband's flat that he shares with his new girl, Grace, and he came out and burned a suit and shouted at you. Charlie got beaten up in Rose Street. My Marvin saw it all. And more. He's seen everything.'

Martha slumped back in her seat, her mouth hanging open. 'My God, he really did follow us. We never noticed. How did he do that?'

'He thinks it's because he's so ordinary. Nobody sees him. He says you and Charlie are easy to follow. You never look behind you and you are too busy talking and bickering and discussing stuff to see anything that's going on. He says when you're driving you never look in your rear-view mirror.'

'I do. I always look.'

'Marvin said you could be tailed by Marlon Brando driving

a gorilla in an open-top orange Cadillac, Beach Boys blasting, and you wouldn't notice. You're too lost in your little world.'

'That's not true.' But Martha worried. She secretly feared it might be the case.

'Marvin said you talk to yourself all the time when you're driving.'

Martha put her hand to her mouth. She did that. She chatted to herself, thinking this conversation excellent. She agreed with everything that was said. Well, she was talking to someone who was always right.

Mrs Hay said, 'Marvin just loved spying on you. He wants to be a detective now. He said it was wonderful. He got paid for being a voyeur.'

'It's not like that. You're uncovering the truth.'

'Well, Marvin had a fine time.'

'And you don't know who he was reporting to?'

'Just a woman he met outside Charlie's office. She quizzed him apparently then offered him money to spy on Charlie. And he took it and spied then buggered off. So, what do you make of that?'

Martha didn't reply. She looked round and recognised the signs of recent sorrow. The fight against grime in here had become a war. Mrs Hay fought her grief and her grievances with elbow grease.

Mrs Hay didn't really care about anything any more. Maybe when scrubbing she imagined she was scrubbing Marvin away. Scrub, scrub, swish, swish, have that, Marvin. Soon you won't exist any more and I'll be free of you.

'My husband ran away,' Martha said. 'He took off and legged it as fast as he could.'

'You actually saw him?'

Martha nodded.

Mrs Hay couldn't believe it. 'You actually saw him running away from you?'

'Yes. I'd just told him I was pregnant with our second child and it was too much for him. He ran off to be with the woman he was seeing who was also expecting his child.' She raised her eyebrows. My small gift to you Mrs Hay; you are not alone. I have also known pain. 'Life's a bitch, is it not?'

Mrs Hay smiled, an odd, slightly squint movement of the lips. 'Oh, thank you, thank you. You've made me feel so much better. I thought it was only me.'

'Glad to have helped,' said Martha.

'That's wonderful. He just took off and left you standing in the street? Oh my, at least my Marvin didn't do that. Oh, that's just fantastic.' She clapped her hands. 'You're worse than me. I love it. And you pregnant, too. And him running off to a pregnant woman he preferred to you. Fabulous.'

'I'm glad you're pleased,' said Martha. Though she wasn't. It was good to know she'd brought some glee into Mrs Hay's life. But she'd been hoping for a bit of bonding and not this triumphal crowing. 'Thanks for the chat. Interesting talking to you. I'll probably go now.'

'I don't believe it,' Martha said to Charlie, 'I've never made someone so happy in my life. And with a confession. Not a kiss, sex, a meal, a wish granted or a song. The woman was practically floating when she showed me to the door.'

'It's not often you get an opportunity to gloat. She must be grateful.'

'I thought telling her my shameful secret would bring us closer. But it didn't.'

'You have to admit there is a certain comfort in discovering someone who is worse off than you are. You done good, kid.' Charlie gave her a nod.

Martha snorted. 'It didn't feel like a good job. I was belittled. It wasn't pleasant.'

They were back in the office comparing notes. Both were comforted to find that the other had done badly.

'This Marvin thing is weird. I had no idea he was following me. He must be good,' said Charlie.

'Or we're crap. Also he must have lost the squeaky shoes.'

'There's that. We can be sure that the woman who hired Marvin was Bernice Stokes. She even mentioned seeing him when she first came to see us. But why would someone hire someone to follow the person they'd hired to find a partner, lover, friend, whatever, who wasn't missing in the first place?'

'When you put it like that, I have no idea.'

'Well,' said Charlie, 'there's a lesson to be learned. When you're out and about and you're pretty bloody happy walking down the street with a good pal, having a cool time, exchanging thoughts, maybe bickering a bit, remember to turn round and look behind you. You'd probably be surprised at what's there.' He raised a thoughtful finger. 'In fact it's a lesson for life. Look back at where you've come from. You just don't know what great big thing you've forgotten about is sneaking up behind you.'

50

I Like You, Charlie Gavin

'Bernice must be finished,' Charlie said. 'Marvin would seem to have disappeared. She'll have paid him off. Her plan must be in place.'

'I think she's poised, ready to pounce,' said Martha. 'If she hasn't already pounced and we missed it.'

Four o'clock on a sunny afternoon and the pair were in Sophie's living room. They'd walked Evie home from school, given her cold milk and biscuits, and were watching her play with Murphy and friends in the garden. There seemed to be no structure to the game going on down on the lawn. There was jumping and running and squealing. Screams and giggles came to them in small squalls as one group pounced on another and, after a brief skirmish involving jumping up and down and pointing, they all scattered in different directions then hurtled back in small colourful waves to jump and scream and giggle once more. It was incomprehensible fun.

Charlie was baffled. 'There is no rhyme or reason to what's going on down there. They're all just squealing. Who are the good guys and who are the bad guys?' He put his forehead on the windowpane and stared at the frenetic players below. 'I never understood little girls. When I was little they scared me. They moved quickly, had squeaky voices and kept their school pencil cases tidy.' He sighed. 'They seemed so positive. I stood looking at them with my mouth open and my hands dangling by my side. They were creatures of mystery, on their way to being bossy. Were you like that?'

'I didn't play with dolls. I wanted to be a cowboy. Cowboys laugh at pencil cases, especially tidy ones. I did do stuff like the rioters on the lawn, though. They're just letting off steam. It's good. They'll eat masses then sleep early. Mothers appreciate mini bouts of running, jumping and squealing.'

'Do you suppose Bernice did stuff like that? I can't imagine it. I think she is one of these people who were born forty-two. I don't think she was ever properly young.'

Martha looked out at the game. 'She'd have been like that little girl there.' She pointed to a girl who was standing apart, keenly watching the goings-on. 'That one is looking for an opening. A moment in the game when she can step in and take over. And that one,' pointing to a shy and anxious girl who was obviously overwhelmed by the wildness and noise, 'is hoping it will all end soon because it's all too much for her and she's out of her depth. She knows it might all turn to tears and she'd be among the weeping.'

'Christ, you know all about girls playing games.'

'It's like life. Everyone wants fun and a slice of cake but there are some, like our first little girl, who want to have most of the fun and all of the cake.'

'I get the feeling you're trying to tell me something. I'm missing the point.'

'Bernice is like that little plotting girl. She's plotting something. And you're like the one who is watching in amazement and shock. Don't you see? What have you been doing all your life?'

'I dunno. Walking about not understanding women, I think.'

'It's not just women. It's men, too. You don't understand people.'

'They can be surprising.'

'They can be mean. They can be nasty and greedy and cruel. They plot against one another. They say vile things about one another. They stab one another. They steal. They can be horrible.'

'Not all of them. I know a lot of the nice ones.'

'That's the thing about you. You invite people into your

house, let them stay and yet you really know nothing about them. I fear for you. You could get horribly hurt. But you're kind.' She reached out, stroked his cheek. 'That's why I like you.'

'You like me?' Charlie 's face reddened slightly. This was pleasing.

'Yes, as a matter of fact, I do.'

'Gosh. And up till now I thought you had really good taste.'

Lucy led Charlie down the hall. This time she passed her messy living room and took him to an even messier kitchen. Dishes piled in the sink, more dishes piled beside the sink waiting their moment of washing, an overflowing waste bin, an old little-used cooker and other signs of a distracted life. He sat at a large table and couldn't stop himself wiping a cluster of toast crumbs into his hand. He held them, wondering what to do with them, and when Lucy turned to put on the kettle, dropped them to the floor. There was, he noticed, a hole in the dark red industrial lino.

The rough white paintwork on the walls was concealed by a collection of Aubrey Beardsley posters. Lucy sighed and made two mugs of instant coffee. Charlie didn't like to mention that he was a coffee freak, very fussy about the drink and not at all pleased about being handed a large mug of instant. He'd come to ask all the questions he'd forgotten to ask the last time he was here. The money to be handed over to Bernice, for example, was there a date for that? A special meeting? Now, though, he wanted to explain to her the joys of sipping a thick dark adult brew as opposed to swigging this warm coffee-flavoured water. Instead he looked round the room and smiled.

Noticing the look, Lucy said, 'I don't cook. I'm not good at kitchens. I don't understand them.'

Charlie said, 'I like to cook. Kitchens are my favourite room.'

'Yes, Bernice said you liked to cook. I thought men didn't. I thought they liked women to do that for them.'

Charlie shook his head. 'Not always. I wanted to know what food tasted like.'

'Didn't you eat before? Didn't anyone cook for you?'

'My Auntie Ella brought me up. She cooked worthy, dutiful dishes for me. I'm grateful. Actually, she wasn't really my auntie. She was a neighbour of my mother's. She abducted me. I never knew my mother.'

'I know, Bernice told me that, too. She told us all.' Lucy came to sit at the table with him and gaze at him in wonder. 'What was it like, being abducted?'

'I don't know. I was a baby, months old. I don't remember.'

'Didn't your mother go to the police? Didn't she go frantic looking for you?'

'Apparently not.'

'Surely she must have wanted to know you were safe?'

'I think so. I'm pretty sure she knew what had happened. She knew who took me. She was young. I was illegitimate. Back then she'd have had a rough time. I mean really bad. People can be cruel.'

'You poor soul.' Lucy put her hand over his. 'You must have been in a dark place.'

Charlie supposed he had been. He nodded. Looked down at the hand touching his. It was pale, translucent, long fingers, dark plum shiny nails. It was beautiful. He considered drawing his finger the length of it. But didn't. It might be misconstrued. The hand fascinated him. Not its owner.

'Is Charlie your real name?' Lucy asked.

'No. I'm a Norman. But I found out too late to take it up. I'm Charlie. That's it.'

'Well, Charlie, I love your reports.'

'Reports?'

'Yes. They're such fun. And it's lovely you send them so often. I don't mind the bill when I think of them.'

'Bill?'

'Well, it is a bit hefty. But your reports are so amusing and you've been through a lot, getting all the information.'

Charlie thought she meant getting beaten up. He was a little ashamed of that. He imagined a real detective would have fought back harder than he had. He'd watched fist-fights at the movies and they seemed easy. No problem at all to John Wayne.

'Sitting outside Brendan's house all night was beyond the call of duty. You found out so much about him,' said Lucy.

Charlie thought, did I do that? No, I didn't.

'And it's good you followed Brendan to Birmingham and Inverness. It was clever, too. He didn't know you were there.'

Charlie thought, that's because I wasn't.

'Do you have the reports?' he asked.

'No. Bernice reads them out at the meetings.'

'Ah, yes. The meetings.'

'We've had a few now. It can be difficult getting everyone together. Claire has to come from Inverness and Millie from Birmingham. But we manage. At first we were all suspicious of one another. You know – does Brendan prefer her or her to me? Is that one with the low-cut dress better in bed than me? But we got to be friends. We can talk about anything. Brendan's penis, anything.'

'Brendan's penis?'

'Well, yes.' Lucy was unaware of Charlie's sudden embarrassment. People in her world spoke openly and honestly about penises and other such things. 'I'd look at it and think, where has that been? And when I mentioned this to the others they all hooted and said they thought the same. It's cool and it's all down to you.'

'Me?' Charlie pointed to himself.

'Well, the reports were your idea.'

Charlie said, 'I sent amusing reports that Bernice read out?'

Lucy said, 'Yes'.

'My reports were so funny you didn't mind paying for them?'

'It wasn't too bad. Not when there're so many of us. We all chipped in fifty quid.'

'Fifty? All of you?'

His usual charge was about thirty pounds. Mrs Florey often pointed out that his invoices were a disgrace. Charlie said he hated taking money from people who were distressed, confused and missing someone they loved. Mrs Florey countered that he was a softie and he should consider his own needs. 'You have to pay bills. You actually have to eat. You have to survive.'

'All fourteen of us,' said Lucy.

'Fourteen. That's . . .' Charlie stared ahead, lips moving, calculating. 'Um, seven hundred pounds. Christ. Some people don't earn that in a year.' How lovely, he thought, if I'd actually got that money.

'I know that. But you looked out for all of us. So we paid. You worked hard.'

Charlie said, 'Promise me you won't pay out any more money.'

'After tomorrow I won't have to.'

He looked at her.

'Tomorrow we all meet and hand over money to our lawyer who is handling the case against Brendan. Breach of promise and emotional exploitation. He's proposed to all of us. It's payback time.'

'Don't,' said Charlie, 'just don't.'

'Oh, but I will. Tomorrow night, dinner at Bernice's place, we finally start the ball rolling.'

Charlie wrestled with his conscience. He ought to tell her the truth. He hadn't written the reports and he hadn't billed Bernice. He was sure she must have pocketed the money. But if he told Lucy about his suspicions she would have to warn the others and someone would tell Bernice. He was a duped man. He wanted revenge. He needed a plan. He had to keep his mouth shut till he formed one.

'You're going to get hurt.'

'I've been hurt. Now it's his turn.' She turned to Charlie. 'No mercy.'

Out on the street Charlie looked round. He was wary,

confused, nervous and cold. The day was warm enough, but he felt malice in the air and pulled his collar up. His demons were following him. And they were up to no good. He was sure of it. Brendan was somewhere watching, Marvin Hay was also watching. And leading the troop, quietly spying, was his mother.

51

It Makes Me Weep, the Fool You Are

He cycled back to the office, to Martha. 'Bastards,' he shouted. 'Bastard bastarding arseholes.'

The old bike, built for comfort not speed, rattled, clanked and shuddered. He wouldn't get paid for his work now that the batch of clients he didn't know about had forked out. They wouldn't pay twice. He'd been duped, taken for a fool. He *was* a fool. He manically pedalled on.

He crashed into the office, stood heaving in air unable to speak. Martha watched. Charlie stormed across the room, opened the third drawer of the filing cabinet and pulled out a bottle of whisky and two glasses. 'Bastards. Bastarding bastards.'

'Actually,' said Martha, 'not for me. It's too early for whisky.'

He poured her one anyway, sat on the sofa and shouted, 'Absobloodylutely amazing. Absobloodyfuckinglutely amazing. Would you believe it?'

'Probably not. What's absobloodylutely amazing? And who is a bastarding bastard?'

'Bloody Bernice and bloody Brendan have bloody got together fourteen women who have been courted by Brendan. He has apparently proposed to them. They all think I've been sending reports about what Brendan's been getting up to.' He stopped, turned to Martha. 'You haven't written any reports and sent them out, have you?'

'No. I absobloodylutely haven't.'

'Now I discover Bernice has charged them all fifty quid each, saying that was my fee.'

Martha said, 'What?' She got up from her desk, picked up the whisky and sat on the sofa with Charlie. 'It beggars belief.'

'How could I have sent them a bill? I don't know who they are. Bernice and Brendan must have written the reports themselves.'

'You have to admit it's a neat little scam. And a good lump of money for the scammers.' She sipped her drink. Felt the raw burn on the back of her throat and knew it was far too early in the day for whisky.

'I'd never charge that much,' said Charlie.

Martha thought Charlie's fees absurdly low but this wasn't the moment to mention it.

'Why me?' Charlie spread his palms.

'Why not you?' said Martha.

'I should be cynical and shrewd. I shouldn't get duped.'

'You keep saying you're a muser and finder of people. A dreamer. Ideal scam fodder, if you ask me.'

'I do not need to be told that.'

Martha thought he did. 'Seven hundred pounds is a lot of money, but it's hardly worth the effort Bernice has put in.'

'That's just the icing on the cake. A little amusing sum. The big crunch comes tomorrow when large chunks of money are handed over.'

'How much?'

Charlie shrugged. 'A lot.'

'Where is this to happen?'

'Bernice's place. They're having dinner.'

'You have to stop it.'

'How do I do that?' He refilled his glass, took a huge swig.

'You just do it. People are getting cheated. You have to.'

The evening was soft, balmy. The car windows were rolled down. Martha and Charlie could hear the sounds of early evening –

people arriving home from work, car doors slamming, voices from front gardens, songs on teatime radios. A sudden squall of sparrows stormed squealing from an untamed hedge, making Charlie jump. He was nervous. They were parked on the opposite side of the road from Bernice's house half an hour before the dinner was to begin so they could watch the arrivals.

Charlie was in a bad mood. He'd hardly eaten all day. He complained his stomach wasn't up to confrontations. 'Food lies uncomfortably on a nervy stomach. It just lies there with no digesting going on. Gases steam and rise. There is embarrassment.'

He wasn't enjoying this. 'When I had to sit an exam at school, I'd wish I'd get run over on the way there. A broken leg would do the trick, I thought. Time off school in bed, sympathy and puddings and no exam. Perfect. I feel that way now.'

'You'd rather have a broken leg than go in there and expose a couple of crooks? What happened to your anger? Sometimes anger is good.'

'I'm just scared. I don't like confrontation. I'm still angry. It's lurking behind my fear.'

'You'll be fine. Vinnie of Vinnie and the Vixens will be by your side.'

'Vinnie of Vinnie and the Vixens is used to confrontation. She relishes it. She's fearless. I'm not. Women en masse terrify me.'

'Charlie, it's part of being grown up. You have to do what's right. You have to stick up for yourself.'

'I don't think of myself as a grown up. Maturity is a façade for me. I have a grown-up body complete with necessary hairy bits. But in my head I'm six and when the going gets tough I want to run away.'

'You'll be fine.' She reached over, put her hand over his and squeezed it.

The touch was lovely, warm, gentle. It was still with him after the hand was withdrawn. But it didn't help. This was going to be awful.

Bernice answered the door. She wasn't pleased to see them. 'What the hell do you want?'

She wore tight-fitting white leather trousers and a shirt with deep ruffles down the front. It was pink. Not a subtle pink. It was violent, sugar-mouse pink. The pink of little girls' fairy tale fantasies. Charlie's nightmare colour. He opened his mouth to say that he and Martha had come to wish all the ladies well. A lie. But one he thought would get him into the house where he could denounce Bernice and warn everyone against parting with money. But instead, to his surprise, the words that came out of his mouth were the ones that formed in his head.

'What a hideous shirt.'

Shocked, Bernice let go of the door and gripped her shirt. 'I love this shirt. Bloody cheek.'

The door swung open and two women lingering in the hallway spotted their hero. 'Charlie!' they hooted. Waved. Signalled others to come. 'It's Charlie.' More women, all wearing pink, appeared from the living room. They smiled, rippled fingers at him. 'Hello, Charlie. Come and say hello to us.'

He was beginning to panic. Too many strange women dressed in pink coming at him. One stepped forward, pushed past Bernice, shook Charlie's hand, giggled and gushed, 'I'm Mary. So pleased to meet you at last. Come in and say hello to everyone. We owe you so much. None of this would be happening if it wasn't for you.'

'Me?' Charlie pointed to himself. 'What did I do?'

'Everything.' Mary spread her arms; everything was huge. 'You brought us together. You pointed the way. This is the night we wind it all up. We get the lawyer started. And we're doing it in pink. Pink outfits. Pink wine. It's fun. Now you come along. It's the icing on the cake.'

The aromas wafting from the house were take-away food, perfume and alcohol. The mood was party warm-up – shrieks of laughter, women holding drinks and waving, the shrill high-volume exchange of gossip, Dusty Springfield singing 'You Don't Own Me'. Charlie didn't like it at all. He sensed developing hysteria.

He turned to Bernice. 'I don't know exactly what you're up to, but it's wrong. I know it's wrong.' And to Mary he shouted, 'It's wrong. It's wrong. Don't do it. Don't part with money. Just don't.'

'Mary,' said Bernice, 'I need a little private word here. If you don't mind.' She shut the door behind her, leaned forward, nudged Charlie off the doorstep and stepped outside to join him and Martha on the path.

'Bugger off, the pair of you. I've put a lot into this. More than you know. Spoil it and you'll be sorry. Both of you. I mean it. Bugger off.' She pushed Charlie's shoulder. 'Turning up here unannounced, shouting don't. Cheek of you.' She turned on Martha. 'I'll put a stop to you both. Bugger off.' Flapping her hand in a shooing motion she stepped towards them. She was a woman accustomed to being obeyed. Martha and Charlie took a step back. She moved forward. They moved further back. The hand flapping and shooing continued. Martha and Charlie backed up to the gate.

'There's the matter of my fee,' said Charlie. He stood his ground.

'You'll get it. Send me the bill.'

'You have already billed all these women. I know that. You charged a fortune. What the hell is that about?'

Bernice folded her arms, gave Charlie a pitying look. 'It's called mark-up. I'm a businesswoman. You bill me, I pass on the charge and make a little something for myself.'

'You're making more than a little something.'

Bernice sighed the dismissive sigh of a woman dealing with a fool. 'It's hardly my fault if you charge peanuts. I checked you out before I hired you. Your fees are pathetic. Laughable. No doubt you feel you are helping people in distress. Being kindly. Where does being kindly get you?' She moved closer and poked

Charlie in the chest. 'I'll tell you where it gets you – nowhere. It gets you laughed at and trampled and beaten down and left lying in life's gutter. Being kindly is for idiots.' She stalked back to her front door, waving her arms. 'Idiots. Fool. Half-baked, soft-hearted twits. God help us all.' She opened the front door, turned. 'You're a fool, Charlie Gavin. It makes me weep, the fool you are.'

52

Good Drunken Walk

Sophie was in the kitchen washing the supper dishes. Evie was in bed sleeping. It was half-past eight. The doorbell rang. Sophie pulled a towel from the rail and, drying her hands, walked to the top of the stairs and shouted, 'Come on in. The door's not locked.' She went back to the sink to finish her chore.

She heard someone coming up the stairs and, assuming it was Duncan, told him to sit. 'I'll make a cup of tea in a minute.'

'Don't want a cup of tea. Brought this.'

Sophie turned. Jamie was standing in the doorway holding a bottle of wine. 'Come to say sorry and goodbye.'

Sophie said, 'Sorry's good. But goodbye?'

'Going away. Australia. New life and all that.'

Sophie said, 'Good for you. You're not planning to take Evie, are you?'

Jamie shook his head. 'Brought a goodbye drink.'

She fetched two glasses and put them on the table.

Jamie looked round. 'This place hasn't changed.'

'Why should it change?' said Sophie. 'It's perfect the way it is.'

Jamie said, 'Perhaps it is. It's homey. I'll get the corkscrew.' He'd almost grown up here and knew where things were kept. He opened the bottle and filled the glasses.

Sophie looked at him. 'You've got older.'

'So have you.'

'You used to be such a nice boy. Kind. Willing to please.

You'd do things for us. Fix things. Carry heavy stuff. Run out for messages, potatoes and the like.'

'I was a bit of a wimp. I got over it. You were always a bossy old bag.' He took a drink.

'You wouldn't know a bossy old bag if she bit you on the bum. I did a lot for you and Martha.'

'You poked about in our lives. You wouldn't leave us alone. You were always at our house.'

'I bought a cot and nappies and clothes and a pram and all sorts of things for the baby. I helped. I cooked. I looked after little Evie when Martha was exhausted. You sat in the shed and smoked dope.'

'Only to get away from you.'

'You've turned nasty.'

'I've always been nasty. So have you. I'm better at hiding it, though.'

Sophie finished her glass, refilled it, passed the bottle to Jamie and waited till he had refilled his before she drank. 'You left my lovely daughter. You actually ran away from her. You're an arse.'

'I panicked. Martha was pregnant and so was Grace. I didn't know what to do. And there had just been an embarrassing chip situation with Evie and it all crowded in on me. I ran. I know. I'm sorry.'

'So you should be. My Martha was ill after that. I grieved with her and for her. I grieved that she'd married a pig like you.'

'She duped me into it. I took a boring nine-to-five job for her. I gave up my dreams. I stopped being me.'

'Dramatic hogwash from a coward. You couldn't stand the strain of parenthood and responsibility.'

'Grace came back. She came for me. I couldn't believe it. Grace is a goddess. I still can't take it in. A woman like that loves me. She's wonderful.'

'So is my Martha.'

He smiled a small, cynical smirk. 'Grace can cook. She has

dress sense. She's a fantastic caring mother. She can sing. She writes songs. She can play the guitar.'

A hard act to follow, Sophie thought. Martha could cook but not well enough to boast about. She couldn't sing or write songs. She could still do the three chords she'd mastered on her old guitar but that didn't qualify as actually playing it. 'Martha is a loving mother. She's kind. She's clever and she does a splendid imitation of Cher when she's had a bit too much to drink.'

Jamie snorted and gave this claim a slow handclap. 'Wowee.'

'If my Martha hadn't started a band, your Grace would be nowhere now. It took Martha's courage and belief for Grace to come out of her shell and find herself.'

'Talent like Grace's will always out. She'd have made it anyway. She's too gifted not to shine.'

Now Sophie snorted. 'Rubbish. You talk bollocks. Always have, always will.'

'You smothered us. You pushed your way into our lives and turned us into horrible versions of you. We became boring. Like you.'

'You are a bullying, swaggering, obnoxious chauvinist.'

'You're a manipulative, pushy old matriarch.'

'Talentless boor.'

'Bumbling, old-fashioned parochial witch.'

The glasses got filled and emptied swiftly.

'Conceited, arrogant lout,' said Sophie.

'Useless, past-it nosey hag.'

Sophie considered the bottle. It was empty. 'I've got another. It's over there. On the rack.'

It was miles and miles away on the other side of the kitchen. She rose and, breathing carefully, keeping a steady eye on her goal, crossed the room, took the bottle and turned to face the trek back to her chair.

Jamie clapped and whistled. 'Good drunken walk.'

Sophie bowed and handed the bottle to him to open. 'Thank

you. I always appreciated being appreciated, even if it is by a garishly dressed failure.'

Jamie smoothed the front of his floral shirt. 'This is how it is with fashion these days. I dress to please myself not you. And I'm not a failure. I own a part-share in a very successful record shop. I manage three up and coming bands. I make enough to feed and clothe my family. Next time you see me, when I come back from Australia, I'll be a millionaire.' He filled her glass.

'I hope you're not driving,' she said.

'Nah, I got the bus.'

They gazed at one another and found themselves smiling.

Sophie said, 'I enjoyed that. I am newly discovering my aggressive side.'

He nodded. 'You're doing well. Another ten or fifteen years and you might even be a virago or Amazon.'

'Here's to me.' She raised her glass. 'I suppose you want to see Evie.'

The child was sleeping. Her jaw was set and it looked as if she slept with the same vigour she used when she was awake.

'She's a beauty,' said Jamie. 'I love her. Martha's done her proud.'

'Indeed,' said Sophie. 'You will note her stunning resemblance to you. She's yours. No question of it.'

'I know,' said Jamie. 'I'll write to her. I'll send her gifts from afar and I'll come back to see her.'

'And you'll be welcome.' She held his face and kissed his cheek. 'I look forward to a return match.'

She watched him walk up the path. He was young and hopeful and probably would become a millionaire. She noted he'd started to swagger. Well, he'd need to where he was going. She clapped. 'Good drunken walk.'

52

Charlie Is My Darling

'My guitar had blood on it. That's how hard I played. I gave it everything,' said Martha. 'My fingers bled. My throat burned raw. I closed my eyes and let the song rip. I was lost in it.'

'Your point is?'

'I never gave up. You did. You ran away from Bernice.'

'So did you.'

'I was following you.'

He considered this. Had a small moment imagining the pair of them scuttling up the garden path elbowing one another aside in their panic to get away. 'I didn't run away. I walked briskly, head held high.'

They'd been sitting in the car for an hour. Across the road the party was hotting up. There were shrieks and whoops and every now and then a party-goer in pink would steam out of the front door and do a crazed, drunken, elbow-flapping Mick Jagger strut.

'Looks fun,' said Martha.

'Looks like the worst party in the world,' said Charlie.

'Actually, we should go over there again and warn these women that they're being conned. It's our duty. You don't have to stay long. Just go in there, make an announcement, tell it like it is and come out again.'

Charlie said, 'No.' He reached over and switched on the radio. 'I won't do that. Absolutely bloody not.'

'I thought you didn't like music on the radio.'

'I like the music. Hate the DJs. They're hearty. There's nothing worse than a hearty DJ when you've just been humiliated. But it's evening now, the DJs will have calmed down.'

This calm DJ said, 'Here's something new – a world first. An all-girl band, Mistral Annie and the End of Time. "Take Me Down Purple" is their first single and you might not think it till you hear it, but they rock.'

Martha glared at the radio. 'Did you hear that? The world's first all-girl band?' She leaned down and shouted at the dial, 'I don't bloody think so. There was Vinnie and the Vixens. We were there long before Mistral Annie. We toured. We went down a storm at the Drop In Youth Club, Aberdeen. We rocked.'

'Actually,' said Charlie, 'they're good. Really good. In fact, I might buy that record.'

Martha punched his shoulder. 'You bastard. You traitor. How could you buy that single? These women are imposters. I, Vinnie of Vinnie and the Vixens, was first. I demand my place in history.'

Charlie thought, perhaps you shouldn't.

Martha got out of the car, slammed the door. 'I've had enough of this. I'm sick of everything. I am a woman. I am fighting for my rights and I'm going over there to that party and I'm going to tell these women the truth. Women unite.'

Hair flying behind her, long cardigan flapping, she ran across the road and up the path to the front door. Charlie called her back. But too late. Without a backward glance, Martha opened the door and stamped inside. Cursing, Charlie went after her.

For the rest of his life pink would be more than a colour for Charlie. It would be the smell of perfume, cigarettes and cheap fizzy wine. And it would be the disturbing sound of drunken female laughter suddenly dying and the thick hostile silence that followed. If he hated pink before he went into that house, he would loathe it to the point of nausea after he came out.

As he stepped cautiously down the hall he heard Bernice say, 'What the hell are you doing here? I told you to go.' He didn't hear Martha's reply. But he knew her well enough to understand that her sudden flush of fury had abated and she was floundering in the face of Bernice's aggression. Her mouth would be open and she'd be making soothing gestures with her hands. His heart went out to her. He would save her.

In the few steps it took to reach the living room he devised a plan. He would quietly reach Martha and stand by her side. He'd swiftly and clearly explain what was happening and strongly advise all the women to go home. He'd take Martha's hand and lead her back to the car. They'd drive back to his place where he'd take her in his arms and tell her he loved her. It was clear. It was simple. There was nothing to it.

There was a ripple of glee as he entered the room – a small gasp of delighted recognition. Charlie later supposed it was the sort of thing that happened to Elvis or John Lennon, should one of them unexpectedly turn up in some fan's living room. But it threw him. He blushed. Women nudged one another and whispered, 'It's Charlie.' A couple waved to him, a shy ripple of fingers. He forgot his planned speech. Bemused, he spread his palms and said, 'Huh?'

A woman he'd never seen before said, 'We know all about you, Charlie. We think you're marvellous. The way you've risen above your circumstances is wonderful.'

'Yes,' someone else agreed. 'Just wonderful.'

A few began to sing, 'Oh, Charlie is my darling.'

Charlie took a step backwards. Every single woman was in pink and singing his name. He said, 'Circumstances?'

A woman nearby reached out and stroked his arm. 'We know you were abducted and brought up in penury by a woman who said she was your aunt. We know how awful it was for you.'

'Do you? It wasn't that bad. I was fed, warm, clothed. Not a lot of money but who had money back then?' Charlie was offended on behalf of his Aunt Ella.

There was a ripple of approval. Of course their hero would

play down his misfortune. Bernice raised her hand, anxious to quell this rush of adoration. 'Time for business, girls.' She turned to Charlie. 'Did you want something?' She was dismissively icy. Cruelly disinterested. Charlie had often met receptionists who were superb at this. But they were nothing compared to Bernice. He took a step back and nearly apologised for being there.

But Martha replied for him. 'We've come to warn you. You are being lied to.' She turned to the company of women. 'You mustn't give her any money. You won't see it again and you won't see her again.' She pointed to Bernice.

Bernice gave her a small burst of applause. 'Oh, well done. Good story. Now will you please leave? We have business to see to.' She flapped her hand, waving Charlie and Martha towards the door.

Martha said, 'We're going. But I need to tell the truth.' She touched her throat. Swallowed. 'I know all of you here have slept with – well, fucked – Brendan and you're angry and you want revenge. Best revenge is to get up and go home, taking your money with you.'

A voice from the women in pink. 'Is this what you've discovered from your detecting? It isn't what any your reports says.'

'We didn't write the reports,' said Martha.

Bernice clapped again. 'Classic.'

'Can we have our money back?' the woman asked Martha.

'If we'd ever got your money, you'd have been welcome to have it back. But we didn't get any money. Bernice wrote all the reports with Brendan, we think. She also invoiced you for our fee and pocketed the payments. They've probably worked this scam before and are already setting it up somewhere else even as I speak.'

'Fantasy. Fantasy,' cried Bernice. 'You two should be writing comic strips.'

'Truth,' said Martha. 'I have a feeling you ladies are beginning to agree with me. Where's Brendan, you may wonder. I don't know.

He's upstairs. He's in a pub somewhere waiting for Bernice to come with the money. He's on a train to the new city, new lovers. The scam goes on. But I'm thinking he might be lying in a darkened room, staring at the ceiling, recovering from all the loveless fucking he's been doing and gathering strength for all the loveless fucking he will have to do in the future.'

She turned to Charlie, who was standing slightly behind her looking puzzled. She took his hand and led him to the door.

'I was going to say that,' he said. 'Yes, definitely that. Only,' he looked back at the women, 'how did you know about me?'

He recognised Lucy. It was quite good to note pink didn't suit her. She wasn't perfect after all. 'She told us.' Her accusing finger pointed at Bernice.

Charlie said, 'Ah, right.'

He followed Martha to the front door. Heard the slow build-up of voices. Women demanding answers.

Once inside the car, he leaned back, took a deep breath and said, 'We certainly handled that well. We told them a thing or two. At least, you did. I said almost nothing. I planned to rescue you and didn't.'

'You saved me. I was about to run away before you turned up. I would never have spoken up if you hadn't been standing behind me. I stopped feeling alone.'

'That's always a good thing.'

Martha made to start the car. 'Time to go. We've had our say. It's all been crap from start to finish. You got beat up. We got duped. We won't get paid. Can it get any worse?'

'I'm hoping not. But on the bright side, the sandwiches were good.'

'What now? Fish and chips? Carbonara?'

Charlie shook his head. 'Not yet. I need to stay here. I need to watch what is going on in that house. Something horrible is happening in my head. A vile notion is intruding into the placid pleasant place where my thoughts live. It is too awful to contemplate.'

'What is it?'

'It's the worst notion I've ever had. I think I might cry.' He stopped speaking and watched a pair of trousers soar out of an upstairs window of the house. They spread into the air and tumbled to the ground. Next came a blue shirt, then a pair of socks. 'Scissors.' A screech from above. 'Cut them up first.'

He jerked his thumb at the pile building up on the lawn. 'Brendan's stuff.'

Martha nodded. 'Hell hath no fury and all that. Only there's a whole bunch of scorned women taking revenge. That's fury too hellish to think about.'

'It's a nightmare. These women cutting up clothes. All the pink. And that dreadful woman Bernice. How could she check up on me? I could hardly check up on myself. I stumbled upon me. Nobody could have found out about the abduction. It wasn't reported anywhere. It happened and only two people knew for sure. Auntie Ella and my mother.'

A slow drizzle started. Tiny soft droplets covered the car windows and the world beyond blurred. The women in the upstairs room across the road fell into a rhythm of work and started to sing. Their soft sweet voices did nothing to ease the nastiness of their intentions. 'Snip, snip, throw, throw, and out you go.' The song echoed through the damp air.

For a moment the rhythmic movement of clothes emerging from the window and the singing distracted Charlie. 'Lot of stuff, Brendan has. I never saw him wearing any of it.'

'A man about town,' said Martha. 'A dandy and a dude. He'd need a lot of gear to attract women.'

He sighed, 'Yeah, he would. Some really cool things. I wonder if Bernice is helping.'

'I doubt it. I think she'll be planning to get away.'

'I'm going to have to confront her. I'm going to have to go in there and talk to her. And I don't know what to say. She'll probably call me Norman. I hate that.'

'Why would she do that?'

He opened the car door. 'It's my name,' said Charlie.

53

Be Kindly

He got out of the car, leaned in, saying, 'Think about it. Bernice picked me. She knew about me. That bloody woman is my mother.'

He stamped off to confront her. He didn't want to, but couldn't stop himself. There were too many things he wanted to know. He had to ask why she hadn't looked for him. Didn't she want him? Had she even thought about him at all? What had she been doing all this time? Had she married? Produced children? He paused on the garden path to watch ruined clothes tumble onto the pile. A pair of red-and-yellow socks stripped of their toes drifted down. Perhaps, he thought, I have a brother or sister somewhere. Someone as lost and bewildered as me. God, there goes a pair of really lurid socks.

Behind him Martha got out of the car and called, 'Be kindly.' Familiar words but they gave him a jolt. He hadn't given kindliness a thought.

Bernice was in the kitchen zipping up a large leather holdall. She shot him a tight smile. 'Thought I'd get away out the back door before you twigged.'

He said, 'Sorry.'

'Don't apologise, Norman. You do that too much. You'll get trampled like Ella.'

'It's true, then?' asked Charlie.

'Yes, it's true. I am your mother and you have just ruined a very nice little scam that took some time to set up.'

'I'm not Norman. I'm Charlie.'

'I know. And I'm not Bernice. I'm Mairi. Of course, I'll have to get a new name when I get busy again somewhere else. Not telling you where.'

'Have you always been like this? Lying, cheating?'

'Yes. I'm afraid so, Charlie. I'll call you Charlie, it's what you're used to. Though when I thought of you, and I thought of you often, I thought of Norman. My little Norman. Anyway, I'm afraid your mother isn't very nice. She's nasty and she does nasty things. I did one good thing. I let you stay with Ella. I knew she'd taken you and I knew she loved you. I let you have love. I didn't have you for long, but I knew you'd need it. Ella had love in her. I didn't. Not really. I could have had the police onto her, but why do that? She was a silly soft old bat but she had a heart. I envied her that. Did you have a good life?'

'It was OK. Yes, she loved me. We lived quietly.'

'You would. Ella would have been terrified of being discovered. But look at you. You're sane. You don't do drugs and you're taller than me. That's parenting at its best. Even if I didn't do it.'

Charlie nodded. 'Did you have a good life?'

'Highs and lows. Highs were high enough to see me through the lows. I survived.'

This wasn't right. This was not how Charlie had envisioned his first meeting with his mother. He'd had many imaginings of this. He'd thought the encounter might be awkward, or loving or even shy. There might be tears, a tender reaching out for one another. It might take place in a quiet bar, or a tiny cosy tearoom. A park would have been good. Anything, anything, but not this forbidding sterile kitchen with its beige Formica worktops and only a polished kettle on show. And this woman was not what he'd longed for. She was hard, embittered, and, he realised, lonely.

'It's hello and goodbye, I'm afraid,' Bernice said. 'I have a feeling the law might be along soon-ish. The ladies have gone on the rampage.' She pointed to the din coming from upstairs.

'It's all got out of hand. I'm more than a bit pissed off, to tell the truth, Charlie.' She picked up her case, gave Charlie a polite little wave.

'I have a question.'

'I bet you have more than one. But no, I didn't remarry. I'm meeting Brendan. Won't give you details. And no, I didn't have any more children. You are the one and only.' She opened the door.

'My question,' said Charlie, 'is did Brendan have any red-and-yellow socks?'

'Good heavens, no. A gentleman should only wear black socks. I don't suppose Ella would have told you such things. Life's finer details slipped past her, but she made excellent stew.' Bernice opened the back door, stepped out, beetled along to the side of the house and disappeared through the garden gate. She probably had a car somewhere nearby. Charlie let her go. She was his mother, after all. He was sure she'd get caught one day. 'Take care,' he said. It was as kindly as he could get.

He walked back up the hall, opened the front door and stepped out into the evening. On the lawn lay a large tangled pile of soaking snipped clothes. In houses across the road, families had gathered at windows to watch the display. One of them, Charlie was sure, would have called the police. The goings-on here had all the makings of rum doings – a party, a lot of drink, women impersonating Mick Jagger, shrieks, loud music, clothes getting thrown out of a window, vandalism. Holding his breath, listening, he was sure he heard a siren in the distance.

He stood on the grass and looked up at the women in pink. 'Ladies,' he called, 'you've got to stop this.'

'Charlie,' they shouted back, 'come on up. We're having fun with Brendan's things.'

Charlie shook his head. 'No. Got to go. I think the police are coming. You should all go. This isn't Bernice's house.' He waved his hand at the heap. 'These aren't Brendan's clothes.'

Several women shouted, 'What?'

'These clothes belong to the man who owns this house. They're not Brendan's. You have to get out of here. Do you all understand? You're cutting up the wrong man's clothes.'

This was all too awful. It was noisy and a little bit scary and he had to get away. In the car, Martha was bristling with anticipation. 'Well? How did it go? You weren't away very long.'

'I had nothing to say. I've waited all my life for that moment. And when it came I sort of stood there thinking, this isn't right. She wasn't the mother I wanted her to be. It wasn't how I planned. I had no control. I will always remember myself standing with my arms dangling by my side and my mouth open.'

Martha took his hand. 'It's all right. It's not your fault.'

Charlie said, 'I'm a mess. I've lived my life so far wondering about meeting my mother. Well, it's happened. So now I'll live the rest of my life wondering why I let it go so badly and why the only question I asked her was about socks.'

'Socks?' said Martha.

'Yes. And all that's left is a tangled knot in my stomach and a feeling like I want to cry. Only I don't cry. I think we ought to go. I definitely hear sirens. Just drive slowly. Act like we're a couple off for an evening at the cinema.'

'I know, pretend we're real people. We're good at that.'

The sex when they finally got round to it was comfort sex. They returned to Charlie's flat and discussed without any real interest what they should eat. They agreed that there wasn't a meal that could follow the bizarre events of the evening.

'I don't think I could stomach anything,' Charlie said. 'I can't get over it. That woman is my mother. I don't like her. I don't like looking at her. I don't like her voice or anything she says. She's vile. What does that say about me, that I come from such a hideous person?'

'It says nothing about you. You're not a hideous person, Charlie. You're lovely.' Martha put her arms round him and kissed his cheek. 'Please don't think you're an awful person. You're the nicest person I know.'

'Am I?'

They were on the sofa, side by side, with a couple of glasses of whisky on the table in front of them.

'Yes, you're lovely.'

And the hug followed by the cheek-kiss happened. This was Charlie's moment. Another chance like this wasn't going to come along soon. So he kissed her – a proper grown-up kiss – and couldn't believe his luck when she responded. The kisses got hotter, the bodies closer. He felt her hand on the back of his head, gently stroking him. When it stopped, when they pulled apart, she stood, held out her hand to him and led him to bed. They undressed slowly, like they'd been doing this for years. But, as Martha was to remark later, it was like that because it was always meant to happen. And Charlie loved her and later loved her again even though he was keen to talk. He was hungry for her kind words.

'Comfort sex,' he said.

'Best sex to start with. Relaxing, no demands. Wild sex will come, as will sleepy sex, I-love-you sex, thank-you sex and make-up sex.'

'You're planning to stick around, then?'

'Oh, yes. I'll phone home and let Sophie know I'll be back in the morning.'

'I don't think I can manage all these different kinds of sex before then.'

'We better stick to comfort sex for the moment. After all the excitement it would be wise.'

Martha woke first. She looked across the pillow at Charlie sleeping. There you are, she thought. He was sound. Sleeping like a man who hadn't slept properly for years. A man who had just discovered the joys of warmth and comfort and slipping, eyes shut, from the world to rest and recover from life's messiness.

She would make him scrambled eggs, toast with butter and bitter marmalade. He could brew the coffee.

Meantime, there were matters to discuss. He would have to come and live with her. 'I am not a woman who would put up with getting up and going home afterwards. I like my sex lying down in a bed followed by eight hours' sleep and a bowl of cereal.' Family life would be good for him. He'd be good for her family and Murphy would be good for Evie. And if it all got too much for him there was a secret place in the garden behind the lilac tree where he could hide.

Brenda could look after this place. She was already queen of the leftover people here.

She thought she could become a partner. Walters and Gavin, she thought. No. Gavin and Walters. Let him go on top. It was the kindly thing to do.